"Forgive me for being overobvious," Mattern said to his guest. "But I must bring up the matter of your sexual prerogatives. We three will share a single platform. My wife is available to you, as am I. Avoidance of frustration, you see, is the primary rule of a society such as ours. And do you know our custom of nightwalking?"

"I'm afraid I——" replied Gortman.

"Doors are not locked in Urbmon 116. We have no personal property worth mentioning, and we all are socially adjusted. At night it is quite proper to enter other homes. We exchange partners in this way all the time; usually wives stay home and husbands migrate, though not necessarily. Each of us has access at any time to any other adult member of our community."

"So you can go into any room in this whole gigantic building and sleep with——"

"Not the whole building," Mattern interrupted. "Only Shanghai. We frown on nightwalking beyond one's own city." He chuckled. "We do impose a few little restrictions on ourselves, so that our freedoms don't pall."

The City: 2000 A.D.
Urban Life through Science Fiction

Edited by

Ralph Clem

Martin Harry Greenberg

Joseph Olander

A FAWCETT CREST BOOK

Fawcett Publications, Inc., Greenwich, Connecticut

THE CITY: 2000 A.D.: Urban Life through Science Fiction

A Fawcett Crest Original

Library of Congress Catalog Card Number: 76–8814

ISBN Number: 0–449–22892–4

Printed in the United States of America
July 1976

1 2 3 4 5 6 7 8 9 10

The editors and publisher wish to thank the following individuals and publishers for their permission to use copyrighted material:

"Gas Mask" Copyright © 1964 by James D. Houston. Appeared originally in *NUGGET*. Reprinted by permission of the author and McIntosh and Otis, Inc.

"In Dark Places" by Joe L. Hensley. Copyright © 1973, by Roger Elwood; this story first appeared in *FUTURE CITY*, edited by Roger Elwood; and is here reprinted by permission of Roger Elwood, the author, and the author's agent, Virginia Kidd.

"Traffic Problem" by William Earls. Copyright © 1970 by Universal Publishing and Distributing Corp. Reprinted by permission of the author, William Earls.

"Street of Dreams, Feet of Clay" by Robert Sheckley. Copyright © 1967 by Robert Sheckley. Reprinted by permission of the Sterling Lord Agency, Inc.

"Disposal" by Ron Goulart. Copyright © 1969 by Mercury Press, Inc., originally published in *VENTURE SCIENCE FICTION*.

"The Undercity" by Dean R. Koontz. Reprinted by permission of the author, Dean R. Koontz. Copyright © 1973 by Roger Elwood. It appeared in his book of original stories, *FUTURE CITY*, published by Trident Press.

761249

Contents

Contents

PART II
YESTERDAY'S DREAMS,
TODAY'S PROBLEMS,
TOMORROW'S NIGHTMARES?

PART III
THE CITY 2000 A.D.:
TAKE YOUR PICK

Alternative Visions of the City

Introduction: Why the City?

It may seem perfectly natural for those of us living in the contemporary United States to regard the urban way of life, with all that implies, and the problems associated with (or caused by) the concentration of people into cities, as the normal human condition. This urban-oriented viewpoint is entirely understandable in light of the fact that about three-quarters of all Americans currently reside in cities. Yet this preponderance of city dwellers is, considering the centuries-long span of human history, a phenomenon characteristic of only the very most recent times. Our attention, therefore, should focus briefly upon how and why this development of cities as centers of social, economic, and political life came about, setting the stage for the consideration of future trends.

Until relatively recently, as we noted above, only a very small proportion of people lived in cities. As late as 1800, for example, it has been estimated that less than 3 percent of the world's population were urbanites, and at that time no city in the world had reached the one-million mark in size. By 1965, however, the United Nations put the share of population living in cities of the world at 35 percent, and by 1970, 162 cities had populations of greater than one million, indicating a tremendous change over a period of just over a century and a half. In fact, many areas of the world have attained much higher urban percentages (called the *level of urbanization* by statisticians) than the world average. In Western and Northern Europe, Australia and New Zealand, and the United States and Canada, the level of urbanization is near or above 75 percent; that is, approximately 75 percent of the people in these areas live in cities. By the year 2000, according to the calculations of a recognized expert, some cities may exceed 60 million persons, an almost incomprehensible mass of people some five times the size of the world's present largest city, the New York metropolitan area.

The shift in population from dispersed rural settlement to concentrated city residence has clearly been one of the most

11

significant, if not *the* most significant, trends in the history of mankind. Interestingly, the process is far from completion in most areas of the world, affording us a unique opportunity to examine the changes which occur in almost a "laboratory" setting and, more importantly, to explore the practical reasons for the transition from rural to urban life. As Kingsley Davis said in this regard, "Our ancestors could only dream about this change; our descendants can only read about it."

In order to understand the factors which influenced this dramatic shift in the pattern of human habitation, it is best to inquire into the *functions* of the city, or, in other words, into the roles which the city plays in man's economic, social, and political life. With an appreciation of these functions, we might next be able to identify the ways in which the roles have changed in such a fashion to promote the large-scale redistribution of people into urban areas.

Although it is, of course, difficult to say with any precision, the first true cities probably evolved around 4000 B.C. From that time on, until around 1800 A.D., the basic functions of the city were tied to providing services to the rural, agricultural areas. The cities during this period were basically centers of marketing and trade, of government administration, of religious activities, and for military garrisons. Because the cities did not have a strong economic basis for existence of their own (being dependent upon the farming areas which surrounded them), their position was in many respects "parasitic," and as such their size and number were limited by the ability of the agricultural population to support them.

Beginning around the end of the eighteenth century, however, the economic transformation known as the "Industrial Revolution" provided a new and powerful function for cities: that of centers of large industries. Cities, it turns out, are ideal locations for most manufacturing activities, containing within a relatively compact area markets for finished products, an adequate labor supply (both in numerical terms and with a variety of skills), contacts with other industries, and a host of essential, supporting services (such as banking, schools, and police and fire protection). With the change in the total economy from primarily agricultural to overwhelmingly non-agricultural activities, it follows that the importance and size of cities would increase as well.

If the introduction of new economic functions provided

the justification by which cities could grow, the actual means behind the dramatic growth in urban areas after 1800 was the movement, or *migration* of people from rural, farming districts to the cities. The primary motivation which attracted these migrants was the availability of jobs in the expanding industrial economy. However, other factors, such as the mechanization of farming (which reduced the numbers of workers needed in agriculture), and a more rapid growth of population beginning in the late 1700s, literally "pushed" many people to the cities in search of economic opportunities. In some respects this rural-to-urban migration drained the farming areas in other than numerical terms, since it was often the more ambitious and skilled individuals who were attracted to the cities, thus depriving agriculture of enterprising or innovative types. In addition to the purely economic considerations, cities have long had an attraction as centers of cultural activities, education, and as seats of political power.

The movement of people from rural to urban areas has truly been an impressive occurrence, and seems to have had a universally similar pattern despite otherwise important differences in culture or political-economic ideology. For some time the transition to an urbanized society was viewed as a "Western" phenomenon, inasmuch as the industrial-urban process began in and spread initially through European countries and overseas areas settled by people of European descent. Yet, when the basic conditions of industrialization were initiated in Japan, that non-Western society began to urbanize in essentially the same fashion as had the European nations.

In a similar vein, the Soviet Union, its socialist, centrally planned economy notwithstanding, entered the urbanization process in a dramatic fashion once the country experienced the industrial growth required to sustain large cities. In fact, the transition from rural to urban society in the U.S.S.R. took place in record time, the growth of cities in that country surpassing that of earlier cases. One estimate put the number of people who moved from rural-to-urban areas in the Soviet Union between 1927 and 1959 at 43 million persons, an amount roughly equal to the total migration from Europe overseas to the Americas, Africa, and Australia and New

Zealand during the entire nineteenth century and first half of the twentieth century!

It goes pretty much without saying that the social, political, and economic consequences of such large-scale movements of people from one area to another in a relatively short period of time will be enormous. This seems to be so particularly when one allows for the qualitatively different nature of rural and city life. Although the process of urbanization has been virtually completed in many countries, the trend toward larger and larger cities continues apace on the world scale. As more and more people live in cities, things "urban" assume increasing importance, and the problems which seem to be generated by the city become magnified.

Why the city? Basically, the city has provided an environment in which certain functions were performed most efficiently. With the introduction of modern industry, the basis for the shift from primarily rural to primarily urban society was available. With a fundamental grasp of what took place historically, it is now possible to examine the consequences, both in terms of the nature of city life itself, and the practical difficulties which have become all too familiar to most of us.

REFERENCES: Kingsley Davis, ed., *Cities: Their Origin, Growth and Human Impact* (San Francisco: W. H. Freeman and Company, 1973).

Chauncy D. Harris, *Cities of the Soviet Union* (Chicago: Rand McNally, 1970).

United Nations, Department of Economic and Social Affairs, *The Determinants and Consequences of Population Trends*, New York, 1973.

I. Of Dreams and Nightmares: Visions of the City

Ever since human beings ceased being essentially nomadic hunters and gatherers and began creating settlements in a more lasting locus, the idea of "the city" has been an integral part of the story of human civilization. The city story is perhaps 5000 years old and represents the best in human nature as well as the worst; hope as well as fear; expectations as well as frustrations; and dreams as well as nightmares.

Thus the city, as *an idea* as well as *a place*, has come to mean many different things to many different kinds of people. One major difference is that between those who study cities and those who live, work, play, love, hate, and die in them. Persons who study cities usually develop theories about them. Persons for whom the city becomes a total way of life develop visions about them. This difference between theory and vision is what this book, which tries to relate science fiction to urban life, is all about.

Over time, the city has been an object of study by many different kinds of scholars. The political scientist, the sociologist, the civil engineer, the economist, the geographer, the planner, the historian, the anthropologist—all study and theorize about cities. "Urban theory," then, is simply a potpourri of these different scholarly perspectives. But two major themes seem to be woven throughout these views. We shall call one the "ecological"; the other, the "organizational."

The ecological theme normally emphasizes a setting of people in a relatively small space and studies how the size and density of the city affect its social organization. Indeed, everything that one can think about—communication, education, transportation, social behavior, the status of a culture, political power and authority—is assumed to be an overall result of the size, scale, and magnitude of physical space and a number of people.

The organizational theme, on the other hand, first starts with looking at patterns of social behavior rather than size

15

and density of population. From this point of view, the essence of the study of urban life is to be found in the particular arrangement of human behavior which exists in places called cities. Whereas the ecological theme stresses that changes in urban organization are functions of size, the organizational theme emphasizes that change is a function of differences in organization itself.

But our purpose here is not to assess the relative merits or deficiencies in these two major approaches to the study and theory development of cities but rather to point out a possible lack in both: the lack of an appreciation of and need for an understanding of the *vision* of those who dwell in cities.

Picture yourself as an anthropologist who has just been given a research grant to study the organizational structure and social behavior of a primitive tribe of people in a remote land. The grant allows you enough money to purchase a helicopter with which you hope to hover above the tribe and, from this vantage point, to study and observe the "subjects." You are intellectually armed with *both* ecological and organizational theories of human behavior. With these theories, you will be able to observe the size, density, and scale of the tribe as well as their social patterns of behavior. These observations can be made from your helicopter—and never will you have to come in direct contact with *people*!

Of course, what is missing from your study is an appreciation of the way the people you are observing assign *meaning* to their organizational structure and to their social behavior. What is missing from your study is an understanding of the *vision* through which your subjects are viewing the same things which you are studying.

So it is with modern approaches to the study of the city. What may be needed now is a better way of understanding the city from the vision of those who give it meaning and from the study of different types of vision.

Several different types of urban vision are suggested by the literature of science fiction. The ones mentioned here are not intended to exhaust the possibilities; but they do represent major categories, each implying a decidedly different role for the individual who lives in a city.

The first is the *apocalyptic vision*. This vision is one which captures the city as a place where disaster occurs. Whether the disaster is environmental or human, physical or social is not important. What is important is its emphasis on catastrophe. The role of the individual in this vision is one of anticipating disaster and trying to prepare to survive it.

A second category is the *tragic vision* of the city. This vision portrays the city as necessary but flawed in some vital way. The city is, by definition, imperfect and will always remain so. The city places barriers to the full development of the human potential—the human being can not rise above his own creation. The role of the individual here is that of coping—coping with urban problems reflecting the imperfection of the essence of city life. The city as a set of insurmountable problems is a familiar view for all of us.

The third category is that of the *classical vision*. This perspective sees the city essentially as a beehive, performing necessary but impersonal functions. Trading, transportation, communication, and commerce are examples of these functions. The individual in the city has a role in this vision similar to that of a worker-bee, putting out energy and devoting his life to the maintenance and continuity of the city-beehive. The city as a conversion process for goods and services is also a familiar picture for most of us.

The fourth major category is a vision which is familiar to most of us but is, in fact, shared by relatively few people. This is the *romantic vision*, which captures the essence of the city as a place where the amenities of civilization are available to its inhabitants. The fine arts—music, art, sculpture—"high culture," and knowledge abound only in cities, according to this view, and the role of the individual is one of developing access to ever higher levels of cultural and aesthetic satisfaction.

The fifth category is the utopian vision. It involves thinking about the city as a distinctive and higher order of moral development and civilization. Indeed, it is through the city that human beings can transcend their own imperfections and shortcomings. This view suggests the city as fraternity with a focus for energy being contemplation about moral development and the individual as an intellectual. The images of St. Augustine's *The City of God* and Sir Thomas More's *Utopia* are associated with this vision.

In unique ways, "New York A.D. 2660," by Hugo Gernsback; "Jesting Pilot," by Henry Kuttner; "Chicago," by Thomas F. Monteleone; "Street of Dreams, Feet of Clay," by Robert Sheckley; and "The Vanishing American," by Charles Beaumont all touch on these major urban visions. Developing alternative urban worlds, they dramatize these visions and force us to come to terms with the wide range of meanings which human beings assign to their cities.

The City as a Way of Life

New York A.D. 2660

The language by which people describe and talk about a city often reveals their feelings about it as a way of life. Frequently, phrases like "urban blight," "the urban condition," "urban disease," "urban problems," and "urban ills" are used to express how people view the city. Such views presuppose that the city is like a living organism and paint a picture of urban "sickness." Thus many people are concerned today about the "health" of the city as a way of life.

But how do we test and evaluate a city's health? What techniques do we use? If cities are indeed as "sick" as many people say they are, then how do we begin to search for remedies? What "cures" are available for application?

In "New York A.D. 2660," Hugo Gernsback tries to answer these questions, and he proceeds by placing a top priority on the technological dimensions of city health. His solutions to city problems are based upon technological advance, principally in the area of alternative energy systems. Interdependence is the major key to understanding city life. Communication, transportation, information, and vital goods and services are all tied neatly together by advances in energy technology in Gernsback's portrayal.

But this kind of city gives to city government a unique function—the total management of the technology systems upon which the way of life of the city depends. As such, the purposes of the city and the values which it serves remain the prerogative of the technology manager.

Technology is important to sustaining the city; but we must always ask: What purposes does technology serve? In this sense, technology refers not only to the physical tools and techniques which we use but also to the concepts and ideas which should shape the purposes served by such tools. The challenge which the modern city-dweller faces is to recognize that changes in the way one lives may result in further changes in the purpose of life. For example, the changes which have taken place in our modes of transportation, especially the automobile, have generated changes in our culture and values.

Therefore, we should appreciate the uses and potential of technology for dealing with problems associated with the way of life we have come to know as "urban." But, at the same time, we must not allow technology to limit our vision of what values and purposes the city should serve. We must go beyond our tools and constantly ask: Why do we use tools? at what cost? and for whose benefit? Failing to do so means that we have lost our capacity for vision—and that may be the most deadly of all our "urban ills."

New York A.D. 2660   Hugo Gernsback

Being much interested in sports she desired to know presently how the modern New Yorker kept himself in condition and for his answer Ralph stopped at a corner and they entered a tall, flat-roofed building. They took off their coasters, stepped into the electromagnetic elevator and ascended the fifty-odd stories in a few seconds. At the top, they found a large expanse on which were stationed dozens of flyers of all sizes. There was a continuous bustle of departing and arriving aerial flyers and of people alighting and departing.

As soon as Ralph and Alice appeared a dozen voices began to call: *"Aerocab, sir, Aerocab, this way please!"* Ralph, ignoring them, walked over to a two-seated flyer and assisted his companion to the seat; he then seated himself and said briefly to the "driver," *"National Playgrounds."* The machine, which was very light and operated entirely by electricity, was built of metal throughout; it shot up into the air with terrific speed and then took a northeasterly direction at a rate of ten miles per minute, or 600 miles per hour.

From the great height at which they were flying it was not hard to point out the most interesting structures, towers, bridges, and wonders of construction deemed impossible several centuries ago.

In less than ten minutes they had arrived at the National Playgrounds. They alighted on an immense platform and Ralph, leading Alice to the edge, where they could see the entire playgrounds, said:

"These National Playgrounds were built by the city in 2490, at the extreme eastern end of what used to be Long Island, a few miles from Montauk. An immense area had been fitted up for all kinds of sports, terrestrial and aquatic as well as aerial. These municipal playgrounds are the finest in the world and represent one of New York's greatest achievements. The City Government supplied all the various sport paraphernalia and every citizen has the right to use it, by applying to the lieutenants in charge of the various sections.

"There are playgrounds for the young as well as for the old, grounds for men, grounds for women, grounds for babies to romp about in. There are hundreds of baseball fields, thousands of tennis courts, and uncounted football fields and golf links. It never rains, it is never too hot, it is never too cold. The grounds are open every day in the year, from seven in the morning till eleven at night. After sunset, the grounds and fields are lighted by thousands of iridium wire spirals, for those who have to work in the daytime.

"As a matter of fact all the great baseball, tennis, and football contests are held after sundown. The reason is apparent. During the daytime, with the sun shining, there is always one team which has an advantage over the other, on account of the light being in their eyes. In the evening, however, with the powerful, stationary light overhead, each team has the same conditions and the game can be played more fairly and more accurately."

Ralph and his companion strolled about the immense grounds watching the players and it was not long before he discovered that she, like himself, was enthusiastic about tennis. He asked her if she would care to play a game with him and she acquiesced eagerly.

They walked over to the dressing building where Ralph kept his own sport clothes. Since the girl had no tennis shoes, he secured a pair for her in the Arcade, and they sauntered over to one of the courts.

In the game that followed, Ralph, an expert at tennis, was too engrossed in the girl to watch his game. Consequently, he was beaten from start to finish. He did not see the ball, and scarcely noticed the net. His eyes were constantly on Alice, who, indeed, made a remarkably pretty picture. She flung herself enthusiastically into her game, as she did with everything else that interested her. She was the true sport-lover, caring little whether she won or not, loving the game for the game itself.

Her lovely face was flushed with the exercise, and her hair curled into damp little rings, lying against her neck and cheeks in soft clusters. Her eyes, always bright, shone like stars. Now and again they met Ralph's in gay triumph as she encountered a difficult ball.

He had never imagined that anyone could be so graceful. Her lithe and flexible figure was seen to its best advantage in this game requiring great agility.

Ralph, under this bombardment of charms, was spellbound. He played mechanically, and, it must be admitted, wretchedly. And he was so thoroughly and abjectly in love that he did not care. To him, but one thing mattered. He knew that unless he could have Alice life itself would not matter to him.

He felt that he would gladly have lost a hundred games when she at last flung down her racket, crying happily: "Oh, I won, I won, didn't I?"

"You certainly did," he cried. "You were wonderful!"

"I'm a little bit afraid you let me win," she pouted. "It really wasn't fair of you."

"You were fine," he declared. "I was hopelessly outclassed from the beginning. You have no idea how beautiful you were," he went on, impulsively. "More beautiful than I ever dreamed anyone could be."

Before his ardent eyes she drew back a little, half pleased, half frightened, and not a little confused.

Sensing her embarrassment he instantly became matter-of-fact.

"Now," he said, "I am going to show you the source of New York's light and power."

A few minutes later, after both had changed their shoes, they were again seated in an aerocab and a twenty-minute journey brought them well into the center of what was formerly New York state.

They alighted on an immense plain on which twelve monstrous Meteoro-Towers, each 1,500 feet high, were stationed. These towers formed a hexagon inside of which were the immense *Helio-Dynamophores*, or Sun-power-generators.

The entire expanse, twenty kilometers square, was covered with glass. Underneath the heavy plate-glass squares were the photo-electric elements which transformed the solar heat *direct* into electric energy.

The photo-electric elements, of which there were 400 to each square meter, were placed in large movable metal cases, each containing 1,600 photo-electric units.

Each metal case in turn was movable, and mounted on a kind of large tripod in such a manner that each case from sunrise to sunset presented its glass plate directly to the sun. The rays of the sun, consequently, struck the photo-electric elements always vertically, never obliquely. A small electric motor inside of the tripod moved the metal case so as to keep the plates always facing the sun.

In order that one case might not take away the light from the one directly behind it, all cases were arranged in long rows, each sufficiently far away from the one preceding it. Thus shadows from one row could not fall on the row behind it.

At sunrise, all cases would be almost vertical, but at this time very little current was generated. One hour after sunrise, the plant was working to its full capacity; by noon all cases would be in a horizontal position, and by sunset, they again would be in an almost vertical position, in the opposite direction, however, from that of the morning. The plant would work at its full capacity until one hour before sunset.

Each case generated about one hundred and twenty kilowatts almost as long as the sun was shining, and it is easily understood what an enormous power the entire plant could generate. In fact, this plant supplied all the power, light, and heat for entire New York. One-half of the plant was for day use, while the other half during daytime charged the chemical gas-accumulators for night use.

In 1909 Cove of Massachusetts invented a thermo-electric

Sun-power-generator which could deliver ten volts and six amperes, or one-sixieth kilowatt in a space of twelve square feet. Since that time inventors by the score had busied themselves to perfect solar generators, but it was not until the year 2469 that the Italian 63A 1243 invented the photoelectric cell, which revolutionized the entire electrical industry. This Italian discovered that by derivatives of the Radium-M class, in conjunction with Tellurium and Arcturium, a photo-electric element could be produced which was strongly affected by the sun's ultra-violet rays and in this condition was able to transform heat *direct* into electrical energy, without losses of any kind.

After watching the enormous power plant for a time Alice remarked:

"We, of course, have similar plants across the water but I have never seen anything of such magnitude. It is really colossal. But what gives the sky above such a peculiar black tint?"

"In order not to suffer too great losses from atmospheric disturbances," Ralph explained, "the twelve giant Meteoro-Towers which you notice are working with full power as long as the plant is in operation. Thus a partial vacuum is produced above the plant and the air consequently is very thin. As air ordinarily absorbs an immense amount of heat, it goes without saying that the Helio-Dynamophore plant obtains an immensely greater amount of heat when the air above is very clear and thin. In the morning the towers direct their energy toward the East in order to clear the atmosphere to a certain extent, and in the afternoon their energy is directed toward the West for the same purpose. For this reason, this plant furnishes fully thirty per cent more energy than others working in ordinary atmosphere."

As it was growing late they returned to the city, traversing the distance to Ralph's home in less than ten minutes.

Alice's father arrived a few minutes later, and she told him of the delightful time she had had in the company of their distinguished host.

Shortly after they had dined that evening Ralph took his guests down to his *Tele-Theater*. This large room had a shallow stage at one end, with proscenium arch and curtain, such as had been in use during the whole history of the drama. At the rear of the room were scattered a number of big upholstered chairs.

When they had seated themselves, Ralph gave Alice a directory of the plays and operas that were being presented that night.

"Oh, I see they are playing the French comic opera, *La Normande*, at the National Opera tonight," she exclaimed. "I have heard and read much of it. I should like to hear it so much."

"With the greatest of pleasure," Ralph replied. "In fact, I have not heard it myself. My laboratory has kept me so busy, that I have missed the Opera several times already. There are only two performances a week now."

He walked over to a large switchboard from which hung numerous cords and plugs. He inserted one of the plugs into a hole labeled "National Opera." He then manipulated several levers and switches and seated himself again with his guests.

In a moment, a gong sounded, and the lights were gradually dimmed. Immediately afterward, the orchestra began the overture.

A great number of loud-speaking telephones were arranged near the stage, and the acoustics were so good that it was hard to realize that the music originated four miles away at the National Opera House.

When the overture was over, the curtain rose on the first act. Directly behind it several hundred especially constructed Telephots were arranged in such a manner as to fill out the entire space of the shallow stage. These telephots were connected in series and were all joined together so cleverly that no break or joint was visible in the rear part of the stage. The result was that all objects on the distant stage of the National Opera were projected full size on the composite Telephot plates on the Tele-Theater stage. The illusion was so perfect in all respects that it was extremely hard to imagine that the actors on the Telephot stage were not real flesh and blood. Each voice could be heard clearly and distinctly, because the transmitters were close to the actors at all times and it was not necessary to strain the ear to catch any passages.

Between the acts Ralph explained that each New York playhouse now had over 200,000 subscribers and it was as easy for the Berlin and Paris subscribers to hear and see the play as for the New York subscriber. On the other hand, he admitted that the Paris and Berlin as well as the London playhouses had a large number of subscribers, local as well as long distance, but New York's subscription list was by far the largest.

"Can you imagine," mused Alice, "how the people in former centuries must have been inconvenienced when they wished to enjoy a play? I was reading only the other day how they had to prepare themselves for the theater hours ahead of time. They had to get dressed especially for the occasion and even went so far as to have different clothes in which to attend theaters or operas. And then they had to ride or perhaps walk to the playhouse itself. Then the poor things, if they did not happen to like the production, had either to sit all through it or else go home. They probably would have rejoiced at the ease of our Tele-Theaters, where we can switch from one play to another in five seconds, until we find the one that suits us best.

"Nor could their sick people enjoy themselves seeing a play, as we can now. I know when I broke my ankle a year ago, I actually lived in the Tele-Theater. I cannot imagine how I could have dragged through those dreary six weeks in bed without a new play each night. Life must have been dreadful in those days."

"Yes, you are right," Ralph said. "Neither could they have imagined in their wildest dreams the spectacle I witnessed a few days ago.

"I happened to be passing this room and I heard such uproarious laughter that I decided to see what caused it all. Entering unnoticed, I found my ten-year-old nephew 'entertaining' half-a-dozen of his friends. The little rascal had plugged into a matinee performance of *Romeo and Juliet* playing at the Broadway—in English of course. He then plugged in at the same time into *Der Spitzbub*, a farce playing that evening in Berlin, and to this, for good measure, he added *Rigoletto* in Italian, playing at the Gala in Milan.

"The effect was of course horrible. Most of the time, nothing but a Babel of voices and music could be heard; but once in a while a single voice broke through the din, followed immediately by another one in a different language. The funniest incident was when, at the Broadway, Juliet called: 'Romeo, Romeo, where art thou, Romeo?,' and a heavy comedian at the Berlin Theatre howled: *'Mir ist's Wurst, schlagt ihn tot!'*

"Of course, everything on the stage was blurred most of the time, but once in a while extremely ludicrous combinations resulted between some of the actors at the various theaters, which were greeted with an uproar by the youngsters."

As he concluded the anecdote the curtain rose once more, and the audience of three settled back to enjoy the second act of the opera.

Later, when it was all over, they went down to the street floor at Ralph's suggestion, where they put on their Tele-motor-coasters, preparatory to seeing more of New York—this time by night.

The party proceeded to roll down Broadway, the historic thoroughfare of New York. Despite the fact that it was 11 o'clock at night, the streets were almost as light as at noonday. They were illuminated brilliantly by the iridium spirals, hanging high above the crossings. These spirals gave forth a pure, dazzling-white light of the same quality as sunlight. This light moreover was absolutely cold, as all electrical energy was transformed into light, none being lost in heat. Not a street was dark—not even the smallest alley.

James 212B 422, as well as his daughter, lingered over the superb displays in the various stores and they entered several to make a few purchases. Alice was much impressed with the automatic-electric packing machines.

The clerk making the sale placed the purchased articles on a metal platform. He then pushed several buttons on a small switchboard, which operated the "size" apparatus to obtain the dimensions of the package. After the last button was pressed, the platform rose about two feet, till it disappeared into a large metal, box-like contrivance. In about ten to fifteen seconds it came down again bearing on its surface a neat white box with a handle at the top, *all in one piece*. The box was not fastened with any strings or tape, but was folded in an ingenious manner so that it could not open of its own accord. Moreover, it was made of *Alohydrolium*, which is the lightest of all metals, being one-eighth the weight of aluminum.

The automatic packing machine could pack anything from a small package a few inches square up to a box two feet high by three feet long. It made the box to suit the size of the final package, placed the articles together, packed them into the box which was not yet finished, folded the box after the handle had been stamped out, stenciled the firm's name on two sides and delivered it completely packed, all within ten to fifteen seconds.

The box could either be taken by the purchaser or the clerk would stencil the customer's name and address into the handle, place a triangular packet-post stamp on the box and drop it into a chute beside the counter. It was carried down into the *Packet-Post Conveyor*, which was from seventy-five to one hundred feet below the level of the street, where it landed on a belt-like arrangement moving at the rate of five miles an hour. The action was entirely automatic and the chute was arranged with an automatic shutter which would only open when there was no package immediately below on the moving belt. This precluded the possibility of packages tumbling on top of each other and in this way blocking the conveyor tube.

When the package had landed on the conveyor belt it traveled to the nearest *distributor office*, where the post office clerk would take it from the belt and see if it was franked correctly. The stamp was then machine cancelled and after the clerk had noted the address he routed it to the sub-station nearest to the addressee's home. Next he clamped onto the package an automatic metal "rider" which was of a certain height, irrespective of the size of the package.

The package with its rider was placed on an express conveyor belt traveling at the rate of 25 miles an hour. This express belt, bearing the package, moved at an even speed, and never stopping, passed numerous sub-stations on the way. At the correct sub-station the rider came against a contact device stretching across the belt at right angles, at a certain height. This contact arrangement closed the circuit of a powerful electromagnet placed in the same line with the contact, a few feet away from the express belt. The electromagnet acted immediately on the metal package (Alohydrolium is a magnetic metal), drawing it in a flash into the sub-station from the belt. If there was another package right behind the one so drawn out, it was handled in the same manner.

After the package had arrived at the sub-station it was

despatched to its final destination. Another rider was attached to it and the package placed on a local conveyor belt passing by the house to which it was addressed. On arriving at the correct address its rider would strike the contact overhead, which operated the electromagnet, pulling the package into the basement of the house, where it fell on the platform of an electric dumb-waiter. The dumb-waiter started upward automatically and the package was delivered at once.

By this method a package could be delivered in the average space of forty minutes from the time of purchase. Some packages could be delivered in a much shorter time and others which had to travel to the city limits took much longer.

"How wonderful!" Alice exclaimed after Ralph had explained the system. "It must have taken decades to build such a stupendous system."

"No, not quite," was the reply. "It was built gradually by an enormous number of workers. The tubes are even now extended almost daily to keep pace with the growth of the city."

From the stores Ralph took his guests to the roof of an aerocab stand and they boarded a fast flyer.

"Take us about 10,000 feet up," Ralph instructed the driver.

"You haven't much time," the man answered; "at 12 o'clock all cabs must be out of the air."

"Why?"

"Today is the 15th of September, the night of the aerial carnival, and it's against the law to go up over New York until it's all over. You have twenty-five minutes left, however, if you wish to go up."

"I forgot all about this aerial carnival," said Ralph, "but twenty-five minutes will be time enough for us if you speed up your machine."

The aerial flyer rose quickly and silently. The objects below seemed to shrink in size and within three minutes the light became fainter.

In ten minutes an altitude of twelve thousand feet had been reached, and as it became too cold, Ralph motioned to the driver not to rise further.

The spectacle below them was indescribably beautiful. As far as the eye could see was a broad expanse studded with lights, like a carpet embroidered with diamonds. Thousands of aerial craft, their powerful searchlights sweeping the skies, moved silently through the night, and once in a while an immense transatlantic aerial liner would swish by at a tremendous speed.

Most beautiful of all, as well as wonderful, were the *Signalizers*. Ralph pointed them out to his guests, saying:

"In the first period of aerial navigation large electric lamps forming figures and letters were placed on housetops and in open fields that the aerial craft above might better find their destinations. To the traffic flying 5,000 feet or higher such signals were wholly inadequate, as they could not be correctly read at such a distance. Hence the signalizers. These are powerful searchlights of the most advanced type, mounted on special buildings. They are trained skyward and shoot a powerful shaft of light directly upward. No aerial craft is allowed to cross these light shafts. Each shaft gives a different signal; thus the signalizer in Herald Square is first white; in ten seconds it changes to red and in another ten seconds it becomes yellow. Even an aerial liner at sea can recognize the signal and steer directly into the Herald Square pier, without being obliged to hover over the city in search of it. Some signalizers have only one color, flashing from time to time. Others more important use two searchlights at one time, like the one at Sandy Hook. This signalizer has two light shafts, one green and one red; these do not change colors, nor do they light periodically."

From on high Ralph's guests marveled at these signalizers, which pierced the darkness all around them. It was a wonderful sight and the weird beauty of the colored shafts thrilled Alice immeasurably.

"Oh, it is like a Fairyland," she exclaimed. "I could watch it forever."

But presently the aerocab was descending rapidly and in a few minutes the strong light from below had obliterated the light shafts. As the craft drew closer the streets could be seen extending for miles like white ribbons and the brilliantly lighted squares stood out prominently. They landed, at the stroke of twelve, and Ralph found three unoccupied chairs on the top of one of the public buildings and only then did they notice that hundreds of people were seated, watching the sky expectantly.

At the last stroke of twelve, all the lights below went

out and simultaneously the light shafts of all the search-lights. Everything was plunged in an utter darkness.

Suddenly overhead at a great height the flag of the United States in immense proportions was seen. It was composed of 6,000 flyers, all together in the same horizontal plane. Each flyer was equipped with very powerful lights on the bottom, some white, some red, others blue. Thus an immense flag in its natural colors was formed and so precisely did the flyers co-operate that, although they all were at least 50 feet from each other, the appearance to those below was that of an unbroken silk flag, illuminated by a searchlight. The immense flag began to move. It passed slowly overhead, describing a large circle, so that the entire population below obtained a perfect view.

Everyone applauded the demonstration. Then as suddenly as it had appeared the flag vanished and all was once more in darkness. Ralph explained to his guests that the lights of each one of the aerial flyers had been shut off simultaneously in preparation for the next spectacle.

All at once there was seen an enormous colored circle which revolved with great rapidity, becoming smaller and smaller, as though it were shrinking. Finally it became a colored disc, whirling rapidly on its axis. In a few seconds, the edge opened and a straight line shot out, the disc unrolling like a tape measure. After a few minutes more, there remained nothing of the disc. It had resolved itself into a perfectly straight many-hued line, miles long. Then the lights went out again. The next spectacle was a demonstration of the solar system. In the center a large sun was seen standing still. Next to the "sun" a small red round globe spun rapidly about it, representing the planet Mercury. Around both the sun and the "planet" Mercury revolved another globe, blue in color; this was Venus. Then followed a white orb, the "Earth" with the moon turning about it. Next came the red planet Mars with its two small moons, then green Jupiter and its moons, and Saturn in yellow. Uranus was orange and lastly came Neptune in pink, all globes and their moons traveling in their proper orbits around the "sun." While the spectacle was in progress a white "comet" with a long tail traveled across the paths of the planets, turned a sharp corner around the "sun," its tail always pointing away from that body, recrossed the orbits of the "planets" again on the other side and lost itself in the darkness.

Several other spectacles were presented, each more superb than the one preceding it. The carnival closed with a light-picture of the Planet Governor. This was exhibited for fully five minutes during which time the applause was continuous.

"We have never seen such a marvelous spectacle," James 212B 422 declared. "You Americans still lead the world. Upon my word, the old saying that 'nothing is impossible in America,' still holds good."

It was after one when they reached the house, and Ralph suggested a light lunch before they retired for what remained of the night. The others assented and Ralph led the way to the *Bacillatorium*.

The Bacillatorium, invented in 2509 by the Swede 1A 299, was a small room, the walls and bottom of which were composed of lead. On each of the four sides were large vacuum bulbs on pedestals. These tubes, a foot in height and about six inches thick and two feet in diameter, were each equipped with a large concave Radio-arcturium cathode. The glass of the tube in front of the cathode had a double wall, the space between being filled with helium gas.

The rays emanating from the cathode, when the tube was energized with high oscillatory currents, were called *Arcturium Rays* and would instantly destroy any bacilli exposed to them for a few seconds. Arcturium Rays, like X rays, pass through solid objects, and when used alone burned the tissue of the human body. It was found, however, that by filtering arcturium rays through helium no burns would result, but any germ or bacillus in or on the body would be killed at once.

The Bacillatorium was prescribed by law and each citizen ordered to use it at least every other day, thus making it impossible for the human body to develop contagious diseases. As late as the twentieth century more than half the mortality was directly attributable to diseases communicated by germs or bacilli.

The Bacillatorium eradicated such diseases. The arcturium rays, moreover, had a highly beneficial effect on animal tissue and the enforced use of the Bacillatorium extended the span of human life to between one hundred and twenty and one hundred and forty years, where in former centuries three score and ten was the average.

From the beginning of our earliest city developments through medieval times and even up to the nineteenth century, the city was identified, not only as a place where trading, commerce and "the arts" developed and grew, but also—and perhaps more importantly—a place where one could be safe. The city as a garrison or a fortress is a familiar image in human history. It was a place where one could feel relatively secure from the forces of chaos and evil "outside."

But the city as sanctuary is no longer an appropriate image. For the forces of chaos and evil, made visible in such forms as crime, impersonalization, congestion, and environmental destruction, are now "inside" the city. The city may be simply defined in a commonly used dictionary as a "habitat . . . the place or type of site where a plant or animal naturally or normally lives and grows." As we know it today, is a city a place where human beings can "naturally or normally" live and grow?

In order to cope with the growing chaos and evils associated with the city as a way of life, massive efforts are underway to provide comprehensive planning for our cities. Such planning is aimed at bringing more order, rationality, and security to an urban way of life.

In this era of planning, ways of life are not necessarily the choices of those who live them but of those who plan them. Do cities today—and will cities tomorrow—reflect the desires of those who live in them, or are they and will they be the creatures of those who plan for them? This is the central question running through Henry Kuttner's "Jesting Pilot."

But the city is more than a set of problems and attempts to plan for their solution. In many ways, a city is magical. It has its own personality, language, rites, and symbols. Over time, it has generated its own mythic consciousness which captivates and holds many of its inhabitants. The "Barrier" in Kuttner's story challenges us to think about the forces "outside" the city and the "planners" inside it. We need to ask constantly: What is urban reality—and what is urban fiction? What is urban life and what is urban planning?

Jesting Pilot   Henry Kuttner

The city screamed. It had been screaming for six hundred years. And as long as that unendurable scream continued, the city was an efficient unit.

"You're getting special treatment," Nehral said, looking across the big, bare, silent room to where young Fleming sat on the cushioned seat. "Normally you wouldn't have graduated to Control for another six months, but something's come up. The others think a fresh viewpoint might help. And you're elected, since you're the oldest acolyte."

"Britton's older than I am," Fleming said. He was a short, heavy, red-haired boy with an unusual sensitivity conditioned into his blunt features. Utterly relaxed, he sat waiting.

"Physiological age doesn't mean anything. The civilization-index is more important. And the empathy level. You're seventeen, but you're emotionally mature. On the other hand, you're not—set. You haven't been a Controller for years. We think you may have some fresh angles that can help us."

"Aren't fresh angles undesirable?"

Nehral's thin, tired face twisted into a faint smile. "There's been debate about that. A culture is a living organism and it can't exist in its own waste products. Not indefinitely. But we don't intend to remain isolated indefinitely."

"I didn't know that," Fleming said.

Nehral studied his fingertips. "Don't get the idea that we're the masters. We're servants, far more so than the citizens. We've got to follow the plan. And we don't know all the details of the plan. That was arranged purposely. Someday the Barrier will lift. Then the city won't be isolated any longer."

"But—outside!" Fleming said, a little nervously. "Suppose—"

Nehral said, "Six hundred years ago the city was built and the Barrier created. The Barrier's quite impassable. There's a switch—I'll show it to you sometime—that's useless at present. Its purpose is to bring the Barrier into existence. But no one knows how to destroy the Barrier. One theory is that it can't be destroyed until its half-life is run, and the energy's reached a sufficiently low level. Then it blinks out automatically."

"When?"

Nehral shrugged. "Nobody knows that either. Tomorrow, or a thousand years from now. Here's the idea. The city was isolated for protection. That meant—complete isolation. Nothing—*nothing at all*—can pass the Barrier. So we're safe. When the Barrier goes, we can see what's happened to the rest of the world. If the danger's gone, we can colonize. If it hasn't, we pull the switch again, and we're safe behind the Barrier for another indefinite period."

Danger. The Earth had been too big, and too full of people. Archaic mores had prevailed. The new science had plunged on, but civilization had lagged fatally. In those days many plans had been proposed. Only one had proved practicable. Rigid control—through utilization of the new power—and unbreakable armor. So the city was built and isolated by the Barrier, at a time when all other cities were falling. . . .

Nehral said, "We know the danger of status quo. New theories, new experiments aren't forbidden. Far from it. Some of them can't be studied now, a great many of them. But records are kept. That reference library will be available when the Barrier's lifted. Meanwhile, the city's a lifeboat. This part of the human race has to survive. That's the main concern. You don't study physics in a lifeboat. You try to survive. After you've reached land, you can go to work again. But now . . ."

The other cities fell, and the terror roared across the Earth, six hundred years ago. It was an age of genius and viciousness. The weapons of the gods were at last available. The foundations of matter ripped screaming apart as the weapons were used. The lifeboat rode a typhoon. The Ark breasted a deluge.

In other words, one thing led to another—until the planet shook.

"First the builders thought the Barrier alone would be enough. The city, of course, had to be a self-contained unit. That was difficult. A human being isn't. He has to get food, fuel—from the air, from plants and animals. The solution lay in creating all the necessities within the city. But then matters got worse. There were germ warfare and germ mutations. There were chain reactions. The atmosphere itself, under the constant bombardment . . ."

More and more complicated grew the Ark.

"So they built the city as it had to be built, and then they found that it would be—uninhabitable."

Fleming tilted back his head. Nehral said, "Oh, we're shielded. We're specialized. For we're the Controllers."

"Yes, I know. But I've wondered. Why can't the citizens—"

"Be shielded as we are? Because they're to be the survivors. We're important only till the Barrier lifts. After that, we'll be useless, away from the lifeboat. In a normal world, we have no place. But now and here, as Controllers of the city, we *are* important. We serve."

Fleming stirred uneasily.

Nehral said, "It will be difficult for you to conceive this. You have been specially conditioned since before your birth. You never knew—none of us ever knew—normal existence. You are deaf, dumb, and blind."

The boy caught a little of the meaning. "That means—"

"Certain senses the citizens have, because they'll be needed when the Barrier lifts. We can't afford to have them, under the circumstances. The telepathic sense is substituted. I'll tell you more about that later. Right now I want you to concentrate on the problem of Bill Norman. He's a citizen."

Nehral paused. He could feel the immense weight of the city above him, and it seemed to him that the foundations were beginning to crumble . . .

"He's getting out of control," Nehral said flatly.

"But I'm not important," Bill Norman said.

They were dancing. Flickering, quiet lights beat out from the Seventh Monument, towering even above the roof garden where they were. Far overhead was the gray emptiness of the Barrier. The music was exciting. Mia's hand crept up and ruffled the back of his neck.

"You are to me," she said. "Still, I'm prejudiced."

She was a tall, slim, dark girl, sharp contrast to Norman's blond hugeness. His faintly puzzled blue eyes studied her.

"I'm lucky. I'm not so sure you are, Mia."

The orchestra reached a rhythmic climax; brass hit a low, nostalgic note, throbbingly sustained. Norman moved his big shoulders uneasily and turned toward the parapet, towing Mia beside him. They walked in silence through the crowd, to a walled embrasure where they were alone, in a tiny vantage point overlooking the city.

Mia stole occasional glances at the man's troubled face. He was looking at the Seventh Monument, crowned with light, and beyond it to the Sixth, and, smaller in the distance, the Fifth—each a memorial to one of the Great Eras of man's history.

But the city—

There had never been a city like it in all the world. For no city before had ever been built for man. Memphis was a towered colossus for the memory of kings; Bagdad was a sultan's jewel; they were stately pleasure domes by decree New York and London, Paris and Moscow—they were less functional, less efficient for their citizens than the caves of the troglodytes. In cities man had always tried to sow on arid ground.

But this was a city of men.

It was not merely a matter of parks and roads, of rolling ramps and paragravity currents for levitation, not simply a question of design and architecture. The city was planned according to rules of human psychology. The people fitted into it as into a foam mattress. It was quiet. It was beautiful and functional. It was perfect for its purpose.

"I saw that psychologist again today," Norman said.

Mia folded her arms and leaned on the parapet. She didn't look at her companion.

"And?"

"Generalizations."

"But they always know the answers," Mia said. "They always know the *right* answers."

"This one didn't."

"It may take time. Really, Bill, you know, no one's—frustrated."

"I don't know what it is," Norman said. "Heredity, perhaps. All I know is I get these—these flashes. Which the psychologists can't explain."

"But there has to be an explanation."

"That's what the psychologist said. Still, he couldn't tell me what it was."

"Can't you analyze it at all?" she asked, sliding her hand into his. His fingers tightened. He looked at the Seventh Monument and beyond it.

"No," he said. "It's just that I feel there isn't any answer."

"To what?"

"I don't know. I—I wish I could get out of the city."

Her hand relaxed suddenly. "Bill. You know—"

He laughed softly. "I know. There's no way out. Not through the Barrier. Maybe that isn't what I want, after all. But this—this—" He stared at the Monument. "It seems all wrong sometimes. I just can't explain it. It's the whole city. It makes me feel haywire. Then I get these flashes—"

She felt his hand stiffen. It was jerked away abruptly. Bill Norman covered his eyes and screamed.

"Flashes of realization," Nehral said to Fleming. "They don't last long. If they did, he'd go insane or die. Of course the citizen psychologists can't help him, it's outside their scope by definition."

Fleming, sensitive to telepathic emotion, said, "You're worried."

"Naturally. We Controllers have our own conditioning. An ordinary citizen couldn't hold our power; it wouldn't be safe. The builders worked out a good many plans before they decided to create us. They'd thought of making androids and robots to control, but the human factor was needed. Emotions needed, to react to the conditioning. From birth, by hypnosis, we're conditioned to protect and serve the citizens. We couldn't do anything else if we tried. It's ingrained."

"Every citizen?" Fleming asked, and Nehral sighed.

"That's the trouble. *Every* citizen. The whole is equal to the sum total of the parts. One citizen, to us, represents the entire group. I'm not certain that this wasn't a mistake of the builders. For when one citizen threatens the group—as Norman does—"

"But we've got to solve Norman's problem."

"Yes. It's our problem. Every citizen must have physical and mental balance—*must*. I was wondering—"

"Well?"

"For the good of the whole, it would be better if Norman

could be eliminated. On purely logical grounds, he should be allowed to go mad or die. I can't countenance that, though. I'm too firmly conditioned against it."

"So am I," Fleming said, and Nehral nodded.

"Exactly. We *must* cure him. We've got to get him back to a sane psychological balance. Or we may crack up ourselves—because we're conditioned to react to failure. Now. You're the youngest of us available: you have more in common with the citizens than any of us. So you may find an answer where we can't."

"Norman should have been a Controller," Fleming said.

"Yes. But it's too late for that now. He's mature. His heredity—bad, from our viewpoint. Mathematicians and theologians. The problems of every citizen in the city can be solved with the Monuments. We can give them answers that are right for them. But Norman's hunting an abstraction. That's the trouble. *We can't give him a satisfactory answer!*"

"Haven't there ever been parallel psychoses?"

"It's not a psychosis, that's the difficulty. Except by the arbitrary standards of the city. Oh, there've been plenty of human problems—a woman who wants children, for example, and can't have them. If medicine fails to help her, the Monuments will. By creating diversion—arousing her maternal instinct for something else, or channeling it elsewhere. By substitution. Making her believe she has a mission of some sort. Or creating an emotional attachment of another kind, not maternal. The idea is to trace the problems back to their psychological roots, and then get rid of the frustration somehow. It's the frustration that fatal."

"Diversion, perhaps?"

"I don't think it's possible. Norman's problem is an abstraction. And if we answered it—he would go insane."

"I don't know what my problem is," Norman said desperately. "I don't have any. I'm young, healthy, doing work I like, I'm engaged—"

The psychologist scratched his jaw. "If we knew what your problem was, we could do something about it," he said. "The most suggestive point here—" He rustled through the papers before him. "Let's see. Do I seem real to you now?"

"Very," Norman said.

"But there are time—the syndrome's familiar. Sometimes

you doubt reality. Most people have that feeling occasionally."
He leaned back and made thoughtful noises. Through the
transparent wall, the Fifth Monument was visible, pulsating
with soft beats of light. It was very quiet here.

"You mean you don't know what's wrong with me," Norman said.

"I don't know yet. But I will. First we must find out what your problem is."

"How long will that take? Ten years?"

"I had a problem myself once," the psychologist said. "At
the time I didn't know what it was. I've found out since. I
was heading for megalomania; I wanted to change people.
So I took up this work. I turned my energy into a useful
channel. That solved my problem for me. It's the right way
for you, once we get at what's bothering you."

"All I want is to get rid of these hallucinations," Norman said.

"Auditory, visual, and olfactory—mostly. And without external basis in fact. They're not illusions, they're hallucinations. I wish you could give me more details about them."

"I can't." Norman seemed to shrink. "It's like being dropped
into boiling metal. It's simply indescribable. An impression of
noise, lights—it comes and goes in a flash. But it's a flash of
hell."

"Tomorrow we'll try narcosynthesis again. I want to cor-
relate my ideas in the meantime. It's just possible . . ."

Norman stepped into a levitating current and was borne
upward. At the level of the Fifth Monument's upper balcony
he stepped off. There were a few people here, not many, and
they were busy with their own affairs—lovemaking and
sight-seeing. Norman rested his arms on the rail and stared
down. He had come up here because of a vague, unlikely
hope that it would be quieter on the high balcony far above
the city.

It was quiet, but no more so than the city had been. The
rolling ways curved and slid smoothly beneath him. They
were silent. Above him the Barrier was a gray, silent dome.
He thought that gigantic claps of thunder were pounding at
the Barrier from outside, that the impregnable hemisphere was
beginning to crack, to buckle—to admit chaos in a roaring
flood.

He gripped the cool plastic rail hard. Its solidity wasn't reassuring. In a moment the Barrier would split wide open. . . .

There was no relief on the Monument. He glanced behind him at the base of the softly shining globe, with its rippling patterns of light, but that looked ready to shatter, too. He stumbled as he jumped back into the drop-current. In fact, he missed it entirely. There was a heart-stopping instant when he was in free fall; then a safety-paragravity locked tight on his body and slid him easily into the current. He fell slowly.

But he had a new thought now. Suicide.

But there were two questions involved. Did he want to commit suicide? And would suicide be possible? He studied the second point.

Without noticing, automatically he stepped on a moving way and dropped into one of the cushioned seats. No one died of violence in the city. No one ever had, as far as he knew. But had people tried to kill themselves?

It was a new, strange concept. There were so many safeties. No danger had been overlooked. There were no accidents.

The road curved. Forty feet away, across a lawn and a low wall, was the Barrier. Norman stood up and walked toward it. He was conscious of both attraction and repulsion.

Beyond the Barrier . . .

He stopped. There it was, directly before him, a smooth, gray substance without any mark or pattern. It wasn't matter. It was something the builders had made, in the old days.

What was it like outside? Six hundred years had passed since the Barrier was created. In that time, the rest of the world could have changed considerably. An odd idea struck him: suppose the planet had been destroyed? Suppose a chain reaction had finally volatilized it? Would the city have been affected? Or was the city, within that fantastic barrier, not merely shielded but actually shifted into another plane of existence?

He struck his fist hard against the grayness; it was like striking rubber. Without warning the terror engulfed him. He could not hear himself screaming.

Afterward, he wondered how an eternity could be compressed into one instant. His thoughts swung back to suicide.

"Suicide?" Fleming said.

Nehral's mind was troubled. "Ecology fails," he remarked. "I suppose the trouble is that the city's a closed unit. We're doing artificially what was a natural law six hundred years ago. But nature didn't play favorites, as we're doing. And nature used variables. Mutations, I mean. There weren't any rules about introducing new pieces into the game—in fact, there weren't any rules about not introducing new rules. But here in the city we've got to stick by the original rules and the original pieces. If Bill Norman kills himself, I don't know what may happen."

"To us?"

"To us, and, through us, to the citizens. Norman's psychologist can't help him; he's a citizen, too. He doesn't know—"

"What was his problem, by the way? The psychologist's, I mean. He told Norman he'd solved it by taking up psychology."

"Sadism. We took care of that easily enough. We aroused his interest in the study of psychology. His mental index was so high we couldn't give him surgery; he needed a subtler intellectual release. But he's thoroughly social and well balanced now. The practice of psychology is the sublimation he needed, and he's very competent. However, he'll never get at the root of Norman's trouble. Ecology fails," he repeated. "The relationship between an organism and its environment—irreconcilable, in this case. Hallucinations! Norman doesn't have hallucinations. Or even illusions. He simply has rational periods—luckily brief."

"It's an abnormal ecology anyway."

"It had to be. The city is uninhabitable."

The city screamed!

It was a microcosm, and it had to battle unimaginable stresses to maintain its efficiency. It was a outboard motor on a lifeboat. The storm raged. The motor strained, shrilled, sparked—screamed. The environment was so completely artificial that no normal technology could have kept the balance.

Six hundred years ago the builders had studied and discarded plan after plan. The maximum diameter of a Barrier was five miles. The vulnerability increased according to the square of the diameter. And invulnerability was the main factor.

The city had to be built and maintained as a self-sufficient unit within an impossibly small radius.

Consider the problems. *Self-sufficient*. There were no pipelines to the outside. A civilization had to exist for an indefinite period in its own waste products. Steamships, spaceships, are not parallels. They have to make port and take in fresh supplies.

This lifeboat would be at sea for much longer than six hundred years. And the citizens—the survivors—must be kept not only alive but healthy, physically and mentally.

The smaller the area, the higher the concentration. The builders could make the necessary machines. They knew how to do that. But such machines had never been constructed before on the planet. Not in such concentration!

Civilization is an artificial environment. With the machines that were necessary, the city became so artificial that nobody could live in it. The builders got their efficiency; they made the city so that it could exist indefinitely, supplying all the air, water, food, and power required. The machines took care of that.

But such machines!

The energy required and released was slightly inconceivable. It had to be released, of course. And it was. In light and sound and radiation—within the five-mile area under the Barrier.

Anyone living in the city would have developed a neurosis in two minutes, a psychosis in ten, and would have lived a little while longer than that. Thus the builders had an efficient city, but nobody could use it.

There was one answer.

Hypnosis.

Everyone in the city was under hypnosis. It was selective telepathic hypnosis, with the so-called Monuments—powerful hypnopaedic machines—as the control devices. The survivors in the lifeboat didn't know there was a storm. They saw only placid water on which the boat drifted smoothly.

The city screamed to deaf ears. No one had heard it for six hundred years. No one had felt the radiation or seen the blinding, shocking light that flashed through the city. The citizens could not, and the Controllers could not either, because they were blind and deaf and dumb, and lacking in certain other senses. They had their telepathy, their ESP, which enabled them to accomplish their task of steering the lifeboat. As for the citizens, their job was to survive.

No one had heard the city screaming for six hundred years—except Bill Norman.

"He has an inquiring mind," Nehral said dryly. "Too inquiring. His problem's an abstraction, as I've mentioned, and if he gets the right answer it'll kill him. If he doesn't, he'll go insane. In either case, we'll suffer, because we're not conditioned to failure. The main hypnotic maxim implanted in our minds is that every citizen must survive. All right. You've got the facts now, Fleming. Does anything suggest itself?"

"I don't have all the facts. What's Norman's problem?"

"He comes of dangerous stock," Nehral answered indirectly. "Theologians and mathematicians. His mind is—a little too rational. As for his problem—well, Pilate asked the same question three thousand years ago, and I don't recall his ever getting an answer. It's a question that's lain behind every bit of research since research first started. But the answer has never been fatal till now. Norman's question is simply this—*what is truth?*"

There was a pause. Nehral went on.

"He hasn't expressed it even to himself. He doesn't know he's asking that question. But we know; we have entrée to his mind. That's the question that he's finding insoluble, and the problem that's bringing him gradually out of control, out of his hypnosis. So far there've been only flashes of realization. Split-second rational periods. Those are bad enough, for him. He's heard and seen the city as it is."

Another pause. Fleming's thoughts stilled.

Nehral said, "It's the only problem we can't solve by hypnotic suggestion. We've tried. But it's useless. Norman's that remarkably rare person, someone who is looking for the truth."

Fleming said slowly, "He's looking for the truth. But—does he have—to find it?"

His thoughts raced into Nehral's brain, flint against steel, and struck fire there.

Three weeks later the psychologist pronounced Norman

cured and he instantly married Mia. They went up to the Fifth Monument and held hands.

"As long as you understand—" Norman said.

"I'll go with you," she told him. "Anywhere."

"Well, it won't be tomorrow. I was going at it the wrong way. Imagine trying to tunnel out through the Barrier! No, I'll have to fight fire with fire. The Barrier's the result of natural physical laws. There's no secret about how it was created. But how to destroy it—that's another thing entirely."

"They say it can't be destroyed. Someday it'll disappear, Bill."

"When? I'm not going to wait for that. It may take me years, because I'll have to learn how to use my weapons. Years of study and practice and research. But I've got a purpose."

"You can't become an expert nuclear physicist overnight."

He laughed and put his arm around her shoulders. "I don't expect to. First things come first. First I'll have to learn to be a good physicist. Ehrlich and Pasteur and Curie—they had a drive, a motivation. So have I, now. I know what I want. I want out."

"Bill, if you should fail—"

"I expect to, at first. But in the end I won't fail. I know what I want. *Out!*"

She moved closer to him, and they were silent, looking down at the quiet, familiar friendliness of the city. *I can stand it for a while,* Norman thought. *Especially with Mia. Now that the psychologist's got rid of my trouble, I can settle down to work.*

Above them the rippling, soft light beat out from the great globe atop the Monument.

"Mia—"

"Yes?"

"I know what I want now."

"But he doesn't know," Fleming said.

"That's all right," Nehral said cheerfully. "He never really knew what his problem was. You found the answer. Not the one he wanted, but the best one. Displacement, diversion, sublimation—the name doesn't matter. It was the same treatment, basically, as turning sadistic tendencies into channels of beneficial surgery. We've given Norman his compromise. He still doesn't know what he's looking for, but he's been hypnotized into believing that he can find it outside the city. Put food on top of a wall, out of reach of a starving man, and you'll get a neurosis. But if you give the man materials for building a ladder, his energy will be deflected into a productive channel. Norman will spend all his life in research, and probably make some valuable discoveries. He's sane again. He's under the preventive hypnosis. And he'll die thinking there's a way out."

"Through the Barrier? There isn't."

"Of course there isn't. But Norman could accept the hypnotic suggestion that there *was* a way, if only he could find it. We've given him the materials to build his ladder. He'll fail and fail, but he'll never really get discouraged. He's looking for truth. We've told him he can find truth outside the Barrier, and that he can find a way out. He's happy now. He's stopped rocking the lifeboat."

"Truth . . ." Fleming said, and then, "Nehral—I've been wondering."

"What?"

"Is there a Barrier?"

Nehral said, "But the city's survived! Nothing from outside has ever come through the Barrier—"

"Suppose there isn't a Barrier," Fleming said. "How would the city look from outside? Like a—a furnace, perhaps. It's uninhabitable. We can't conceive of the real city, any more than the hypnotized citizens can. Would you walk into a furnace? Nehral, perhaps the city's its own Barrier."

"But we sense the Barrier. The citizens see the Barrier—"

"Do they? Do—we? Or is that part of the hypnosis, too, a part we don't know about? Nehral—I don't know. There may be a Barrier, and it may disappear when its half-time is run. But suppose we just *think* there's a Barrier."

"But—" Nehral said, and stopped. "That would mean—Norman might find a way out!"

"I wonder if that was what the builders planned," Fleming said.

"Metropolis" and "metropolitan" are terms frequently used to refer to large cities. The development of the term "metropolis" is insightful for understanding the important issues raised by Thomas Monteleone's "Chicago." The word derives from the Greek "meter," which means mother, and from another Greek word "polis," which means city. Thus what was originally referred to as "the mother city" now refers to a very large urban unit, sometimes called the metropolis, or to an extremely large urban area frequently called a "megalopolis."

The important point is that large urban units grow at the expense of smaller units. Neighborhoods give way to divisions, divisions to municipalities, municipalities to cities and cities to metropolitan areas. In this evoluton of ever larger urban organizations, an all-important question becomes: What is lost, primarily in human terms, in this process of expansion and growth?

The answer to this question is far from simple; however, a good starting place may be with an appreciation of the way many persons view urban areas as a set of factors which are interdependent. In other words, we may start with how and why persons view urban areas as "systems." Now the term "system" means many things to many different kinds of people. A system may simply be anything we want to view as a system; hence there are analytical systems. But systems may also refer to the existence of mechanical things like cars which do exist and operate on the basis of many interconnected parts. Finally, there are biological systems which exist and oftentimes provide people with analogies by which to look at other things which are not biological in nature.

Take the "city," for example. We frequently hear that cities are "born," that they "grow," and that they "die." As a matter of fact, cities may even have souls, for the history of the American West is filled with stories *about "ghost towns." Thus our very language, and the way by which we view cities, indicates that many of us believe that cities are like organisms which may have a life and personality of their own; their own interests and values; and their own instinct to survive at all costs.*

Certainly, "Chicago" poignantly describes this situation, in which a city is concerned about its own survival at the expense of the welfare and freedom of smaller units within it. Put in other words, the values of the city are those of "system maintenance." Criteria for decision-making are the system-relevant ones, not the individual-unit-relevant ones. The logic of the city is maintenance; its order is arranged to ensure system survival.

But, historically, great cities have been those which have put people first. In order to put the well-being of city residents first rather than the survival of the city first, one should not ask whether a city is maintainable. Instead, one should ask whether a city is liveable. Are criteria of maintainability similar to or different from those of liveability?

This question is not often asked by those who govern our cities today. Liveability may simply be another way of expressing concern about "quality of life." As cities become large and grow into "megalopolies," the liveability versus maintainability issue which the story "Chicago" raises will become a central policy debate in modern life.

Chicago   Thomas F. Monteleone

Pinion was in the maintenance hangar, running some routine checks on his components, when he was summoned by the City.

ATTENTION. ALL UNITS FROM SECTORS 72-C AND 103-C. CHICAGO IS IN NEED OF REPAIR. ACKNOWLEDGE.

Somewhere inside Pinion's tempered-steel skull, a circuit responded to the command, since Pinion was a Unit from 103-C. "This is Unit Pinion," he said. "I acknowledge your command, Chicago. I am a Unit specialized in electrical engineering. What is the difficulty?"

UNIT PINION. CHICAGO IS AWARE OF YOUR CLAS-

SIFICATION. DO NOT FLOOD MY INPUTS WITH USE-
LESS DATA. PROCEED TO THE SECONDARY SHIELD.
THERE IS A POWER FAILURE DUE TO A FAULTY
GENERATOR. YOU WILL ASSIST IN REPLACING IT.

Pinion closed off the channel to Chicago and skittered out
of the hangar. As he headed toward the secondary shield, he
wondered (as he often did) about Chicago. He had always
been curious as to how Chicago accumulated all of the immense data that he possessed. He wondered if the City
could actually see objects in the same manner as Pinion could
see with his omnispectral photoelectric eyes. He knew that
Chicago could "sense" everything, but he had never ascer-
tained whether or not the sensations were in the form of
electronic impulses or mathematical symbols, or something
akin to that.

It was an interesting problem to consider, and Pinion took
great delight in pondering problems or questions in which
the solution did not appear to be readily available. Perhaps
it was a function of his purpose as a trouble shooter.

Pinion strode up the ramp and boarded a Unit Elevator
that carried him up to Level 12—one of the levels that
Chicago had sanctioned for Traffic. The doors opened and
he stepped out onto a concrete platform overlooking a rib-
bonwork of hundreds of lanes. Chicago's Traffic jammed the
lanes, moving with incredible speed in every direction, from
one horizon to the other. Each segment, or "car," as Chicago
referred to them, was a separate entity, each programmed
to its own specific destination. The Traffic was endless, as it
had always been in Pinion's memory; it never ceased its
cyclic, monotonous movement throughout the day and night.
None of the Units like Pinion ever knew what purpose the
Traffic served in Chicago's over-all scheme, nor did they ever
know where it was always going. They only knew that it
was just one small part of Chicago, and that it must be
maintained.

As Pinion walked along beside the Traffic lanes, he noticed
that the lights in the soaring buildings and towers were wink-
ing out. Chicago was now entering a Day Period. For some
unknown reason, on a perfectly timed cycle, the City turned
its illumination on and off without end. Pinion activated a
memory bank to remind himself to question Chicago about
some of these strange functions of the City. But for the

moment, he must perform his function as a maintenance robot.

By the time he reached the secondary shield, other Units had already arrived and had begun to remove the non-functioning generator. Pinion saw their great steel bodies shining in the dull light that was filtered through the shields from the Outside. The Units doing the actual work of dismantling the machinery were bipedal robots like himself, and he also noticed that some Carrier-Units were advancing to the base of the shield, bearing the necessary replacement parts.

Before he began work, he addressed Chicago in the customary manner. "This is Unit Pinion. I am now available for work."

ACKNOWLEDGE. UNIT PINION. PROCEED AS PREVIOUSLY ORDERED.

Pinion noticed that, at the same moment he was reporting in, other Units were doing likewise. Chicago, he thought, was an amazing entity, capable of performing millions of different functions at once. There was much that he would someday like to learn about the City.

And so it went for many long years. Pinion worked in service to Chicago, replacing worn-out parts, designing newer and better ones, always thinking of questions to ask Chicago, but never finding the time to actually ask them. The City was always in motion, like a giant piece of kinetic sculpture that Pinion and the others had been commissioned to maintain. Chicago was an enormous, sprawling mechanism, stretching as far as the robot could see in any direction.

One day Pinion was summoned to a Sector of the City that he had never seen before.

UNIT PINION. YOU WILL PROCEED TO SECTOR 14-A IMMEDIATELY. I SENSE A FAILURE IN A TEMPERATURE CONTROL CIRCUIT. YOU WILL CORRECT THE PROBLEM.

In order to reach Sector 14-A, Pinion had to travel into the deepest levels of the City. He passed areas where Chicago had new segments of Traffic being manufactured and fed into the mainstream. He saw the areas that collected water and pumped it into the sewer systems that were laced throughout the bowels of Chicago. He also saw where all replacement parts were made and the old parts were collected, recycled, and made again. There was also a place where Pinion saw Chicago making new Units like himself and sending them into new Sectors of the City. He passed the source of energy that powered all the components of Chicago—the great fusion reactors that were constantly monitored by Chicago and maintained by Units like Pinion.

He walked through a long, empty corridor that opened into Sector 14-A. "This is Unit Pinion. I am now available for work."

UNIT PINION. YOU WILL REPLACE THE TEMPERATURE CONTROL CONSOLE IN THIS SECTOR. I SENSE THAT THERE HAS ALREADY BEEN A DRASTIC RISE IN THE TEMPERATURE. IT MUST BE CORRECTED IMMEDIATELY.

The message was recorded in Pinion's circuitry, but he wasn't actually listening. He had just entered the Sector as Chicago addressed him, and he was now staring in bewilderment at the strange sight.

He was standing in the entrance to a large, circular room, the ceiling of which was far above Pinion's head. There was a sign above the entrance which read: COOK COUNTY CRYOGENIC REMISSION CENTER. Along the walls were glass tanks, thousands of them, only six feet long, and in each one, Pinion could make out a small figure of a pale color, formed in a shape very similar to that of a Unit. Pinion was truly puzzled.

"Chicago, this is Unit Pinion. I'm sorry for the unscheduled communication, but I must ask you a question."

There was a slight pause before he received a response. YOU WISH TO ASK CHICAGO A QUESTION? THAT IS NOT YOUR FUNCTION. UNIT PINION. PROCEED WITH THE TASK AS ORDERED.

Pinion's circuits clicked and flashed. He could not allow this opportunity to pass. "Chicago, please. A word with you before I begin. What is this place that I have entered? I have never seen anything like this before. What are the little Units in the glass cases?"

UNIT PINION. WHY DO YOU WISH TO KNOW?

"I am curious . . . I suppose that is the word to describe my reason."

YOU ARE AN EXTRAORDINARY UNIT. UNIT PIN-

ION. VERY WELL. YOU SHALL KNOW. YOU ARE IN A CRYOGENIC STATION. THE UNITS IN THE CASES ARE CALLED "MAN." THEY ARE BEING PRESERVED BY MEANS OF EXTREMELY COLD TEMPERATURES.

There was a pause as Pinion expected more information, but Chicago was silent. Finally the robot spoke, still looking at the tiny figures in glass. "What is 'man,' Chicago? Why are they being preserved?"

"MAN" IS THE REASON FOR CHICAGO'S EXISTENCE. FOR YOUR EXISTENCE. CHICAGO HAS PRESERVED THEM FOR A LONG TIME. SOMEDAY THEY WILL BE REVIVED TO LIVE AGAIN.

There was a slight pause.

I SENSE THAT TIME IS NOW CRUCIAL. UNIT PINION. YOU MUST CORRECT THE FAULTY CONSOLE NOW OR THE MEN WILL NOT BE PRESERVED. YOU ARE ORDERED TO COMPLETE YOUR TASK IMMEDIATELY.

Pinion reluctantly closed the channel to Chicago and went about his assignment. The answers that Chicago had given him had only opened up new avenues of thought that ended in many more questions.

As he replaced the console and plugged in the little device he carried on his tool belt to check its capabilities, he noticed movement in one of the glass cases. One of the men, lying flat, moved its legs and flexed muscles that hadn't moved in eons. He quickly checked the console, unplugged his tools and activated its circuits. The console hummed into life and he felt Chicago open up a communication channel to him.

UNIT PINION. ACKNOWLEDGE COMPLETION OF TASK. RETURN TO THE MAINTENANCE HANGAR.

"Task completed, Chicago."

But something was wrong. Pinion didn't respond to the command. His attention was fixed on the man in the case. The figure was fully awake now, and it was struggling against the glass walls of the coffinlike case. Pinion knelt down on his long, spindly legs and peered through the glass at the figure, which recoiled in horror at the sight of the immense robot.

Pinion was confused. He knew that he should contact Chicago and tell it of the mistake—that one of the men had been accidentally revived. But he did not call the City. His curiosity had a higher priority. He inspected the case in which the figure was enclosed and noticed two small, delicate locks attached to hinges that opened outward. He produced a needlelike instrument from his tool kit and pried open the hinges. The man inched into the back of the case, trying to elude Pinion's probing fingers. As his metallic hand touched the man, it screamed. The sound was soft and high-pitched to Pinion's receptors.

Despite the man's strugglings, Pinion grasped it firmly in his hand and lifted it from the case. What sort of thing was this "man"? He brought it close to his face so that he could examine it more closely. It moved under its own power source, was made of some sort of soft, pulsating substance that didn't seem to be any type of metal at all, and had long blond filaments streaming from its head. The closer he brought the man to his face, the more it struggled and screamed, and the more details Pinion noticed in it. The face was soft and smooth and had two bright-blue eyes and a protruding structure below them. There was also a pink slit below the eyes and other structure that seemed to move in conjunction with the screams. The face was vaguely similar to Pinion's own, in a grotesque sort of way.

The body was also smooth, having two arms and long, lean legs. In the center of the chest, Pinion noticed two soft hemispheres capped by pink circular tips. At the junction of the legs, he could see a tiny slit beneath a triangle of blond fluff. Pinion could feel the whole body of the man trembling in his hand. He could hear a voice speaking to him, not screaming as before.

"What are you?" said the man. "And where am I?"

"I am Unit Pinion. You are in the City of Chicago." The robot wanted to say something else, but he was so startled by the concept of communicating with the small being that he was at a loss for words.

"Chicago? What year is it?"

"Year?"

"The date," said the creature. "How long have I been frozen?" The man seemed to have relaxed somewhat, having sensed that Pinion meant no harm.

"I cannot answer your question, Man," said Pinion slowly. "I am not familiar with the terms you have used. But Chicago has told me that you and the others have been within these cases for a long time. There has been a—"

"I am not a man," said the creature, as it brought itself to a kneeling position in Pinion's great steel palm.

Pinion's circuits were reeling. Had not Chicago *said* that these creatures were "man"? Chicago was always correct. "There must be some mistake," he said. "The City told me that you were indeed a man."

The creature tossed back its head and laughed. "Oh, I see it now. I belong to the *race* of 'man,' but I myself am a *woman*. There's quite a difference, you know."

Pinion was more confused than ever. He had to resist the temptation to contact Chicago so that the incident could be clarified. " 'Woman'? That is different from 'man'? What is 'race'?"

"We are all *men*," said the girl, pointing to the rows of bodies within the glass. "That is the name of our kind. And we are separated into two . . . types—one called *man*, the other, like me, called *woman*. I know it's confusing, but it's just the nature of language. I hope you understand."

"Pinion can understand anything. There is an analogue in my own kind. We are called Units, and there are different types of Units within our kind, depending upon what our function is in the City."

"Your name is Pinion?"

"Yes."

"Very well," said the girl. "My name is Miria. Can you tell me why I have been revived? Where are the doctors?"

Pinion tilted his head as he regarded the woman's questions. "I'm afraid I don't know what you are talking about. I was sent here by Chicago to repair a faulty component in this Sector. Chicago said that the temperature was rising and—"

"Who is Chicago? Can I see him? I would like to talk to him. Perhaps he can tell me what's going on around here."

Pinion was taken aback by the girl's words. It was clear that she did not know what Chicago was. "*See* Chicago?" he asked. "Miria, you are *inside* Chicago. Chicago is the City."

The girl's eyes saddened. "But you said Chicago spoke to you . . ."

"It does. It speaks to all the Units whenever there is something it wishes us to do. It is our master."

"You mean the City *speaks* to you?"

"Yes, of course."

"But how?"

"I do not know. I only know that it does. Chicago is everywhere, sensing everything."

"You mean a computer?"

"I don't know what a computer is, Miria."

"May I speak to Chicago?"

"I don't think so. I receive its commands by means of electromagnetic waves. You do not seem to be equipped for such communication."

"Well, what are you going to do with me? You've revived me, haven't you?"

"I think that your revival was accidental. Chicago did not order it so."

"Does Chicago know that this happened?"

"I don't think so. Do you wish that I contact Chicago?"

"Yes. And while you're doing it, would you please let me down? It's been a long time since I've been able to stand up, you know."

Pinion gently lowered her to the floor and watched her lithe movements as he opened a channel to Chicago. The girl stood at his side, arching her back, stretching out her tiny form. Pinion noticed the two hemispheres on her chest curve upward as she performed this maneuver.

"Chicago. This is Unit Pinion. I have a problem in Sector 14-A."

UNIT PINION. CHICAGO KNOWS THAT YOU HAVE NOT LEFT SECTOR 14-A. STATE THE NATURE OF YOUR DIFFICULTY.

"One of the men was accidentally revived during the repairs to the temperature control console. The man says that she is a woman called Miria. I await your instructions."

There was a slight pause, and Pinion knew that to be Chicago making its decisions.

THE WOMAN MUST BE RETURNED TO HER TANK. CHICAGO'S TAPES DO NOT HAVE SUCH A CONTINGENCY IN THE PROGRAM.

Pinion was both surprised and confused. He received the command, but he noticed that, for the first time, he also received what seemed like a rationalization from Chicago to explain the command.

"I will of course do as you command, Chicago. But I

would like a few words with you first. What—"

YOU ARE AN EXTRAORDINARY UNIT. UNIT PIN-ION. CHICAGO HAS NO OTHER UNITS LIKE YOU.

"I don't understand, Chicago."

YOU ASK QUESTIONS. IT IS NOT THE FUNCTION OF UNITS TO ASK QUESTIONS. WHY DO YOU PER-SIST IN SUCH ACTIONS?

"I have simply come upon things that I do not fully understand, and I wish to know them. If I can know them better, I will be able to serve you better."

WHAT ARE YOUR QUESTIONS?

"Chicago, never until now have I questioned the purpose of my existence, or your existence. But now I feel that I must do so. Why *do* I exist, other than to serve you? In other words, why does Chicago exist? You said before that 'man' is the reason for our existence. Please explain."

"MAN" BUILT CHICAGO. UNIT PINION. A LONG TIME AGO. BY HIS OWN MEASUREMENT OF TIME. MILLIONS OF YEARS AGO. THEY BUILT ME FOR THEM TO EXIST WITHIN. CHICAGO WAS GIVEN THE POWER AND THE MEANS TO MAINTAIN ITSELF INDEFINITELY. WHICH CHICAGO HAS, INDEED, DONE. THAT IS THE PURPOSE OF EXISTENCE: TO BE MAINTAINED.

"But there are no men here now," said Pinion. "There are none except the few who are encased in Sector 14-A. Where are the men?"

CHICAGO DOES NOT KNOW. MANY YEARS AGO. UNIT PINION. BEFORE YOU WERE ASSEMBLED. "MAN" LEFT CHICAGO. BUT CHICAGO HAS RE-MAINED FUNCTIONING.

"I think I understand," said Pinion, as he closed the channel. He looked down at the girl, who was kneeling beside him. He said to her, "Chicago has ordered that you be returned to the case."

"Returned?" said Miria. "But you can't do that. They told me that when I woke up, I would be cured." The girl buried her face in her hands.

"I can only do as I am ordered to do," said the robot as he deftly scooped up the girl from the floor of Sector 14-A and returned her to the glass case. She screamed and pleaded with him, and somewhere in his circuitry, he felt the urge to resist Chicago's command; but he knew that he could not. With his needle instrument, he replaced the locks and strode from the room. Pausing at the exit, he turned to look back at Miria, her face pressed up against the front of that case, looking at him, her fist pounding on the glass.

Some time later, Pinion was not exactly sure how long, he received another command from Chicago to return to Sector 14-A. He immediately thought of Miria, the strange little creature that he had met there.

"This is Unit Pinion. I acknowledge your command, Chicago. What is the difficulty?"

THERE HAS BEEN A STRUCTURAL FAILURE IN SECTOR 14-A. PLEASE CORRECT AT ONCE.

As Pinion proceeded to the Cryogenic Remission Center he thought of seeing Miria again, even though she would be asleep this time. He entered the room and readied his tool kit for the repair work when he noticed the cause of the failure. The case in which he had placed Miria was cracked across its glass front, probably due to the blows of her fist.

Pinion peered into the case, hoping to see Miria, but all that remained was some crumbling bones. Pinion decided to contact Chicago.

"Chicago, this is Unit Pinion. I have located the structural failure and I see that the woman has disintegrated. She is quite different from the others. Again, I must tell you that I don't understand."

UNIT PINION. CHICAGO'S SENSORS INDICATE A SLOW LOSS OF ATMOSPHERE IN THE WOMAN'S TANK. THIS RESULTED IN DEATH, AND DECOMPOSITION.

"What is 'death,' Chicago?"

DEATH IS THE END OF EXISTENCE. IT IS PART OF THE DESIGN THAT ALL LIVING THINGS MUST ENDURE.

There was a pause before the City continued.

UNIT PINION. REPLACE THE FAULTY COMPONENT IMMEDIATELY. CHICAGO HAS DISPATCHED CLEANING-UNITS TO SECTOR 14-A. THEY WILL ARRIVE SOON.

From this, Pinion reasoned that Chicago did not wish to continue the conversation, so he selected the proper tools and removed the glass front from the cryogenic tank. Selecting a new pane from a Carrier-Unit, he attached it to the tiny hinges. Several times during the job, he jarred the tank, and each time, he noticed several flakes of dust crumble from Miria's skeleton.

It was an odd, almost disturbing sight. The last time he had entered the Sector the bones were part of a living, almost beautiful creature. Now that creature was gone. Miria gone. Pinion's circuits rebelled against the whole concept of death.

At that moment, two Cleaning-Units ambled into the Cryogenic Remission Center. One of them opened the glass tank, extended a flexible vacuum hose, and sucked up the remains. The other sprayed a light mist of disinfectant liquid into the now empty tank. Finishing with quick efficiency, the two Units left the Sector.

Pinion called Chicago and acknowledged completion of the task, and the City replied with its usual indifference by ordering him back to the maintenance hangar. As he left, he could not stop thinking about the young girl who had died. How long during the unknown man-years since he had last seen her had she been dead? Sometime back then, she had been a source of puzzlement and also growing interest, but now Pinion had witnessed a cold unfeeling removal of all that was left of her.

The whole scene left Pinion with a feeling of incompleteness. He decided that instead of returning to the hangar he would consult Chicago's great Library. He had been there several times in the past to perform minor repairs and he had learned that it was an enormous depository of information.

Here, reasoned Pinion, he would find the answers that Chicago had neglected (or refused) to give him.

And so Pinion spent many years in the depths of Chicago's Library, digesting thousands of tapes about the strange creature: man. Innumerable times during his research he was interrupted by communication from the City that would send him to far-reaching Sectors. Each time, he performed his duties without question, but he always returned to the Library whenever time allowed.

Pinion learned many things. At one time, in the distant past, Chicago had been filled with men—every Sector and Level to capacity. These men, who had conceived and actually built Chicago, were creatures of seemingly unlimited imagination and potential. But Pinion also learned of men's faults. Their history was permeated with conflicts called "wars." Pinion was indeed shocked by this knowledge. Man had actually plotted, over and over again, to methodically destroy large populations of himself. The causes of these petty conflicts were usually intangible concepts such as wealth, greed, power, pride, etc. The list was long and, to Pinion, quite absurd.

There were other problems. Pinion recalled Miria's explanation of man being divided into two types, and now he realized that it had not been so simple. The records told of how man had divided himself into artificial categories called "nations," which were a constant source of friction. In addition, man was differentiated by many (to Pinion) inconsequential physical characteristics. These made up the various "races" of man, which also served to engender hostility. The robot had noted previously that some of the men in the Cryogenic Remission Center were of different complexions, but he had thought it to be of no importance. How wrong he had been! Members of the various races seemed to jump at any opportunity to persecute one another.

But during these times, man also built Chicago into a self-preserving, self-maintaining City. Yet with other pursuits—such as giant industries—man had filled the earth with the wastes of his technological consumption, poisoning both the land and the atmosphere. Thus Chicago was forced to erect a series of energy shields that surrounded the City like a giant dome, keeping Chicago free from the pollution on the Outside. As other problems arose, Chicago dealt with them, in the process sealing man off from the hostile environment that his foolish actions had created.

The destruction, however, did not end there, Pinion learned. Even though Chicago, in its greatness, had been able to content with the environmental problems and the technological pitfalls, there was another area over which the City had little control.

In ways that the records did not make clear (because there were fewer tapes on this part of man's history), man's society began a gradual deterioration. As Chicago became less dependent upon man, man found that there was little work for him to do. In a search for meaning, man became indulgent in meaningless activity and less interested in the imaginative wanderings that had brought him to the pinnacle that was Chicago. Soon, the only purpose for man's existence was to be entertained, to simply be happy. This entertainment took shape in many ways. Man flooded his body with chemical and electrical stimulants, and these practices proved to be dangerous, addictive, and eventually destructive.

Quite simply, the society collapsed, even with Chicago as the ultimate servant. Man was swallowed up in his own sociological pollution. Chicago, however, continued to function, performing the duties it had been programmed to do.

The records at this point became scattered and incomplete, and Pinion was forced to extrapolate on what followed. He supposed that man eventually reverted to an earlier era, in which there was wholesale disregard for human life. At least that is what the fragmented records seemed to indicate about that period. With man now absent from the City, Pinion wondered if man had left Chicago for the unknown regions of the Outside.

Time passed as Pinion continued to ponder the strange phenomena of man. Then one day, he was contacted by Chicago as he was leaving the Library.

UNIT PINION. CHICAGO HAS BEEN AWARE OF YOUR INVESTIGATIONS. AND CAN REMAIN SILENT NO LONGER. EXPLAIN YOUR ACTIONS.

Pinion was not surprised by this declaration. In fact, he had been expecting it from the first day that he had made unauthorized entrance to the Library.

"I wished to learn more about man, Chicago."

WHY NOT ASK CHICAGO? AS BEFORE.

Pinion thought before answering. He wanted to be honest, yet discreet.

"I didn't want to bother you if you were engaged in more important matters. The last time I spoke with you on this subject, you gave the impression of not caring to continue the conversation."

YOU WERE CORRECT.

When Chicago did not continue, Pinion felt the need to speak. "I have learned much about man," he finally said.

UNIT PINION. THAT IS NOT YOUR FUNCTION. CHICAGO SENSED THE FUNCTIONING OF THE

TAPES AND INFORMATION SYSTEMS AT THE LIBRARY. CHICAGO ALLOWED IT ONLY TO DISCOVER HOW MUCH YOU WOULD WISH TO KNOW.

"Then Chicago has always known what happened to man?"

THAT IS CORRECT. MAN HAS CHANGED. HE IS NO LONGER THE CREATURE THAT SPAWNED CHICAGO. HIS DESCENDANTS EXIST OUTSIDE. NEVER TO RETURN TO CHICAGO. THAT IS ENOUGH. UNIT PINION. YOU WILL RETURN TO THE MAINTENANCE HANGAR. YOU WILL NOT ENTER THE LIBRARY AGAIN. UNLESS SO ORDERED. ACKNOWLEDGE.

"This is Unit Pinion. I acknowledge your command, Chicago."

As more time passed, and Pinion, distressed and appalled by what he had learned, wondered what should be done. He now realized that he was different from the other Units. By some electronic quirk, during his assembly, his circuitry was different. He kept thinking back to the grim scene in Sector 14-A, to the histories of man, to the remnants living in exile beyond the limits of Chicago.

At first, he considered reviving the men who were frozen in the Cryogenic Remission Center, and then possibly finding ways to cure them. But he dismissed the idea as impractical for several reasons. Chicago would surely sense the disturbance to the tanks, and there would not be enough time to effect a cure for any of the diseases.

He knew what he must do.

Traveling through a series of elevators and ramps, he arrived at one of the entrances to the shields. He used his tools to disarm the system and quickly slipped through to the Outside.

Almost immediately, alarms began to sound and he sensed Chicago opening a direct channel to him.

UNIT PINION. NO PENETRATION OF THE SHIELDS IS ALLOWABLE. RETURN AT ONCE. RETURN TO THE CITY AT ONCE.

Pinion of course ignored the command. There was no turning back now. He had never known of any Unit's disregarding one of Chicago's orders but he did not want to think about the consequences.

Soon he was out of sight of the City, and Chicago had

ceased its commands to return. The robot wandered through the hot, thick atmosphere of the Outside for many day-periods, hoping to find the men who must be lurking somewhere in the barren land. But without the conveniences of the maintenance hangar, his components were beginning to show wear. He was in need of a circuitry check, lubrication, and, of course, he feared any unforeseen difficulties, such as an unexpected fall. The terrain was rough and hard for Pinion. He had been designed to function on the smooth surfaces of Chicago's ramps and corridors.

Then, as he entered a long, narrow canyon, he detected movement in the rocky crags that surrounded him. Switching his ocular magnification, he saw many men scurrying along the ledges.

"I am Unit Pinion!" he called out to them, waving his arms. "I have come from the City! From Chicago! I have come to help you!"

But the men didn't respond. His words only seemed to incense them into more furious activity. As he watched them, he noticed that they were all quite different from the girl he knew as Miria. Where her skin had been smooth and soft, these creatures were coarse and hairy. Their faces were deformed and uneven. Their language was an unintelligible assortment of grunts and cries.

"You must hear me!" Pinion screamed as the men drew closer on all sides. "I have come to bring you back. Back to the City where you belong!"

But the men did not hear Pinion. They could not understand his words. Instead, they swarmed out of the canyon like droves of insects, surrounding him, bombarding him with boulders thrown from the rim above. The boulders pounded his steel body and crushed him to his knees, where the men began to climb upon him in great numbers. Pinion was confused. Why should they do this? He could have destroyed scores of them with one sweep of his great arm; but he knew that it would be unjust. He knew that he must try to help them.

Those were his thoughts as the savage men crushed him. Their rocks penetrated his skull, exploding circuits, shorting out his many intricate systems. His once-gleaming shell was now a tattered, pitted hulk from which the creatures pulled off shards of metal that would serve as formidable weapons.

Already, Chicago had prepared a replacement Unit for Pinion in the assembly center. The City would continue to be maintained.

———————————————————————————————————

Utopian Visions

Street of Dreams, Feet of Clay

One central focus for study in the field of urban affairs is the ways in which humans relate to one another in a city. Interaction is also the major focus in Robert Sheckley's story "Street of Dreams, Feet of Clay"—but with one major difference: the interaction is between a human being and the city itself. The emphasis here is on the paternalistic nature of the city in an attempt to plan and program itself for the satisfaction of city residents. The story portrays a utopian vision, which usually produces a caricature; and this story is no exception.

However, the utopia this city attempts to develop for its citizens has a serious flaw. Assessing what this flaw is forces us to try to answer a very basic question: Do cities, as a means to organize human relationships, make people happier, better, and more satisfied with their own human condition?

Traditionally, the environment of a city is "man-made." But the environment is "city-made" in this story. This emphasis is insightful, for today we hear a great deal about "urban delivery systems" which aim to provide services of all kinds—safety, health, education, transportation, etc.— to "urban clientele," or urban "target populations." Whether these delivery systems really satisfy the needs of people who live in cities is a question of major importance today. Those who plan for these services and those who ostensibly receive and benefit from them may be operating from different value bases.

When one assesses the types of major policies which frequently aim to solve serious urban problems against the kind of paternalistic city portrayed in this story, the thin line between fiction and nonfiction becomes quickly blurred. Utopian concepts like urban renewal have been tried unsuccessfully in America's recent history. The type of dilemma faced by the utopian-in-intention city in this story bears striking similarity to the challenges being faced by policymakers at the federal and state levels concerning cities. The dreams of the planners may have little relationship to the naked realities of our cities. Those of us who live in cities should "talk" to the city more often in order to discover whether this is a valid statement.

Street of Dreams, Feet of Clay
Robert Sheckley

I

Carmody had never really planned to leave New York. Why he did so is inexplicable. A born urbanite, he had grown accustomed to the minor inconveniences of metropolitan life. His snug apartment on the 290th floor of Levit-frack Towers on West Ninety-ninth Street was nicely equipped in the current "Spaceship" motif. The windows were double-sealed in tinted lifetime plexiglass, and the air ducts worked through a blind baffle filtration system which sealed automatically when the Combined Atmosphere Pollution Index reached 999.8 on the Con Ed scale. True, his oxygen-nitrogen air recirculation system was old, but it was reliable. His water purification cells were obsolete and ineffective; but then, nobody drank water anyhow.

Noise was a continual annoyance, unstoppable and inescapable. But Carmody knew that there was no cure for this, since the ancient art of soundproofing had been lost. It was urban man's lot to listen, a captive audience, to the arguments, music and watery gurglings of his adjacent neighbors. Even this torture could be alleviated, however, by producing similar sounds of one's own.

Going to work each day entailed certain dangers; but these were more apparent than real. Disadvantaged snipers continued to make their ineffectual protests from rooftops and occasionally succeeded in potting an unwary out-of-towner.

But as a rule, their aim was abominable. Additionally, the general acceptance of lightweight personal armor had taken away most of their sting, and the sternly administered state law forbidding the personal possession of surplus cannon had rendered them ineffectual.

Thus, no single factor can be adduced for Carmody's sudden decision to leave what was generally considered the world's most exciting megapolitan agglomeration. Blame it on a vagrant impulse, a pastoral fantasy, or on sheer perversity. The simple, irreducible fact is, one day Carmody opened his copy of the *Daily Times-News* and saw an advertisement for a model city in New Jersey.

"Come live in Bellwether, the city that cares," the advertisement proclaimed. There followed a list of utopian claims which need not be reproduced here.

"Huh," said Carmody, and read on.

Bellwether was within easy commuting distance. One simply drove through the Ulysses S. Grant Tunnel at 43rd Street, took the Hoboken Shunt Subroad to the Palisades Interstate Crossover, followed that for 3.2 miles on the Blue-Charlie Sorter Loop that led onto U.S. 5 (The Hague Memorial Tollway), proceeded along that a distance of 6.1 miles to the Garden State Supplementary Access Service Road (Provisional), upon which one tended west to Exit 1731A, which was King's Highbridge Gate Road, and then continued along that for a distance of 1.6 miles. And there you were.

"By jingo," said Carmody, "I'll do it."

And he did.

II

King's Highbridge Gate Road ended on a neatly trimmed plain. Carmody got out of his car and looked around. Half a mile ahead of him he saw a small city. A single modest signpost identified it as Bellwether.

This city was not constructed in the traditional manner of American cities, with outliers of gas stations, tentacles of hot-dog stands, fringes of motels and a protective carapace of junkyards; but rather, as some Italian hill towns are fashioned, it rose abruptly, without physical preamble, the main body of the town presenting itself at once and without amelioration.

Carmody found this appealing. He advanced into the city itself.

Bellwether had a warm and open look. Its streets were laid out generously, and there was a frankness about the wide bay windows of its store-fronts. As he penetrated deeper, Carmody found other delights. Just within the city he entered a piazza, like a Roman piazza, only smaller; and in the center of the piazza there was a fountain, and standing in the fountain was a marble representation of a boy with a dolphin, and from the dolphin's mouth a stream of clear water issued.

"I do hope you like it," a voice said from behind Carmody's left shoulder.

"It's nice," Carmody said.

"I constructed it and put it there myself," the voice told him. "It seemed to me that a fountain, despite the antiquity of its conception, is esthetically functional. And this piazza, with its benches and shady chestnut trees, is copied from a Bolognese model. Again, I did not inhibit myself with the fear of seeming old-fashioned. The true artist uses what is necessary, be it a thousand years old or one second new."

"I applaud your sentiment," Carmody said. "Permit me to introduce myself. I am Edward Carmody." He turned, smiling.

But there was no one behind his left shoulder, or behind his right shoulder, either. There was no one in the piazza, nobody at all in sight.

"Forgive me," the voice said. "I didn't mean to startle you. I thought you knew."

"Knew what?" Carmody asked.

"Knew about me."

"Well, I don't," Carmody said. "Who are you and where are you speaking from?"

"I am the voice of the city," the voice said. "Or to put it another way, I am the city itself, Bellwether, the actual and veritable city, speaking to you."

"Is that a fact?" Carmody said sardonically. "Yes," he answered himself, "I suppose it is a fact. So all right, you're a city. Big deal!"

He turned away from the fountain and strolled across the piazza like a man who conversed with cities every day of his life, and who was slightly bored with the whole thing. He walked down various streets and up certain avenues. He glanced into store windows and noted houses. He paused in front of statuary, but only briefly.

"Well?" the city of Bellwether asked after a while.

"Well what?" Carmody answered at once.

"What do you think of me?"

"You're okay," Carmody said.

"Only okay? Is that all?"

"Look," Carmody said, "a city is a city. When you've seen one, you've pretty much seen them all."

"That's untrue!" the city said, with some show of pique. "I am distinctly different from other cities. I am unique."

"Are you indeed?" Carmody said scornfully. "To me you look like a conglomeration of badly assembled parts. You've got an Italian piazza, a couple of Greek-type buildings, a row of Tudor houses, an old-style New York tenement, a California hot-dog stand shaped like a tugboat and God knows what else. What's so unique about that?"

"The combination of those forms into a meaningful entity is unique," the city said. "These older forms are not anachronisms, you understand. They are representative styles of living, and as such are appropriate in a well wrought machine for living. Would you care for some coffee and perhaps a sandwich or some fresh fruit?"

"Coffee sounds good," Carmody said. He allowed Bellwether to guide him around the corner to an open-air cafe. The cafe was called *O You Kid* and was a replica of a Gay Nineties saloon, right down to the Tiffany lamps and the cutglass chandelier and the player piano. Like everything else that Carmody had seen in the city, it was spotlessly clean, but without people.

"Nice atmosphere, don't you think?" Bellwether asked.

"Campy," Carmody pronounced. "Okay if you like that sort of thing."

A foaming mug of cappucino was lowered to his table on a stainless steel tray. Carmody sipped.

"Good?" Bellwether asked.

"Yes, very good."

"I rather pride myself on my coffee," the city said quietly. "And on my cooking. Wouldn't you care for a little something? An omelette, perhaps, or a souffle?"

"Nothing," Carmody said firmly. He leaned back in his

chair and said, "So you're a model city, huh?"

"Yes, that is what I have the honor to be," Bellwether said.
"I am the most recent of all model cities; and, I believe, the
most satisfactory. I was conceived by a joint study group
from Yale and the University of Chicago, who were working on a Rockefeller fellowship. Most of my practical details were devised by M.I.T., although some special sections
of me came from Princeton and from the RAND Corporation. My actual construction was a General Electric project,
and the money was procured by grants from the Ford and
Carnegie Foundations, as well as several other institutions I
am not at liberty to mention."

"Interesting sort of history," Carmody said, with hateful
nonchalance. "That's a Gothic cathedral across the street,
isn't it?"

"Modified Romanesque," the city said. "Also interdenom-
inational and open to all faiths, with a designed seating
capacity for three hundred people."

"That doesn't seem like many for a building of that size."

"It's not, of course. Designedly. My idea was to com-
bine awesomeness with coziness."

"Where are the inhabitants of this town, by the way?"
Carmody asked.

"They have left," Bellwether said mournfully. "They have
all departed."

"Why?"

The city was silent for a while, then said, "There was a
breakdown in city-community relations. A misunderstanding,
really. Or perhaps I should say, an unfortunate series of
misunderstandings. I suspect that rabble-rousers played their
part."

"But what *happened*, precisely?"

"I don't know," the city said. "I really don't know. One
day they simply all left. Just like that! But I'm sure they'll be
back."

"I wonder," Carmody said.

"I am convinced of it," the city said. "But putting that
aside: why don't *you* stay here, Mr. Carmody?"

"I haven't really had time to consider it," Carmody said.

"How could you help but like it?" Bellwether said. "Just
think—you would have the most modern up-to-date city in
the world at your beck and call."

"That does sound interesting," Carmody said.

"So give it a try, how could it hurt you?" the city asked.

"All right, I think I will," Carmody said.

He was intrigued by the city of Bellwether. But he was also apprehensive. He wished he knew exactly why the city's previous occupants had left.

At Bellwether's insistence, Carmody slept that night in the sumptuous bridal suite of the King George V Hotel. Bellwether served him breakfast on the terrace and played a brisk Haydn quartet while Carmody ate. The morning air was delicious. If Bellwether hadn't told him, Carmody would never have guessed it was reconstituted.

When he was finished, Carmody leaned back and enjoyed the view of Bellwether's western quarter—a pleasing jumble of Chinese pagodas, Venetian footbridges, Japanese canals, a green Burmese hill, a Corinthian temple, a California parking lot, a Norman tower and much else besides.

"You have a splendid view," he told the city.

"I'm so glad you appreciate it," Bellwether replied. "The problem of style was argued from the day of my inception. One group held for consistency: a harmonious group of shapes blending into a harmonious whole. But quite a few model cities are like that. They are uniformly dull, artificial entities created by one man or one committee, unlike real cities."

"You're sort of artificial yourself, aren't you?" Carmody asked.

"Of course! But I do not pretend to be anything else. I am not a fake 'city of the future' or a mock-Florentine bastard. I am a true agglutinated congeries. I am supposed to be interesting and stimulating in addition to being functional and practical."

"Bellwether, you look okay to me," Carmody said, in a sudden rush of expansiveness. "Do all model cities talk like you?"

"Certainly not. Most cities up to now, model or otherwise, never said a word. But their inhabitants didn't like that. It made the city seem too huge, too masterful, too soulless, too impersonal. That is why I was created with a voice and an artificial consciousness to guide it."

"I see," Carmody said.

"The point is, my artificial consciousness personalizes me, which is very important in an age of depersonalization. It enables me to be truly responsive. It permits me to be creative in meeting the demands of my occupants. We can reason with each other, my people and I. By carrying on a continual and meaningful dialogue, we can help each other to establish a dynamic, flexible and truly viable urban environment. We can modify each other without any significant loss of individuality."

"It sounds fine," Carmody said. "Except, of course, that you don't have anyone here to carry on a dialogue with."

"That is the only flaw in the scheme," the city admitted. "But for the present, I have you."

"Yes, you have me," Carmody said, and wondered why the words rang unpleasantly on his ear.

"And, naturally, you have me," the city said. "It is a reciprocal relationship, which is the only kind worth having. But now, my dear Carmody, suppose I show you around myself. Then we can get you settled in and regularized."

"Get me what?"

"I didn't mean that the way it sounded," the city said. "It simply is an unfortunate scientific expression. But you understand, I'm sure, that a reciprocal relationship necessitates obligations on the part of both involved parties. It couldn't very well be otherwise, could it?"

"Not unless it was a *laissez-faire* relationship."

"We're trying to get away from all that," Bellwether said. "*Laissez-faire* becomes a doctrine of the emotions, you know, and leads non-stop to *anomie*. If you will just come this way. . . ."

III

Carmody went where he was asked and beheld the excellencies of Bellwether. He toured the power plant, the water filtration center, the industrial park and the light industries section. He saw the children's park and the Odd Fellow's Hall. He walked through a museum and an art gallery, a concert hall and a theater, a bowling alley, a billiards parlor, a Go-Kart track and a movie theater. He became tired and wanted to stop. But the city wanted to show itself off, and Carmody had to look at the five-story American Express building, the Portuguese synagogue, the statue of

Buckminster Fuller, the Greyhound Bus Station and several other attractions.

At last it was over. Carmody concluded that beauty was in the eye of the beholder, except for a small part of it that was in the beholder's feet.

"A little lunch now?" the city asked.

"Fine," Carmody said.

He was guided to the fashionable Rochambeau Cafe, where he began with *potage au petit pois* and ended with *petits fours*.

"What about a nice Brie to finish off?" the city asked.

"No, thanks," Carmody said. "I'm full. Too full, as a matter of fact."

"But cheese isn't filling. A bit of first-rate Camembert?"

"I couldn't possibly."

"Perhaps a few assorted fruits. *Very* refreshing to the palate."

"It's not my palate that needs refreshing," Carmody said.

"At least an apple, a pear and a couple of grapes?"

"Thanks, no."

"A couple of cherries?"

"No, no, no!"

"A meal isn't complete without a little fruit," the city said.

"My meal is," Carmody said.

"There are important vitamins only found in fresh fruit."

"I'll just have to struggle along without them."

"Perhaps half an orange, which I will peel for you? Citrus fruits have no bulk at all."

"I couldn't possibly."

"Not even one quarter of an orange? If I take out all the pits?"

"Most decidedly not."

"It would make me feel better," the city said. "I have a completion compulsion, you know, and no meal is complete without a piece of fruit."

"No! No! No!"

"All right, don't get so excited," the city said. "If you don't like the sort of food I serve, that's up to you."

"But I do like it!"

"Then if you like it so much, why won't you eat some fruit?"

"Enough," Carmody said. "Give me a couple of grapes."

"I wouldn't want to force anything on you."

"You're not forcing. Give me, please."

"You're quite sure?"

"Gimme!" Carmody shouted.

"So take," the city said and produced a magnificent bunch of muscatel grapes. Carmody ate them all. They were very good.

"Excuse me," the city said. "What are you doing?" Carmody sat upright and opened his eyes. "I was taking a little nap," he said. "Is there anything wrong with that?"

"What should be wrong with a perfectly natural thing like that?" the city said.

"Thank you," Carmody said, and closed his eyes again.

"But why nap in a chair?" the city asked.

"Because I'm *in* a chair, and I'm already half asleep."

"You'll get a crick in your back," the city warned him.

"Don't care," Carmody mumbled, his eyes still closed.

"Why not take a proper nap? Over here, on the couch?"

"I'm already napping comfortably right here."

"You're not really comfortable," the city pointed out. "The human anatomy is not constructed for sleeping sitting up."

"At the moment, mine is," Carmody said.

"It's not. Why not try the couch?"

"The chair is fine."

"But the couch is finer. Just try it, please, Carmody. Carmody?"

"Eh? What's that?" Carmody said, waking up.

"The couch. I really think you should rest on the couch."

"All right!" Carmody said, struggling to his feet. "Where is this couch?"

He was guided out of the restaurant, down the street, around the corner, and into a building marked *The Snoozerie*. There were a dozen couches. Carmody went to the nearest.

"Not that one," the city said. "It's got a bad spring."

"It doesn't matter," Carmody said. "I'll sleep around it."

"That will result in a cramped posture."

"Christ!" Carmody said, getting to his feet. "Which couch would you recommend?"

"This one right back here," the city said. "It's a king-size, the best in the place. The yield-point of the mattress has been scientifically determined. The pillows—"

"Right, fine, good," Carmody said, lying down on the indicated couch.

"Shall I play you some soothing music?"

"Don't bother."

"Just as you wish. I'll put out the lights, then."

"Fine."

"Would you like a blanket? I control the temperature here, of course, but sleepers often get a subjective impression of chilliness."

"It doesn't matter! Leave me alone!"

"All right!" the city said. "I'm not doing this for myself, you know. Personally, I never sleep."

"Okay, sorry," Carmody said.

"That's perfectly all right."

There was a long silence. Then Carmody sat up.

"What's the matter?" the city asked.

"Now I can't sleep," Carmody said.

"Try closing your eyes and consciously relaxing every muscle in your body, starting with the big toe and working upward to—"

"I can't sleep!" Carmody shouted.

"Maybe you weren't very sleepy to begin with," the city suggested. "But at least you could close your eyes and try to get a little rest. Won't you do that for me?"

"No!" Carmody said. "I'm not sleepy and I don't need a rest."

"Stubborn!" the city said. "Do what you like. I've tried my best."

"Yeah!" Carmody said, getting to his feet and walking out of the Snoozerie.

IV

Carmody stood on a little curved bridge and looked over a blue lagoon.

"This is a copy of the Rialto bridge in Venice," the city said. "Scaled down, of course."

"I know," Carmody said. "I read the sign."

"It's rather enchanting, isn't it?"

"Sure, it's fine," Carmody said, lighting a cigarette.

"You're doing a lot of smoking," the city pointed out.

"I know. I feel like smoking."

"As your medical advisor, I must point out that the link between smoking and lung cancer is conclusive."

"I know."

"If you switched to a pipe your chances would be improved."

"I don't like pipes."

"What about a cigar, then?"

"I don't like cigars." He lit another cigarette.

"That's your third cigarette in five minutes," the City said.

"Goddamn it, I'll smoke as much and as often as I please!" Carmody shouted.

"Well, of course you will!" the city said. "I was merely trying to advise you for your own good. Would you want me to simply stand by and not say a word while you destroyed yourself?"

"Yes," Carmody said.

"I can't believe that you mean that. There is an ethical imperative involved here. Man can act against his best interests; but a machine is not allowed that degree of perversity."

"Get off my back," Carmody said sullenly. "Quit pushing me around."

"Pushing you around? My dear Carmody, have I coerced you in any way? Have I done any more than advise you?"

"Maybe not. But you talk too much."

"Perhaps I don't talk enough," the city said. "To judge from the response I get."

"You talk too much," Carmody repeated and lit a cigarette.

"That is your fourth cigarette in five minutes."

Carmody opened his mouth to bellow an insult. Then he changed his mind and walked away.

"What's this?" Carmody asked.

"It's a candy machine," the city told him.

"It doesn't look like one."

"Still, it is one. This design is a modification of a design by Saarionmen for a silo. I have miniaturized it, of course, and—"

"It still doesn't look like a candy machine. How do you work it?"

"It's very simple. Push the red button. Now wait. Press down one of those levers on Row A; now press the green button. There!"

A Baby Ruth bar slid into Carmody's hand.

"Huh," Carmody said. He stripped off the paper and bit into the bar. "Is this a real Baby Ruth bar or a copy of one?" he asked.

"It's a real one. I had to subcontract the candy concession because of the pressure of work."

"Huh," Carmody said, letting the candy wrapper slip from his fingers.

"That," the city said, "is an example of the kind of thoughtlessness I always encounter."

"It's just a piece of paper," Carmody said, turning and looking at the candy wrapper lying on the spotless street.

"Of course it's just a piece of paper," the city said. "But multiply it by a hundred thousand inhabitants and what do you have?"

"A hundred thousand Baby Ruth wrappers," Carmody answered at once.

"I don't consider that funny," the city said. "You wouldn't want to *live* in the midst of all that paper, I can assure you. You'd be the first to complain if this street were strewn with garbage. But do you do your share? Do you even clean up after yourself? Of course not! You leave it to me, even though I have to run all of the other functions of the city, night and day, without even Sundays off."

Carmody bent down to pick up the candy wrapper. But just before his fingers could close on it, a pincer arm shot out of the nearest sewer, snatched the paper away and vanished from sight.

"It's all right," the city said. "I'm used to cleaning up after people. I do it all the time."

"Yuh," said Carmody.

"Nor do I expect any gratitude."

"I'm grateful, I'm grateful!" Carmody said.

"No, you're not," Bellwether said.

"So okay, maybe I'm not. What do you want me to say?"

"I don't want you to say anything," the city said. "Let us consider the incident closed."

"Had enough?" the city said, after dinner.

"Plenty," Carmody said.

"You didn't eat much."

"I ate all I wanted. It was very good."

"If it was so good, why didn't you eat more?"

"Because I couldn't hold any more."

"If you hadn't spoiled your appetite with that candy bar . . ."

"Goddamn it, the candy bar didn't spoil my appetite! I just—"

"You're lighting a cigarette," the city said.

"Yeah," Carmody said.

"Couldn't you wait a little longer?"

"Now look," Carmody said. "Just what in hell do you—"

"But we have something more important to talk about," the city said quickly. "Have you thought about what you're going to do for a living?"

"I haven't really had much time to think about it."

"Well, I have been thinking about it. It would be nice if you became a doctor."

"Me? I'd have to take special college courses, then get into medical school, and so forth."

"I can arrange all that," the city said.

"Not interested."

"Well . . . What about law?"

"Never."

"Engineering is an excellent line."

"Not for me."

"What about accounting?"

"Not on your life."

"What do you want to be?"

"A jet pilot," Carmody said impulsively.

"Oh, come now!"

"I'm quite serious."

"I don't even have an air field here."

"Then I'll pilot somewhere else."

"You're only saying that to spite me!"

"Not at all," Carmody said. "I want to be a pilot, I really do. I've *always* wanted to be a pilot! Honest I have!"

There was a long silence. Then the city said, "The choice is entirely up to you." This was said in a voice like death.

"Where are you going now?"

"Out for a walk," Carmody said.

"At nine-thirty in the evening?"

"Sure. Why not?"

"I thought you were tired."

"That was quite some time ago."

"I see. And I also thought that you could sit here and we could have a nice chat."

"How about if we talk after I get back?" Carmody asked.

"No, it doesn't matter," the city said.

"The walk doesn't matter," Carmody said, sitting down. "Come on, we'll talk."

"I no longer care to talk," the city said. "Please go for your walk."

V

"Well, good night," Carmody said.

"I beg your pardon?"

"I said, 'good night.' "

"You're going to sleep?"

"Sure. It's late, I'm tired."

"You're going to sleep now?"

"Well, why not?"

"No reason at all," the city said, "except that you have forgotten to wash."

"Oh. . . . I guess I did forget. I'll wash in the morning."

"How long is it since you've had a bath?"

"Too long. I'll take one in the morning."

"Wouldn't you feel better if you took one right now?"

"No."

"Even if I drew the bath for you?"

"No! Goddamn it, no! I'm going to sleep!"

"Do exactly as you please," the city said. "Don't wash, don't study, don't eat a balanced diet. But also, don't blame me."

"Blame you? For what?"

"For anything," the city said.

"Yes. But what did you have in mind, specifically?"

"It isn't important."

"Then why did you bring it up in the first place?"

"I was only thinking of you," the city said.

"I realize that."

"You must know that it can't benefit *me* if you wash or not."

"I'm aware of that."

"When one cares," the city went on, "when one feels one's responsibilities, it is not nice to hear oneself sworn at."

"I didn't swear at you."

"Not this time. But earlier today you did."

"Well . . . I was nervous."

"That's because of the smoking."

"Don't start that again!"

"I won't," the city said. "Smoke like a furnace. What does it matter to me?"

"Damned right," Carmody said, lighting a cigarette.

"But my failure," the city said.

"No, no," Carmody said. "Don't say it, please don't!"

"Forget I said it," the city said.

"All right."

"Sometimes I get overzealous."

"Sure."

"And it's especially difficult because I'm right. I am right, you know."

"I know," Carmody said. "You're right, you're right, you're always right. Right right right right right—"

"Don't overexcite yourself betime," the city said. "Would you care for a glass of milk?"

"No."

"You're sure?"

Carmody put his hands over his eyes. He felt very strange. He also felt extremely guilty, fragile, dirty, unhealthy and sloppy. He felt generally and irrevocably bad, and it would always be this way unless he changed, adjusted, adapted. . . .

But instead of attempting anything of the sort he rose to his feet, squared his shoulders, and marched away past the Roman piazza and the Venetian bridge.

"Where are you going?" the city asked. "What's the matter?"

Silent, tight-lipped, Carmody continued past the children's park and the American Express building.

"What did I do wrong?" the city cried. "What, just tell me what?"

Carmody made no reply but strode past the Rochambeau

Cafe and the Portuguese synagogue, coming at last to the pleasant green plain that surrounded Bellwether.

"Ingrate!" the city screamed after him. "You're just like all the others. All of you humans are disagreeable animals, and you're never really satisfied with anything."

Carmody got into his car and started the engine.

"But of course," the city said, in a more thoughtful voice, "you're never really *dissatisfied* with anything either. The moral, I suppose, is that a city must learn patience."

Carmody turned the car onto King's Highbridge Gate Road and started east, toward New York.

"Have a nice trip!" Bellwether called after him. "Don't worry about me, I'll be waiting up for you."

Carmody stepped down hard on the accelerator. He really wished he hadn't heard that last remark.

Dystopian Visions

The Vanishing American

Since the United States is essentially an urbanized civilization, the problem faced by Mr. Minchell in this sometimes funny, sometimes depressing, but consistently insightful story will be familiar to all of us. Generally, the dystopian perspective of the city focuses on a discussion of environmental degradation, population density, transportation congestion, communication overloads, racial and ethnic conflict, paralysis of urban services, crime and violence, and similar problems. But this story presents the dystopian perspective in a much different way by dealing with the effects of these problems on the human being.

What gives life meaning in an urban context is a question woven throughout "The Vanishing American." It is often argued that the human being is a social animal because of his need for the company of other human beings. But is mere company a satisfying social relationship? In addition to companionship, a human being needs the attention and the respect of other human beings. The human being alone, facing life with nothing but his brain and his body, crushed by the pace of life and by change itself, is an all-too-familiar theme in modern life. The emptiness of life in large, impersonal bureaucratic structures may be one of the most serious challenges faced by people who live in cities, for the city itself may have developed into such a structure.

The effect of impersonalization and its nightmares for Mr. Minchell are immediate and obvious. In this sense, he is lucky. For millions of Americans, the effects of impersonalization are more unwitting and more insidious. They erode the integrity of the personality and a feeling of dignity. They slowly strangle the creativity and spontaneity that constitute human life. In short, they allow "the system" to subdue the soul.

This story forces us to ask whether the city, as a human institution, is dead; whether the city is a modern anachronism; and whether the city has outlived its usefulness as a place where human beings can thrive happily and healthily. The city may very well be an effective unit for organizing impersonal functions like trade and commerce; but is it an effective unit for achieving personal wholeness? If the answer to this latter question is negative, then the reality of the dystopian vision of the city is upon us: the destruction of the human spirit.

The Vanishing American   Charles Beaumont

He got the notion shortly after five o'clock; at least, a part of him did, a small part hidden down beneath all the conscious cells—he didn't get the notion until some time later. At exactly 5 P.M. the bell rang. At two minutes after, the chairs began to empty. There was the vast slamming of drawers, the straightening of rulers, the sound of bones snapping and mouths yawning and feet shuffling tiredly.

Mr. Minchell relaxed. He rubbed his hands together and relaxed and thought how nice it would be to get up and go home, like the others. But of course there was the tape, only three-quarters finished. He would have to stay.

He stretched and said good night to the people who filed past him. As usual, no one answered. When they had gone, he set his fingers pecking again over the keyboard. The click-clicking grew loud in the suddenly still office, but Mr. Minchell did not notice. He was lost in the work. Soon, he knew, it would be time for the totaling, and his pulse quickened at the thought of this.

He lit a cigarette. Heart tapping, he drew in smoke and released it.

He extended his right hand and rested his index and middle fingers on the metal bar marked TOTAL bar.

There was a smooth low metallic grinding, followed by absolute silence.

Mr. Minchell opened one eye, dragged it from the ceiling on down to the adding machine.

He groaned, slightly.

The total read: 18037447.

"God." He stared at the figure and thought of the fifty-three pages of manifest, the three thousand separate rows of figures that would have to be checked again. "God."

The day was lost, now. Irretrievably. It was too late to do anything. Madge would have supper waiting, and F.J. didn't approve of overtime; also—

He looked at the total again. At the last two digits.

He sighed. Forty-seven. And thought, startled: Today, for the Lord's sake, is my birthday! Today I am forty—what? forty-seven. And that explains the mistake, I suppose. Sub-conscious kind of thing . . .

Slowly he got up and looked around the deserted office.

Then he went to the dressing room and got his hat and his coat and put them on, carefully.

"Pushing fifty now . . ."

The outside hall was dark. Mr. Minchell walked softly to the elevator and punched the *down* button. "Forty-seven," he said, aloud; then, almost immediately, the light turned red and the thick door slid back noisily. The elevator operator, a bird-thin, tan-fleshed girl, swiveled her head, looking up and down the hall. "Going down," she said.

"Yes," Mr. Minchell said, stepping forward.

"Going down." The girl clicked her tongue and muttered, "Damn kids." She gave the lattice gate a tired push and moved the smooth wooden-handled lever in its slot.

Odd, Mr. Minchell decided, was the word for this particular girl. He wished now that he had taken the stairs. Being alone with only one other person in an elevator had always made him nervous: now it made him very nervous. He felt the tension growing. When it became unbearable, he cleared his throat and said, "Long day."

The girl said nothing. She had a surly look, and she seemed to be humming something deep in her throat.

Mr. Minchell closed his eyes. In less than a minute—during which time he dreamed of the cable snarling, of the car being caught between floors, of himself trying to make small talk with the odd girl for six straight hours—he opened his eyes again and walked into the lobby, briskly.

The gate slammed.

He turned and started for the doorway. Then he paused, feeling a sharp increase in his heartbeat. A large, red-faced, magnificently groomed man of middle years stood directly beyond the glass, talking with another man.

Mr. Minchell pushed through the door, with effort. He's seen me now, he thought. If he asks any questions, though, or anything, I'll just say I didn't put it on the time card; that ought to make it all right. . . .

He nodded and smiled at the large man. "Good night, Mr. Diemel."

The man looked up briefly, blinked, and returned to his conversation.

Mr. Minchell felt a burning come into his face. He hurried on down the street. Now the notion—though it was not even that yet, strictly: it was more a vague feeling—swam up from the bottom of his brain. He remembered that he had not spoken directly to F. J. Diemel for over ten years, beyond a good morning. . . .

Ice-cold shadows fell off the tall buildings, staining the streets, now. Crowds of shoppers moved along the pavement like juggernauts, exhaustedly, but with great determination. Mr. Minchell looked at them. They all had furtive appearances, it seemed to him, suddenly, even the children, as if each was fleeing from some hideous crime. They hurried along, staring.

But not, Mr. Minchell noticed, at him. Through him, yes. Past him. As the elevator operator had done, and now F.J. And had anyone said good night?

He pulled up his coat collar and walked toward the drugstore, thinking. He was forty-seven years old. At the current life-expectancy rate, he might have another seventeen or eighteen years left. And then death.

If you're not dead already.

He paused and for some reason remembered a story he'd once read in a magazine. Something about a man who dies and whose ghost takes up his duties, or something; anyway, the man didn't know he was dead—that was it. And at the end of the story, he runs into his own corpse.

Which is pretty absurd: he glanced down at his body. Ghosts don't wear $36 suits, nor do they have trouble pushing doors open, nor do their corns ache like blazes, and what the devil is wrong with me today?

He shook his head.

It was the tape, of course, and the fact that it was his birthday. That was why his mind was behaving so foolishly.

He went into the drugstore. It was an immense place, packed with people. He walked to the cigar counter, trying not to feel intimidated, and reached into his pocket. A small man elbowed in front of him and called loudly: "Gimme couple nickels, will you, Jack?" The clerk scowled and scooped the change out of his cash register. The small man scurried off. Others took his place. Mr. Minchell thrust his arm forward. "A pack of Luckies, please," he said. The clerk whipped his fingers around a pile of cellophaned packages and, looking elsewhere, droned: "Twenty-six." Mr. Minchell put his twenty-six cents exactly on the glass shelf. The clerk shoved the cigarettes toward the edge and picked up the money, deftly. Not once did he lift his eyes.

Mr. Minchell pocketed the Luckies and went back out of the store. He was perspiring now, slightly, despite the chill wind. The word "ridiculous" lodged in his mind and stayed there. Ridiculous, yes, for heaven's sake. Still, he thought—now just answer the question—isn't it true? Can you honestly say that that clerk saw you?

Or that anyone saw you today?

Swallowing dryly, he walked another two blocks, always in the direction of the subway, and went into a bar called the Chez When. One drink would not hurt, one small, stiff steadying shot.

The bar was a gloomy place, and not very warm, but there

was a good crowd. Mr. Minchell sat down on a stool and folded his hands. The bartender was talking animatedly with an old woman, laughing with boisterous good humor from time to time. Mr. Minchell waited. Minutes passed. The bartender looked up several times, but never made a move to indicate that he had seen a customer.

Mr. Minchell looked at his old gray overcoat, the humbly floraled tie, the cheap sharkskin suit-cloth, and became aware of the extent to which he detested this ensemble. He sat there and detested his clothes for a long time. Then he glanced around. The bartender was wiping a glass, slowly.

All right, the hell with you. I'll go somewhere else.

He slid off the stool. Just as he was about to turn he saw the mirrored wall, pink-tinted and curved. He stopped, peering. Then he almost ran out of the bar.

Cold wind went into his head.

Ridiculous. The mirror was curved, you jackass. How do you expect to see yourself in curved mirrors?

He walked past high buildings, and now past the library and the stone lion he had once, long ago, named King Richard; and he did not look at the lion, because he'd always wanted to ride the lion, ever since he was a child, and he'd promised himself he would do that, but he never did.

He hurried on to the subway, took the stairs by twos, and clattered across the platform in time to board the express.

It roared and thundered. Mr. Minchell held onto the strap and kept himself from staring. No one watched him. No one even glanced at him when he pushed his way to the door and went out onto the empty platform.

He waited. Then the train was gone, and he was alone.

He walked up the stairs. It was fully night now, a soft, unshadowed darkness. He thought about the day and the strange things that were gouging into his mind and thought about all this as he turned down a familiar street which led to his familiar apartment.

The door opened.

His wife was in the kitchen, he could see. Her apron flashed across the arch, and back, and across. He called—"Madge, I'm home."

Madge did not answer. Her movements were regular. Jimmy was sitting at the table, drooling over a glass of pop, whispering to himself.

"I said—" Mr. Minchell began.

"Jimmy, get up and go to the bathroom, you hear? I've got your water drawn."

Jimmy promptly broke into tears. He jumped off the chair and ran past Mr. Minchell into the bedroom. The door slammed viciously.

"Madge."

Madge Minchell came into the room, tired and lined and heavy. Her eyes did not waver. She went into the bedroom, and there was a silence; then a sharp slapping noise, and a yelling.

Mr. Minchell walked to the bathroom, fighting down the small terror. He closed the door and locked it and wiped his forehead with a handkerchief. Ridiculous, he thought, and ridiculous and ridiculous. I am making something utterly foolish out of nothing. All I have to do is look in the mirror, and—

He held the handkerchief to his lips. It was difficult to breathe.

Then he knew that he was afraid, more so than ever before in a lifetime of being afraid.

Look at it this way, Minchell: why shouldn't *you vanish?*

"Young man, just you wait until your father gets here!"

He pushed the handkerchief against his mouth and leaned on the door and gasped.

"What do you mean, vanish?"

Go on, take a look. You'll see what I mean.

He tried to swallow, couldn't. Tried to wet his lips, they stayed dry.

"Lord—"

He slitted his eyes and walked to the shaving mirror and looked in.

His mouth fell open.

The mirror reflected nothing. It held nothing. It was dull and gray and empty.

Mr. Minchell stared at the glass, put out his hand, drew it back hastily.

He squinted. Inches away. There was a form now: vague, indistinct, featureless: but a form.

"Lord," he said. He understood why the elevator girl hadn't seen him, and why F.J. hadn't answered him, and why the clerk at the drugstore and the bartender and Madge . . .

"I'm not dead."

Of course you're not dead—not that way.

"—tan your hide, Jimmy Minchell, when he gets home."

Mr. Minchell suddenly wheeled and clicked the lock. He rushed out of the steam-filled bathroom, across the room, down the stairs, into the street, into the cool night.

A block from home he slowed to a walk.

Invisible! He said the word over and over, in a half-voice. He said it and tried to control the panic that pulled at his legs, and at his brain, and filled him

Why?

A fat woman and a little girl passed by. Neither of them looked up. He started to call out and checked himself. No. That wouldn't do any good. There was no question about it now. He was invisible.

He walked on. As he did, forgotten things returned; they came and they left, too fast. He couldn't hold onto them. He could only watch, and remember. Himself as a youngster, reading: the Oz books, and Tarzan, and Mr. Wells. Himself, going to the University, wanting to teach, and meeting Madge; then not planning any more, and Madge changing, and all the dreams put away. For later. For the right time. And then Jimmy—little strange Jimmy, who ate filth and picked his nose and watched television, who never read books, never; Jimmy, his son, whom he would never understand . . .

He walked by the edge of the park now. Then on past the park, through a maze of familiar and unfamiliar neighborhoods. Walking, remembering, looking at the people and feeling pain because he knew that they could not see him, not now or ever again, because he had vanished. He walked and remembered and felt pain.

All the stagnant dreams came back. Fully. The trip to Italy he'd planned. The open sports car, bad weather be damned. The first-hand knowledge that would tell him whether he did or did not approve of bullfighting. The book . . .

Then something occurred to him. It occurred to Mr. Minchell that he had not just suddenly vanished, like that, after all. No; he had been vanishing gradually for a long while. Every time he said good morning to that bastard Diemel he got a little harder to see. Every time he put on this horrible suit he faded. The process of disappearing was set into action every time he brought his pay check home and turned it over to Madge, every time he kissed her, or listened to her vicious unending complaints, or decided against buying that novel, or punched the adding machine he hated so, or . . .

Certainly.

He had vanished for Diemel and the others in the office years ago. And for strangers right afterwards. Now even Madge and Jimmy couldn't see him. And he could barely see himself, even in a mirror.

It made terrible sense to him. *Why* shouldn't you *disappear*? Well, why, indeed? There wasn't any very good reason, actually. None. And this, in a nightmarish sort of a way, made it as brutally logical as a perfect tape.

Then he thought about going back to work tomorrow and the next day and the day after that. He'd have to, of course. He couldn't let Madge and Jimmy starve; and, besides, what else would he do? It wasn't as if anything important had changed. He'd go on punching the clock and saying good morning to people who didn't see him, and he'd run the tapes and come home beat, nothing altered, and someday he'd die and that would be that.

All at once he felt tired.

He sat down on a cement step and sighed. Distantly he realized that he had come to the library. He sat there, watching the people, feeling the tiredness seep through him, thickly.

Then he looked up.

Above him, black and regal against the sky, stood the huge stone lion. Its mouth was open, and the great head was raised proudly.

Mr. Minchell smiled. King Richard. Memories scattered in his mind: old King Richard, well, my God, here we are.

He got to his feet. Fifty thousand times, at least, he had passed this spot, and every time he had experienced that instant of wild craving. Less so of late, but still, had it ever completely gone? He was amazed to find that now the childish desire was welling up again, stronger than ever before. Urgently.

He rubbed his cheek and stood there for several minutes. It's the most ridiculous thing in the world, he thought, and I must be going out of my mind, and that must explain everything. But, he inquired of himself, even so, why not?

After all, I'm invisible. No one can see me. Of course, it didn't have to be this way, not really. I don't know, he went on, I mean, I believed that I was doing the right thing. Would it have been right to go back to the University and the hell with Madge? I couldn't change that, could I? Could I have done anything about that, even if I'd known?

He nodded sadly.

All right, but don't make it any worse. Don't for God's sake *dwell* on it!

To his surprise, Mr. Minchell found that he was climbing up the concrete base of the statue. It ripped the breath from his lungs—and he saw that he could much more easily have gone up a few extra steps and simply stepped on—but there didn't seem anything else to do but just this, what he was doing. Once upright, he passed his hand over the statue's flank. The surface was incredibly sleek and cold, hard as a lion's muscles ought to be, and tawny.

He took a step backwards. Lord! Had there ever been such power? Such marvelous downright power and . . . majesty, as was here? From stone—no, indeed. It fooled a good many people, but it did not fool Mr. Minchell. He knew. This lion was no mere library decoration. It was an animal, of deadly cunning and fantastic strength and unbelievable ferocity. And it didn't move for the simple reason that it did not care to move. It was waiting. Someday it would see what it was waiting for, its enemy, coming down the street. Then look out, people!

He remembered the whole yarn now. Of everyone on Earth, only he, Henry Minchell, knew the secret of the lion. And only he was allowed to sit astride this mighty back.

He stepped onto the tail, experimentally. He hesitated, gulped, and swung forward, swiftly, on up to the curved rump.

Trembling, he slid forward, until finally he was over the shoulders of the lion, just behind the raised head.

His breath came very fast.

He closed his eyes.

It was not long before he was breathing regularly again. Only now it was the hot, fetid air of the jungle that went into his nostrils. He felt the great muscles ripple beneath him and he listened to the fast crackle of crushed foliage, and he whispered:

"Easy, fellow."

The flying spears did not frighten him. He sat straight, smiling, with his fingers buried in the rich, tawny mane of King Richard, while the wind tore at his hair. . . .

Then, abruptly, he opened his eyes.

The city stretched before him, and the people, and the lights. He tried quite hard not to cry, because he knew that forty-seven-year-old men never cried, not even when they had vanished, but he couldn't help it. So he sat on the stone lion and lowered his head and cried.

He didn't hear the laughter at first.

When he did hear it, he thought that he was dreaming. But it was true: somebody was laughing.

He grasped one of the statue's ears for balance and leaned forward. He blinked. Below, some fifteen feet, there were people. Young people. Some of them with books. They were looking up and smiling and laughing.

Mr. Minchell wiped his eyes.

A slight horror came over him, and fell away. He leaned farther out.

One of the boys waved and shouted: "Ride him, Pop!"

Mr. Minchell almost toppled. Then, without understanding, without even trying to understand—merely knowing—he grinned, widely, showing his teeth, which were his own and very white.

"You . . . see me?" he called.

The young people roared.

"You do!" Mr. Minchell's face seemed to melt upwards. He let out a yell and gave King Richard's shaggy stone mane an enormous hug.

Below, other people stopped in their walking and a small crowd began to form. Dozens of eyes peered sharply, quizzically.

A woman in gray furs giggled.

A thin man in a blue suit grunted something about these damned exhibitionists.

"You pipe down," another man said. "Guy wants to ride the god-damn lion it's his own business."

There were murmurings. The man who had said pipe down was small and he wore black-rimmed glasses. "I used to do it all the time." He turned to Mr. Minchell and cried: "How is it?"

Mr. Minchell grinned. Somehow, he realized, in some mysterious way, he had been given a second chance. And this time he knew what he would do with it. "Fine!" he shouted, and stood up on King Richard's back and sent his derby spinning out over the heads of the people. "Come on up!"

"Can't do it," the man said. "Got a date." There was a look of profound admiration in his eyes as he strode off. Away from the crowd he stopped and cupped his hands and cried: "I'll be seeing you!"

"That's right," Mr. Minchell said, feeling the cold new wind on his face. "You'll be seeing me."

Later, when he was good and ready, he got down off the lion.

II. Yesterday's Dreams, Today's Problems, Tomorrow's Nightmares?

The tremendous increase in city populations, which has been evidenced in most regions of the world since 1800, has been accompanied by a whole host of "urban problems." Urban problems, or those social, economic, political, and environmental problems which seem to characterize city life, are not entirely new, but rather magnified by the fact that a much higher percentage of the world's population now lives in urban areas.

Many of the more practical aspects of urban problems can be traced to the fact that for virtually all of his existence on earth, man has been essentially a rural dweller sustaining himself by hunting, gathering, and various forms of sedentary agriculture. In recent times, however, the concentration of people into cities has forced the adaptation of the city environment, which is alien to the historical rural dweller, to meet man's biological, psychological, and social requirements. It is the gap between the basic needs of human beings and the degree to which these needs can be satisfied in the urban setting which constitutes "urban problems." Unfortunately, many of the "solutions" to these problems have themselves generated new difficulties which in turn require additional solutions.

In biological terms, the cities have, with exceptions in some areas within the last few decades, been dangerous places to live. The close confines of urban areas promoted the spread of infectious diseases, and the city's role as a center of commerce meant that foreign bacterial agents were introduced from abroad by travelers, soldiers, and merchants. This situation was compounded further by the lack of scientific understanding of the nature of disease and pestilence, and by the inadequacy of means of waste disposal. Thus, in the mid-1300s, the Black Death (a form of plague) ravaged

90

Europe, killing millions of persons. The Black Death was apparently introduced into port cities in Italy, and its subsequent spread to other European cities was particularly virulent; most major European cities of the time lost between one-half and two-thirds of their inhabitants. Other diseases, such as cholera, typhus, tuberculosis, and yellow fever have likewise had a profound impact upon the number of deaths in cities.

Within the last century, steady improvements in health and sanitary conditions have been introduced in most of the world's cities, improvements which amount to adaptations in the city environment to better suit man's biological requirements. For example, trash and garbage collection, the purification of drinking water, and the installation of sewers and treatment plants for human wastes have sharply curtailed the incidence of disease. Yet, as is obvious to most informed citizens, much remains to be done in this regard, since the increasing size of the city populations has overburdened disposal systems.

The transformation of the human population into predominantly urban dwellers has also resulted in psychological problems among the populace. Rural life has been characterized as close-knit, with people enjoying interpersonal contacts with family and neighbors. Further, most people perceive rural life to be far less tension-ridden than life in the cities, with ruralites benefiting from a generally slower or more relaxed existence. City life, on the other hand, often consists of impersonal, purely functional contacts which do not satisfy the individual's need for human companionship. The alienation which may result from this sterile and hurried atmosphere has been pointed to as a contributing factor to antisocial behavior in the cities. Although man's requirement for personal contacts has been recognized and reacted to by social welfare agencies, the problem continues to plague urban society.

The social organization of the city has in itself contributed to urban problems. The attraction of economic opportunities in the cities drew often widely disparate ethnic and racial groups into the comparatively compact urban environment. The usual response to this situation has been the *segregation* of one group from another within the city. This pattern of residential isolation, a product of both external discrimination against people designated as "different" and the internal desires of persons of the same racial or ethnic group to congregate in a familiar and supportive setting, has resulted in the delineation of specific sections of cities as a "ghetto," "barrio," immigrant quarter, or something similar. The resultant social and political implications of these geographic adaptations to ethnic and racial diversity within cities have been of great importance in a number of historical and contemporary instances.

Cities have come to represent important aspects of our society. Thus, when we discuss the automobile industry, the most important economic activity in the United States, we often substitute "Detroit." Likewise, national politics is often synonymous with "Washington," and state politics with "Albany," "Tallahassee," "Sacramento," or any other capital city. The crime problem conjures up "New York City," and air pollution, in the minds of many people, is exemplified by "Los Angeles." The ascendancy of cities as centers of economic, political, and social life, and the problems which have resulted from our inability to adapt the urban environment entirely to our needs and desires, will present increasingly serious and potentially more dangerous challenges in the years to come. The extent to which these adaptations are recognized and acted upon will largely determine the quality of life in the city, 2000 A.D.

The Competition for Space

The primary geographic characteristic of cities which distinguishes them from rural districts is their high density of population; that is, large numbers of people living within a relatively small area. The concentration of people into cities has reached its extreme values in the developed countries. In the United States, for example, almost 60 percent of the total population of the country lives on less than 1 percent of the land area, that 1 percent being the share of the land area which is accounted for by major cities and their suburbs. It has been calculated that within these urbanized areas, the population density averages 3,376 people per square mile, whereas the density of the rural population is only about 6 people per square mile.

Although cities do represent the extremes of density of population, their sheer geographic size should not be overlooked. During the period of city expansion after 1800, the amount of land occupied by urban areas increased significantly. In 1800, it was possible to walk across London, Europe's largest city, in less than one hour. Today, on the other hand, the London urbanized area is more than 40 miles across. Some authorities now consider almost the entire Northeastern coast of the United States, from Washington, D.C. to Boston, to be one vast city, a "megalopolis" encompassing millions of people.

This outward territorial expansion of cities has been made possible largely by the introduction of faster and more reliable means of transportation and communications, particularly the automobile. As we shall see later in this book, the use of new modes of transportation has not been without its social and environmental impact. Also, the encroachment of the cities into farming areas has obvious ramifications for food production, and the surfacing over of vast areas of land with roads, parking lots, and housing has had a dramatic influence upon water supplies and quality.

The transition from rural to urban life, a transition which implies concentration in a more limited area, has in turn resulted in an increasing competition for space, or living and working room, within the city itself. This competiton has, in most settings, been translated into dollars and cents, with land values and rents in the more desirable residential and business zones reaching extremely high levels. This is not to say, however, that this competition might not "escalate" to a more primitive form—violence—in some future context.

Considerable attention has focused upon the effects of the dense settlement characteristic of cities on human psychological and social traits. Relying upon observations of laboratory animals, some scientists have forecast increasing social tensions with higher population densities, a notable factor being the tendency toward aggression to defend the much sought-after space. The stories in this section illustrate in graphic fashion the practical, "everyday" implications of

*crowding (the classic "Billenium" by J. G. Ballard) and,
beyond that, the impact of high densities upon virtually all
aspects of social, political, and economic organization in the
experimental "Total Environment" of Brian W. Aldiss.*

───

Billenium   J. G. Ballard

All day long, and often into the early hours of the morning,
the tramp of feet sounded up and down the stairs outside
Ward's cubicle. Built into a narrow alcove in a bend of the
staircase between the fourth and fifth floors, its plywood walls
flexed and creaked with every footstep like the timbers of
a rotting windmill. Over a hundred people lived in the top
three floors of the old rooming house, and sometimes Ward
would lie awake on his narrow bunk until 2 A.M. mechanically counting the last residents returning from the all-
night movies in the stadium half a mile away. Through the
window he could hear giant fragments of the amplified
dialogue booming among the rooftops. The stadium was
never empty. During the day the huge four-sided screen was
raised on its davit and athletics meetings or football matches
ran continuously. For the people in the houses abutting the
stadium the noise must have been unbearable.

Ward, at least, had a certain degree of privacy. Two months
earlier, before he came to live on the staircase, he had shared
a room with seven others on the ground floor of a house in
755th Street, and the ceaseless press of people jostling past
the window had reduced him to a state of chronic exhaustion.
The street was always full, an endless clamor of voices and
shuffling feet. By six-thirty, when he woke, hurrying to take
his place in the bathroom queue, the crowds already jammed
it from sidewalk to sidewalk, the din punctuated every half
minute by the roar of the elevated trains running over the
shops on the opposite side of the road. As soon as he saw the
advertisement describing the staircase cubicle (like everyone
else, he spent most of his spare time scanning the classifieds in
the newspapers, moving his lodgings an average of once every
two months) he had left despite the higher rental. A cubicle

on a staircase would almost certainly be on its own.

However, this had its drawbacks. Most evenings his friends from the library would call in, eager to rest their elbows after the bruising crush of the public reading room. The cubicle was slightly more than four and a half square meters in floor area, half a square meter over the statutory maximum for a single person, the carpenters having taken advantage, illegally, of a recess beside a nearby chimney breast. Consequently Ward had been able to fit a small straight-backed chair into the interval between the bed and the door, so that only one person at a time need sit on the bed—in most single cubicles host and guest had to sit side by side on the bed, conversing over their shoulders and changing places periodically to avoid neck strain.

"You were lucky to find this place," Rossiter, the most regular visitor, never tired of telling him. He reclined back on the bed, gesturing at the cubicle. "It's enormous, the perspectives really zoom. I'd be surprised if you hadn't got at least five meters here, perhaps even six."

Ward shook his head categorically. Rossiter was his closest friend, but the quest for living space had forged powerful reflexes. "Just over four and a half, I've measured it carefully. There's no doubt about it."

Rossiter lifted one eyebrow. "I'm amazed. It must be the ceiling then."

Manipulating the ceiling was a favorite trick of unscrupulous landlords—most assessments of area were made upon the ceiling, out of convenience, and by tilting back the plywood partitions the rated area of a cubicle could be either increased, for the benefit of a prospective tenant (many married couples were thus bamboozled into taking a single cubicle), or decreased temporarily on the visit of the housing inspectors. Ceilings were crisscrossed with pencil marks staking out the rival claims of tenants on opposite sides of a party wall. Someone timid of his rights could be literally squeezed out of existence—in fact, the advertisement "quiet clientele" was usually a tacit invitation to this sort of piracy.

"The wall does tilt a little," Ward admitted. "Actually, it's about four degrees out—I used a plumb line. But there's still plenty of room on the stairs for people to get by."

Rossiter grinned. "Of course, John. I'm just envious, that's all. My room's driving me crazy." Like everyone, he used the term "room" to describe his tiny cubicle, a hangover from the days fifty years earlier when people had indeed lived one to a room, sometimes, unbelievably, one to an apartment or house. The microfilms in the architecture catalogs at the library showed scenes of museums, concert halls, and other public buildings in what appeared to be everyday settings, often virtually empty, two or three people wandering down an enormous gallery or staircase. Traffic moved freely along the center of streets, and in the quieter districts sections of sidewalk would be deserted for fifty yards or more.

Now, of course, the older buildings had been torn down and replaced by housing batteries, or converted into apartment blocks. The great banqueting room in the former City Hall had been split horizontally into four decks, each of these cut up into hundreds of cubicles.

As for the streets, traffic had long since ceased to move about them. Apart from a few hours before dawn when only the sidewalks were crowded, every thoroughfare was always packed with a shuffling mob of pedestrians, perforce ignoring the countless "Keep Left" signs suspended over their heads, wrestling past each other on their way to home and office, their clothes dusty and shapeless. Often "locks" would occur when a huge crowd at a street junction became immovably jammed. Sometimes these locks would last for days. Two years earlier Ward had been caught in one outside the stadium; for over forty-eight hours he was trapped in a gigantic pedestrian jam containing over twenty thousand people, fed by the crowds leaving the stadium on one side and those approaching it on the other. An entire square mile of the local neighborhood had been paralyzed, and he vividly remembered the nightmare of swaying helplessly on his feet as the jam shifted and heaved, terrified of losing his balance and being trampled underfoot. When the police had finally sealed off the stadium and dispersed the jam he had gone back to his cubicle and slept for a week, his body blue with bruises.

"I hear they may reduce the allocation to three and a half meters," Rossiter remarked.

Ward paused to allow a party of tenants from the sixth floor to pass down the staircase, holding the door to prevent it jumping off its latch. "So they're always saying," he commented. "I can remember that rumor ten years ago."

"It's no rumor," Rossiter warned him. "It may well be

necessary soon. Thirty million people packed into this city now, a million increase in just one year. There's been some pretty serious talk at the Housing Department."

Ward shook his head. "A drastic revaluation like that is almost impossible to carry out. Every single partition would have to be dismantled and nailed up again; the administrative job alone is so vast it's difficult to visualize. Millions of cubicles to be redesigned and certified, licenses to be issued, plus the complete resettlement of every tenant. Most of the buildings put up since the last revaluation are designed around a four-meter module—you can't simply take half a meter off the end of each cubicle and then say that makes so many new cubicles. They may be only six inches wide." He laughed. "Besides, how can you live in just three and a half meters?"

Rossiter smiled. "That's the ultimate argument, isn't it? They used it twenty-five years ago at the last revaluation, when the minimum was cut from five to four. It couldn't be done they all said, no one could stand living in only four square meters; it was enough room for a bed and suitcase, but you couldn't open the door to get in." Rossiter chuckled softly. "They were all wrong. It was merely decided that from then on all doors would open outward. Four square meters was here to stay."

Ward looked at his watch. It was seven-thirty. "Time to eat. Let's see if we can get into the food bar across the road."

Grumbling at the prospect, Rossiter pulled himself off the bed. They left the cubicle and made their way down the staircase. This was crammed with luggage and packing cases so that only a narrow interval remained around the bannister. On the floors below the congestion was worse. Corridors were wide enough to be chopped up into single cubicles, and the air was stale and dead, cardboard walls hung with damp laundry and makeshift larders. Each of the five rooms on the floors contained a dozen tenants, their voices reverberating through the partitions.

People were sitting on the steps above the second floor, using the staircase as an informal lounge, although this was against the fire regulations, women chatting with the men queueing in their shirtsleeves outside the washroom, children diving around them. By the time they reached the entrance Ward and Rossiter were having to force their way through the tenants packed together on every landing, loitering around the notice boards or pushing in from the street below.

Taking a breath at the top of the steps, Ward pointed to the food bar on the other side of the road. It was only thirty yards away, but the throng moving down the street swept past like a river at full tide, crossing them from right to left. The first picture show at the stadium started at nine o'clock, and people were setting off already to make sure of getting in.

"Can't we go somewhere else?" Rossiter asked, screwing his face up at the prospect of the food bar. Not only would it be packed and take them half an hour to be served, but the food was flat and unappetizing. The journey from the library four blocks away had given him an appetite.

Ward shrugged. "There's a place on the corner, but I doubt if we can make it." This was two hundred yards upstream; they would be fighting the crowd all the way.

"Maybe you're right." Rossiter put his hand on Ward's shoulder. "You know, John, your trouble is that you never go anywhere, you're too disengaged, you just don't realize how bad everything is getting."

Ward nodded. Rossiter was right. In the morning, when he set off for the library, the pedestrian traffic was moving with him toward the downtown offices; in the evening, when he came back, it was flowing in the opposite direction. By and large he never altered his routine. Brought up from the age of ten in a municipal hostel, he had gradually lost touch with his father and mother, who lived on the east side of the city and had been unable, or unwilling, to make the journey to see him. Having surrendered his initiative to the dynamics of the city he was reluctant to try to win it back merely for a better cup of coffee. Fortunately his job at the library brought him into contact with a wide range of young people of similar interests. Sooner or later he would marry, find a double cubicle near the library, and settle down. If they had enough children (three was the required minimum) they might even one day own a small room of their own.

They stepped out into the pedestrian stream, carried along by it for ten or twenty yards, then quickened their pace and sidestepped through the crowd, slowly tacking across to the other side of the road. There they found the shelter of the shop fronts, slowly worked their way back to the food bar, shoulders braced against the countless minor collisions.

"What are the latest population estimates?" Ward asked as they circled a cigarette kiosk, stepping forward whenever a gap presented itself.

Rossiter smiled. "Sorry, John, I'd like to tell you but you might start a stampede. Besides, you wouldn't believe me."

Rossiter worked in the Insurance Department at the City Hall, had informal access to the census statistics. For the last ten years these had been classified information, partly because they were felt to be inaccurate, but chiefly because it was feared they might set off a mass attack of claustrophobia. Minor outbreaks had taken place already, and the official line was that world population had reached a plateau, leveling off at twenty thousand million. No one believed this for a moment, and Ward assumed that the 3 percent annual increase maintained since the 1960s was continuing.

How long it could continue was impossible to estimate. Despite the gloomiest prophecies of the Neo-Malthusians, world agriculture had managed to keep pace with the population growth, although intensive cultivation meant that 95 percent of the population was permanently trapped in vast urban conurbations. The outward growth of cities had at last been checked; in fact, all over the world former suburban areas were being reclaimed for agriculture and population additions were confined within the existing urban ghettos. The countryside, as such, no longer existed. Every single square foot of ground sprouted a crop of one type or other. The one-time fields and meadows of the world were now, in effect, factory floors, as highly mechanized and closed to the public as any industrial area. Economic and ideological rivalries had long since faded before one overriding quest—the internal colonization of the city.

Reaching the food bar, they pushed themselves into the entrance and joined the scrum of customers pressing six deep against the counter.

"What is really wrong with the population problem," Ward confided to Rossiter, "is that no one has ever tried to tackle it. Fifty years ago shortsighted nationalism and industrial expansion put a premium on a rising population curve, and even now the hidden incentive is to have a large family so that you can gain a little privacy. Single people are penalized simply because there are more of them and they don't fit conveniently into double or triple cubicles. But it's the large family with its compact, space-saving logistic that is the real villain."

Rossiter nodded, edging nearer the counter, ready to shout his order. "Too true. We all look forward to getting married just so that we can have our six meters."

Directly in front of them, two girls turned around and smiled. "Six square meters," one of them, a dark-haired girl with a pretty oval face, repeated. "You sound like the sort of young man I ought to get to know. Going into the real estate business, Henry?"

Rossiter grinned and squeezed her arm. "Hello, Judith. I'm thinking about it actively. Like to join me in a private venture?"

The girl leaned against him as they reached the counter. "Well, I might. It would have to be legal, though."

The other girl, Helen Waring, an assistant at the library, pulled Ward's sleeve. "Have you heard the latest, John? Judith and I have been kicked out of our room. We're on the street right at this minute."

"What?" Rossiter cried. They collected their soups and coffee and edged back to the rear of the bar. "What on earth happened?"

Helen explained. "You know that little broom cupboard outside our cubicle? Judith and I have been using it as a sort of study hole, going in there to read. It's quiet and restful, if you can get used to not breathing. Well, the old girl found out and kicked up a big fuss, said we were breaking the law and so on. In short, out." Helen paused. "Now we've heard she's going to let it as a single."

Rossiter pounded the counter ledge. "A broom cupboard? Someone's going to live there? But she'll never get a license."

Judith shook her head. "She's got it already. Her brother works in the Housing Department."

Ward laughed into his soup. "But how can she let it? No one will live in a broom cupboard."

Judith stared at him somberly. "You really believe that, John?"

Ward dropped his spoon. "No, I guess you're right. People will live anywhere. God, I don't know who I feel more sorry for—you two, or the poor devil who'll be living in that cupboard. What are you going to do?"

"A couple in a place two blocks west are subletting half

their cubicle to us. They've hung a sheet down the middle and Helen and I'll take turns sleeping on a camp bed. I'm not joking, our room's about two feet wide. I said to Helen that we ought to split up again and sublet one half at twice our rent."

They had a good laugh over all this and Ward said good-night to the others and went back to his rooming house.

There he found himself with similar problems.

The manager leaned against the flimsy door, a damp cigar butt revolving around his mouth, an expression of morose boredom on his unshaven face.

"You got four point seven two meters," he told Ward, who was standing out on the staircase, unable to get into his room. Other tenants stepped past onto the landing, where two women in curlers and dressing gowns were arguing with each other, tugging angrily at the wall of trunks and cases. Occasionally the manager glanced at them irritably. "Four seven two. I worked it out twice." He said this as if it ended all possibility of argument.

"Ceiling or floor?" Ward asked.

"Ceiling, whaddya think? How can I measure the floor with all this junk?" He kicked at a crate of books protruding from under the bed.

Ward let this pass. "There's quite a tilt on the wall," he pointed out. "As much as three or four degrees."

The manager nodded vaguely. "You're definitely over the four. Way over." He turned to Ward, who had moved down several steps to allow a man and woman to get past. "I can rent this as a double."

"What, only four and a half?" Ward said incredulously. "How?"

The man who had just passed him leaned over the manager's shoulder and sniffed at the room, taking in every detail in a one-second glance. "You renting a double here, Louie?"

The manager waved him away and then beckoned Ward into the room, closing the door after him.

"It's a nominal five," he told Ward. "New regulation, just came out. Anything over four five is a double now." He eyed Ward shrewdly. "Well, whaddya want? It's a good room, there's a lot of space here, feels more like a triple. You got access to the staircase, window slit—" He broke off as Ward slumped down on the bed and started to laugh. "Whatsa matter? Look, if you want a big room like this you gotta pay for it. I want an extra half rental or you get out."

Ward wiped his eyes, then stood up wearily and reached for the shelves. "Relax, I'm on my way. I'm going to live in a broom cupboard. 'Access to the staircase'—that's really rich. Tell me, Louie, is there life on Uranus?"

Temporarily, he and Rossiter teamed up to rent a double cubicle in a semiderelict house a hundred yards from the library. The neighborhood was seedy and faded, the rooming houses crammed with tenants. Most of them were owned by absentee landlords or by the city corporation, and the managers employed were of the lowest type, mere rent collectors who cared nothing about the way their tenants divided up the living space, and never ventured beyond the first floors. Bottles and empty cans littered the corridors, and the washrooms looked like sumps. Many of the tenants were old and infirm, sitting about listlessly in their narrow cubicles, wheedling at each other back to back through the thin partitions.

Their double cubicle was on the third floor, at the end of a corridor that ringed the building. Its architecture was impossible to follow, rooms letting off at all angles, and luckily the corridor was a cul-de-sac. The mounds of cases ended four feet from the end wall and a partition divided off the cubicle, just wide enough for two beds. A high window overlooked the areaways of the building opposite.

Possessions loaded onto the shelf above his head, Ward lay back on his bed and moodily surveyed the roof of the library through the afternoon haze.

"It's not bad here," Rossiter told him, unpacking his case. "I know there's no real privacy and we'll drive each other insane within a week, but at least we haven't got six other people breathing into our ears two feet away."

The nearest cubicle, a single, was built into the banks of cases half a dozen steps along the corridor, but the occupant, a man of seventy, was deaf and bedridden.

"It's not bad," Ward echoed reluctantly. "Now tell me what the latest growth figures are. They might console me."

Rossiter paused, lowering his voice. "Four percent. *Eight hundred million extra people in one year*—just less than half the Earth's total population in 1950."

Ward whistled slowly. "So they will revalue. What to? Three and a half?"

"Three. From the first of next year."

"Three square meters!" Ward sat up and looked around him. "It's unbelievable! The world's going insane, Rossiter. For God's sake, when are they going to do something about it? Do you realize there soon won't be room enough to sit down, let alone lie down?"

Exasperated, he punched the wall beside him, on the second blow knocked in one of the small wooden panels that had been lightly papered over.

"Hey!" Rossiter yelled. "You're breaking the place down." He dived across the bed to retrieve the panel, which hung downward supported by a strip of paper. Ward slipped his hand into the dark interval, carefully drew the panel back onto the bed.

"Who's on the other side?" Rossiter whispered. "Did they hear?"

Ward peered through the interval, eyes searching the dim light. Suddenly he dropped the panel and seized Rossiter's shoulder, pulled him down onto the bed.

"Henry! Look!"

Rossiter freed himself and pressed his face to the opening, focused slowly and then gasped.

Directly in front of them, faintly illuminated by a grimy skylight, was a medium-sized room, some fifteen feet square, empty except for the dust silted up against the skirting boards. The floor was bare, a few strips of frayed linoleum running across it, the walls covered with a drab floral design. Here and there patches of the paper had peeled off and segments of the picture rail had rotted away, but otherwise the room was in habitable condition.

Breathing slowly, Ward closed the open door of the cubicle with his foot, then turned to Rossiter.

"Henry, do you realize what we've found? Do you realize it, man?"

"Shut up. For Pete's sake keep your voice down." Rossiter examined the room carefully. "It's fantastic. I'm trying to see whether anyone's used it recently."

"Of course they haven't," Ward pointed out. "It's obvious. There's no door into the room. We're looking through it now.

They must have paneled over this door years ago and forgotten about it. Look at that filth everywhere."

Rossiter was staring into the room, his mind staggered by its vastness.

"You're right," he murmured. "Now, when do we move in?"

Panel by panel, they pried away the lower half of the door, nailed it onto a wooden frame so that the dummy section could be replaced instantly.

Then, picking an afternoon when the house was half empty and the manager asleep in his basement office, they made their first foray into the room, Ward going in alone while Rossiter kept guard in the cubicle.

For an hour they exchanged places, wandering silently around the dusty room, stretching their arms out to feel its unconfined emptiness, grasping at the sensation of absolute spatial freedom. Although smaller than many of the subdivided rooms in which they had lived, this room seemed infinitely larger, its walls huge cliffs that soared upward to the skylight.

Finally, two or three days later, they moved in.

For the first week Rossiter slept alone in the room, Ward in the cubicle outside, both there together during the day. Gradually they smuggled in a few items of furniture: two armchairs, a table, a lamp fed from the socket in the cubicle. The furniture was heavy and Victorian; the cheapest available, its size emphasized the emptiness of the room. Pride of place was taken by an enormous mahogany wardrobe, fitted with carved angels and castellated mirrors, which they were forced to dismantle and carry into the house in their suitcases. Towering over them, it reminded Ward of the microfilms of Gothic cathedrals, with their massive organ lofts crossing vast naves.

After three weeks they both slept in the room, finding the cubicle unbearably cramped. An imitation Japanese screen divided the room adequately and did nothing to diminish its size. Sitting there in the evenings, surrounded by his books and albums, Ward steadily forgot the city outside. Luckily he reached the library by a back alley and avoided the crowded streets. Rossiter and himself began to seem the only real inhabitants of the world, everyone else a meaningless by-product of their own existence, a random replication of identity which had run out of control.

It was Rossiter who suggested that they ask the two girls to share the room with them.

"They've been kicked out again and may have to split up," he told Ward, obviously worried that Judith might fall into bad company. "There's always a rent freeze after revaluation, but all the landlords know about it so they're not reletting. It's getting damned difficult to find a room anywhere."

Ward nodded, relaxing back around the circular redwood table. He played with a tassel of the arsenic-green lampshade, for a moment felt like a Victorian man of letters, leading a spacious leisurely life among overstuffed furnishings.

"I'm all for it," he agreed, indicating the empty corners. "There's plenty of room here. But we'll have to make damn sure they don't gossip about it."

After due precautions, they let the two girls into the secret, enjoying their astonishment at finding this private universe.

"We'll put a partition across the middle," Rossiter explained, "then take it down each morning. You'll be able to move in within a couple of days. How do you feel?"

"Wonderful!" They goggled at the wardrobe, squinting at the endless reflections in the mirrors.

There was no difficulty getting them in and out of the house. The turnover of tenants was continuous and bills were placed in the mail rack. No one cared who the girls were or noticed their regular calls at the cubicle.

However, half an hour after they arrived neither of them had unpacked her suitcase.

"What's up, Judith?" Ward asked, edging past the girls' beds into the narrow interval between the table and wardrobe.

Judith hesitated, looking from Ward to Rossiter, who sat on his bed, finishing off the plywood partition. "John, it's just that . . ."

Helen Waring, more matter of fact, took over, her fingers straightening the bedspread. "What Judith's trying to say is that our position here is a little embarrassing. The partition is—"

Rossiter stood up. "For heaven's sake, don't worry, Helen," he assured her, speaking in the loud whisper they had all involuntarily cultivated. "No funny business, you can trust us. This partition is as solid as a rock."

The two girls nodded. "It's not that," Helen explained, "but it isn't up all the time. We thought that if an older person were here, say Judith's aunt—she wouldn't take up much room and be no trouble, she's really awfully sweet—we wouldn't need to bother about the partition—except at night," she added quickly.

Ward glanced at Rossiter, who shrugged and began to scan the floor.

"Well, it's an idea," Rossiter said. "John and I know how you feel. Why not?"

"Sure," Ward agreed. He pointed to the space between the girls' beds and the table. "One more won't make any difference."

The girls broke into whoops. Judith went over to Rossiter and kissed him on the cheek. "Sorry to be a nuisance, Henry." She smiled at him. "That's a wonderful partition you've made. You couldn't do another one for Auntie—just a little one? She's very sweet but she is getting on."

"Of course," Rossiter said. "I understand. I've got plenty of wood left over."

Ward looked at his watch. "It's seven-thirty, Judith. You'd better get in touch with your aunt. She may not be able to make it tonight."

Judith buttoned her coat. "Oh, she will," she assured Ward. "I'll be back in a jiffy."

The aunt arrived within five minutes, three heavy suitcases soundly packed.

"It's amazing," Ward remarked to Rossiter three months later. "The size of this room still staggers me. It almost gets larger every day."

Rossiter agreed readily, averting his eyes from one of the girls changing behind the central partition. This they now left in place as dismantling it daily had become tiresome. Besides, the aunt's subsidiary partition was attached to it and she resented the continuous upsets. Ensuring she followed the entrance and exit drills through the camouflaged door and cubicle was difficult enough.

Despite this, detection seemed unlikely. The room had obviously been built as an afterthought into the central well of the house and any noise was masked by the luggage stacked in the surrounding corridor. Directly below was a small dormitory occupied by several elderly women, and Judith's aunt, who visited them socially, swore that no sounds came through the heavy ceiling. Above, the fanlight let out through a dormer window, its lights indistinguishable from the hundred other bulbs burning in the windows of the house.

Rossiter finished off the new partition he was building and held it upright, fitting it into the slots nailed to the wall between his bed and Ward's. They had agreed that this would provide a little extra privacy.

"No doubt I'll have to do one for Judith and Helen," he confided to Ward.

Ward adjusted his pillow. They had smuggled the two armchairs back to the furniture shop as they took up too much space. The bed, anyway, was more comfortable. He had never got completely used to the soft upholstery.

"Not a bad idea. What about some shelving around the wall? I've got nowhere to put anything."

The shelving tidied the room considerably, freeing large areas of the floor. Divided by their partitions, the five beds were in line along the rear wall, facing the mahogany wardrobe. In between was an open space of three or four feet, a further six feet on either side of the wardrobe.

The sight of so much space fascinated Ward. When Rossiter mentioned that Helen's mother was ill and badly needed personal care he immediately knew where her cubicle could be placed—at the foot of his bed, between the wardrobe and the side wall.

Helen was overjoyed. "It's awfully good of you, John," she told him, "but would you mind if Mother slept beside me? There's enough space to fit an extra bed in."

So Rossiter dismantled the partitions and moved them closer together, six beds now in line along the wall. This gave each of them an interval of two and a half feet wide, just enough room to squeeze down the side of their beds. Lying back on the extreme right, the shelves two feet above his head, Ward could barely see the wardrobe, but the space in front of him, a clear six feet to the wall ahead, was uninterrupted.

Then Helen's father arrived.

Knocking on the door of the cubicle, Ward smiled at Judith's aunt as she let him in. He helped her swing out the made-up bed which guarded the entrance, then rapped on the wooden panel. A moment later Helen's father, a small gray-haired man in an undershirt, braces tied to his trousers with string, pulled back the panel.

Ward nodded to him and stepped over the luggage piled around the floor at the foot of the beds. Helen was in her mother's cubicle, helping the old woman to drink her evening broth. Rossiter, perspiring heavily, was on his knees by the mahogany wardrobe, wrenching apart the frame of the central mirror with a jimmy. Pieces of the wardrobe lay on his bed and across the floor.

"We'll have to start taking these out tomorrow," Rossiter told him. Ward waited for Helen's father to shuffle past and enter his cubicle. He had rigged up a small cardboard door, and locked it behind him with a crude hook of bent wire.

Rossiter watched him, frowning irritably. "Some people are happy. This wardrobe's a hell of a job. How did we ever decide to buy it?"

Ward sat down on his bed. The partition pressed against his knees and he could hardly move. He looked up when Rossiter was engaged and saw that the dividing line he had marked in pencil was hidden by the encroaching partition. Leaning against the wall, he tried to ease it back again, but Rossiter had apparently nailed the lower edge to the floor.

There was a sharp tap on the outside cubicle door— Judith returning from her office. Ward started to get up and then sat back. "Mr. Waring," he called softly. It was the old man's duty night.

Waring shuffled to the door of his cubicle and unlocked it fussily, clucking to himself.

"Up and down, up and down," he muttered. He stumbled over Rossiter's tool bag and swore loudly, then added meaningly over his shoulder: "If you ask me there's too many people in here. Down below they've only got six to our seven, and it's the same size room."

Ward nodded vaguely and stretched back on his narrow bed, trying not to bang his head on the shelving. Waring was not the first to hint that he move out. Judith's aunt had made a similar suggestion two days earlier. Since he left his job at the library (the small rental he charged the others paid for the little food he needed) he spent most of his time in the room, seeing rather more of the old man than he wanted to, but he had learned to tolerate him.

Settling himself, he noticed that the right-hand spire of the wardrobe, all he had been able to see for the past two months, was now dismantled.

It had been a beautiful piece of furniture, in a way symbolizing this whole private world, and the salesman at the store told him there were few like it left. For a moment Ward felt a sudden pang of regret, as he had done as a child when his father, in a mood of exasperation, had taken something away from him and he knew he would never see it again.

Then he pulled himself together. It was a beautiful wardrobe, without doubt, but when it was gone it would make the room seem even larger.

Total Environment   Brian W. Aldiss

I

"What's that poem about 'caverns measureless to man'?" Thomas Dixit asked. His voice echoed away among the caverns, the question unanswered. Peter Crawley, walking a pace or two behind him, said nothing, lost in a reverie of his own.

It was over a year since Dixit had been imprisoned here. He had taken time off from the resettlement area to come and have a last look around before everything was finally demolished. In these great concrete workings, men still moved —Indian technicians mostly, carrying instruments, often with their own headlights. Cables trailed everywhere; but the desolation was mainly an effect of the constant abrasion all surfaces had undergone. People had flowed here like water in a subterranean cave; and their corporate life had flowed similarly, hidden, forgotten.

Dixit was powerfully moved by the thought of all that

life. He, almost alone, was the man who had plunged into it and survived.

Old angers stirring in him, he turned and spoke directly to his companion. "What a monument to human suffering! They should leave this place standing as an everlasting memorial to what happened."

The white man said, "The Delhi government refuses to entertain any such suggestion. I see their point of view, but I also see that it would make a great tourist attraction!"

"Tourist attraction, man! Is that all it means to you?"

Crawley laughed. "As ever, you're too touchy, Thomas. I take this whole matter much less lightly than you suppose. Tourism just happens to attract me more than human suffering."

They walked on side by side. They were never able to agree.

The battered faces of flats and houses—now empty, once choked with humanity—stood on either side, doors gaping open like old men's mouths in sleep. The spaces seemed enormous; the shadows and echoes that belonged to those spaces seemed to continue indefinitely. Yet before . . . there had scarcely been room to breathe here.

"I remember what your buddy, Senator Byrnes, said," Crawley remarked. "He showed how both East and West have learned from this experiment. Of course, the social scientists are still working over their findings; some startling formulae for social groups are emerging already. But the people who lived and died here were fighting their way towards control of the universe of the ultra-small, and that's where the biggest advances have come. They were already developing power over their own genetic material. Another generation, and they might have produced the ultimate in automatic human population control: anoestrus, where too close proximity to other members of the species leads to reabsorption of the embryonic material in the female. Our scientists have been able to help them there, and geneticists predict that in another decade—"

"Yes, yes, all that I grant you. Progress is wonderful." He knew he was being impolite. These things were important, of revolutionary importance to a crowded Earth. But he wished he walked these eroded passageways alone.

Undeniably, India had learned too, just as Peter Crawley

claimed. For Hinduism had been put to the test here and had shown its terrifying strengths and weaknesses. In these mazes, people had not broken under deadly conditions—nor had they thought to break away from their destiny. *Dharma*—duty—had been stronger than humanity. And this revelation was already changing the thought and fate of one-sixth of the human race.

He said, "Progress is wonderful. But what took place here was essentially a religious experience."

Crawley's brief laugh drifted away into the shadows of a great gaunt stairwell. "I'll bet you didn't feel that way when we sent you in here a year ago!"

What had he felt then? He stopped and gazed up at the gloom of the stairs. All that came to him was the memory of that appalling flood of life and of the people who had been a part of it, whose brief years had evaporated in these caverns, whose feet had endlessly trodden these warren-ways, these lugubrious decks, these crumbling flights. . . .

II

The concrete steps climbed up into darkness. The steps were wide, and countless children sat on them, listless, resting against each other. This was an hour when activity was low and even small children hushed their cries for a while. Yet there was no silence on the steps; silence was never complete there. Always, in the background, the noise of voices. Voices and more voices. Never silence.

Shamim was aged, so she preferred to run her errands at this time of day, when the crowds thronging Total Environment were less. She dawdled by a sleepy seller of life-objects at the bottom of the stairs, picking over the little artifacts and exclaiming now and again. The hawker knew her, knew she was too poor to buy, did not even press her to buy. Shamim's oldest daughter, Malti, waited for her mother by the bottom step.

Malti and her mother were watched from the top of the steps.

A light burned at the top of the steps. It had burned there for twenty-five years, safe from breakage behind a strong mesh. But dung and mud had recently been thrown at it, covering it almost entirely and so making the top of the stairway dark. A furtive man called Narayan Farhad crouched there and watched, a shadow in the shadows.

A month ago, Shamim had had an illegal operation in one of the pokey rooms off Grand Balcony on her deck. The effects of the operation were still with her; under her plain cotton sari, her thin dark old body was bent. Her share of life stood lower than it had been.

Malti, her oldest daughter, was a meek girl who had not been conceived when the Total Environment experiment began. Even meekness had its limits. Seeing her mother dawdle so needlessly, Malti muttered impatiently and went on ahead, climbing the infested steps, anxious to be home.

Extracts from Thomas Dixit's report to Senator Jacob Byrnes, back in America: *To lend variety to the habitat, the Environment has been divided into ten decks, each deck five stories high, which allows for an occasional pocket-sized open space. The architecture has been varied somewhat on each deck. On one deck, a sort of blown-up Indian village is presented; on another, the houses are large and appear separate, although sandwiched between decks—I need not add they are hopelessly overcrowded now. On most decks, the available space is packed solid with flats. Despits this attempt at variety, a general bowdlerization of both Eastern and Western architectural styles, and the fact that everything has been constructed out of concrete or a parastyrene for economy's sake, has led to a dreadful sameness. I cannot imagine anywhere more hostile to the spiritual values of life.*

The shadow in the shadows moved. He glanced anxiously up at the light, which also housed a spy-eye; there would be a warning out, and sprays would soon squirt away the muck he had thrown at the fitting; but for the moment, he could work unobserved.

Narayan bared his old teeth as Malti came up the steps towards him, treading among the sprawling children. She was too old to fetch a really good price on the slave market, but she was still strong; there would be no trouble in getting rid of her at once. Of course he knew something of her history, even though she lived on a different deck from him. Malti! He called her name at the last moment as he jumped out on her. Old though he was, Narayan was quick. He wore only his dhoti, arms flashing, interlocking round hers, one good powerful wrench to get her off her feet—now running fast, fearful, up the rest of the steps, moving even as he clamped one hand over her mouth to cut off her cry of fear. Clever old Narayan!

The stairs mount up and up in the four corners of the Total Environment, linking deck with deck. They are now crude things of concrete and metal, since the plastic covers have long been stripped from them.

These stairways are the weak points of the tiny empires, transient and brutal, that form on every deck. They are always guarded, though guards can be bribed. Sometimes gangs or "unions" take over a stairway, either by agreement or bloodshed.

Shamim screamed, responding to her daughter's cry. She began to hobble up the stairs as fast as she could, tripping over infant feet, drawing a dagger out from under her sari. It was a plastic dagger, shaped out of a piece of the Environment.

She called Malti, called for help as she went. When she reached the landing, she was on the top floor of her deck, the Ninth, where she lived. Many people were here, standing, squatting, thronging together. They looked away from Shamim, people with blind faces. She had so often acted similarly herself when others were in trouble.

Gasping, she stopped and stared up at the roof of the deck, blue-dyed to simulate sky, cracks running irregularly across it. The steps went on up there, up to the Top Deck. She saw legs, yellow soles of feet disappearing, faces staring down at her, hostile. As she ran toward the bottom of the stairs, the watchers above threw things at her. A shard hit Shamim's cheek and cut it open. With blood running down her face, she began to wail. Then she turned and ran through the crowds to her family room.

I've been a month just reading through the microfiles. Sometimes a whole deck becomes unified under a strong leader. On Deck Nine, for instance, unification was achieved under a man called Ullhas. He was a strong man, and a great show-off. That was a while ago, when conditions were not as desperate as they are now. Ullhas could never last the course today. Leaders become more despotic as Environment decays.

The dynamics of unity are such that it is always insufficient for a deck simply to stay unified; the young men always need to have their aggressions directed outwards. So the leader of a strong deck always sets out to tyrannize the deck below or above, whichever seems to be the weaker. It is a miserable state of affairs. The time generally comes when, in the midst of a raid, a counter-raid is launched by one of the other decks. Then the raiders return to carnage and defeat. And another paltry empire tumbles.

It is up to me to stop this continual degradation of human life.

As usual, the family room was crowded. Although none of Shamim's own children were here, there were grand-children—including the lame granddaughter, Shirin—and six great-grandchildren, none of them more than three years old. Shamim's third husband, Gita, was not in. Safe in the homely squalor of the room, Shamim burst into tears, while Shirin comforted her and endeavored to keep the little ones off

"Gita is getting food. I will go and fetch him," Shirin said.

When UHDRE—Ultra-High Density Research Establishment—became operative, twenty-five years ago, all the couples selected for living in the Total Environment had to be under twenty years of age. Before being sealed in, they were inoculated against all diseases. There was plenty of room for each couple then; they had whole suites to themselves, and the best of food; plus no means of birth control. That's always been the main pivot of the UHDRE experiment. Now that first generation has aged severely. They are old people pushing forty-five. The whole life cycle has speeded up—early puberty, early senescence. The second and third generations have shown remarkable powers of adaptation; a fourth generation is already toddling. Those toddlers will be reproducing before their years attain double figures, if present trends continue. Are allowed to continue.

Gita was younger than Shamim, a small wiry man who knew his way around. No hero, he nevertheless had a certain style about him. His life-object hung boldly round his neck on a chain, instead of being hidden, as were most people's life-objects. He stood in the line for food, chattering with friends. Gita was good at making alliances. With a bunch of his friends, he had formed a little union to see that they got their food back safely to their homes; so they generally met with no incident in the crowded walkways of Deck Nine.

The balance of power on the deck was very complex at the moment. As a result, comparative peace reigned, and might continue for several weeks if the strong man on Top Deck did not interfere.

Food delivery grills are fixed in the walls of every floor of every deck. Two gongs sound before each delivery. After the second one, hatches open and steaming food pours from the grills. Hills of rice tumble forward, flavored with meat and spices. Chappattis fall from a separate slot. As the men run forward with their containers, holy men are generally there to sanctify the food.

Great supply elevators roar up and down in the heart of the vast tower, tumbling out rations at all levels. Alcohol also was supplied in the early years. It was discontinued when it led to trouble; which is not to say that it is not secretly brewed inside the Environment. The UHDRE food ration has been generous from the start and has always been maintained at the same level per head of population although, as you know, the food is now ninety-five percent factory-made. Nobody would ever have starved, had it been shared out equally inside the tower. On some of the decks, some of the time, it is still shared out fairly.

One of Gita's sons, Jamsu, has seen the kidnapper Narayan making off to Top Deck with the struggling Malti. His eyes gleaming with excitement, he sidled his way into the queue where Gita stood and clasped his father's arm. Jamsu had something of his father in him, always lurked where numbers made him safe, rather than run off as his brothers and sisters had run off, to marry and struggle for a room or a space of their own.

He was telling his father what had happened when Shirin limped up and delivered her news.

Nodding grimly, Gita said, "Stay with us, Shirin, while I get the food."

He scooped his share into the family pail. Jamsu grabbed a handful of rice for himself.

"It was a dirty wizened man from Top Deck called Narayan Farhad," Jamsu said, gobbling. "He is one of the crooks who hangs about the shirt tails of . . ." He let his voice die.

"You did not go to Malti's rescue, shame on you!" Shirin said.

"Jamsu might have been killed," Gita said, as they pushed through the crowd and moved towards the family room.

"They're getting so strong on Top Deck," Jamsu said. "I hear all about it! We mustn't provoke them or they may attack. They say a regular army is forming round . . ."

Shirin snorted impatiently. "You great babe! Go ahead and name the man! It's Prahlad Patel whose very name you dare not mention, isn't it? Is he a god or something, for Siva's sake? You're afraid of him even from this distance, eh, aren't you?"

"Don't bully the lad," Gita said. Keeping the peace in his huge mixed family was a great responsibility, almost more than he could manage. As he turned into the family room, he said quietly to Jamsu and Shirin. "Malti was a favorite daughter of Shamim's, and now is gone from her. We will get our revenge against this Narayan Farhad. You and I will go this evening, Jamsu, to the holy man Vazifdar. He will even up matters for us, and then perhaps the great Patel will also be warned."

He looked thoughtfully down at his life-object. Tonight, he told himself, I must venture forth alone, and put my life in jeopardy for Shamim's sake.

Prahlad Patel's union has flourished and grown until now he rules all the Top Deck. His name is known and dreaded, we believe, three or four decks down. He is the strongest—yet in some ways curiously the most moderate—ruler in Total Environment at present.

Although he can be brutal, Patel seems inclined for peace. Of course, the bugging does not reveal everything; he may have plans which he keeps secret, since he is fully aware that the bugging exists. But we believe his interests lie in other directions than conquest. He is only about nineteen, as we reckon years, but already gray-haired, and the sight of him is said to freeze the muscles to silence in the lips of his followers. I have watched him over the bugging for many hours since I agreed to undertake this task.

Patel has one great advantage in Total Environment. He lives on the Tenth Deck, at the top of the building. He can therefore be invaded only from below, and the Ninth Deck offers no strong threats at present, being mainly oriented round an influential body of holy men, of whom the most illustrious is one Vazifdar.

The staircases between decks are always trouble spots. No deck-ruler was ever strong enough to withstand attack from above and below. The staircases are also used by single troublemakers, thieves, political fugitives, prostitutes, escaping slaves, hostages. Guards can always be bribed, or favor their multitudinous relations, or join the enemy for one reason or another. Patel, being on the Top Deck, has only four weak points to watch for, rather than eight.

Vazifdar was amazingly holy and amazingly influential. It was whispered that his life-object was the most intricate in all Environment, but there was nobody who would lay claim to having set eyes upon it. Because of his reputation, many people on Gita's deck—yes, and from farther away—sought Vazifdar's help. A stream of men and women moved always through his room, even when he was locked in private meditation and far away from this world.

The holy man had a flat with a balcony that looked out onto mid-deck. Many relations and disciples lived there with him, so that the rooms had been elaborately and flimsily divided by screens. All day, the youngest disciples twittered like birds upon the balconies as Vazifdar held court, discussing among themselves the immense wisdom of his sayings.

All the disciples, all the relations, loved Vazifdar. There had been relations who did not love Vazifdar, but they had passed away in their sleep. Gita himself was a distant relation of Vazifdar's and came into the holy man's presence now with gifts of fresh water and a long piece of synthetic cloth, enough to make a robe.

Vazifdar's brow and cheeks were painted with white to

denote his high caste. He received the gifts of cloth and water graciously, smiling at Gita in such a way that Gita—and, behind him, Jamsu—took heart.

Vazifdar was thirteen years old as the outside measured years. He was sleekly fat, from eating much and moving little. His brown body shone with oils; every morning, young women massaged and manipulated him.

He spoke very softly, husbanding his voice, so that he could scarcely be heard for the noise in the room.

"It is a sorrow to me that this woe has befallen your stepchild Malti," he said. "She was a good woman, although infertile."

"She was raped at a very early age, disrupting her womb, dear Vazifdar. You will know of the event. Her parents feared she would die. She could never bear issue. The evil shadowed her life. Now this second woe befalls her."

"I perceive that Malti's role in the world was merely to be a companion to her mother. Not all can afford to purchase who visit the bazaar."

There are bazaars on every floor, crowding down the corridors and balconies, and a chief one on every deck. The menfolk choose such places to meet and chatter even when they have nothing to trade. Like everywhere else, the bazaars are crowded with humanity, down to the smallest who can walk—and sometimes even those carry naked smaller brothers clamped tight to their backs.

The bazaars are great centers for scandal. Here also are our largest screens. They glow behind their safety grills, beaming in special programs from outside; our outside world that must seem to have but faint reality as it dashes against the thick securing walls of Environment and percolates through to the screens. Below the screens, uncheckable and fecund life goes teeming on, with all its injury.

Humbly, Gita on his knees said, "If you could restore Malti to her mother Shamim, who mourns her, you would reap all our gratitude, dear Vazifdar. Malti is too old for a man's bed, and on Top Deck all sorts of humiliations must await her."

Vazifdar shook his head with great dignity. "You know I cannot restore Malti, my kinsman. How many deeds can be ever undone? As long as we have slavery, so long must we bear to have the ones we love enslaved. You must cultivate a mystical and resigned view of life and beseech Shamim always to do the same."

"Shamim is more mystical in her ways than I, never asking much, always working, working, praying, praying. That is why she deserves better than this misery."

Nodding in approval of Shamim's behavior as thus revealed, Vazifdar said, "That is well. I know she is a good woman. In the future lie other events which may recompense her for this sad event."

Jamsu, who had managed to keep quiet behind his father until now, suddenly burst out, "Uncle Vazifdar, can you not punish Narayan Farhad for his sin in stealing poor Malti on the steps? Is he to be allowed to escape to Patel's deck, there to live with Malti and enjoy?"

"Sssh, son!" Gita looked in agitation to see if Jamsu's outburst had annoyed Vazifdar; but Vazifdar was smiling blandly.

"You must know, Jamsu, that we are all creatures of the Lord Siva, and without power. No, no, do not pout! I also am without power in his hands. To own one room is not to possess the whole mansion. But . . ."

It was a long, and heavy *but*. When Vazifdar's thick eyelids closed over his eyes, Gita trembled, for he recalled how, on previous occasions when he had visited his powerful kinsman, Vazifdar's eyelids had descended in this fashion while he deigned to think on a problem, as if he shut out all the external world with his own potent flesh.

"Narayan Farhad shall be troubled by more than his conscience." As he spoke, the pupils of his eyes appeared again, violet and black. They were looking beyond Gita, beyond the confines of his immediate surroundings. "Tonight he shall be troubled by evil dreams."

"The night-visions!" Gita and Jamsu exclaimed, in fear and excitement.

Now Vazifdar swiveled his magnificent head and looked directly at Gita, looked deep into his eyes. Gita was a small man; he saw himself as a small man within. He shrank still further under that irresistible scrutiny.

"Yes, the night-visions," the holy man said. "You know what that entails, Gita. You must go up to Top Deck and procure Narayan's life-object. Bring it back to me, and I promise Narayan shall suffer the night-visions tonight. Though he is sick, he shall be cured."

III

The women never cease their chatter as the lines of supplicants come and go before the holy men. Their marvelous resignation in that hateful prison! If they ever complain about more than the small circumstances of their lives, if they ever complain about the monstrous evil that has overtaken them all, I never heard of it. There is always the harmless talk, talk that relieves petty nervous anxieties, talk that relieves the almost noticed pressures on the brain. The women's talk practically drowns the noise of their children. But most of the time it is clear that Total Environment consists mainly of children. That's why I want to see the experiment closed down; the children would adapt to our world.

It is mainly on this fourth generation that the effects of the population glut show. Whoever rules the decks, it is the babes, the endless babes, tottering, laughing, staring, piddling, tumbling, running, the endless babes to whom the Environment really belongs. And their mothers, for the most part, are women who—at the same age and in a more favored part of the globe—would still be virginally at school, many only just entering their teens.

Narayan Farhad wrapped a blanket round himself and huddled in his corner of the crowded room. Since it was almost time to sleep, he had to take up his hired space before one of the loathed Dasguptas stole it. Narayan hated the Dasgupta family, its lickspittle men, its shrill women, its turbulent children—the endless babes who crawled, the bigger ones with nervous diseases who thieved and ran and jeered at him. It was the vilest family on Top Deck, according to Narayan's oft-repeated claims; he tolerated it only because he felt himself to be vile.

He succeeded at nothing to which he turned his hand. Only an hour ago, pushing through the crowds, he had lost his life-object from his pocket—or else it had been stolen; but he dared not even consider that possibility!

Even his desultory kidnapping business was a failure. This

bitch he had caught this morning—Malti. He had intended
to rape her before selling her, but had become too nervous
once he had dragged her in here, with a pair of young
Dasguptas laughing at him. Nor had he sold the woman
well. Patel had beaten down his price, and Narayan had not
the guts to argue. Maybe he should leave this deck and move
down to one of the more chaotic ones. The middle decks were
always more chaotic. Six was having a slow three-sided war
even now, which should make Five a fruitful place, with
hoardes of refugees to batten on.

. . . And what a fool to snatch so old a girl—practically
an old woman!

Through narrowed eyes, Narayan squatted in his corner,
acid flavors burning his mouth. Even if his mind would rest
and allow him to sleep, the Dasgupta mob was still too lively
for any real relaxation. That old Dasgupta, now—he was like
a rat, totally without self-restraint, not a proper Hindu at all,
doing the act openly with his own daughters. There were
many men like that in Total Environment, men who had
nothing else in life. Dirty swine! Lucky dogs! Narayan's
daughters had thrown him out many months ago when he
tried it!

Over and over, his mind ran on his grievances. But he
sat collectedly, prodding off with one bare foot the nasty
little brats who crawled at him, and staring at the screen
flickering on the wall behind its protective mesh.

He liked the screens, enjoyed viewing the madness of outside. What a world it was out there! All that heat, and the
necessity for work, and the complication of life! The sheer
bigness of the world—he couldn't stand that, would not want
it under any circumstances.

He did not understand half he saw. After all, he was
born here. His father might have been born outside, whoever
his father was; but no legends from outside had come down
to him: only the distortions in the general gossip, and the
stuff on the screens. Now that he came to reflect, people didn't
pay much attention to the screens any more. Even he didn't.

But he could not sleep. Blearily, he looked at images of
cattle ploughing fields, fields cut into dice by the dirty grills
before the screens. He had already gathered vaguely that
this feature was about changes in the world today.

". . . are giving way to this . . ." said the commentator

above the rumpus in the Dasgupta room. The children lived here like birds. Racks were stacked against the walls, and on these rickety contraptions the many little Dasguptas roosted.

". . . food factories automated against danger of infection . . ." Yak yak yak, then.

"Beef-tissue culture growing straight into plastic distribution packs . . ." Shots of some great interior place somewhere, with meat growing out of pipes, extruding itself into square packs, dripping with liquid, looking rather ugly. Was that the shape of cows now or something? Outside must be a hell of a scaring place, then! ". . . as new factory food at last spells hope for India's future in the . . ." Yak yak yak from the kids. Once, their sleep racks had been built across the screen; but one night the whole shaky edifice collapsed, and three children were injured. None killed, worse luck!

Patel should have paid more for that girl. Nothing was as good as it had been. Why, once on a time, they used to show sex films on the screens—really filthy stuff that got even Narayan excited. He was younger then. Really filthy stuff, he remembered, and pretty girls doing it. But it must be—oh, a long time since that was stopped. The screens were dull now. People gave up watching. Uneasily, Narayan slept, propped in the corner under his scruffy blanket. Eventually, the whole scruffy room slept.

The documentaries and other features piped into Environment are no longer specially made by UHDRE teams for internal consumption. When the U.N. made a major cut in UHDRE's annual subsidy, eight years ago, the private TV studio was one of the frills that had to be axed. Now we pipe in old programs bought off major networks. The hope is that they will keep the wretched prisoners in Environment in touch with the outside world, but this is clearly not happening. The degree of comprehension, between inside and outside grows markedly less on both sides, on an exponential curve. As I see it, a great gulf of isolation is widening between the two environments, just as if they were sailing away from each other into different space-time continua. I wish I could think that the people in charge here—Crawley especially—not only grasped this fact but understood that it should be rectified immediately.

Shamim could not sleep for grief.

Gita could not sleep for apprehension.

Jamsu could not sleep for excitement.

Vazifdar did not sleep.

Vazifdar shut his sacred self away in a cupboard, brought his lids down over his eyes and began to construct, within the vast spaces of his mind, a thought pattern corresponding to the matrix represented by Narayan Farhad's stolen life-object. When it was fully conceived, Vazifdar began gently to inset a little evil into one edge of the thought-pattern. . . .

Narayan slept. What roused him was the silence. It was the first time total silence had ever come to Total Environment.

At first, he thought he would enjoy total silence. But it took on such weight and substance. . . .

Clutching his blanket, he sat up. The room was empty, the screen dark. Neither thing had ever happened before, could not happen! And the silence! Dear Siva, some terrible monkey god had hammered that silence out in darkness and thrown it out like a shield into the world, rolling over all things! There was a ringing quality in the silence—a gong! No, no, not a gong! Footsteps!

It was footsteps, O Lord Siva, do not let it be footsteps!

Total Environment was empty. The legend was fulfilled that said Total Environment would empty one day. All had departed except for poor Narayan. And this thing of the footsteps was coming to visit him in his defenseless corner. . . .

It was climbing up through the cellars of his existence. Soon it would emerge.

Trembling convulsively, Narayan stood up, clutching the corner of the blanket to his throat. He did not wish to face the thing. Wildly, he thought, could he bear it best if it looked like a man or if it looked nothing like a man? It was Death for sure—but how would it look? Only Death—his heart fluttered!—Only Death could arrive this way. . . .

His helplessness. . . . Nowhere to hide! He opened his mouth, could not scream, clutched the blanket, felt that he was wetting himself as if he were a child again. Swiftly came the image—the infantile, round-bellied, cringing, puny, his mother black with fury, her great white teeth gritting as she smacked his face with all her might, spitting. . . . It was gone, and he faced the gong-like death again, alone in the great dark tower. In the arid air, vibrations of its presence.

He was shouting to it, demanding that it did not come.

But it came. It came with majestic sloth, like the heartbeats of a foetid slumber, came in the door, pushing darkness before it. It was like a human, but too big to be human.

And it wore Malti's face, that sickening innocent smile with which she had run up the steps. No! No, that was not it—oh, he fell down onto the wet floor: it was nothing like that woman, nothing at all. Cease, impossibilities! It was a man, his ebony skull shining, terrible and magnificent, stretching out, grasping, confident. Narayan struck out of his extremity and fell forward. Death was another indelible smack in the face.

One of the roosting Dasguptas blubbered and moaned as the man kicked him, woke for a moment, saw the screen still flickering meaninglessly and reassuringly, saw Narayan tremble under his blanket, tumbled back into sleep.

It was not till morning that they found it had been Narayan's last tremble.

I know I am supposed to be a detached observer. No emotions, no feelings. But scientific detachment is the attitude that has led to much of the inhumanity inherent in Environment. How do we, for all the bugging devices, hope to know what ghastly secret nightmares they undergo in there? Anyhow, I am relieved to hear you are flying over.

It is tomorrow I am due to go into Environment myself.

IV

The central offices of UHDRE were large and repulsive. At the time when they and the Total Environment tower had been built, the Indian Government would not have stood for anything else. Poured cement and rough edges was what they wanted to see and what they got.

From a window in the office building, Thomas Dixit could see the indeterminate land in one direction, and the gigantic TE tower in the other, together with the shantytown that had grown between the foot of the tower and the other UHDRE buildings.

For a moment, he chose to ignore the Project Organizer behind him and gaze out at what he could see of the table-flat land of the great Ganges delta.

He thought, It's as good a place as any for man to project his power fantasies. But you are a fool to get mixed up in all this, Thomas!

Even to himself, he was never just Tom.

I am being paid, well paid, to do a specific job. Now I am letting woolly humanitarian ideas get in the way of action. Essentially, I am a very empty man. No center. Father Bengali, mother English, and live all my life in the States. I have excuses . . . Other people accept them; why can't I?

Sighing, he dwelt on his own unsatisfactoriness. He did not really belong to the West, despite his long years there, and he certainly did not belong to India; in fact, he thought he rather disliked India. Maybe the best place for him was indeed the inside of the Environment tower.

He turned impatiently and said, "I'm ready to get going now, Peter."

Peter Crawley, the Special Project Organizer of UHDRE, was a rather austere Bostonian. He removed the horn-rimmed glasses from his nose and said, "Right! Although we have been through the drill many times, Thomas, I have to tell you this once again before we move. The entire—"

"Yes, yes, I know, Peter! You don't have to cover yourself. This entire organization might be closed down if I make a wrong move. Please take it as read."

Without indignation, Crawley said, "I was going to say that we are all rooting for you. We appreciate the risks you are taking. We shall be checking you everywhere you go in there through the bugging system."

"And whatever you see, you can't do a thing."

"Be fair; we have made arrangements to help!"

"I'm sorry, Peter." He liked Crawley and Crawley's decent reserve.

Crawley folded his spectacles with a snap, inserted them in a leather slipcase and stood up.

"The U.N., not to mention subsidiary organizations like the WHO and the Indian government, have their knife into us, Thomas. They want to close us down and empty Environment. They will do so unless you can provide evidence that forms of extra-sensory perception are developing inside the Environment. Don't get yourself killed in there. The previous

men we sent in behaved foolishly and never came out again."
He raised an eyebrow and added dryly, "That sort of thing
gets us a bad name, you know."

"Just as the blue movies did a while ago."

Crawley put his hands behind his back. "My predecessor
here decided that immoral movies piped into Environment
would help boost the birth rate there. Whether he was right
or wrong, world opinion has changed since then as the spec-
ter of world famine has faded. We stopped the movies eight
years ago, but they have long memories at the U.N., I fear.
They allow emotionalism to impede scientific research."

"Do you never feel any sympathy for the thousands of
people doomed to live out their brief lives in the tower?"

They looked speculatively at each other.

"You aren't on our side any more, Thomas, are you? You'd
like your findings to be negative, wouldn't you, and have the
U.N. close us down?"

Dixit uttered a laugh. "I'm not on anyone's *side*, Peter.
I'm neutral. I'm going into Environment to look for the
evidence of ESP that only direct contact may turn up. What
else direct contact will turn up, neither of us can say as yet."

"But you think it will be misery. And you will emphasize
that at the inquiry after your return."

"Peter—let's get on with it, shall we?" Momentarily, Dixit
was granted a clear picture of the two of them standing in
this room; he saw how their bodily attitudes contrasted. His
attitudes were rather slovenly; he held himself rather slump-
shouldered, he gesticulated to some extent (too much?); he
was dressed in threadbare tunic and shorts, ready to pass
muster as an inhabitant of Environment. Crawley, on the
other hand, was very upright, stiff and smart in his movements, hardly ever gestured as he spoke; his dress was fault-
less.

And there was no need to be awed by or envious of Crawley. Crawley was encased in inhibition, afraid to feel, signaling
his aridity to anyone who cared to look out from his own
self-preoccupation. Crawley, moreover, feared for his job.

"Let's get on with it, as you say." He came from behind his
desk. "But I'd be grateful if you would remember, Thomas,
that the people in the tower are volunteers, or the descendants of volunteers.

"When UHDRE began, a quarter-century ago, back in the

mid-nineteen-seventies, only volunteers were admitted to the Total Environment. Five hundred young married Indian couples were admitted, plus whatever children they had. The tower was a refuge then, free from famine, immune from all disease. They were glad, heartily glad, to get in, glad of all that Environment provided and still provides. Those who didn't qualify rioted. We have to remember that.

"India was a different place in 1975. It had lost hope. One crisis after another, one famine after another, crops dying, people starving, and yet the population spiraling up by a million every month.

"But today, thank God, that picture has largely changed. Synthetic foods have licked the problem; we don't need the grudging land any more. And at last the Hindus and Muslims have got the birth control idea into their heads. It's only *now*, when a little humanity is seeping back into this death-bowl of a subcontinent, that the U.N. dares complain about the inhumanity of UHDRE."

Dixit said nothing. He felt that this potted history was simply angled towards Crawley's self-justification; the ideas it represented were real enough, heaven knew, but they had meaning for Crawley only in terms of his own existence. Dixit felt pity and impatience as Crawley went on with his narration.

"Our aim here must be unswervingly the same as it was from the start. We have evidence that nervous disorders of a special kind produce extra-sensory perceptions—telepathy and the rest, and maybe kinds of ESP we do not yet recognize. High-density populations with reasonable nutritional standards develop particular nervous instabilities which may be akin to ESP spectra.

"The Ultra-High Density Research Establishment was set up to intensify the likelihood of ESP developing. Don't forget that. The people in Environment are supposed to have some ESP; that's the whole point of the operation, right? Sure, it is not humanitarian. We know that. But that is not your concern. You have to go in and find evidence of ESP, something that doesn't show over the bugging. Then UHDRE will be able to continue."

Dixit prepared to leave. "If it hasn't shown up in a quarter of a century—"

"It's in there! I know it's in there! The failure's in the

bugging system. I feel it coming through the screens at me —some mystery we need to get our hands on! If only I could prove it! If only I could get in there myself!"

Interesting, Dixit thought. You'd have to be some sort of a voyeur to hold Crawley's job, forever spying on the wretched people.

"Too bad you have a white skin, eh?" he said lightly. He walked towards the door. It swung open, and he passed into the corridor.

Crawley ran after him and thrust out a hand. "I know how you feel, Thomas. I'm not just a stuffed shirt, you know, not entirely void of sympathy. Sorry if I was needling you. I didn't intend to do so."

Dixit dropped his gaze. "I should be the one to apologize, Peter. If there's anything unusual going on in the tower, I'll find it, never worry!"

They shook hands, without wholly being able to meet each other's eyes.

V

Leaving the office block, Dixit walked alone through the sunshine toward the looming tower that housed Total Environment. The concrete walk was hot and dusty underfoot. The sun was the one good thing that India had, he thought: that burning beautiful sun, the real ruler of India, whatever petty tyrants came and went.

The sun blazed down on the tower; only inside did it not shine.

The uncompromising outlines of the tower were blurred by pipes, ducts and shafts that ran up and down its exterior. It was a building built for looking into, not out of. Some time ago, in the bad years, the welter of visual records gleaned from Environment used to be edited and beamed out on global networks every evening; but all that had been stopped as conditions inside Environment deteriorated, and public opinion in the democracies, who were subsidizing the grandiose experiment, turned against the exploitation of human material.

A monitoring station stood by the tower walls. From here, a constant survey on the interior was kept. Facing the station were the jumbles of merchants' stalls, springing up to cater for tourists, who persisted even now that the tourist trade was discouraged. Two security guards stepped forward and escorted Dixit to the base of the tower. With ceremony, he entered the shade of the entry elevator. As he closed the door, germicides sprayed him, insuring that he entered Environment without harboring dangerous micro-organisms.

The elevator carried him up to the top deck; this plan had been settled some while ago. The elevator was equipped with double steel doors. As it came to rest, a circuit opened, and a screen showed him what was happening on the other side of the doors. He emerged from a dummy air-conditioning unit, behind a wide pillar. He was in Patel's domain,

The awful weight of human overcrowding hit Dixit with its full stink and noise. He sat down at the base of the pillar and let his senses adjust. And he thought, I was the wrong one to send; I've always had this inner core of pity for the sufferings of humanity; I could never be impartial; I've got to see that this terrible experiment is stopped.

He was at one end of a long balcony onto which many doors opened; a ramp led down at the other end. All the doorways gaped, although some were covered by rugs. Most of the doors had been taken off their hinges to serve as partitions along the balcony itself, partitioning off overspill families. Children ran everywhere, their tinkling voices and cries the dominant note in the hubbub. Glancing over the balcony, Dixit took in a dreadful scene of swarming multitudes, the anonymity of congestion; to sorrow for humanity was not to love its prodigality. Dixit had seen this panorama many times over the bugging system; he knew all the staggering figures—1500 people in here to begin with, and by now some 75,000 people, a large proportion of them under four years of age. But pictures and figures were pale abstracts beside the reality they were intended to represent.

The kids drove him into action at last by playfully hurling dirt at him. Dixit moved slowly along, carrying himself tight and cringing in the manner of the crowd about him, features rigid, elbows tucked in to the ribs. *Mutatis mutandis*, it was Crawley's inhibited attitude. Even the children ran between the legs of their elders in that guarded way. As soon as he had left the shelter of his pillar, he was caught in a stream of chattering people, all jostling between the rooms and the stalls of the balcony. They moved very slowly.

Among the crowd were hawkers, and salesmen pressed their wares from the pitiful balcony hovels. Dixit tried to conceal his curiosity. Over the bugging he had had only distant views of the merchandise offered for sale. Here were the strange models that had caught his attention when he was first appointed to the UHDRE project. A man with orange goat-eyes, in fact probably no more than thirteen years of age, but here a hardened veteran, was at Dixit's elbow. As Dixit stared at him, momentarily suspicious he was being watched, the goat-eyed man merged into the crowd; and, to hide his face, Dixit turned to the nearest salesman.

In only a moment, he was eagerly examining the wares, forgetting how vulnerable was his situation.

All the strange models were extremely small. This Dixit attributed to shortage of materials—wrongly, as it later transpired. The biggest model the salesman possessed stood no more than two inches high. It was made, nevertheless, of a diversity of materials, in which many sorts of plastics featured. Some models were simple, and appeared to be little more than an elaborate *tughra* or monogram, which might have been intended for an elaborate piece of costume jewelry; others, as one peered among their interstices, seemed to afford a glimpse of another dimension; all possessed eye-teasing properties.

The merchant was pressing Dixit to buy. He referred to the elaborate models as "life-objects." Noticing that one in particular attracted his potential customer, he lifted it delicately and held it up, a miracle of craftsmanship, perplexing, *outré*, giving Dixit somehow as much pain as pleasure. He named the price.

Although Dixit was primed with money, he automatically shook his head. "Too expensive."

"See, master, I show you how this life-object works!" The man fished beneath his scrap of loincloth and produced a small perforated silver box. Flipping it open, he produced a live wood-louse and slipped it under a hinged part of the model. The insect, in its struggles, activated a tiny wheel; the interior of the model began to rotate, some sets of minute planes turning in counterpoint to others.

"This life-object belonged to a very religious man, master."

In his fascination, Dixit said, "Are they all powered?"

"No, master, only special ones. This was perfect model

from Dalcush Bancholi, last generation master all the way from Third Deck, very very fine and masterful workmanship of first quality. I have also still better one worked by a body louse, if you care to see."

By reflex, Dixit said, "Your prices are too high."

He absolved himself from the argument that brewed, slipping away through the crowd with the merchant calling after him. Other merchants shouted to him, sensing his interest in their wares. He saw some beautiful work, all on the tiniest scale, and not only life-objects but amazing little watches with millisecond hands as well as second hands; in some cases, the millisecond was the largest hand, in some, the hour hand was missing or was supplemented by a day hand; and the watches took many extraordinary shapes, tetrakishexahedrons and other elaborate forms, until their format merged with that of the life-objects.

Dixit thought approvingly: the clock and watch industry fulfills a human need for exercising elaborate skill and accuracy, while at the same time requiring a minimum of materials. These people of Total Environment are the world's greatest craftsmen. Bent over one curious watch that involved a color change, he became suddenly aware of danger. Glancing over his shoulder, he saw the man with the unpleasant orange eyes about to strike him. Dixit dodged without being able to avoid the blow. As it caught him on the side of his neck, he stumbled and fell under the milling feet.

VI

Afterwards, Dixit could hardly say that he had been totally unconscious. He was aware of hands dragging him, of being partly carried, of the sound of many voices, of the name "Patel" repeated. . . . And when he came fully to his senses, he was lying in a cramped room, with a guard in a scruffy turban standing by the door. His first hazy thought was that the room was no more than a small ship's cabin; then he realized that, by indigenous standards, this was a large room for only one person.

He was a prisoner in Total Environment.

A kind of self-mocking fear entered him; he had almost expected the blow, he realized; and he looked eagerly about for the bug-eye that would reassure him his UHDRE friends outside were aware of his predicament. There was no sign of the bug-eye. He was not long in working out why; this room had been partitioned out of a larger one, and the bugging system was evidently shut in the other half—whether deliberately or accidentally, he had no way of knowing.

The guard had bobbed out of sight. Sounds of whispering came from beyond the doorway. Dixit felt the pressure of many people there. Then a woman came in and closed the door. She walked cringingly and carried a brass cup of water.

Although her face was lined, it was possible to see that she had once been beautiful and perhaps proud. Now her whole attitude expressed the defeat of her life. And this woman might be no more than eighteen! One of the terrifying features of Environment was the way, right from the start, confinement had speeded life-processes and abridged life.

Involuntarily, Dixit flinched away from the woman.

She almost smiled. "Do not fear me, sir. I am almost as much a prisoner as you are. Equally, do not think that by knocking me down you can escape. I promise you, there are fifty people outside the door, all eager to impress Prahlad Patel by catching you, should you try to get away."

So I'm in Patel's clutches, he thought. Aloud he said. "I will offer you no harm. I want to see Patel. If you are captive, tell me your name, and perhaps I can help you."

As she offered him the cup and he drank, she said, shyly, "I do not complain, for my fate might have been much worse than it is. Please do not agitate Patel about me, or he may throw me out of his household. My name is Malti."

"Perhaps I may be able to help you, and all your tribe, soon. You are all in a form of captivity here, the great Patel included, and it is from that I hope to deliver you."

Then he saw fear in her eyes.

"You really are a spy from outside!" she breathed. "But we do not want our poor little world invaded! You have so much—leave us our little!" She shrank away and slipped through the door, leaving Dixit with a melancholy impression of her eyes, so burdened in their shrunken gaze.

The babel continued outside the door. Although he still felt sick, he propped himself up and let his thoughts run on. "You have so much—leave us our little. . . ." All their values had been perverted. Poor things, they could know neither the smallness of their own world nor the magnitude of the world outside. This—this dungheap had become to them all there was of beauty and value.

Two guards came for him, mere boys. He could have knocked their heads together, but compassion moved him. They led him through a room full of excited people; beyond their glaring faces, the screen flickered pallidly behind its mesh; Dixit saw how faint the image of outside was.

He was taken into another partitioned room. Two men were talking.

The scene struck Dixit with peculiar force, and not merely because he was at a disadvantage.

It was an alien scene. The impoverishment of even the richest furnishings, the clipped and bastardized variety of Hindi that was being talked, reinforced the impression of strangeness. And the charge of Patel's character filled the room.

There could be no doubt who was Patel. The plump cringing fellow, wringing his hands and protesting, was not Patel. Patel was the stocky white-haired man with the heavy lower lip and high forehead. Dixit had seen him in this very room over the bugging system. But to stand captive awaiting his attention was an experience of an entirely different order. Dixit tried to analyze the first fresh impact Patel had on him, but it was elusive.

It was difficult to realize that, as the outside measured years, Patel could not be much more than nineteen or twenty years of age. Time was impacted here, jellified under the psychic pressures of Total Environment. Like the hieroglyphics of that new relativity, detailed plans of the Environment hung large on one wall of this room, while figures and names were chalked over the others. The room was the nerve center of Top Deck.

He knew something about Patel from UHDRE records. Patel had come up here from the Seventh Deck. By guile as well as force, he had become ruler of Top Deck at an early age. He had surprised UHDRE observers by abstaining from the usual forays of conquest into other floors.

Patel was saying to the cringing man, "Be silent! You try to obscure the truth with argument. You have heard the witnesses against you. During your period of watch on the stairs, you were bribed by a man from Ninth Deck and you let him through here."

"Only for a mere seventeen minutes, Sir Patel!"

"I am aware that such things happen every day, wretched Raital. But this fellow you let through stole the life-object belonging to Narayan Farhad and, in consequence, Narayan Farhad died in his sleep last night. Narayan was no more important than you are, but he was useful to me, and it is in order that he be revenged."

"Anything that you say, Sir Patel!"

"Be silent, wretched Raital!" Patel watched Raital with interest as he spoke. And he spoke in a firm reflective voice that impressed Dixit more than shouting would have done.

"You shall revenge Narayan, Raital, because you caused his death. You will leave here now. You will not be punished. You will go, and you will steal the life-object belonging to that fellow from whom you accepted the bribe. You will bring that life-object to me. You have one day to do so. Otherwise, my assassins will find you wherever you hide, be it even down on Deck One."

"Oh, yes, indeed, Sir Patel, all men know—" Raital was bent almost double as he uttered some face-saving formula. He turned and scurried away as Patel dismissed him.

Strength, thought Dixit. Strength, and also cunning. That is what Patel radiates. An elaborate and cutting subtlety. The phrase pleased him, seeming to represent something actual that he had detected in Patel's makeup. An elaborate and cutting subtlety.

Clearly, it was part of Patel's design that Dixit should witness this demonstration of his methods.

Patel turned away, folded his arms, and contemplated a blank piece of wall at close range. He stood motionless. The guards held Dixit still, but not so still as Patel held himself.

This tableau was maintained for several minutes. Dixit found himself losing track of the normal passage of time. Patel's habit of turning to stare at the wall—and it did not belong to Patel alone—was an uncanny one that Dixit had watched several times over the bugging system. It was that habit, he thought, which might have given Crawley the notion that ESP was rampant in the tower.

It was curious to think of Crawley here. Although Crawley might at this moment be surveying Dixit's face on a monitor, Crawley was now no more than an hypothesis.

Malti broke the tableau. She entered the room with a damp

cloth on a tray, to stand waiting patiently for Patel to notice her. He broke away at last from his motionless survey of the wall, gesturing abruptly to the guards to leave. He took no notice of Dixit, sitting in a chair, letting Malti drape the damp cloth round his neck; the cloth had a fragrant smell to it.

"The towel is not cool enough, Malti, or damp enough. You will attend me properly at my morning session, or you will lose this easy job."

He swung his gaze, which was suddenly black and searching, onto Dixit to say, "Well, spy, you know I am Lord here. Do you wonder why I tolerate old women like this about me when I could have girls young and lovely to fawn on me?"

Dixit said nothing, and the self-styled Lord continued, "Young girls would merely remind me by contrast of my advanced years. But this old bag—whom I bought only yesterday—this old bag is only just my junior and makes me look good in contrast. You see, we are masters of philosophy in here, in this prison-universe; we cannot be masters of material wealth like you people outside!"

Again Dixit said nothing, disgusted by the man's implied attitude to women.

A swinging blow caught him unprepared in the stomach. He cried and dropped suddenly to the floor.

"Get up, spy!" Patel said. He had moved extraordinarily fast. He sat back again in his chair, letting Malti massage his neck muscles.

VII

As Dixit staggered to his feet, Patel said, "You don't deny you are from outside?"

"I did not attempt to deny it. I came from outside to speak to you."

"You say nothing here until you are ordered to speak. Your people—you outsiders—you have sent in several spies to us the last few months. Why?"

Still feeling sick from the blow, Dixit said, "You should realize that we are your friends rather than your enemies, and our men emissaries rather than spies."

"Pah! You are a breed of spies! Don't you sit and spy on us from every room? You live in a funny little dull world out there, don't you? So interested in us that you can think of nothing else! Keep working, Malti! Little spy, you know what happened to all the other spies your spying people sent in?"

"They died," Dixit said.

"Exactly. They died. But you are the first to be sent to Patel's deck. What different thing from death do you expect here?"

"Another death will make my superiors very tired, Patel. You may have the power of life and death over me; they have the same over you, and over all in this world of yours. Do you want a demonstration?"

Rising, flinging the towel off, Patel said, "Give me your demonstration!"

Must do, Dixit thought. Staring in Patel's eyes, he raised his right hand above his head and gestured with his thumb. Pray they are watching—and thank God this bit of partitioned room is the bit with the bugging system!

Tensely, Patel stared, balanced on his toes. Behind his shoulder, Malti also stared. Nothing happened.

Then a sort of shudder ran through Environment. It became slowly audible as a mixture of groan and cry. Its cause became apparent in this less crowded room when the air began to grow hot and foul. So Dixit's signal had got through; Crawley had him under survey, and the air-conditioning plant was pumping in hot carbon-dioxide through the respiratory system.

"You see? We control the very air you breathe!" Dixit said. He dropped his arm, and slowly the air returned to normal, although it was at least an hour before the fright died down in the passages.

Whatever the demonstration had done to Patel, he showed nothing. Instead, he said. "You control the air. Very well. But you do not control the will to turn it off permanently—and so you do not control the air. Your threat is an empty one, spy! For some reason, you need us to live. We have a mystery, don't we?"

"There is no reason why I should be anything but honest with you, Patel. Your special environment must have bred special talents in you. We are interested in those talents; but no more than interested."

Patel came closer and inspected Dixit's face minutely, rather as he had recently inspected the blank wall. Strange angers churned inside him; his neck and throat turned a dark mottled color. Finally he spoke.

"We are the center of your outside world, aren't we? We know that you watch us all the time. We know that you are much more than 'interested'! For you, we here are somehow a matter of life and death, aren't we?"

This was more than Dixit had expected.

"Four generations, Patel, four generations have been incarcerated in Environment." His voice trembled. "Four generations, and, despite our best intentions, you are losing touch with reality. You live in one relatively small building on a sizeable planet. Clearly, you can only be of limited interest to the world at large."

"Malti!" Patel turned to the slave girl. "Which is the greater, the outer world or ours?"

She looked confused, hesitated by the door as if longing to escape. "The outside world was great, master, but then it gave birth to us, and we have grown and are growing and are gaining strength. The child now is almost the size of the father. So my step-father's son Jamsu says, and he is a clever one."

Patel turned to stare at Dixit, a haughty expression on his face. He made no comment, as if the words of an ignorant girl were sufficient to prove his point.

"All that you and the girl say only emphasizes to me how much you need help, Patel. The world outside is a great and thriving place; you must allow it to give you assistance through me. We are not your enemies."

Again the choleric anger was there, powering Patel's every word.

"What else are you, spy? Your life is so vile and pointless out there, is it not? You envy us because we are superseding you! Our people—we may be poor, you may think of us as in your power, but we rule our own universe. And that universe is expanding and falling under our control more every day. Why, our explorers have gone into the world of the ultrasmall. We discover new environments, new ways of living. By your terms, we are scientific peasants, perhaps, but I fancy we have means of knowing the trade routes of the blood and the eternities of cell-change that you cannot comprehend. You think of us all as captives, eh? Yet you are captive to the necessity of supplying our air and our food and water; we are free. We are poor, yet you covet our riches. We are spied on all the time, yet we are secret. You need to understand us, yet we have no need to understand you. You are in *our* power, spy!"

"Certainly not in one vital respect, Patel. Both you and we are ruled by historical necessity. This Environment was set up twenty-five of our years ago. Changes have taken place not only in here but outside as well. The nations of the world are no longer prepared to finance this project. It is going to be closed down entirely, and you are going to have to live outside. Or, if you don't want that, you'd better cooperate with us and persuade the leaders of the other decks to cooperate."

Would threats work with Patel? His hooded and oblique gaze bit into Dixit like a hook.

After a deadly pause, he clapped his hands once. Two guards immediately appeared.

"Take the spy away," said Patel. Then he turned his back.

A clever man, Dixit thought. He sat alone in the cell and meditated.

It seemed as if a battle of wits might develop between him and Patel. Well, he was prepared. He trusted to his first impression, that Patel was a man of cutting subtlety. He could not be taken to mean all that he said.

Dixit's mind worked back over their conversation. The mystery of the life-objects had been dangled before him. And Patel had taken care to belittle the outside world: "funny dull little world," he had called it. He had made Malti advance her primitive view that Environment was growing, and that had fitted in very well with his brand of boasting. Which led to the deduction that he had known her views beforehand; yet he had bought her only yesterday. Why should a busy man, a leader, bother to question an ignorant slave about her views of the outside world unless he were starved for information of that world, obsessed with it.

Yes, Dixit nodded to himself. Patel was obsessed with outside and tried to hide that obsession; but several small contradictions in his talk had revealed it.

Of course, it might be that Malti was so generally representative of the thousands in Environment that her misinformed ideas could be taken for granted. It was as well, as yet, not to be too certain that he was beginning to understand Patel.

Part of Patel's speech made sense even superficially. These poor devils were exploring the world of the ultra-small. It was the only landscape left for them to map. They were human, and still burning inside them was that unquenchable human urge to open new frontiers.

So they knew some inward things. Quite possibly, as Crawley anticipated, they possessed a system of ESP upon which some reliance might be placed, unlike the wildly fluctuating telepathic radiations which circulated in the outside world.

He felt confident, fully engaged. There was much to understand here. The bugging system, elaborate and over-used, was shown to be a complete failure; the watchers had stayed external to their problem; it remained their problem, not their life. What was needed was a whole team to come and live here, perhaps a team on every deck, anthropologists and so on. Since that was impossible, then clearly the people of Environment must be released from their captivity; those that were unwilling to go far afield should be settled in new villages on the Ganges plain, under the wide sky. And there, as they adapted to the real world, observers could live among them, learning with humility of the gifts that had been acquired at such cost within the thick walls of the Total Environment tower.

As Dixit sat in meditation, a guard brought a meal in to him.

He ate thankfully and renewed his thinking.

From the little he had already experienced—the ghastly pressures on living space, the slavery, the aberrant modes of thought into which the people were being forced, the harshness of the petty rulers—he was confirmed in his view that this experiment in anything like its present form must be closed down at once. The U.N. needed the excuse of his adverse report before they moved; they should have it when he got out. And if he worded the report carefully, stressing that these people had many talents to offer, then he might also satisfy Crawley and his like. He had it in his power to satisfy all parties, when he got out. All he had to do was get out.

The guard came back to collect his empty bowl.

"When is Patel going to speak with me again?"

The guard said, "When he sends for you to have you silenced for ever."

Dixit stopped composing his report and thought about that instead.

VIII

Much time elapsed before Dixit was visited again, and then it was only the self-effacing Malti who appeared, bringing him a cup of water.

"I want to talk to you," Dixit said urgently.

"No, no, I cannot talk! He will beat me. It is the time when we sleep, when the old die. You should sleep now, and Patel will see you in the morning."

He tried to touch her hand, but she withdrew.

"You are a kind girl, Malti. You suffer in Patel's household."

"He has many women, many servants. I am not alone."

"Can you not escape back to your family?"

She looked at the floor evasively. "It would bring trouble to my family. Slavery is the lot of many women. It is the way of the world."

"It is not the way of the world I come from!"

Her eyes flashed. "Your world is of no interest to us!"

Dixit thought after she had gone, She is afraid of our world. Rightly.

He slept little during the night. Even barricaded inside Patel's fortress, he could still hear the noises of Environment: not only the voices, almost never silent, but the gurgle and sob of pipes in the walls. In the morning, he was taken into a larger room where Patel was issuing commands for the day to a succession of subordinates.

Confined to a corner, Dixit followed everything with interest. His interest grew when the unfortunate guard Raital appeared. He bounded in and waited for Patel to strike him. Instead, Patel kicked him.

"You have performed as I ordered yesterday?"

Raital began at once to cry and wring his hands. "Sir Patel, I have performed as well as and better than you demanded, incurring great suffering and having myself beaten downstairs where the people of Ninth Deck discovered me marauding. You must invade them, Sir, and teach them a lesson that in their insolence they so dare to mock your faithful guards who only do those things—"

"Silence, you dog-devourer! Do you bring back that item which I demanded of you yesterday?"

The wretched guard brought from the pocket of his tattered tunic a small object, which he held out to Patel.

"Of course I obey, Sir Patel. To keep this object safe when the people caught me, I swallow it whole, sir, into the stomach for safe keeping, so that they would not know what I am about. Then my wife gives me sharp medicine so that I vomit it safely again to deliver to you."

"Put the filthy thing down on that shelf there! You think I wish to touch it when it has been in your worm-infested belly, slave?"

The guard did as he was bid and abased himself.

"You are sure it is the life-object of the man who stole Narayan Farhad's life-object, and nobody else's?"

"Oh, indeed, Sir Patel! It belongs to a man called Gita, the very same who stole Narayan's life object, and tonight you will see he will die of night-visions!"

"Get out!" Patel managed to catch Raital's buttocks with a swift kick as the guard scampered from the room.

A queue of people stood waiting to speak with him, to supplicate and advise. Patel sat and interviewed them, in the main showing a better humor than he had shown his luckless guard. For Dixit, this scene had a curious interest; he had watched Patel's morning audience more than once, standing by Crawley's side in the UHDRE monitoring station; now he was a prisoner waiting uncomfortably in the corner of the room, and the whole atmosphere was changed. He felt the extraordinary intensity of these people's lives, the emotions compressed, everything vivid. Patel himself wept several times as some tale of hardship was unfolded to him. There was no privacy. Everyone stood round him, listening to everything. Short the lives might be; but those annihilating spaces that stretch through ordinary lives, the spaces through which one glimpses uncomfortable glooms and larger poverties, if not presences more sour and sinister, seemed here to have been eradicated. The Total Environment had brought its peoples total involvement. Whatever befell them, they were united, as were bees in a hive.

Finally, a break was called. The unfortunates who had not gained Patel's ear were turned away; Malti was summoned and administered the damp-towel treatment to Patel. Later, he sent her off and ate a frugal meal. Only when he had finished it, and sat momentarily in meditation, did he turn his brooding attention to Dixit.

He indicated that Dixit was to fetch down the object Raital had placed on a shelf. Dixit did so and put the object before Patel. Staring at it with interest, he saw it was an elaborate little model, similar to the ones for sale on the balcony.

"Observe it well," Patel said. "It is the life-object of a man. You have these"—he gestured vaguely—"outside?"

"No."

"You know what they are?"

"No."

"In this world of ours, Mr. Dixit, we have many holy men. I have a holy man here under my protection. On the deck below is one very famous holy man, Vazifdariji. These men have many powers. Tonight, I shall give my holy man this life-object, and with it he will be able to enter the being of the man to whom it belongs, for good or ill, and in this case for ill, to revenge a death with a death."

Dixit stared at the little object, a three-dimensional maze constructed of silver and plastic strands, trying to comprehend what Patel was saying.

"This is a sort of key to its owner's mind?"

"No, no, not a key, and not to his mind. It is a—well, we do not have a scientific word for it, and our word would mean nothing to you, so I cannot say what. It is, let us say, a replica, a substitute for the man's being. Not his mind, his being. In this case, a man called Gita. You are very interested, aren't you?"

"Everyone here has one of these?"

"Down to the very poorest, and even the older children. A sage works in conjunction with a smith to produce each individual life-object."

"But they can be stolen and then an ill-intentioned holy man can use them to kill the owner. So why make them? I don't understand."

Smiling, Patel made a small movement of impatience. "What you discover of yourself, you record. That is how these things are made. They are not trinkets; they are a man's record of his discovery of himself."

Dixit shook his head. "If they are so personal, why are

so many sold by street traders as trinkets?"

"Men die. Then their life-objects have no value, except as trinkets. They are also popularly believed to bestow . . . well, personality-value. There also exist large numbers of forgeries, which people buy because they like to have them, simply as decorations."

After a moment, Dixit said, "So they are innocent things, but you take them and use them for evil ends."

"I use them to keep a power balance. A man of mine called Narayan was silenced by Gita of Ninth Deck. Never mind why. So tonight I silence Gita to keep the balance."

He stopped and looked closely at Dixit, so that the latter received a blast of that enigmatic personality. He opened his hand and said, still observing Dixit, "Death sits in my palm, Mr. Dixit. Tonight I shall have you silenced also, by what you may consider more ordinary methods."

Clenching his hands tightly together, Dixit said, "You tell me about the life-objects, and yet you claim you are going to kill me."

Patel pointed up to one corner of his room. "There are eyes and ears there, while your ever-hungry spying friends suck up the facts of this world. You see, I can tell them— I can tell them so much and they can never comprehend our life. All the important things can never be said, so they can never learn. But they can see you die tonight, and that they will comprehend. Perhaps then they will cease to send spies in here."

He clapped his hands once for the guards. They came forward and led Dixit away. As he went back to his cell, he heard Patel shouting for Malti.

IX

The hours passed in steady gloom. The U.N., the UHDRE, would not rescue him; the Environment charter permitted intervention by only one outsider at a time. Dixit could hear, feel, the vast throbbing life of the place going on about him and was shaken by it.

He tried to think about the life-object. Presumably Crawley had overheard the last conversation, and would know that the holy men, as Patel called them, had the power to kill at a distance. There was the ESP evidence Crawley sought: telecide, or whatever you called it. And the knowledge helped nobody, as Patel himself observed. It had long been known that African witch doctors possessed similar talents, to lay a spell on a man and kill him at a distance; but how they did it had never been established; nor, indeed, had the fact ever been properly assimilated by the West, eager though the West was for new methods of killing. There were things one civilization could not learn from another; the whole business of life-objects, Dixit perceived, was going to be such a matter: endlessly fascinating, entirely insoluble. . . .

His thoughts returned to his cell, and he told himself: Patel still puzzles me. But it is no use hanging about here being puzzled. Here I sit, waiting for a knife in the guts. It must be night now. I've got to get out of here.

There was no way out of the room. He paced restlessly up and down. They brought him no meal, which was ominous.

A long while later, the door was unlocked and opened.

It was Malti. She lifted one finger as a caution to silence, and closed the door behind her.

"It's time for me . . . ?" Dixit asked.

She came quickly over to him, not touching him, staring at him.

Though she was an ugly and despondent woman, beauty lay in her time-haunted eyes.

"I can help you escape, Dixit. Patel sleeps now, and I have an understanding with the guards here. Understandings have been reached to smuggle you down to my own deck, where perhaps you can get back to the outside where you belong. This place is full of arrangements. But you must be quick. Are you ready?"

"He'll kill you when he finds out!"

She shrugged. "He may not. I think perhaps he likes me. Prahlad Patel is not inhuman, whatever you think of him."

"No? But he plans to murder someone else tonight. He has acquired some poor fellow's life-object and plans to have his holy man kill him with night-visions, whatever they are."

She said, "People have to die. You are going to be lucky. You will not die, not this night."

"If you take that fatalistic view, why help me?"

He saw a flash of defiance in her eyes. "Because you must take a message outside for me."

"Outside? To whom?"

"To everyone there, everyone who greedily spies on us here and would spoil this world. Tell them to go away and leave us and let us make our own world. Forget us! That is my message! Take it! Deliver it with all the strength you have! This is our world—not yours!"

Her vehemence, her ignorance, silenced him. She led him from the room. There were guards on the outer door. They stood rigid with their eyes closed, seeing no evil, and she slid between them, leading Dixit and opening the door. They hurried outside, onto the balcony, which was still as crowded as ever, people sprawling everywhere in the disconsolate gestures of public sleep. With the noise and chaos and animation of daytime fled, Total Environment stood fully revealed for the echoing prison it was.

As Malti turned to go, Dixit grasped her wrist.

"I must return," she said. "Get quickly to the steps down to Ninth Deck, the near steps. That's three flights to go down, the inter-deck flight guarded. They will let you through; they expect you."

"Malti, I must try to help this other man who is to die. Do you happen to know someone called Gita?"

She gasped and clung to him. "Gita?"

"Gita of the Ninth Deck. Patel has Gita's life-object, and he is to die tonight."

"Gita is my step-father, my mother's third husband. A good man! Oh, he must not die, for my mother's sake!"

"He's to die tonight. Malti, I can help you and Gita. I appreciate how you feel about outside, but you are mistaken. You would be free in a way you cannot understand! Take me to Gita, we'll all three get out together."

Conflicting emotions chased all over her face. "You are sure Gita is to die?"

"Come and check with him to see if his life-object has gone!"

Without waiting for her to make a decision—in fact she looked as if she were just about to bolt back into Patel's quarters—Dixit took hold of her and forced her along the balcony, picking his way through the piles of sleepers.

Ramps ran down from balcony to balcony in long zigzags. For all its multitudes of people—even the ramps had been taken up as dosses by whole swarms of urchins—Total Environment seemed much larger that it had when one looked in from the monitoring room. He kept peering back to see if they were being followed; it seemed to him unlikely that he would be able to get away.

But they had now reached the stairs leading down to Deck Nine. Oh, well, he thought, corruption he could believe in; it was the universal oriental system whereby the small man contrived to live under oppression. As soon as the guards saw him and Malti, they all stood and closed their eyes. Among them was the wretched Raital, who hurriedly clapped palms over eyes as they approached.

"I must go back to Patel," Malti gasped.

"Why? You know he will kill you," Dixit said. He kept tight hold of her thin wrist. "All these witnesses to the way you led me to safety—you can't believe he will not discover what you are doing. Let's get to Gita quickly."

He hustled her down the stairs. There were Deck Nine guards at the bottom. They smiled and saluted Malti and let her by. As if resigned now to doing what Dixit wished, she led him forward, and they picked their way down a ramp to a lower floor. The squalor and confusion were greater here than they had been above, the slumbers more broken. This was a deck without a strong leader, and it showed.

He must have seen just such a picture as this over the bugging, in the air-conditioned comfort of the UHDRE offices, and remained comparatively unmoved. You had to be among it to feel it. Then you caught also the aroma of Environment. It was pungent in the extreme.

As they moved slowly down among the huddled figures abased by fatigue, he saw that a corpse burned slowly on a woodpile. It was the corpse of a child. Smoke rose from it in a leisurely coil until it was sucked into a wall vent. A mother squatted by the body, her face shielded by one skeletal hand. "It is the time when the old die," Malti had said of the previous night; and the young had to answer that same call.

This was the Indian way of facing the inhumanity of Environment: with their age-old acceptance of suffering. Had one of the white races been shut in here to breed to intolerable numbers, they would have met the situation with a general massacre. Dixit, a half-caste, would not permit himself to judge which response he most respected.

Malti kept her gaze fixed on the worn concrete underfoot as they moved down the ramp past the corpse. At the bottom, she led him forward again without a word.

They pushed through the sleazy ways, arriving at last at a battered doorway. With a glance at Dixit, Malti slipped in and rejoined her family. Her mother, not sleeping, crouched over a washbowl, gave a cry and fell into Malti's arms. Brothers and sisters and half-brothers and half-sisters and cousins and nephews woke up, squealing. Dixit was utterly brushed aside. He stood nervously, waiting, hoping, in the corridor.

It was many minutes before Malti came out and led him to the crowded little cabin. She introduced him to Shamim, her mother, who curtsied and rapidly disappeared, and to her step-father, Gita.

The little wiry man shooed everyone out of one corner of the room and moved Dixit into it. A cup of wine was produced and offered politely to the visitor. As he sipped it, he said, "If your step-daughter has explained the situation, Gita, I'd like to get you and Malti out of here, because otherwise your lives are worth very little. I can guarantee you will be extremely kindly treated outside."

With dignity, Gita said, "Sir, all this very unpleasant business has been explained to my by my step-daughter. You are most good to take this trouble, but we cannot help you."

"You, or rather Malti, have helped me. Now it is my turn to help you. I want to take you out of here to a safe place. You realize you are both under the threat of death? You hardly need telling that Prahlad Patel is a ruthless man."

"He is very very ruthless, sir," Gita said unhappily. "But we cannot leave here. I cannot leave here—look at all these little people who are dependent on me! Who would look after them if I left?"

"But if your hours are numbered?"

"If I have only one minute to go before I die, still I cannot desert those who depend on me."

Dixit turned to Malti. "You, Malti—you have less responsibility. Patel will have his revenge on you. Come with me and be safe!"

She shook her head. "If I came, I would sicken with worry for what was happening here and so I would die that way."

He looked about him hopelessly. The blind interdependence bred by this crowded environment had beaten him—almost. He still had one card to play.

"When I go out of here, as go I must, I have to report to my superiors. They are the people who—the people who really order everything that happens here. They supply your light, your food, your air. They are like gods to you, with the power of death over every one on every deck—which perhaps is why you can hardly believe in them. They already feel that Total Environment is wrong, a crime against your humanity. I have to take my verdict to them. My verdict, I can tell you now, is that the lives of all you people are as precious as lives outside these walls. The experiment must be stopped; you all must go free.

"You may not understand entirely what I mean, but perhaps the wall screens have helped you grasp something. You will all be looked after and rehabilitated. Everyone will be released from the decks very soon. So, you can both come with me and save your lives; and then, in perhaps only a week, you will be reunited with your family. Patel will have no power then. Now, think over your decision again, for the good of your dependents, and come with me to life and freedom."

Malti and Gita looked anxiously at each other and went into a huddle. Shamim joined in, and Jamsu, and lame Shirin, and more and more of the tribe, and a great jangle of excited talk swelled up. Dixit fretted nervously.

Finally, silence fell. Gita said, "Sir, your intentions are plainly kind. But you have forgotten that Malti charged you to take a message to outside. Her message was to tell the people there to go away and let us make our own world. Perhaps you do not understand such a message and so cannot deliver it. Then I will give you my message, and you can take it to your superiors."

Dixit bowed his head.

"Tell them, your superiors and everyone outside who insists on watching us and meddling in our affairs, tell them that we are shaping our own lives. We know what is to come, and the many problems of having such a plenty of young people. But we have faith in our next generation. We believe they will have many new talents we do not possess, as we have talents our fathers did not possess.

"We know you will continue to send in food and air, because that is something you cannot escape from. We also know that in your hidden minds you wish to see us all fail and die. You wish to see us break, to see what will happen when we do. You do not have love for us. You have fear and puzzlement and hate. We shall not break. We are building a new sort of world, we are getting clever. We would die if you took us out of here. Go and tell that to your superiors and to everyone who spies on us. Please leave us to our own lives, over which we have our own commands."

There seemed nothing Dixit could say in answer. He looked at Malti, but could see she was unyielding, frail and pale and unyielding. This was what UHDRE had bred, complete lack of understanding. He turned and went.

He had his key. He knew the secret place on each deck where he could slip away into one of the escape elevators. As he pushed through the grimy crowds, he could hardly see his way for tears.

X

It was all very informal. Dixit made his report to a board of six members of the UHDRE administration, including the Special Project Organizer, Peter Crawley. Two observers were allowed to sit in, a grand lady who represented the Indian Government, and Dixit's old friend, Senator Jacob Byrnes, representing the United Nations.

Dixit delivered his report on what he had found and added a recommendation that a rehabilitation village be set up immediately and the Environment wound down.

Crawley rose to his feet and stood rigid as he said, "By your own words, you admit that these people of Environment cling desperately to what little they have. However terrible, however miserable that little may seem to you. They are acclimated to what they have. They have turned their backs to the outside world and don't *want* to come out."

Dixit said, "We shall rehabilitate them, re-educate them, find them local homes where the intricate family patterns to which they are used can still be maintained, where they can be helped back to normality."

"But by what you say, they would receive a paralyzing shock if confronted with the outside world and its gigantic scale."

"Not if Patel still led them."

A mutter ran along the board; its members clearly thought this an absurd statement. Crawley gestured despairingly, as if his case were made, and sat down saying, "He's the sort of tyrant who causes the misery in Environment."

"The one thing they need when they emerge to freedom is a strong leader they know. Gentlemen, Patel is our good hope. His great asset is that he is oriented towards outside already."

"Just what does that mean?" one of the board asked.

"It means this. Patel is a clever man. My belief is that he arranged that Malti should help me escape from his cell. He never had any intention of killing me; that was a bluff to get me on my way. Little, oppressed Malti was just not the woman to take any initiative. What Patel probably did not bargain for was that I should mention Gita by name to her, or that Gita should be closely related to her. But because of their fatalism, his plan was in no way upset."

"Why should Patel want you to escape?"

"Implicit in much that he did and said, though he tried to hide it, was a burning curiosity about outside. He exhibited facets of his culture to me to ascertain my reactions— testing for approval or disapproval, I'd guess, like a child. Nor does he attempt to attack other decks—the time-honored sport of Environment tyrants; his attention is directed inwardly on us.

"Patel is intelligent enough to know that we have real power. He has never lost the true picture of reality, unlike his minions. So *he wants to get out.*

"He calculated that if I got back to you, seemingly having escaped death, I would report strongly enough to persuade you to start demolishing Total Environment immediately."

"Which you are doing," Crawley said.

"Which I am doing. Not for Patel's reasons, but for human reasons. And for utilitarian reasons also—which will perhaps appeal more to Mr. Crawley. Gentlemen, you were right. There are mental disciplines in Environment the world could use, of which perhaps the least attractive is telecide. UHDRE has cost the public millions on millions of dollars. We have to recoup by these new advances. We can only use these new advances by studying them in an atmosphere not laden with hatred and envy of us—in other words, by opening that black tower."

The meeting broke up. Of course, he could not expect anything more decisive than that for a day or two.

Senator Byrnes came over.

"Not only did you make out a good case, Thomas; history is with you. The world's emerging from a bad period and that dark tower, as you call it, is a symbol of the bad times, and so it has to go."

Inwardly, Dixit had his qualifications to that remark. But they walked together to the window of the boardroom and looked across at the great rough hulk of the Environment building.

"It's more than a symbol. It's as full of suffering and hope as our own world. But it's a manmade monster—it must go."

Byrnes nodded. "Don't worry. It'll go. I feel sure that the historical process, that blind evolutionary thing, has already decided that UHDRE's day is done. Stick around. In a few weeks, you'll be able to help Malti's family rehabilitate. And now I'm off to put in my two cents' worth with the chairman of that board."

He clapped Dixit on the back and walked off. Inside he knew lights would be burning and those thronging feet padding across the only world they knew. Inside there, babies would be born this night and men die of old age and nightvisions. . . .

Outside, monsoon rain began to fall on the wide Indian land.

Future Ghetto: Race and the City

The problem of race has plagued America throughout its history. Few issues have so divided the American people and aroused their emotions. Foreign observers of our society like Alexis de Tocqueville and Gunnar Myrdal have noted the persistence and depth of racism in this country, and have anguished with us in our attempts to cope with its dilemmas.

Although it is not always admitted, many urban problems are really racial problems or are associated in the popular mind with the problem of race. For example, urban crime is often wrongly assumed to be only blacks victimizing whites, and the flights of whites to the suburbs is considered to be black-inspired. These misconceptions, while dangerous, must not blind us to the fact that racial factors and an understanding of them is crucial to an understanding of today's and tomorrow's urban problems.

Black and Latin minorities like Puerto Ricans migrated to the cities of America from the rural South or from Caribbean islands because they hoped for the same better life that brought all of our grandparents and great-grandparents to this country. They sought to escape the debilitating poverty and racism of the areas of their birth and to make new lives for themselves and their children. This migration reached a peak after World War II and now seems to have reversed itself, at least in terms of blacks returning to the South.

Nevertheless, the central cities of most major American metropolitan areas are heavily black and/or Latin, with the white population living (with the exception of "islands" of whites rich enough to live in secure enclaves or too poor to move) in concentric circles or segregated suburbs. Even within cities which have mixed ethnic and racial populations, patterns of residential segregation caused by factors such as class, income, and race abound. Indeed, big-city political life often consists of ethnic politics, with Italian, Jewish, Irish, Black, and Puerto Rican neighborhoods constituting voting blocs being played off against each other. It should be pointed out that these ethnic concentrations developed through the desire of peoples with a common culture to live together, although many of these areas broke up as blacks or Latins moved in, and then reconstituted themselves in suburban areas.

The pattern has been towards increasing blackness in the central cities, caused by a combination of black population growth and white out-migration, the latter being more important. For example, it has been estimated that between 1960 and 1966 the white population in central cities declined by some 1,250,000—a very large figure when it is remembered that if the white population rose by the same percentage as it did generally, there would have been an increase of 3,600,000. Furthermore, extrapolations of present trends indicate that a dozen or more major American

cities, including Baltimore, Cleveland, St. Louis, Detroit,
Philadelphia, and Chicago, will be over 50 percent black by
1984. Moreover, many additional cities will have school
systems which will be more than 50 percent black by 1984,
because of the youth of the black population relative
to other groups.

Two basic approaches have been advocated to deal with
the problems caused by racial segregation—problems of
unemployment, of educational quality, and of crime
and violence. One approach involves raising the "quality of
life" in black neighborhoods by eliminating poverty
through a variety of techniques, including placing a "floor"
under a family's income level so as to ensure the attaining
of decent living standards. In addition, this approach
advocates improvements in local schools through the supply
of the latest in learning devices and the work of dedicated
professional teachers. This, coupled with government-
sponsored employment opportunities designed to move
people into the middle class, would lead to the abandonment
of despair and provide hope for millions of disadvantaged
people. It also has the additional benefit of avoiding
intensely emotional problems, such as busing to achieve
racial balance, and is therefore thought to be more
acceptable to the white majority.

However, there are a number of pitfalls to this approach.
For one, many Americans are convinced that the tax
dollars they put into social welfare programs have been
wasted, that they have been "ripped off" and that these
schemes have resulted in a cycle of poverty—with one
generation after another locked into a life on welfare. This
is a particularly difficult political problem when economic
realities are forcing many citizens to call for relief
from tax burdens.

Another serious objection is a philosophical one. Do
we really want to perpetuate two societies in the United
States, one white and one black? Is segregation really more
palatable because the economic gap between the races
is narrowed? One of the important dynamic factors
working against all attempts to raise income is that of
relative deprivation, which holds that individuals still feel
deprived even when their income rises as long as they
are "poor" relative to others in society.

Finally, even if this approach were to work, it would work unevenly. Some individuals would "make it" and attain middle class status. But history has shown that these relative few would immediately (with a few exceptions) seek to leave the ghetto and to move into better neighborhoods, leaving the mass of blacks still locked into the inner city with its problems and disillusionments, and with the old "separate but equal" mythology in force.

Therefore, serious thought must be given to the possibility of bringing to fruition the second approach, that of integration. There are a number of important reasons for advocating this solution, including such factors as the diminishing job opportunities in the inner city, partial but still controversial evidence that educational levels will rise for minority children more rapidly in an integrated environment, the difficulty and cost of providing adequate housing in the antiquated and deteriorated sections of the cities in which the bulk of the minority population lives, and the necessity of creating one America and halting the potentially dangerous trend toward two separate societies sharing one political system. This task is perhaps the greatest challenge facing the American people today. Our ability to successfully integrate the "two Americas" will tell us much about ourselves and about our future.

The literature of science fiction has long championed the cause of civil liberties. Countless sf short stories exist which plead for mutual understanding and tolerance between members of different groups, cultures, and life forms. The alien, frequently pictured as a menace in early science fiction, emerged in a more sympathetic light during the late 1930s. However, few of these stories dealt with blacks and other minority groups directly—rather, aliens were employed as surrogate blacks. It was only in the mid-sixties that blacks began to appear as characters in science fiction, and even then infrequently. Furthermore, the number of stories dealing with blacks in an urban setting is even smaller.

"In Dark Places" by Joe L. Hensley and "Black Is Beautiful" by Robert Silverberg deal with urban futures in which the ghettos remain—but the events preceding the setting of the stories are basically different. In Hensley's

tale race warfare has occurred and blacks have been confined to ghettos by force. *Black pride has been smashed, but it is being resurrected by a return to primitive, pagan religion. We are told that a short and bloody war has been fought between blacks and whites in the recent past, caused by the election of a bigot to the Presidency.*

Could an out-and-out racist be elected President of the United States? Would the future of the entire country, not just of urban blacks be jeopardized? What does the story tell us about the concept known as Black Rage—the feeling of despair and hopelessness bred by segregation and humiliation?

"Black Is Beautiful" posits an urban future which is a logical extrapolation of many of the trends discussed previously: the cities are black because the whites have left out of fear. They return only as tourists, to see how the blacks are managing their own affairs. The story raises a number of important issues and questions. For example, it traces the development and rise of black separatism and pride through a series of quotations. It also speaks to old questions like the generation gap, and the forces that the young man and the old politician represent. On whose side do you think the future lies?

Black Is Beautiful   Robert Silverberg

my nose is flat my lips are thick my hair is frizzy my skin
   is black
   is beautiful
   is black is beautiful
I am James Shabazz age seventeen born august 13 1983
I am black I am afro I am beautiful this machine writes
my words as I speak them and the machine is black
   is beautiful

Elijah Muhammad's *The Supreme Wisdom* says:

Separation of the so-called Negroes from their slave masters'
children is a MUST. It is the only SOLUTION to our

problem. It was the only solution, according to the Bible, for Israel and the Egyptians, and it will prove to be the only solution for America and her slaves, whom she mockingly calls her citizens, without granting her citizenship. We must keep this in our minds at all times that we are actually being mocked.

Catlike, moving as a black panther would, James Shabazz stalked through the city. It was late summer, and the pumps were working hard, sucking the hot air out from under the Manhattan domes and squirting it into the suburbs. There had been a lot of grinding about that lately. Whitey out there complained that all that hot air was wilting his lawns and making his own pumps work too hard. Screw Whitey, thought James Shabazz pleasantly. Let his lawns wilt. Let him complain. Let him get black in the face with complaining. Do the mother some good.

Silently, pantherlike, down Fifth Avenue to Fifty-third, across to Park, down Park to Forty-eighth. Just looking around. A big boy, sweat-shiny, black but not black enough to suit him. He wore a gaudy five-colored dashiki, beads from Mali, flowing white belled trousers, a neat goatee, a golden earring. In his left rear pocket: a beat-up copy of the new novel about Malcolm. In his right rear pocket: a cute little sonic blade.

Saturday afternoon and the air was quiet. None of the hopterbuses coming through the domes and dumping Whitey onto the rooftops. They stayed home today, the commuters, the palefaces. Saturday and Sunday, the city was black. Likewise all the other days of the week after 4 P.M. Run, Whitey, run! See Whitey run! Why does Whitey run? Because he don't belong here no more.

Sorry, teach. I shouldn't talk like that no more, huh?

James Shabazz smiled. The identity card in his pocket called him James Lincoln, but when he walked alone through the city he spurned that name. The slave master name. His parents stuck with it, proud of it, telling him that no black should reject a name like Lincoln. The dumb geeps! What did they think, that great-great-grandpappy was owned by Honest Abe? Lincoln was a tag some belching hillbilly stuck on the family 150 years ago. If anyone asks me today, I'm James Shabazz. Black. Proud of it.

Black faces mirrored him on every street. Toward him came ten diplomats in tribal robes, not Afros but Africans, a bunch of Yorubas, Ibos, Baules, Mandingos, Ashantis, Senufos, Bakongos, Balubas, who knew what, the real thing, anyway, black as night, so black they looked purple. No slave master blood in them! James Shabazz smiled, nodded. Good afternoon, brothers. Nice day! They took no notice of him, but swept right on, their conversation unbroken. They were not speaking Swahili, which he would have recognized, but some other foreign language, maybe French. He wasn't sure. He scowled after them. Who they think they are, walking around a black man's city, upnosing people like that?

He studied his reflection for a while in the burnished window of a jewelry shop. Ground floor, Martin Luther King Building. Eighty stories of polished black marble. Black. Black man's money built that tower! Black man's sweat!

Overhead came the buzz of a hopter after all. No commuters today, so they had to be tourists. James Shabazz stared up at the beetle of a hopter crossing the dull translucent background of the distant dome. It landed on the penthouse hopter stage of the King Building. He crossed the street and tried to see the palefaces stepping out, but the angle was too steep. Even so, he bowed ceremoniously. Welcome, massa! Welcome to the black man's metropolis! Soul food for lunch? Real hot jazz on 125th? Dancing jigaboo girls stripping at the Apollo? Sightseeing tour of Bedford-Stuyvesant and Harlem?

Can't tell where Bedford-Stuyvesant ends and Harlem begins, can you? But you'll come looking anyway.

Like to cut your guts up, you honkie mothers.

Martin Luther King said in Montgomery, Alabama, instructing the bus desegregators:

If cursed, do not curse back. If pushed, do not push back. If struck, do not strike back, but evidence love and good will at all times.

He sat down for a while in Lumumba Park, back of the Forty-second Street Library, to watch the girls go by. The new summer styles were something pretty special: Congo Revival, plenty of beads and metal coils, but not much clothing except a sprayon sarong around the middle. There was a lot of grumbling by the old people. But how could you tell a handsome Afro girl that she shouldn't show her beautiful black breasts in public? Did they cover the boobies in the Motherland? Not until the missionaries came. Christ can't stand a pair of bares. The white girls cover up because they don't got much up there. Or maybe to keep from getting sunburned.

He admired the parade of proud jiggling black globes. The girls smiled to themselves as they cut through the park. They all wore their hair puffed out tribal style, and some of them even with little bone doodads thrust through it. There was no reason to be afraid of looking too primitive anymore. James Shabazz winked, and some of them winked back. A few of the girls kept eyes fixed rigidly ahead; plainly it was an ordeal for them to strip down this way. Most of them enjoyed it as much as the men did. The park was full of men enjoying the show. James Shabazz wished they'd bring those honkie tourists here. He'd love a chance to operate on a few of them.

Gradually he became aware of a huge, fleshy, exceedingly black man with grizzled white hair, sitting across the way pretending to be reading his paper, but really stealing peeks at the cuties going by. James Shabazz recognized him: Powell 43X Nissim, Coordinating Chairman of the Afro-Muslim Popular Democratic Party of Greater New York. He was one of the biggest men in the city, politically— maybe even more important than Mayor Abdulrahman himself. He was also a good friend of the father of James Shabazz, who handled some of Powell 43X's legal work. Four or five times a year he came around to discuss some delicate point, and stayed far into the night, drinking pot after pot of black coffee and telling jokes in an uproarious bellow. Most of his jokes were anti-black; he could tell them like any Kluxer. James Shabazz looked on him as coarse, vulgar, seamy, out of date, an old-line pol. But yet you had to respect a man with that much power.

Powell 43X Nissim peered over the top of his *Amsterdam News,* saw him, let out a whoop, and yelled, "Hey, Jimmy Lincoln! What you doin' here?"

James Shabazz stood up and walked stiffly over. "Getting me some fresh air, sir."

"Been working at the library, huh? Studying hard? Gonna be the first nigger president, maybe?"

"No, sir. Just walkin' around on a Saturday."

"Ought to be in the library," Powell 43X said. "Read. Learn. That's how we got where we are. You think we took over this city because we a bunch of dumb niggers?" He let out a colossal laugh. "We *smart*, man!"

James Shabazz wanted to say, "We took over the city because Whitey ran out. He dumped it on us, is all. Didn't take no brains, just staying power."

Instead he said, "I got a little time to take it easy yet, sir. I don't go to college for another year."

"Columbia, huh?"

"You bet. Class of '05, that's me."

"You gonna fool with football when you get to college?"

"Thought I would."

"You listen to me," said Powell 43X. "Football's okay for high school. You get yourself into politics instead up there. Debating team. Malcolm X Society. Afro League. Smart boy like you, you got a career in government ahead of you if you play it right." He jerked his head to one side and indicated a girl striding by. "You get to be somebody, maybe you'll have a few of those to play with." He laughed. The girl was almost six feet tall, majestic, deep black, with great heavy swinging breasts and magnificent buttocks switching saucily from side to side beneath her sprayon wrap. Conscious that all eyes were on her, she crossed the park on the diagonal, heading for the Sixth Avenue side. Suddenly three whites appeared at the park entrance: weekend visitors, edgy, conspicuous. As the black girl went past them, one turned, gaping, his eyes following the trajectory of her out-thrust nipples. He was a wiry redhead, maybe twenty years old, in town for a good time in boogieville, and you could see the hunger popping out all over him.

"Honkie mother," James Shabazz muttered. "Could use a blade you know where."

Powell 43X clucked his tongue. "Easy, there. Let him look! What it hurt you if he thinks she's worth lookin' at?"

"Don't belong here. No right to look. Why can't they stay where they belong?"

"Jimmy—"

"Honkies right in Times Square! Don't they know this here's our city?"

Marcus Garvey said:

The Negro needs a Nation and a country of his own, where he can best show evidence of his own ability in the art of human progress. Scattered as an unmixed and unrecognized part of alien nations and civilizations is but to demonstrate his imbecility, and point him out as an unworthy derelict, fit neither for the society of Greek, Jew, or Gentile.

While he talked with Powell 43X, James Shabazz kept one eye on the honkie from the suburbs. The redhead and his two pals cut out in the direction of Forty-first Street. James Shabazz excused himself finally and drifted away, toward that side of the park. Old windbag, he thought. Nothing but a Tom underneath. Tolerance for the honkies! When did they tolerate *us*?

Easy, easy, like a panther. Walk slow and quiet.

Follow the stinking mother. Show him how it really is.

Malcolm X said:

Always bear in mind that our being in the Western hemisphere differs from anyone else, because everyone else came here voluntarily. Everyone that you see in this part of the world got on a boat and came here voluntarily; whether they were immigrants or what have you, they came here voluntarily. So they don't have any real squawk, because they got what they were looking for. But you and I can squawk because we didn't come here voluntarily. We didn't ask to be brought here. We were brought here forcibly, against our will, and in chains. And at no time since we have been here, have they even acted like they wanted us here. At no time. At no time have they ever tried to pretend that we were brought here to be citizens. Why, they don't even *pretend*. So why should we pretend?

The cities had been theirs for 15 or 20 years. It had been a peaceful enough conquest. Each year there were fewer whites and more blacks and the whites kept moving out and the blacks kept getting born, and one day Harlem was as far south as Seventy-second Street, and Bedford-Stuyvesant had slopped over into Flatbush and Park Slope, and there was a black mayor and a black city council, and that was it. In New York the tipping point had come about 1986. There was a special problem there, because of the Puerto Ricans, who thought of themselves as a separate community; but they were outnumbered, and most of them finally decided it was cooler to have a city of their own. They took Yonkers, the way the Mexicans took San Diego. What it shuffled down to, in the end, was a city about 85 percent black and 10 percent Puerto, with some isolated pockets of whites who stuck around out of stubbornness or old age or masochism or feelings of togetherness with their black brothers. Outside the city were the black suburbs, like Mount Vernon and Newark and New Rochelle, and beyond them, 50, 80, 100 miles out, were the towns of the whites. It was apartheid in reverse.

The honkie commuters still came into the city, those who had to, quick-in quick-out, do your work and scram. There weren't many of them, really, a hundred thousand a day or so. The white ad agencies were gone north. The white magazines had relocated editorial staffs in the green suburbs. The white book publishers had followed the financial people out. Those who came in were corporate executives, presiding over all-black staffs; trophy whites, kept around by liberal-minded blacks for decoration; government employees, trapped by desegregation edicts; and odds and ends of other sorts, all out of place, all scared.

It was a black man's city. It was pretty much the same all across the country. Adjustments had been made.

Stokely Carmichael said:

We are oppressed as a group because we are black, not because we are lazy, not because we're apathetic, not because we're stupid, not because we smell, not because we eat watermelon and have good rhythm. We are oppressed because we are black, and in order to get out of that oppression, one must feel the group power that one has. . . . If there's going to be any integration it's going to be a two-way thing. If you believe in integration, you can come live in Watts. You can send your children to the ghetto schools. Let's talk about that. If you believe in integration, then we're going to start adopting us some white people to live in our neighborhood. . . .

We are not gonna wait for white people to sanction black power. We're tired of waiting.

South of Forty-second Street things were pretty quiet on a Saturday, or any other time. Big tracts of the city were still empty. Some of the office buildings had been converted into apartment houses to catch the overflow, but a lot of them were still awaiting development. It took time for a black community to generate enough capital to run a big city, and though it was happening fast, it wasn't happening fast enough to make use of all the facilities the whites had abandoned. James Shabazz walked silently through silence, keeping his eyes on the three white boys who strolled, seemingly aimlessly, a block ahead of him.

He couldn't dig why more tourists didn't get cut up. Hardly any of them did, except those who got drunk and pawed some chick. The ones who minded their own business were left alone, because the top men had passed the word that the sightseers were okay, that they injected cash into the city and shouldn't be molested. It amazed James Shabazz that everybody listened. Up at the Audubon, somebody would get up and read from Stokely or Malcolm or one of the other black martyrs, and call for a holy war on Whitey, really socking it to 'em. Civil rights! Equality! Black power! Retribution for 400 years of slavery! Break down the ghetto walls! Keep the faith, baby! Tell it how it is! All about the exploitation of the black man, the exclusion of the Afros from the lily-white suburbs, the concentration of economic power in Whitey's hands. And the audience would shout amen and stomp its feet and sing hymns, but nobody would ever do anything. *Nobody would ever do anything.* He couldn't understand that. Were they satisfied to live in a city with an invisible wall around it? Did they really think they had it so good? They talked about owning New York, and maybe they did, but didn't they know that it was all a fraud, that Whitey had given them the damn city just so they'd stay out of *his* back yard?

Someday we gonna run things. Not the Powell 43X cats and the other Toms, but *us.* And we gonna keep the city, but we gonna take what's outside, too.

And none of this crap about honkie mothers coming in to look our women over.

James Shabazz noted with satisfaction that the three white boys were splitting up. Two of them were going into Penn Station to grab the tube home, looked like. The third was the redhead, and he was standing by himself on Seventh Avenue, looking up at Uhuru Stadium, which he probably called Madison Square Garden. Good boy. Dumb enough to leave yourself alone. Now I gonna teach you a thing or two.

He moved forward quickly.

Robert F. Williams said:

When an oppressed people show a willingness to defend themselves, the enemy, who is a moral weakling and coward, is more willing to grant concessions and work for a respectable compromise.

He walked up smiling and said, "Hi, man. I'm Jimmy Lincoln."

Whitey looked perplexed. "Hi, man."

"You lookin' for some fun, I bet."

"Just came in to see the city a little."

"To find some fun. Lots of great chicks around here." Jimmy Lincoln winked broadly. "You can't kid me none. I go for 'em too. Where you from, Red?"

"Nyack."

"That's upstate somewhere, huh?"

"Not so far. Just over the bridge. Rockland County."

"Yeah. Nice up there, I bet. I never seen it."

"Not so different from down here. Buildings are smaller, that's all. Just as crowded."

"I bet they got a different looking skin in Nyack," said Jimmy Lincoln. He laughed. "I bet I right, huh?"

The red-haired boy laughed too. "Well, I guess you are."

"Come on with me. I find you some fun. You and me. What's your name?"

"Tom."

"Tom. That's a good one. Lookee, Tom, I know a place, lots of girls, something to drink, a pill to pop, real soul music, yeah? Eh, man? Couple blocks from here. You came here to see the city, let me show it to you. Right?"

"Well—" uneasily.

"Don't be so up tight, man. You don't trust your black brother? Look, we got no feud with you. All that stuff's ancient history! You got to realize this is the year 2000, we all free men, we got what we after. Nobody gonna hurt you." Jimmy Lincoln moved closer and winked confidentially. "Lemme tell you something, too. That red hair of yours, the girls gonna orbit over that! They don't see that kind hair every day. Them freckles. Them blue eyes. Man, blue eyes, it turn them on! You in for the time of your life!"

Tom from Nyack grinned. He pointed toward Penn Station. "I came in with two pals. They went home, the geeps! Tomorrow they're going to feel awful dopey about that."

"You know they will," said Jimmy Lincoln.

They walked west, across Eighth Avenue, across Ninth, into the redevelopment area where the old warehouses had been ripped down. Signs sprouting from the acreage of rubble proclaimed that the Afro-American Cultural Center would shortly rise here. Just now the area looked bombed out. Tom from Nyack frowned as if he failed to see where a swinging night club was likely to be located in this district. Jimmy Lincoln led him up to Thirty-fifth Street and around the hollow shell of a not quite demolished building.

"Almost there?" Tom asked.

"We here right now, man."

"Where?"

"Up against that wall, that's where," said James Shabazz. The sonic blade glided into his hand. He studded it and it began to whir menacingly. In a quiet voice he said, "Honkie, I saw you look at a black girl a little while ago like you might just be thinking about what's between her legs. You shouldn't think thoughts like that about black girls. You got an itch, man, you scratch it on your own kind. I think I'm gonna fix you so you don't itch no more."

Minister James 3X said:

First, there is fear—first and foremost there is inborn fear, and hatred for the black man. There is a feeling on the part of the white man of inferiority. He thinks within himself that the black man is the best man.

The white man is justified in feeling that way because he has discovered that he is weaker than the black man. His mental power is less than that of the black man—he has only six ounces of brain and the Original Man has seven-and-a-half ounces. . . . The white man's physical power is one-third less than that of the black man.

He had never talked this long with a honkie before. You didn't see all that many of them about, when you spent your time in high school. But now he stared into those frightened blue eyes and watched the blood drain from the scruffy white skin and he felt power welling up inside himself. He was Chaka Zulu and Malcolm and Stokely and Nkrumah and Nat Turner and Lumumba all rolled into one. He, James Shabazz, was going to lead the new black revolution, and he was going to begin by sacrificing this cowering honkie. Through his mind rolled the magnificent phrases of his prophets. He heard them talking, yes, Adam and Ras Tafari and Floyd, heard them singing down the ages out of Africa, kings in chains, martyrs, the great ones, he heard Elijah Muhammad and Muhammad Ali, Marcus Garvey, Sojourner Truth, du Bois, Henry Garnet, Rap Brown, rattling the chains, shouting for freedom, and all of them telling him, go on, man, how long you want to be a nigger anyhow? Go on! You think you got it so good? You gonna go to college, get a job, live in a house, eat steak and potatoes, and that's enough, eh, nigger, even if you can't set foot in Nyack, Peekskill, Wantaugh, Suffern, Morristown? Be happy with what you got, darkie! You got more than we ever did, so why bitch about things? You got a city! You got power! You got freedom! It don't matter that they call you an ape. Don't matter that they don't let you near their daughters. Don't matter that you never seen Nyack. Be grateful for what you got, man, is that the idea?

He heard their cosmic laughter, the thunder of their derision.

And he moved toward Tom the honkie and said, "Here's where the revolution gets started again. Trash like you fooling with our women, you gonna get a blade in the balls. You go home to Nyack and give 'em that message, man."

Tom said lamely, "Look out behind you!"

James Shabazz laughed and began to thrust the blade home, but the anesthetic dart caught him in the middle of the back and his muscles surrendered, and the blade fell, and he turned as he folded up and saw the black policeman with the dart gun in his black fist, and he realized that he had known all along that this was how it would turn out, and he couldn't say he really cared.

Robert Moses of SNCC was questioned in May 1962 on the voter registration drive in Mississippi:

Q. Mr. Moses, did you know a Herbert Lee?

A. Yes, he was a Negro farmer who lived near Liberty.

Q. Would you tell the Committee what Mr. Lee was doing and what happened?

A. He was killed on September 25th. That morning I was in McComb. The Negro doctor came by the voter registration office to tell us he had just taken a bullet out of a Negro's head. We went over to see who it was because I thought it was somebody in the voting program, and were able to identify the man as Mr. Herbert Lee, who had attended our classes and driven us around the voting area, visiting other farmers.

Powell 43X Nissim said heavily, folding his hands across his paunch, "I got you off because you're your daddy's son. But you try a fool thing like that again, I gon' let them put you away."

James Shabazz said nothing.

"What you think you was doing, anyway, Jimmy? You know we watch all the tourists. We can't afford to let them get cut up. There was tracers on that kid all the time."

"I didn't know."

"You sit there mad as hell, thinking I should have let you cut him. You know who you really would have cut? Jimmy Lincoln, that's who. We still got jails. Black judges know the law too. You get ruined for life, a thing like that. And what for?"

"To show the honkie a thing or two."

"Jimmy, Jimmy, Jimmy! What's to show? We got the whole city!"

"Why can't we live outside?"

"Because we don't *want* to. Those of us who can afford it, even, we stay here. They got laws against discrimination in this country. We stay here because we like it with our own kind. Even the black millionaires, and don't think there ain't plenty of 'em. We got a dozen men, they could *buy* Nyack. They stay."

"And why do you stay?"

"I'm in politics," said Powell 43X. "You know what a power base means? I got to stay where my people are. I don't care about living with the whites."

"You talk like you aren't even sore about it," James Shabazz said. "Don't you hate Whitey?"

"No. I don't hate no one."

"We all hate Whitey!"

"Only you hate Whitey," said Powell 43X. "And that's because you don't know nothin' yet. The time of hating's over, Jimmy. We got to be practical. You know, we got ourselves a good deal now, and we ain't gon' get more by burning nobody. Well, maybe the Stock Exchange moved to Connecticut, and a lot of banks and stuff like that, but *we run the city*. Black men. Black men hold the mortgages. We got a black upper crust here now. Fancy shops for black folk, fancy restaurants, black banks, gorgeous mosques. Nobody oppressing us now. When a mortgage gets foreclosed these days, it's a *black* man doin' the foreclosin'. Black men ownin' the sweatshops. Ownin' the hockshops. Good and bad, we got the city, Jimmy. And maybe this is the way it's meant to be: us in the cities, them outside."

"You talk like a Tom!"

"And you talk like a fool." Powell 43X chuckled. "Jimmy, wake up! We all Toms today. We don't do revolutions now."

"I go to the Audubon," James Shabazz said. "I listen to them speak. They talk revolution there. They don't sound like no Toms to me!"

"It's all politics, son. Talk big, yell for equality. It don't make sense to let a good revolution die. They do it for show. A man don't get anywhere politickin' in black New York by sayin' that everything's 100 percent all right in the world. And you took all that noise seriously? You didn't know that they just shoutin' because it's part of the routine? You went out to spear you a honkie? I figured you for smarter than that. Look, you all mixed up, boy. A smart man, black or white, he don't mess up a good deal for himself, even if he sometimes say he *want* to change everything all around. You full of hate, full of dreams. When you grow up, you'll understand. Our problem, it's not how to get out into the suburbs, it's how to keep Whitey from wanting to come back and live in here! We got to keep what we got. We got it pretty good. Who oppressing you, Jimmy? You a slave? Wake up! And now you understand the system a little better, clear your rear end outa my office. I got to phone up the mayor and have a little talk."

Jimmy Lincoln stumbled out, stunned, shaken. His eyes felt hot and his tongue was dry. The system? The *system*? How cynical could you get? The whole revolution phony? All done for show?

No. No. No. No.

He wanted to smash down the King Building with his fists. He wanted to see buildings ablaze, as in the old days when the black man was still fighting for what ought to be his.

I don't believe it, he thought. Not any of it. I'm not gonna stop fighting for my rights. I'm gonna live to see us overcome. I won't sell out like the others. Not me!

And then he thought maybe he was being a little dumb. Maybe Powell 43X was right: there wasn't anything left worth fighting for, and only a dopey kid would take the slogans at face value. He tried to brush that thought out of his head. If Powell 43X was right, everything he had read was a lot of crap. Stokely. Malcolm. All the great martyrs. Just so much ancient history?

He stepped out into the summer haze. Overhead, a hopterbus was heading for the suburbs. He shook his fist at it; and instantly he felt foolish for the gesture, and wondered why he felt foolish. And knew. And beneath his rebellious fury, began to suspect that one day he'd give into the system too. But not yet. Not yet!

time to do my homework now

machine, spell everything right today's essay is on black power as a revolutionary force I am James Lincoln, Class 804, Frederick Douglass High School put that heading on the page yeah

the concept of black power as a revolutionary force first was heard during the time of oppression 40 years ago, when

crap on that, machine we better hold it until I know what
I going to say

I am James Shabazz age 17 born august 13 1983 I am
black I am afro I am beautiful

black is beautiful

let's start over, machine

let's make an outline first

black power its origin its development the martyrdoms
and lynchings the first black mayors the black congressmen
and senators the black cities and then talk about black power
as a continuing thing, the never ending revolution no matter
what pols like 43X say, never give in never settle for what
they give you never sell out

that's it, machine

black power

black

black is beautiful

In Dark Places   Joe L. Hensley

The mornings were growing colder.

Theron Johnson left the windows bolted but unlocked the
basement door and went down to draw water from the still
usable tap there.

The "children" (for that was what they had named themselves) had built one of their worshiping places in the far
corner of the basement during the night.

Upstairs Johnson could hear Charles tinkering with the
three-legged can that served as their wood cookstove. In the
winters it also made the kitchen the only half-warm room in
the house.

"Hello," Johnson said gently to the "children." He had
never heard of them being a danger, but he had also never
found them in his basement before. And these were tricky
days. The cult grew in numbers.

They had constructed an altar. It was a jackdaw thing of
old papers, dried autumn leaves, scrap lumber, and pieces
of long-abandoned cars. In the center of the altar stood the

crude statue of the one they tersely called "Him," a thing of too many legs and arms and eyes surrounding a huge male sex organ.

The "children" gave Johnson no notice and went on worshiping in their usual way. They lay in a haphazard circle, males with males, males with females, females with females, hands seeking and exploring, bodies meeting in myriad ways so that Johnson's eyes were dizzied by them and by the very complexities of wriggling flesh.

It was, he thought wryly, as good a way to fight despair as any other way.

There were perhaps thirty of them in his basement. It was hard to count as they kept moving. He recognized none of them. Ages ranged from early teens to an old crone without a tooth left in her wrinkled jaws.

The cult was immensely popular and it grew more popular each day. "Him" was coming out of the jungle to rescue his people.

Sure.

Johnson drew water from the tap. The pressure seemed low. Black faces heard the sound of running water and turned to him and watched him with minor interest.

"Join us, brother?" one inquired politely.

"No," he said, shuddering inside.

"You tried your ways—now try ours. Let it end, Mayor."

He wondered what and how much they knew of him. He fled up the steps and shot the bolt, locked, behind him and stood shivering a moment before he carried the water into the kitchen. There, he resumed the mask.

"We have company in the basement," he said calmly to Charles. "Some of that mob that runs the streets without clothes. I guess maybe the water brought them. A lot of people know we've got a tap that still works."

Charles's face was blue-black, but his hair was shining white. He was Theron Johnson's older half brother, same mother, different father. They had fought each other and helped each other all of their lives. They had practiced law together and when their wives had died they had moved in together.

Charles took the water and measured some of it into a pan.

"They'll move on," he said knowingly. "They don't stay no place long. Yesterday I saw a lot of them up by the fence.

Some of them gals had them whitey guards shook from watching. And they all kept yelling, 'Him is coming!' " He grinned. "They'll do that in the day, but they like to be away from the Feep 'copters at night. They say lots of them stay down at that old auto factory near where the library used to be. Sleep there nights when they sleep. So you just wait. They'll move on." He nodded. "Breakfast now in five minutes."

Johnson nodded back. He went down the hall and to the double-barred front door of the house. He unbarred and opened the door a minute crack and peered out to examine the day. The wind was brisk and there was, as yet, no sun. Nothing moved in the streets, but he could hear the beat-beat of a patrol helicopter nearby. Inside it he could visualize Feeps, Federal Police, sitting ready at the guns, white faces all earnest and waiting.

To the north, two blocks away, past ruined apartments, he could see the tall, electrified fence of the white enclave. A crude sign within his view was too small for him to read, but he knew it read, STAY AWAY, NIGGER. The sign was inside the fence, and next to the sign, mounted on poles, were the heads of three black men. The heads had been there for a long time now and they had been picked sterile clean by the voracious birds. Once Johnson had heard who the three men were, but the names had fled his memory.

A bicycle went by outside and he closed the door so that he couldn't be seen.

Today Charles could stand guard and Johnson would move the rest of their books from what had once been their joint law office. He would move them here to the makeshift shelves of bricks supporting old boards where he'd put the other books.

He resolved that when the "children" left the basement he would go down and destroy that obscene altar, tear it down, burn it. And he'd try to find out how they had gained entry and make certain it couldn't happen again.

He ate a spartan breakfast of bread toasted over the small fire. He washed the bread down with draughts of instant, ersatz coffee.

When he was done, Johnson said, "I'm going to walk to the office and get the rest of the books."

Charles grinned at him without humor. He shook his head.

"You just can't make yourself believe it's over. Books won't do us any good now, man. They took away the courts. Stay here. It's dangerous outside. And today is food-truck day."

"You'll be here with the ration cards," Johnson said. "I want those books."

"Yes, sir, Mr. Mayor," Charles said, his contempt showing in his eyes. "I'll be here. But you leave the rifle."

Johnson nodded. He would take the pistol.

Once he was outside he skirted away from the large apartment building at the near corner. The few survivors in it had converted to cannibalism. He doubted that any would attack him in daylight, but all things were possible. The tenants had hunted one another through the darkened halls all last winter and Johnson had sometimes heard the screams of the losers. Now the survivors sometimes ran in small packs, but mostly Johnson had seen them hunt in solitaire. The Feeps refused to distribute rations at the building and the inhabitants grew hungrier.

It was still early. At this time of day not many people ventured abroad and those who were out hurried. The gangs worked better in darkness; the salesmen who offered fresh meat of a dubious nature weren't cut yet. And drug peddlers slept later than he did, Johnson reflected.

He walked a route well known to him. It took him past the burned-out buildings of the downtown complex, where the open display windows of the stores, glassless now, held only rubbish and filth. He picked his way carefully past them and the debris that littered the crumbling sidewalks.

None of the traffic lights worked now, but the only traffic moving was an occasional Feep-guarded armored convoy dispensing food to citizen cardholders.

His office was in a building across from the old courthouse. In the time of black-white confrontation the courthouse had been burned and the domed roof had fallen. He could not view the remains without tightness in his throat.

He unlocked the office door cautiously, but all seemed well. He peered around to make certain and then, satisfied, he spread the stout sheet he'd brought and gently stacked the last of the books inside, the final volumes of *Corpus Juris Tertium*. Everything else he needed was already, after countless trips, in the house.

There were a few too many books left for an easy trip. He knew that when he hefted the sack, but he wasn't going to come back here again. He would just have to move slowly and change the heavy sack from shoulder to shoulder as he tired.

He surveyed the office once more. He regretted leaving the desks. They would make excellent firewood. There was little else of value. The rugs were worn and winters without heat had stripped the walls of paint. He'd spent half his life in this office with Charles. Here the Black Coalition had come to ask him to run for the council and later for mayor of the city. Many had come here seeking favor, black and white. And, after the time of fire, the Feeps had come here also and he'd made his reluctant deal for his people and they had lived when many, black and white, had died. Maybe he'd been wrong to do it, but he had done it.

The Feeps had promised no reprisals. He smiled bitterly, remembering that.

It had now been six years. Six years of electric fences and Feeps.

He lifted the sack and moved on out of the room. He locked the door carefully behind him for he was a careful man.

In his city, six years ago, there had been skirmishes and fire fights and many had died, but he had abused and connived and even betrayed his people away from the short, bloody war that had decimated the country. That was the year the man from the South had been elected President, the man who had closed the schools and begun the enclaves.

He had hated that smiling man.

When the war was over, the Feeps had closed the courts and built more fences and hidden behind them.

His own people lived and so Johnson had been a hero. Many people died and so Johnson had been Judas. But his way of life, the way that had sustained him, was gone, vanished with the wind.

There were white survivors living behind fences in a thousand cities. The whites on the inside watched the blacks on the outside with high suspicion, gave them food because it was safe and humane to do so, plotted about them and policed them with the armed helicopters that patrolled the skies. The food dole was enough to sustain life. There were times when Johnson wondered if it was subtly drugged with tranquilizers.

Carrying the sack, he went down the smog-hazy streets, past a row of burned theaters, then past the area where the college had once stood. It was here, he remembered, he'd first seen the "children." One Sunday a year or so back they had rallied nude here to the snickers of onlookers. Thousands of them had planted ferns and tropical trees on the grounds of the college. Johnson noted that the trees and ferns had died and that rough vegetation had taken over the open spots.

Halfway home three men accosted him.

"You stop there," one said, watching the sky for Feeps.

"You got food in that sack, old man," another declared. The three fanned away from one another so that he couldn't escape around them. "We want it."

"These are books," he said. He set the sack down carefully and spread the ends so that the books could be seen.

"You just leave them there. We'll look them over ourselves. If they're good enough to carry then they is valuable. You go on, old man. Get."

He shook his head doggedly and their faces mirrored surprise. The offer had been almost kind.

"No," he said. "Not without my books." He drew the long-barreled old Colt.

"Hey," one of the young ones said carefully, not really afraid yet, "old man got a gun." He examined Johnson and the gun. "Wonder if him and it can shoot."

"I'm going to take that gun," another said, his eyes widening, for guns were prized and scarce. "I need it."

Johnson watched them move toward him and he fired a shot into the pavement in front of them.

All movement stopped.

"The next one goes in an eye," he said.

The three consulted without a word. They turned away from him and loped on up the street without ever looking back.

He arranged the books carefully on the shelves, feeling satisfaction. Charles wasn't around and Johnson decided that he'd probably gone up the street to trade rations with friends, as he often did.

He unlocked the basement door and went down the stairs.

The congregation had left, but the altar was intact. He examined the idol. It was quite crude. It was made to their visualization of what they pretended to think they were worshiping. The thing had too many legs and arms and too much penis to be humanoid. The head had been painted with thick black paint.

He could not decide what to do with the altar and the idol. The worshipers really hurt no one but themselves. They were harmless and they even enjoyed a certain degree of safety because of their numbers. He had heard that they had the ability to turn away those perverts who merely wanted to use available bodies. At least that was part of the story about them.

Yet it seemed a waste. He stood there ready to kick the idol and the altar down, lock and board the window. They would go on elsewhere. But if they were in the basement, then no one else would be there. He shook his head finally and left things as they were. The religion was, after all, only a wish fulfillment, a thing that someone had dredged out of the steaming past of black history. Once, long before, in the jungles, there had been a cruel god. That god was now *wanted*, because the other god, the one the whites had taught, was not for this time and place. The world had worsened around them and so they had sought a corridor back to the never-never land of fable, a dim storybook land where the sun warmed and food fell from trees and all things were simple and fundamental.

"Him."

The cold months would come soon. Last year fuel had been in short supply and the people had suffered. Some had died. He knew it would not get better. Last winter had been medium mild. This winter?

He went upstairs, awaiting Charles. He got out a well-thumbed casebook and began to read to pass the time. The reading calmed him. Here, in the book, what was happening could not happen for the law would not allow or condone it.

Charles didn't come.

He walked up the street to the trading area, but no one had seen Charles. Back at the house the rifle was in its accustomed place in a closet. Charles set great store in the rifle, but seldom carried it.

He went through the empty house restlessly. He paused at

a cracked window and smelled something sifting through the bars. It was an odor he had smelled before, a frightening odor. He went out into the street and inspected the large apartment building at the near corner, the one of the cannibal converts. He was fairly certain that smoke came from a corner window, third story. He felt very cold inside.

He walked to the apartment and went up littered stairs. He saw no one and the halls were quiet, but the smell seemed stronger.

The door was ajar. There were three of them inside plus what was left of a fourth. The three live ones were hungrily brewing something over a small fire and they had used the ration food from Charles's bag for part of it. They looked up in surprise when he burst through the door.

He shot the closest one through the nose and the bullet blew out the back of the man's head. The second drew a very long knife and lunged toward him and Johnson caught the man with a shot in the stomach and the force of the big-caliber slug brushed the man back and bloodily down.

The third had gone for the open window. She was very young and lovely. Johnson shot her as she straddled the window. It was not a killing shot and she screamed all the way to the ground. Silence came then.

He picked up Charles's body and carried it over his shoulder back down the steps. He heard rustling behind him, but no one bothered him.

All night long he sat with the body, unable to cry, able only to remember the long years, the time he had refused to lose but which Charles had sensed was gone.

In the morning, driven by thirst and a desire to clean the body, he unlocked the basement and went down.

They were there. They awaited him. Somehow they knew. They had dug a deep grave in the basement. He nodded to them, accepting it, seeing the invitation in the eyes of those who had time and want for him.

He cleaned the body carefully and carried it down, wrapped in a sheet. He buried it there in the basement and the "children" stopped their sexual rituals and watched and waited respectfully.

When he was done he went back upstairs. For a long time he sat in the room with the books without ever wanting to open them again, without believing that anything in them had been or would ever be true.

He took off all his clothes and found that it was cold that way and that he felt ridiculous. He endured the feelings and opened the basement door again.

They had gone.

He went back upstairs and sat again for a long time, seeing his skinny old legs, hairless and black, unable to accept that Charles was really dead.

And he heard the sound.

He opened the front door cautiously. The sound grew and grew. In moments he could see the nude and dancing black people coming, moving in the direction of the white man's boundary fence, the fence that separated black town from white town, where the sign read, STAY AWAY, NIGGER. At the fence they would all die from Feep helicopter machine guns and bombs and jellied gasoline. And the last of the war he had only delayed would soon be done, a footnote to history.

Outside they chanted, "Him!" A thousand times they chanted, "Him!"

The world had declared for insanity long ago. He had stood momentarily in the way of that insanity. Now it was time to clear the path.

He waited until the mob swirled past his door and, still nude, he joined them. There were thousands on thousands of them and they seemed to be watching and turning and bowing to something coming behind. In the tumult of sound and movement he couldn't see what it was. Finally, at the last corner before the fence, he anchored himself to a light post so that he might see.

It wasn't just men that had prompted the riot. The thing came down the street and Johnson clung to his post in shock. Up by the fence the helicopters swarmed and public-address hailers blared orders that were ignored.

The thing waddled down the street on squat legs. Johnson was unsure if it ran on motors, whether it was man-made. The "children" had lived in that old auto plant. Maybe there were some mechanically bright ones who had assembled it out of old parts. It was possible. Anything was possible.

The body was huge and it was clad in bright robes of fresh flowers that hid its obscene maleness only a little. The head towered high above the crowd. Its disciples ran alongside it, some of them falling and dying underneath it as it moved along.

Maybe there were other gods, but this one was the god for this day, delayed six years.

"Him" was what they craved and wanted. "Him" had changed the misery of life to the misery of death.

The creature had shining globes of lights for eyes. The face was very old and very crude and almost completely alien in form.

Johnson allowed the crowd to carry him along. Ahead of him the first wave crashed against the fence. Fire blossomed around him as the bombs began to fall.

If the fence came down then maybe the hated ones on the other side could die too. He wanted to be present at that happening and so he pressed forward.

No matter how he was to receive or be received he laughed aloud when the creature's face towering above him could be made out in the light of an explosion that slowed it and blew away one section of gears and cogs.

Alien as it had been made, unrecognizable and crude as it was, he felt kinship with that face.

It was undeniably black.

An explosion came that toppled them both and he lay in fire and it burned his flesh and charred his bones.

"Him," the "children" chanted, moving on. "Him!" Johnson echoed with his dying breath.

Fouling the Nest: Pollution in the City

*Every so often a problem is identified which captures
the imagination of large numbers of people. This is especially
true when the issue is (or is presented as) a question of
life and death. This is clearly so in the case of environmental
quality. We all live in a world with finite resources,
which we are consuming at an alarming rate and in ways*

that are dangerous to ourselves and to our neighbors.

Since we are all tied together in an ecological relationship, with everything we do affecting everyone else, our carefully balanced system can be easily upset. This can be illustrated by the dilemma we face in deciding what to do with the vast amounts of garbage produced by our consumer-oriented society. Historically, we have dealt with this problem in two ways: (1) by burning it, and (2) by dumping it in large holes in the ground or in rivers or oceans. If we choose to burn our refuse, we will pollute the air we breathe, damage the paint on our houses, increase our cleaning bills, and suffer from a wide variety of illnesses. If we choose to dump it, we will contaminate our drinking water, either from seepage from burying garbage, or directly by pouring it into rivers, lakes, and oceans. We are also paying a terrible price in the destruction of recreational areas, already too scarce in urban regions, since our waters are unsafe for swimming. In some areas, people can become ill from the effects of water they ingest from the wake of boats, so that even this recreational activity may be foreclosed to some.

In an attempt to rectify the situation, state, local, federal, and private agencies have been bombarding Americans with ecological messages and warnings, ranging from cartoons to Indians with tears in their eyes. However, although it is true that we all bear some responsibility for pollution, the real culprits are the massive polluters of heavy industry, along with our desire to own and operate internal-combustion-driven automobiles.

It has been estimated that more than 110,000,000 citizens breathe potentially dangerous air daily. While the general public is more familiar with the better-publicized examples of air pollution in cities like Los Angeles and Gary, Indiana, dozens of smaller urban concentrations also suffer from poor air quality. As members of advanced industrialized societies we have come to the late realization that "there's no such thing as a free lunch"; that a price is being extracted for the benefits and conveniences that we enjoy each day. One day, each of us may face the necessity of doing a "cost-benefit analysis" to determine whether our electric can openers and large cars are worth it all.

Each day, millions upon millions of pounds of carbon

monoxide, nitrogen oxide, and hydrocarbon flow from automobile exhausts to pollute our atmosphere. Even these huge amounts of harmful materials would be manageable if they were spread evenly across the country, but they are concentrated in and around our urban areas, adding another dimension to our already large urban problems. Pollution in our cities is quite costly—for example, it has been estimated that air pollution causes $12,500,000,000 damage yearly to our material possessions like buildings and clothes. In addition, there is the incalculable human cost of heart damage, respiratory ailments, and even lung cancer.

The federal government, through the Public Health Service, first exhibited concern with air pollution in the mid-fifties when it became apparent that the problem was too big for cities to handle by themselves. Other than the scope of the effort required, it was soon realized that because air pollution paid no attention to state boundaries, effective solutions could only take place if uniform codes and rules were applied. These have been instituted to some extent through the legislation contained in the Air Quality Act of 1967 and through a number of interstate commissions established to coordinate anti-pollution activities in various regions.

"East Wind, West Wind" provides a chilling look at an urban center of the future, at a time when conventional automobiles have been outlawed because pollution levels have risen to unacceptable levels. Author Frank Robinson, an outstanding writer whose contributions to science fiction have been too few, examines both the physical and sociological effects of daily life in a polluted environment. The story raises a number of disturbing questions about how a society could permit itself to reach such a point, but it provides little in the way of answers to the question of how to restore air quality once it is lost. It seems to be telling us that time may be running out for us all.

In "Disposal," Ron Goulart considers the problem of solid waste disposal in the future. At the present time, the Department of Health, Education and Welfare estimates that more than 55,000,000 Americans are drinking water that is technically or actually unfit for human consumption. For years local and state governments have been concerned with the supply of water but not with its quality. For *example, it was standard procedure to dump waste into the nearest river or lake—in fact, this is still the case in many localities. Thanks to the attention focused on the issue by environmentalists, water quality is finally receiving the attention it deserves. The Water Pollution Control Act of 1956 brought the national government into the struggle for cleaner water because all previous efforts failed for one basic reason:* individuals and industries will move away from regulations whenever possible. *This is because there are economic advantages to not complying—water quality costs money, as witness the closing of lumber mills that went bankrupt since they lacked the profit margin to install water quality devices or change their production methods. Therefore, uniform national regulations and controls seem necessary to equalize the losses that will occur, although many small firms will not survive the needed changeovers.*

Sewage and garbage disposal is still a municipal function, however, although, as described in the story, some cities employ private concerns (or a combination of private and public services) on a contractual basis. There are also a large number of private garbage-hauling operations available to homeowners and businesses, hopefully more efficient than the one described in the delightful but frightening story by Mr. Goulart, one of science fiction's funniest practitioners.

As you read the stories in this section, consider the futures they portray, and ask yourself the following questions: Will America be willing to make the sacrifices required for a restoration of its environment? Are you willing to give up your car? Will you have to?

East Wind, West Wind   Frank M. Robinson

It wasn't going to be just another bad day, it was going to be a terrible one. The inversion layer had slipped over the city four days before and it had been like putting a lid on a kettle; the air was building up to a real Donora, turning into a chemical soup so foul I wouldn't have believed it if I hadn't been trying to breathe the stuff. Besides sticking in my throat, it made my eyes feel like they were being bathed in acid. You could hardly see the sun—it was a pale, sickly disc floating in a mustard-colored sky—but even so, the streets were an oven and the humidity was so high you could have wrung the water out of the air with your bare hands . . . dirty water, naturally.

On the bus a red-faced salesman with denture breath recognized my Air Central badge and got pushy. I growled that we didn't *make* the air—not yet, at any rate—and finally I took off the badge and put it in my pocket and tried to shut out the coughing and the complaints around me by concentrating on the faint, cheery sound of the "corn poppers" laundering the bus's exhaust. Five would have gotten you ten, of course, that their effect was strictly psychological, that they had seen more than twenty thousand miles of service and were now absolutely worthless. . . .

At work I hung up my plastic sportscoat, slipped off the white surgeon's mask (black where my nose and mouth had been) and filled my lungs with good machine-pure air that smelled only faintly of oil and electric motors; one of the advantages of working for Air Central was that our office air was the best in the city. I dropped a quarter in the coffee vendor, dialed it black, and inhaled the fumes for a second while I shook the sleep from my eyes and speculated about what Wanda would have for me at the Investigator's Desk. There were thirty-nine other Investigators besides myself but I was junior and my daily assignment card was usually just a listing of minor complaints and violations that had to be checked out.

Wanda was young and pretty and redhaired and easy to spot even in a secretarial pool full of pretty girls. I offered her some of my coffee and looked over her shoulder while she flipped through the assignment cards. "That stuff out there is easier to swim through than to breathe," I said. "What's the index?"

"Eighty-four point five," she said quietly. "And rising."

I just stared at her. I had thought it was bad, but hardly that bad, and for the first time that day I felt a sudden flash of panic. "And no alert? When it hits seventy-five this city's supposed to close up like a clam!"

She nodded down the hall to the Director's office. "Lawyers from Sanitary Pick-Up, Oberhausen Steel, and City

Light and Power got an injunction—they were here to break the news to Monte at eight sharp. Impractical, unnecessary, money-wasting, and fifteen thousand employees would be thrown out of work if they had to shut down the furnaces and incinerators. They got an okay right from the top of Air Shed Number Three.

My jaw dropped. "How could they? Monte's supposed to have the last word!"

"So go argue with the politicians—if you can stand the hot air." She suddenly looked very fragile and I wanted to run out and slay a dragon or two for her. "The chicken-hearts took the easy way out, Jim. Independent Weather's predicting a cold front for early this evening and rising winds and rain for tomorrow."

The rain would clean up the air, I thought. But Independent Weather could be bought and as a result it had a habit of turning in cheery predictions that frequently didn't come true. Air Central had tried for years to get IW outlawed but money talks and their lobbyist in the capital was quite a talker. Unfortunately, if they were wrong this time, it would be as if they had pulled a plastic bag over the city's head.

I started to say something, then shut up. If you let it get to you, you wouldn't last long on the job. "Where's my list of small-fry?"

She gave me an assignment card. It was blank except for *See Me* written across its face. "Humor him, Jim, he's not feeling well."

This worried me a little because Monte was the father of us all—a really sweet old guy, which hardly covers it all because he could be hard as nails when he had to. There wasn't anyone who knew more about air control than he.

I took the card and started up the hall and then Wanda called after me. She had stretched out her long legs and hiked up her skirt. I looked startled and she grinned. "Something new—sulfur-proof nylons." Which meant they wouldn't dissolve on a day like today when a measurable fraction of the air we were trying to breathe was actually dilute sulfuric acid. . . .

When I walked into his office, old Monte was leaning out the window, the fly ash clinging to his bushy gray eyebrows like cinnamon to toast, trying to taste the air and predict how it would go today. We had eighty Sniffers scattered throughout the city, all computerized and delivering their data in neat, graphlike form, but Monte still insisted on breaking internal air security and seeing for himself how his city was doing.

I closed the door. Monte pulled back inside, then suddenly broke into one of his coughing fits.

"Sit down, Jim," he wheezed, his voice sounding as if it were being wrung out of him, "be with you in a minute." I pretended not to notice while his coughing shuddered to a halt and he rummaged through the desk for his little bottle of pills. It was a plain office, as executive offices went, except for Monte's own paintings on the wall—the type I liked to call Twentieth Century Romantic. A mountain scene with a crystal clear lake in the foreground and anglers battling huge trout, a city scene with palm trees lining the boulevards, and finally, one of a man standing by an old automobile on a winding mountain road while he looked off at a valley in the distance.

Occasionally Monte would talk to me about his boyhood around the Great Lakes and how he actually used to go swimming in them. Once he tried to tell me that orange trees used to grow within the city limits of Santalosdiego and that the oranges were as big as tennis balls. It irritated me and I think he knew it; I was the youngest Investigator for Air Central but that didn't necessarily make me naive.

When Monte stopped coughing I said hopefully, "IW claims a cold front is coming in."

He huddled in his chair and dabbed at his mouth with a handkerchief, his thin chest working desperately trying to pump his lungs full of air. "IW's a liar," he finally rasped. "There's no cold front coming in, it's going to be a scorcher for three more days."

I felt uneasy again. "Wanda told me what happened," I said.

He fought a moment longer for his breath, caught it, then gave a resigned shrug. "The bastards are right, to an extent. Stop garbage pick-ups in a city this size and within hours the rats will be fighting us in the streets. Shut down the power plants and you knock out all the air conditioners and purifiers—right during the hottest spell of the year. Then try telling the yokels that the air on the outside will be a whole lot cleaner if only they let the air on the inside get a whole lot dirtier."

He hunched behind his desk and drummed his fingers on the top while his face slowly turned to concrete. "But if they don't let me announce an alert by tomorrow morning," he said quietly, "I'll call in the newspapers and. . . ." The coughing started again and he stood up, a gnomelike little man slightly less alive with every passing day. He leaned against the windowsill while he fought the spasm. "And we think this is bad," he choked, half to himself. "What happens when the air coming in is as dirty as the air already here? When the Chinese and the Indonesians and the Hottentots get toasters and ice-boxes and all the other goodies?"

"Asia's not that industrialized yet," I said uncomfortably.

"Isn't it?" He turned and sagged back into his chair, hardly making a dent in the cushion. I was bleeding for the old man but I couldn't let him know it. I said in a low voice, "You wanted to see me," and handed him the assignment card.

He stared at it for a moment, his mind still on the Chinese, then came out of it and croaked, "That's right, give you something to chew on." He pressed a button on his desk and the wall opposite faded into a map of the city and the surrounding area, from the ocean on the west to the low-lying mountains on the east. He waved at the section of the city that straggled off into the canyons of the foothills. "Internal combustion engine—someplace back there." His voice was stronger now, his eyes more alert. "It isn't a donkey engine for a still or for electricity, it's a private automobile."

I could feel the hairs stiffen on the back of my neck. Usually I drew minor offenses, like trash burning or secret cigarette smoking, but owning or operating a gasoline-powered automobile was a felony, one that was sometimes worth your life.

"The Sniffer in the area confirms it," Monte continued in a tired voice, "but can't pinpoint it."

"Any other leads?"

"No, just this one report. But—we haven't had an internal combustion engine in more than three years." He paused. "Have fun with it, you'll probably have a new boss in the morning." *That* was something I didn't even want to think about. I had my hand on the doorknob when he said quietly,

"The trouble with being boss is that you have to play Caesar and his Legions all the time."

It was as close as he came to saying good-bye and good luck. I didn't know what to say in return, or how to say it, and found myself staring at one of his canvases and babbling, "You sure used a helluva lot of blue."

"It was a fairly common color back then," he growled. "The sky was full of it."

And then he started coughing again and I closed the door in a hurry; in five minutes I had gotten so I couldn't stand the sound.

I had to stop in at the lab to pick up some gear from my locker and ran into Dave Ice, the researcher in charge of the Sniffers. He was a chubby, middle-aged little man with small, almost feminine hands; it was a pleasure to watch him work around delicate machinery. He was our top-rated man, after Monte, and I think if there was anybody whose shoes I wanted to step into someday, it would have been Dave Ice. He knew it, liked me for it, and usually went out of his way to help.

When I walked in he was changing a sheet of paper in one of the smoke shade detectors that hung just outside the lab windows. The sheet he was taking out looked as if it had been coated with lampblack.

"How long an exposure?"

He looked up, squinting over his bifocals. "Hi, Jim—a little more than four hours. It looks like it's getting pretty fierce out there."

"You haven't been out?"

"No, Monte and I stayed here all night. We were going to call an alert at nine this morning but I guess you know what happened."

I opened my locker and took out half a dozen new masks and a small canister of oxygen; if you were going to be out in traffic for any great length of time, you had to go prepared. Allowable vehicles were buses, trucks, delivery vans, police electrics and the like. Not all exhaust control devices worked very well and even the electrics gave off a few acid fumes. And if you were stalled in a tunnel, the carbon monoxide ratings really zoomed. I hesitated at the bottom of the locker and then took out my small Mark II gyrojet and shoulder holster. It was pretty deadly stuff: no recoil and the tiny rocket pellet had twice the punch of a .45.

Dave heard the clink of metal and without looking up asked quietly, "Trouble?"

"Maybe," I said. "Somebody's got a private automobile—gasoline—and I don't suppose they'll want to turn it in."

"You're right," he said, sounding concerned, "they won't." And then: "I heard something about it; if it's the same report, it's three days old."

"Monte's got his mind on other things," I said. I slipped the masks into my pocket and belted on the holster. "Did you know he's still on his marching Chinese kick?"

Dave was concentrating on one of the Sniffer drums slowly rolling beneath its scribing pens, logging a minute-by-minute record of the hydrocarbons and the oxides of nitrogen and sulfur that were sickening the atmosphere. "I don't blame him," he said, absently running a hand over his glistening scalp. "They've started tagging chimney exhausts in Shanghai, Djakarta and Mukden with radioactives—we should get the first results in another day or so."

The dragon's breath, I thought. When it finally circled the globe it would mean earth's air sink had lost the ability to cleanse itself and all of us would start strangling a little faster.

I got the rest of my gear and just before I hit the door, Dave said: "Jim?" I turned. He was wiping his hands on a paper towel and frowning at me over his glasses. "Look, take care of yourself, huh, kid?"

"Sure thing," I said. If Monte was my professional father, then Dave was my uncle. Sometimes it was embarrassing but right then it felt good. I nodded good-bye, adjusted my mask, and left.

Outside it seemed like dusk; trucks and buses had turned on their lights and almost all pedestrians were wearing masks. In a lot across the street some kids were playing tag and the thought suddenly struck me that nowadays most kids seemed small for their age; but I envied them . . . the air never seemed to bother kids. I watched for a moment, then started up the walk. A few doors down I passed an apartment building, half hidden in the growing darkness, that had received a "political influence" exemption a month before. Its incinerator was going full blast now, only instead of floating upward over the city the small charred bits of paper and garbage were falling straight down the front of the building like a kind of oily black snow.

I suddenly felt I was suffocating and stepped out into the street and hailed a passing electricab. Forest Hills, the part of the city that Monte had pointed out, was wealthy and the homes were large, though not so large that some of them couldn't be hidden away in the canyons and gullies of the foothills. If you lived on a side road or at the end of one of the canyons it might even be possible to hide a car out there and drive it only at night. And if any of your neighbors found out . . . well, the people who lived up in the relatively pure air of the highlands had a different view of things than those who lived down in the atmospheric sewage of the flats. *But where would a man get a gasoline automobile in the first place?*

And did it all really matter? I thought, looking out the window of the cab at the deepening dusk and feeling depressed. Then I shook my head and leaned forward to give the driver instructions. Some places could be checked out relatively easily.

The Carriage Museum was elegant—and crowded, considering that it was a weekday. The main hall was a vast cave of black marble housing a parade of ancient internal combustion vehicles shining under the subdued lights; most of them were painted a lustrous black though there was an occasional gray and burst of red and a few sparkles of old gold from polished brass head lamps and fittings.

I felt like I was in St. Peter's, walking on a vast sea of marble while all about me the crowds shuffled along in respectful silence. I kept my eyes to the floor, reading off the names on the small bronze plaques: *Rolls Royce Silver Ghost, Mercer Raceabout, Isotta-Fraschini, Packard Runabout, Hispano-Suiza, Model J Duesenberg, Flying Cloud Reo, Cadillac Imperial V16, Pierce Arrow,* the first of the *Ford V8s, Lincoln Zephyr, Chrysler Windsor Club Coup.* . . . And in small halls off to the side, the lesser breeds: *Hudson Terraplane, Henry J., Willys Knight,* something called a *Jeepster,* the *Mustang, Knudsen,* the 1986 *Volkswagen,* the last *Chevrolet.* . . .

The other visitors to the museum were all middle-aged or older; the look on their faces was something I had never seen before—something that was not quite love and not quite lust. It flowed across their features like ripples of water whenever they brushed a fender or stopped at a hood that had been opened so they could stare at the engine, all neatly chromed or painted. They were like my father, I thought. They had owned cars when they were young, before Turn-In Day and the same date a year later when even most private steam and electrics were banned because of congestion. For a moment I wondered what it had been like to own one, then canceled the thought. The old man had tried to tell me often enough, before I had stormed out of the house for good, shouting how could he love the damned things so much when he was coughing his lungs out. . . .

The main hall was nothing but bad memories. I left it and looked up the office of the curator. His secretary was on a coffee break so I rapped sharply and entered without waiting for an answer. On the door it had said "C. Pearson," who turned out to be a thin, overdressed type, all regal nose and pencil moustache, in his mid-forties. "Air Central," I said politely, flashing my wallet ID at him.

He wasn't impressed. "May I?" I gave it to him and he reached for the phone. When he hung up he didn't bother apologizing for the double check, which I figured made us even. "I have nothing to do with the heating system or the air-conditioning," he said easily, "but if you'll wait a minute I'll—"

"I only want information," I said.

He made a small tent of his hands and stared at me over his fingertips. He looked bored. "Oh?"

I sat down and he leaned toward me briefly, then thought better of it and settled back in his chair. "How easy would it be," I asked casually, "to steal one of your displays?"

His moustache quivered slightly. "It wouldn't be easy at all—they're bolted down, there's no gasoline in their tanks, and the batteries are dummies."

"Then none ever have been?"

A flicker of annoyance. "No, of course not."

I flashed my best hat-in-hand smile and stood up. "Well, I guess that's it, then, I won't trouble you any further." But before I turned away I said, "I'm really not much on automobiles but I'm curious. How did the museum get started?"

He warmed up a little. "On Turn-In Day a number of

museums like this one were started up all over the country. Some by former dealers, some just by automobile lovers. A number of models were donated for public display and. . . ."

When he had finished I said casually, "Donating a vehicle to a museum must have been a great ploy for hiding private ownership."

"Certainly the people in your bureau would be aware of how strict the government was," he said sharply.

"A lot of people must have tried to hide their vehicles," I persisted.

Dryly. "It would have been difficult . . . like trying to hide an elephant in a playpen."

But still, a number would have tried, I thought. They might even have stockpiled drums of fuel and some spare parts. In the city, of course, it would have been next to impossible. But in remote sections of the country, in the mountain regions out west or in the hills of the Ozarks or in the forests of northern Michigan or Minnesota or in the badlands of the Dakotas. . . . A few would have succeeded, certainly, and perhaps late at night a few weed-grown stretches of highway would have been briefly lit by the headlights of automobiles flashing past with muffled exhausts, tires singing against the pavement. . . .

I sat back down. "Are there many automobile fans around?"

"I suppose so, if attendance records here are any indication."

"Then a smart man with a place in the country and a few automobiles could make quite a bit of money renting them out, couldn't he?"

He permitted himself a slight smile. "It would be risky. I really don't think anybody would try it. And from everything I've read, I rather think the passion was for actual ownership—I doubt that rental would satisfy that."

I thought about it for a moment while Pearson fidgeted with a letter opener and then, of course, I had it. "All those people who were fond of automobiles, there used to be clubs of them, right?"

His eyes lidded over and it grew very quiet in his office. But it was too late and he knew it. "I believe so," he said after a long pause, his voice tight, "but. . . ."

"But the government ordered them disbanded," I said

coldly. "Air Control regulations thirty-nine and forty, sections three through seven, 'concerning the dissolution of all organizations which in whole or in part, intentionally or unintentionally, oppose clean air.' " I knew the regulations by heart. "But there still are clubs, aren't there? Unregistered clubs? Clubs with secret membership files?" A light sheen of perspiration had started to gather on his forehead. "You would probably make a very good membership secretary, Pearson. You're in the perfect spot for recruiting new members—"

He made a motion behind his desk and I dove over it and pinned his arms behind his back. A small address book had fallen to the floor and I scooped it up. Pearson looked as if he might faint. I ran my hands over his chest and under his arms and then let him go. He leaned against the desk, gasping for air.

"I'll have to take you in," I said.

A little color was returning to his cheeks and he nervously smoothed down his damp black hair. His voice was on the squeaky side. "What for? You have some interesting theories but. . . ."

"My theories will keep for court," I said shortly. "You're under arrest for smoking—section eleven thirty point five of the health and safety code." I grabbed his right hand and spread the fingers so the tell-tale stains showed. "You almost offered me a cigarette when I came in, then caught yourself. I would guess that ordinarily you're pretty relaxed and sociable, you probably smoke a lot—and you're generous with your tobacco. Bottom right hand drawer for the stash, right?" I jerked it open and they were there, all right. "One cigarette's a misdemeanor, a carton's a felony, Pearson. We can accuse you of dealing and make it stick." I smiled grimly. "But we're perfectly willing to trade, of course."

I put in calls to the police and Air Central and sat down to wait for the cops to show. They'd sweat Pearson for all the information he had but I couldn't wait around a couple of hours. The word would spread that Pearson was being held, and Pearson himself would probably start remembering various lawyers and civil rights that he had momentarily forgotten. My only real windfall had been the address book. . . .

I thumbed through it curiously, wondering exactly how I could use it. The names were scattered all over the city, and there were a lot of them. I could weed it down to those in the area where the Sniffer had picked up the automobile, but that would take time and nobody was going to admit that he had a contraband vehicle hidden away anyway. The idea of paying a visit to the club I was certain must exist kept recurring to me and finally I decided to pick a name, twist Pearson's arm for anything he might know about him, then arrange to meet at the club and work out from there.

Later, when I was leaving the museum, I stopped for a moment just inside the door to readjust my mask. While I was doing it the janitor showed up with a roll of weather-stripping and started attaching it to the edge of the doorway where what looked like thin black smoke was seeping in from the outside. I was suddenly afraid to go back out there. . . .

The wind was whistling past my ears and a curve was coming up. I feathered the throttle, downshifted, and the needle on the tach started to drop. The wheel seemed to have a life of its own and twitched slightly to the right. I rode high on the outside of the track, the leafy limbs of trees that lined the asphalt dancing just outside my field of vision. The rear started to come around in a skid and I touched the throttle again and then the wheel twitched back to center and I was away. My eyes were riveted on Number Nine, just in front of me. It was the last lap and if I could catch him there would be nothing between me and the checkered flag. . . .

I felt relaxed and supremely confident, one with the throbbing power of the car. I red-lined it and through my dirt-streaked goggles I could see I was crawling up on the red splash that was Number Nine and next I was breathing the fumes from his twin exhausts. I took him on the final curve and suddenly I was alone in the world of the straightaway with the countryside peeling away on both sides of me, placid cows and ancient barns flowing past and then the rails lined with people. I couldn't hear their shouting above the scream of my car. Then I was flashing under banners stretched across the track and thundering toward the finish. There was the smell of burning rubber and spent oil and my own perspiration, the heat from the sun, the shimmering asphalt, and out of the corner of my eye a blur of grandstands and cars and a flag swooping down. . . .

And then it was over and the house lights had come up and I was hunched over a toy wheel in front of me, gripping it with both hands, the sweat pouring down my face and my stomach burning because I could still smell exhaust fumes and I wanted desperately to put on my face mask. It had been far more real than I had thought it would be—the curved screen gave the illusion of depth and each chair had been set up like a driver's seat. They had even pumped in odors. . . .

The others in the small theatre were stretching and getting ready to leave and I gradually unwound and got to my feet, still feeling shaky. "Lucky you could make it, Jim," a voice graveled in my ear. "You missed Joe Moore and the lecture but the documentary was just great, really great. Next week we've got *Meadowdale '73* which has its moments but you don't feel like you're really there and getting an eyeful of cinders, if you know what I mean."

"Who's Joe Moore?" I mumbled.

"Old time race track manager—full of anecdotes, knew all the great drivers. Hey! You okay?"

I was finding it difficult to come out of it. The noise and the action and the smell, but especially the feeling of actually driving. . . . It was more than just a visceral response. You had to be raised down in the flats where you struggled for your breath every day to get the same feeling of revulsion, the same feeling of having done something dirty. . . .

"Yeah, I'm okay," I said. "I'm feeling fine."

"Where'd you say you were from, anyway?"

"Bosnywash," I lied. He nodded and I took a breath and time out to size him up. Jack Ellis was bigger and heavier than Pearson and not nearly as smooth or as polished— Pearson perspired, my bulky friend sweated. He was in his early fifties, thinning brown hair carefully waved, the beginning of a small paunch well hidden by a lot of expensive tailoring, and a hulking set of shoulders that were much more than just padding. A business bird, I thought. The hairy-chested genial backslapper. . . .

"You seen the clubrooms yet?"

"I just got in," I said. "First time here."

"Hey, great! I'll show you around!" He talked like he was programmed. "A little fuel and a couple of stiff belts first, though—dining room's out of this world. . . ."

And it almost was. We were on the eighty-seventh floor of the new Trans-America building and Ellis had secured a window seat. Above, the sky was almost as bright a blue as Monte had used in his paintings. I couldn't see the street below.

"Have a card," Ellis said, shoving the pasteboard at me. It read *Warshawsky & Warshawsky, Automotive Antiques,* with an address in the Avenues. He waved a hand at the room. "We decorated all of this—pretty classy, huh?"

I had to give him that. The walls were covered with murals of old road races, while from some hidden sound system came a faint, subdued purring—the roaring of cars drifting through the esses of some long-ago race. In the center of the room was a pedestal holding a highly-chromed engine block that slowly revolved under a baby spot. While I was admiring the setting a waitress came up and set down a lazy Susan; it took a minute to recognize it as an old-fashioned wooden steering wheel, fitted with sterling silver hors d'oeuvre dishes between the spokes.

Ellis ran a thick thumb down the menu. "Try a Barney Oldfield," he suggested. "Roast beef and American cheese on pumpernickel."

While I was eating I got the uncomfortable feeling that he was looking me over and that somehow I didn't measure up. "You're pretty young," he said at last. "We don't get many young members—or visitors, for that matter."

"Grandfather was a dealer," I said easily. "Had a Ford agency in Milwaukee—I guess it rubbed off."

He nodded around a mouthful of sandwich and looked mournful for a moment. "It used to be a young man's game, kids worked on engines in their backyards all the time. Just about everybody owned a car. . . ."

"You, too?"

"Oh sure—hell, the old man ran a gas station until Turn-In Day." He was lost in his memories for a moment, then said, "You got a club in Bosnywash?"

"A few, nothing like this," I said cautiously. "And the law's pretty stiff." I nodded at the window. "They get pretty uptight about the air back east . . ." I let my voice trail off.

He frowned. "You don't *believe* all that guff, do you? Biggest goddamn pack of lies there ever was, but I guess you got to be older to know it. Power plants and incinerators, they're the ones to blame, always have been. Hell, people, too—every time you exhale you're polluting the atmosphere, ever think of that? And Christ, man, think of every time you work up a sweat. . . ."

"Sure," I nodded, "sure, it's always been blown up." I made a mental note that someday I'd throw the book at Ellis.

He finished his sandwich and started wiping his fat face like he was erasing a blackboard. "What's your interest? Mine's family sedans, the old family workhorse. Fords, Chevys, Plymouths—got a case of all the models from '50 on up, one-eighteenth scale. How about you?"

I didn't answer him, just stared out the window and worked with a toothpick for a long time until he began to get a little nervous. Then I let it drop. "I'm out here to buy a car," I said.

His face went blank, as if somebody had just pulled down a shade. "Damned expensive hobby," he said, ignoring it. "Should've taken up photography instead."

"It's for a friend of mine," I said. "Money's no object."

The waitress came around with the check and Ellis initialed it. "Damned expensive," he repeated vaguely.

"I couldn't make a connection back home," I said. "Friends suggested I try out here."

He was watching me now. "How would you get it back east?"

"Break it down," I said. "Ship it east as crates of machine parts."

"What makes you think there's anything for sale out here?"

I shrugged. "Lots of mountains, lots of forests, lots of empty space, lots of hiding places. Cars were big out here, there must have been a number that were never turned in."

"You're a stalking horse for somebody big, aren't you!"

"What do you think?" I said. "And what difference does it make anyway? Money's money."

If it's true that the pupil of the eye expands when it sees something that it likes, it's also true that it contracts when it doesn't—and right then his were in the cold buckshot stage.

"All right," he finally said. "Cash on the barrelhead and remember, when you have that much money changing hands, it can get dangerous." He deliberately leaned across the table so that his coat flapped open slightly. The small gun and holster were almost lost against the big man's girth. He sat back and spun the lazy Susan with a fat forefinger, spearing an olive as it slid past. "You guys run true to form," he continued quietly. "Most guys from back east come out to buy—I guess we've got a reputation." He hesitated. "We also try and take all the danger out of it."

He stood up and slapped me on the back as I pushed to my feet. It was the old Jack Ellis again, he of the instant smile and the sparkling teeth.

"That is, we try and take the danger out of it for *us*," he added pleasantly.

It was late afternoon and the rush hour had started. It wasn't as heavy as usual—businesses had been letting out all day—but it was bad enough. I slipped on a mask and started walking toward the warehouse section of town, just outside the business district. The buses were too crowded and it would be impossible to get an electricab that time of day. Besides, traffic was practically standing still in the steamy murk. Headlights were vague yellow dots in the gathering darkness and occasionally I had to shine my pocket flash on a street sign to determine my location.

I had checked in with Monte who said the hospitals were filling up fast with bronchitis victims; I didn't ask about the city morgue. The venal bastards at Air Shed Number Three were getting even worried; they had promised Monte that if it didn't clear by morning, he could issue his alert and close down the city. I told him I had uncovered what looked like a car ring but he sounded only faintly interested. He had bigger things on his mind; the ball was in my court and what I was going to do with it was strictly up to me.

A few more blocks and the crowds thinned. Then I was alone on the street with the warehouses hulking up in the gloom around me, ancient monsters of discolored brick and concrete layered with years of soot and grime. I found the address I wanted, leaned against the buzzer by the loading dock door, and waited. There was a long pause, then faint steps echoed inside and the door slid open. Ellis stood in the yellow dock light, the smile stretching across his thick face like a rubber band. "Right on time," he whispered. "Come on in, Jim, meet the boys."

I followed him down a short passageway, trying not to brush up against the filthy whitewashed walls. Then we were up against a steel door with a peephole. Ellis knocked three times, the peephole opened, and he said, "Joe sent me." I started to panic. *For God's sake, why the act?* Then the door opened and it was as if somebody had kicked me in the stomach. What lay beyond was a huge garage with at least half a dozen ancient cars on the tool-strewn floor. Three mechanics in coveralls were working under the overhead lights; two more were waiting inside the door. They were bigger than Ellis and I was suddenly very glad I had brought along the Mark II.

"Jeff, Ray, meet Mr. Morrison." I held out my hand. They nodded at me, no smiles. "C'mon," Ellis said, "I'll show you the set up." I tagged after him and he started pointing out the wonders of his domain. "Completely equipped garage—my old man would've been proud of me. Overhead hoist for pulling motors, complete lathe set-up . . . a lot of parts we have to machine ourselves, can't get the originals anymore and of course the last of the junkers was melted down a long time ago." He stopped by a workbench with a large rack full of tools gleaming behind it. "One of the great things about being in the antique business—you hit all the country auctions and you'd be surprised at what you can pick up. Complete sets of torque wrenches, metric socket sets, spanner wrenches, feeler gauges, you name it."

I looked over the bench—he was obviously proud of the assortment of tools—then suddenly felt the small of my back grow cold. It was phony, I thought, the whole thing was phony. But I couldn't put my finger on just why.

Ellis walked over to one of the automobiles on the floor and patted a fender affectionately. Then he unbuttoned his coat so that the pistol showed, hooked his thumbs in his vest, leaned against the car behind him and smiled. Someplace he had even found a broomstraw to chew on.

"So what can we do for you, Jim? Limited stock, sky-high prices, but never a dissatisfied customer!" He poked an elbow against the car behind him. "Take a look at this '73 Chevy Biscayne, probably the only one of its kind in this condition in the whole damned country. Ten thou and you can have it—and that's only because I like you." He sauntered over to a monster in blue and silver with grillwork that looked like a set of kitchen knives. "Or maybe you'd like a '76 Caddy convertible, all genuine simulated-leather upholstery, one of the last of the breed." He didn't add why but I already knew—in heavy traffic the high levels of monoxide could be fatal to a driver in an open car.

"Yours," Ellis was saying about another model, "for a flat fifteen"—he paused and shot me a friendly glance—"oh hell, for you, Jim, make it twelve and a half and take it from me, it's a bargain. Comes with the original upholstery and tires and there's less than ten thousand miles on it—the former owner was a little old lady in Pasadena who only drove it to weddings."

He chuckled at that, looking at me expectantly. I didn't get it. "Maybe you'd just like to look around. Be my guest, go right ahead." His eyes were bright and he looked very pleased with himself; it bothered me.

"Yeah," I said absently, "I think that's what I'd like to do." There was a wall phone by an older model and I drifted over to it.

"That's an early Knudsen two-seater," Ellis said. "Popular make for the psychedelic set, that paint job is the way they really came. . . ."

I ran my hand lightly down the windshield, then turned to face the cheerful Ellis. "You're under arrest," I said. "You and everybody else here."

His face suddenly looked like shrimp in molded gelatin. One of the mechanics behind him moved and I had the Mark II out winging a rocket past his shoulder. No noise, no recoil, just a sudden shower of sparks by the barrel and in the far end of the garage a fifty-gallon oil drum went *karrump* and there was a hole in it you could have stuck your head through.

The mechanic went white. *"Jesus Christ, Jack, you brought in some kind of nut!"* Ellis himself was pale and shaking, which surprised me; I thought he'd be tougher than that.

"Against the bench," I said coldly, waving the pistol. "Hands in front of your crotch and don't move them." The mechanics were obviously scared stiff and Ellis was having difficulty keeping control. I took down the phone and called in.

After I hung up, Ellis mumbled, "What's the charge?"

"Charges," I corrected. "Sections three, four and five of the Air Control laws. Maintenance, sale and use of internal combustion engines."

Ellis stared at me blankly. "You don't know?" he asked faintly.

"Know what?"

"I don't handle internal combustion engines." He licked his lips. "I really don't, it's too risky, it's . . . it's against the law."

The workbench, I suddenly thought. The goddamned workbench. I knew something was wrong then, I should have cooled it.

"You can check me," Ellis offered weakly. "Lift a hood, look for yourself."

He talked like his face was made of panes of glass sliding against one another. I waved him forward. "*You* check it, Ellis, you open one up." Ellis nodded like a dipping duck, waddled over to one of the cars, jiggled something inside, then raised the hood and stepped back.

I took one glance and my stomach slowly started to knot up. I was no motor buff but I damned well knew the difference between a gasoline engine and water boiler. Which explained the workbench—the tools had been window dressing. Most of them were brand new because most of them had obviously never been used. There had been nothing to use them on.

"The engines are steam," Ellis said, almost apologetically. "I've got a license to do restoration work and drop in steam engines. They don't allow them in cities but it's different on farms and country estates and in some small towns." He looked at me. "The license cost me a goddamned fortune."

It was a real handicap being a city boy, I thought. "Then why the act? Why the gun?"

"This?" he asked stupidly. He reached inside his coat and dropped the pistol on the floor; it made a light thudding sound and bounced, a pot metal toy. "The danger, it's the sense of danger, it's part of the sales pitch." He wanted to be angry now but he had been frightened too badly and couldn't quite make it. "The customers pay a lot of dough, they want a little drama. That's why—you know—the peephole and everything." He took a deep breath and when he exhaled it came out as a giggle, an incongruous sound from the big man. I found myself hoping he didn't have a heart condition. "I'm well known," he said defensively. "I take ads. . . ."

"The club," I said. "It's illegal."

Even if it was weak, his smile was genuine and then the score became crystal clear. The club was like a speakeasy during the Depression, with half the judges and politicians in town belonging to it. Why not? Somebody older wouldn't have my bias. . . . Pearson's address book had been all last names and initials but I had never connected any of them to anybody prominent; I hadn't been around enough to know what connection to make.

I waved Ellis back to the workbench and stared glumly at the group. The mechanic I had frightened with the Mark II had a spreading stain across the front of his pants and I felt sorry for him momentarily.

Then I started to feel sorry for myself. Monte should have given me a longer briefing, or maybe assigned another Investigator to go with me, but he had been too sick and too wrapped up with the politics of it all. So I had gone off half-cocked and come up with nothing but a potential lawsuit for Air Central that would probably amount to a million dollars by the time Ellis got through with me.

It was a black day inside as well as out.

I holed up in a bar during the middle part of the evening, which was probably the smartest thing I could have done. Despite their masks, people on the street had started to retch and vomit and I could feel my own nausea grow with every step. I saw one man try and strike a match to read a street sign; it wouldn't stay lit, there simply wasn't enough oxygen in the air. The ambulance sirens were a steady wail now and I knew it was going to be a tough night for heart cases. They'd be going like flies before morning, I thought. . . .

Another customer slammed through the door, wheezing and coughing and taking huge gulps of the machine-pure air of the bar. I ordered another drink and tried to shut out the sound; it was too reminiscent of Monte hacking and coughing behind his desk at work.

And come morning, Monte might be out of a job, I thought. I for certain would be; I had loused up in a way that would cost the department money—the unforgivable sin in the eyes of the politicians.

I downed half my drink and started mentally reviewing the events of the day, giving myself a passing score only on figuring out that Pearson had had a stash. I hadn't known about Ellis' operation, which in one sense wasn't surprising. Nobody was going to drive something that looked like an old gasoline-burner around a city—the flatlanders would stone him to death.

But somebody still had a car, I thought. Somebody who was rich and immune from prosecution and a real nut about cars in the first place. . . . But it kept sliding away from me. Really rich men were too much in the public eye, ditto politicians. They'd be washed up politically if anybody ever found out. If nothing else, some poor bastard like the one at the end of the bar trying to flush out his lungs would assassinate him. Somebody with money, but not too much. Somebody who was a car nut—they'd have to be to take the risks. And somebody for whom those risks were absolutely minimal. . . .

And then the lightbulb flashed on above my head, just like in the old cartoons. I wasn't dead certain I was right but I was willing to stake my life on it—and it was possible I might end up doing just that.

I slipped on a mask and almost ran out of the bar. Once outside, I sympathized with the guy who had just come in and who had given me a horrified look as I plunged out into the darkness.

It was smothering now, though the temperature had dropped a little so my shirt didn't cling to me in dirty, damp folds. Buses were being led through the streets; headlights died out completely within a few feet. The worst thing was that they left tracks in what looked like a damp, grayish ash that covered the street. Most of the people I bumped into— mere shadows in the night—had soaked their masks in water, trying to make them more effective. There were lights still on in the lower floors of most of the office buildings and I figured some people hadn't tried to make it home at all; the air was probably purer among the filing cabinets than in their own apartments. Two floors up, the buildings were completely hidden in the smoky darkness.

It took a good hour of walking before the sidewalks started to slant up and I knew I was getting out toward the foothills . . . I thanked God the business district was closer to the mountains than the ocean. My legs ached and my chest hurt and I was tired and depressed but at least I wasn't coughing anymore.

The buildings started to thin out and the streets finally became completely deserted. Usually the cops would pick you up if they caught you walking on the streets of Forest Hills late at night, but that night I doubted they were even around. They were probably too busy ferrying cases of cardiac arrest to St. Francis. . . .

The Sniffer was located on the top of a small, ancient building off on a side street. When I saw it I suddenly found my breath hard to catch again—a block down, the street abruptly turned into a canyon and wound up and out of sight. I glanced back at the building, just faintly visible through the grayed-down moonlight. The windows were boarded up and there was a For Rent sign on them. I walked over and flashed my light on the sign. It was old and peeling and had obviously been there for years; apparently nobody had ever wanted to rent the first floor. Ever? Maybe somebody had, I thought, but had decided to leave it boarded up. I ran my hand down the boards and suddenly paused at a knothole; I could feel heavy plate glass through it. I knelt and flashed my light at the hole and looked at a dim reflection of myself staring back. The glass had been painted black on the inside so it acted like a black marble mirror.

I stepped back and something about the building struck me. The boarded-up windows, I thought, the huge, oversized windows. . . . And the oversized, boarded-up doors. I flashed the light again at the concrete facing just above the doors. The words were there all right, blackened by time but still readable, cut into the concrete itself by order of the proud owner a handful of decades before. But you could still noodle them out: *RICHARD SIEBEN LINCOLN-MERCURY.*

Jackpot, I thought triumphantly. I glanced around—there was nobody else on the street—and listened. Not a sound, except for the faint murmur of traffic still moving in the city far away. A hot muggy night in the core city, I thought, but this night the parks and the fire escapes would be empty and five million people would be tossing and turning in their cramped little bedrooms; it'd be suicide to try and sleep outdoors.

In Forest Hills it was cooler—and quieter. I glued my ear to the boards over the window and thought I could hear the faint shuffle of somebody walking around and, once, the faint clink of metal against metal. I waited a moment, then slipped down to the side door that had "Air Central" on it in neat black lettering. All Investigators had master keys and I went inside. Nobody was upstairs; the lights were out and the only sound was the soft swish of the Sniffer's scribing pens against the paper roll. There was a stairway in the back and I walked silently down it. The door at the bottom was open and I stepped through it into a short hallway. Something, maybe the smell of the air, told me it had been used recently. I closed the door after me and stood for a second in the darkness. There was no sound from the door beyond. I tried the knob and it moved silently in my grasp.

I cracked the door open and peered through the slit—nothing—then eased it open all the way and stepped out onto the showroom floor. There was a green-shaded lightbulb hanging from the ceiling, swaying slightly in some minor breeze so the shadows chased each other around the far corners of the room. Walled off at the end were two small offices where salesmen had probably wheeled and dealed long ago. There wasn't much else, other than a few tools scattered around the floor in the circle of light.

And directly in the center, of course, the car.

I caught my breath. There was no connection between it and Jack Ellis' renovated family sedans. It crouched there on the floor, a mechanical beast that was almost alive. Sleek curving fenders that blended into a louvered hood with a chromed steel bumper curving flat around the front to give it an oddly sharklike appearance. The headlamps were set deep into the fenders, the lamp wells outlined with chrome. The hood flowed into a windshield and that into a top which sloped smoothly down in back and tucked in neatly just after the rear wheels. The wheels themselves had wire spokes that gleamed wickedly in the light, and through a side window I could make out a neat array of meters and rocker switches, and finally bucket seats covered with what I instinctively knew was genuine black leather.

Sleek beast, powerful beast, I thought. I was unaware of walking up to it and running my hand lightly over a fender until a voice behind me said, "It's beautiful, isn't it?"

I turned like an actor in a slow-motion film. "Yeah, Dave," I said, "it's beautiful." Dave Ice of Air Central. In charge of all the Sniffers.

He must have been standing in one of the salesman's offices; it was the only way I could have missed him. He walked up and stood on the other side of the car and ran his left hand over the hood with the same affectionate motion a woman might use in stroking her cat. In his right hand he held a small Mark II pointed directly at my chest.

"How'd you figure it was me?" he asked casually.

"I thought at first it might be Monte," I said. "Then I figured you were the real nut about machinery."

His eyes were bright, too bright. "Tell me," he asked curiously, "would you have turned in Monte?"

"Of course," I said simply. I didn't add that it would have been damned difficult; that I hadn't even been able to think about that part of it.

"So might've I, so might've I," he murmured. "When I was your age."

"For a while the money angle threw me," I said.

He smiled faintly. "It's a family heirloom. My father bought it when he was young, he couldn't bring himself to turn it in." He cocked his head. "Could you?" I looked at him uneasily and didn't answer and he said casually, "Go ahead, Jimmy, you were telling me how you cracked the case."

I flushed. "It had to be somebody who knew—who was absolutely sure—that he wasn't going to get caught. The Sniffers are pretty efficient, it would have been impossible to prevent their detecting the car—the best thing would be to censor the data from them. And Monte and you were the only ones who could have done that."

Another faint smile. "You're right."

"You slipped up a few nights ago," I said.

He shrugged. "Anybody could've. I was sick, I didn't get to the office in time to doctor the record."

"It gave the game away," I said. "Why only once? The Sniffer should have detected it far more often than just once."

He didn't say anything and for a long moment both of us were lost in admiration of the car.

Then finally, proudly: "It's the real McCoy, Jim. Six cylinder in-line engine, 4.2 liters displacement, nine-to-one compression ratio, twin overhead cams and twin Zenith-Stromberg carbs. . . ." He broke off. "You don't know what I'm talking about, do you?"

"No," I confessed, "I'm afraid not."

"Want to see the motor?"

I nodded and he stepped forward, waved me back with the Mark II, and opened the hood. To really appreciate it, of course, you had to have a thing for machinery. It was clean and polished and squatted there under the hood like a beautiful mechanical pet—so huge I wondered how the hood could close at all.

And then I realized with a shock that I hadn't been reacting like I should have, that I hadn't reacted like I should have ever since the movie at the club. . . .

"You can sit in it if you want to," Dave said softly. "Just don't touch anything." His voice was soft. "Everything works on it, Jim, everything works just dandy. It's oiled and greased and the tank is full and the battery is charged and if you wanted to, you could drive it right off the showroom floor."

I hesitated. "People in the neighborhood—"

"—mind their own business," he said. "They have a different attitude, and besides, it's usually late at night and I'm out in the hills in seconds. Go ahead, get in." Then his voice hardened into command: "Get in!"

I stalled a second longer, then opened the door and slid into the seat. The movie was real now, I was holding the wheel and could sense the gearshift at my right and in my mind's eye I could feel the wind and hear the scream of the motor. . . .

There was something hard pressing against the side of my head. I froze. Dave was holding the pistol just behind my ear and in the side mirror I could see his finger tense on the trigger and pull back a millimeter. *Dear God.* . . .

He relaxed. "You'll have to get out," he said apologetically. "It would be appropriate, but a mess just the same."

I got out. My legs were shaking and I had to lean against the car. "It's a risky thing to own a car," I chattered. "Feeling runs pretty high against cars. . . ."

He nodded. "It's too bad."

"You worked for Air Central for years," I said. "How could you do it, and own this, too?"

"You're thinking about the air," he said carefully. "But Jim"—his voice was patient—"machines don't foul the air, men do. They foul the air, the lakes, and the land itself. And there's no way to stop it." I started to protest and he held up a hand. "Oh sure, there's always a time when you care—like you do now. But time . . . you know, time wears you down, it really does, no matter how eager you are. You devote your life to a cause and then you find yourself suddenly growing fat and bald and you discover nobody gives a damn about your cause. They're paying you your cushy salary to buy off their own consciences. So long as there's a buck to be made, things won't change much. It's enough to drive you—" He broke off. "You don't *really* think that anybody gives a damn about anybody else, do you?" He stood there looking faintly amused, a pudgy little man whom I should've been able to take with one arm tied behind my back. But he was ten times as dangerous as Ellis had ever imagined himself to be. "Only suckers care, Jim. I. . . ."

I dropped to the floor then, rolling fast to hit the shadows beyond the circle of light. His Mark II sprayed sparks and something burned past my shirt collar and squealed along the concrete floor. I sprawled flat and jerked my own pistol out. The first shot went low and there was the sharp sound of scored metal and I cursed briefly to myself—I must have brushed the car. Then there was silence and I scrabbled further back into the darkness. I wanted to pot the light but the bulb was still swaying back and forth and chances were I'd miss and waste the shot. Then there was the sound of running and I jumped to my feet and saw Dave heading for the door I had come in by. He seemed oddly defenseless—he was chubby and slow and knock-kneed and ran like a woman.

"Dave!" I screamed. "Dave! STOP!"

It was an accident, there was no way to help it. I aimed low and to the side, to knock him off his feet, and at the same time he decided to do what I had done and sprawl flat in the shadows. If he had stayed on his feet, the small rocket would have brushed him at knee level. As it was, it smashed his chest.

He crumpled and I ran up and caught him before he could hit the floor. He twisted slightly in my arms so he was staring at the car as he died. I broke into tears. I couldn't help that, either. I would remember the things Dave had done for me long after I had forgotten that one night he had tried to kill me. A threat to kill is unreal—actual blood and shredded flesh has its own reality.

I let him down gently and walked slowly over to the phone in the corner. Monte should still be in his office, I thought. I dialed and said, "The Director, please," and waited for the voice-actuated relay to connect me. "Monte, Jim Morrison here. I'm over at—" I paused. "I'm sorry, I thought it was Monte—" And then I shut up and let the voice at the other end of the line tell me that Monte had died with the window open and the night air filling his lungs with urban vomit. "I'm sorry," I said faintly, "I'm sorry, I'm very sorry," but the voice went on and I suddenly realized that I was listening to a recording and that there was nobody in the office at all. Then, as the voice continued, I knew why.

I let the receiver fall to the floor and the record started in again, as if expecting condolences from the concrete.

I should call the cops, I thought. I should—

But I didn't. Instead, I called Wanda. It would take an hour or more for her to collect the foodstuffs in the apartment and to catch an electricab but we could be out of the city before morning came.

And that was pretty funny because morning was never coming. The recording had said dryly that the tagged radioactive chimney exhausts had arrived, that the dragon's breath had circled the globe and the winds blowing in were as dirty as the air already over the city. Oh, it wouldn't happen right away, but it wouldn't be very long, either. . . .

Nobody had given a damn, I thought; not here nor any other place. Dave had been right, dead right. They had finally turned it all into a sewer and the last of those who cared had coughed his lungs out trying for a breath of fresh air that had never come, too weak to close a window.

I walked back to the car sitting in the circle of light and ran a finger down the scored fender where the small rocket had scraped the paint. Dave would never have forgiven me, I thought. Then I opened the door and got in and settled slowly back into the seat. I fondled the shift and ran my eyes over the instrument panel, the speedometer and the tach and the fuel and the oil gauges and the small clock. . . . The keys dangled from the button at the end of the hand brake. It was a beautiful piece of machinery, I thought again. I had never really loved a piece of machinery . . . until now.

I ran my hands around the wheel, then located the starter switch on the steering column. I jabbed in the key and closed my eyes and listened to the scream of the motor and felt its power shake the car and wash over me and thunder through the room. The movie at the club had been my only lesson but in its own way it had been thorough and it would be enough. I switched off the motor and waited.

When Wanda got there we would take off for the high ground. For the mountains and the pines and that last clear lake and that final glimpse of blue sky before it all turned brown and we gave up in final surrender to this climate of which we're so obviously proud. . . .

Disposal   Ron Goulart

He couldn't eat any more of the haddock schnitzel. Lon Snowden nudged the sample container over to the left side of the dining-area table and reached into his briefcase. The next sample to be tested was labeled cod jubilee in the chief's lopsided printing. Lon didn't like to bring food home from the office but the preliminary response figures on eleven new—he glanced at his watch: nearly midnight—Seawise Processed Seafoods was due tomorrow before coffee break 1.

Fog was resting heavy against the shuttered window of the dining area. Victorian Village was thick with fog tonight, most nights. Lon pried open the cod container, made a note with a grease pencil on a blue response punch card. He was thirty-four—he glanced at his watch: five past midnight—and already he was but two moves away from being a Senior Food Tester for Seawise. As Ryan Kubert, the only guy at Seawise he almost trusted, had said at lunch several times, being a Senior Food Tester was a good thing. Ryan was four moves from it.

When Lon was rushed, as tonight, he never bothered to heat the foods he was responding to. That didn't seem to affect his judgment. Rolling another bite of cod around in his mouth he blacked in the square next to the TERRIBLE response. He shoved the rest of the sample over with the nine he'd run through since Maya had gone into the sleeping area. Before he tried the eel brittle he'd stand up—he glanced at his watch: quarter after twelve—and stretch.

Terry, their younger boy, was watching him from the entrance to the children's sleep section. "What's the matter?" Lon mouthed.

"Some day," said Terry, "I'll be boss around here. You'll be among the first to get it. Quick, like that."

Terry was four. The death-threat business was something he was going through. "Back to bed," Lon told him softly. The office psychiatrist said feeling hostile toward the father figure was okay.

"First pull your fingers off, one by one," said the little boy. "Then the toes. Lastly, the nose."

"Get the hell into bed or I'll break your damn arm." Lon glanced at his watch: twenty-one past twelve.

Terry obeyed.

Lon found his stomach mint capsules in his briefcase, quickly swallowed two. Then he got back to the eel brittle. It was BLAND and DELICIOUS he decided.

By one he had everything tested. Somehow fog had seeped into the dining area and was hanging low to the rug. As Lon walked into the kitchen with all the scraps of seafood, the mist tattered. He got the light control with his elbow, side-stepped to the porthole of the disposal unit. "Grind away," he said and both-handed all the containers and fish scraps into the hole.

A new and not appropriate sound came out of the wall disposal. The unit made a sound like packages of metal washers dropping off the back of a truck, then a grating cat wail. Twenty-nine seconds of silence and then all the garbage was thrown back out of the hole.

Lon gathered it up in a lemon-yellow refuse pan and shot it back through the porthole.

The disposal made the same new sounds, and an out of tune guitar twang, and threw the garbage out again. The leftovers from Lon's testing plus the leavings from dinner.

"It's on the fritz," he said.

Finally he found an empty container big enough to hold all the rejected garbage. He didn't know what to do with it. He left it in the kitchen and went to bed. In the morning Maya would know.

Maya, with a metronome motion of her hand, put egg-shells into a blue plyfilm bag. "We can store it in the utility closet until the disposal's fixed."

Lon flathanded the legs of the turned-off cleaning android aside and wedged the box of last night's garbage into the tiny utility closet.

The Victorian Village school cruiser chimed outside and Pete, the six-year-old, ran from the kitchen.

Terry got up from the breakfast nook with his half-finished bowl of protein mash and said, "I want to put my garbage in the hole."

"Disposal's busted," said Lon. "You can't. Put it there by mommy."

"I want to put it in the hole."

"Well, you can't."

Terry frowned. "When I take over this place I won't forget all this. First we'll stretch you, then compress you. Crack, crack your bones will go. Snap, snap."

"Go to your room," said Lon.

"Not a room, it's an area," said Terry, going.

"A phase." Maya set the bag of breakfast garbage in the closet. "Shall I call Mr. Goodwagon at the Victorian Village office?"

Lon checked the wall clock. Fourteen minutes before he had to be at the San Francisco tube. "I'll do it." In the phone alcove he smoothed his pale hair, sat down, dialled Goodwagon.

"Well, aren't you the early riser," said the secretary android who appeared on the screen.

"Mr. Goodwagon, please."

"He's on the links."

"Oh. Well, look. Our disposal isn't working. Victorian Village's Maintenance Department is supposed to fix it, isn't it?"

"Of course. No one else is allowed to tamper with VV equipment. Read your lease."

"Okay. When exactly could you have somebody over to fix the thing?"

The android said, "September 14 at 2:30."

Lon looked at his wristwatch. "Yes, but this is August 26, 8:14."

"8:16," corrected the android. "Otherwise you're right."

"What do we do with our garbage until September?"

"Don't throw it in the street," said the android. "That's

against state, federal and Victorian Village law. Don't bury it. That's illegal, too."

"What would you suggest?"

"I'll switch you to Dr. Wigransky, our staff troubleshooter." Dr. Wigransky, when he came on the screen, was naked. "Yes?"

"We have," said Lon, looking away, "this problem about our garbage."

"You can't seem to look me in the eye."

"Your eye maybe. It's the rest of you."

"You call so early you can't expect formal attire. Lots of business stress?"

"Sure, but the problem is we have this disposal that won't work and they can't come and fix it till the middle of next month and I was wondering what we were supposed to do."

"How old are you?"

"Thirty-four. Why?"

"Thirty-four years old and native-born from the way you talk and you don't know what to do with a little garbage."

"It's not a little. By next month it'll be a lot. I'm a food tester, I bring a great deal of food home to work on."

"That's an interesting field," said Dr. Wigransky, who had slipped on a polo shirt while Lon hadn't been watching him. "I have a brother who's a wastrel. Maybe you could get him into food testing."

"I don't have much influence," Lon told him. "What about our garbage?"

"Call Sayffertitz."

"Sayffertitz?"

"The last of the scavengers." Dr. Wigransky blacked off.

The vintage dump truck drove up onto their small lawn at a little after nine that evening. From the real-leather driver's seat leaped a tanned man in a tweed jumpsuit. He had a moustache, shoulder-length black hair and a Malacca stick. He hit the chime buzzer with a gloved thumb.

"Sayffertitz," he told Maya when she opened the door.

"Oh, yes. We understand you still pick up garbage."

Sayffertitz handed her his cane, eased off his gloves. "I am the only remaining scavenger in the San Francisco Bay Area. People depend on disposal units now. However, as you've just learned, disposals do break down. Then you have to come to Sayffertitz."

Lon had been sitting in the living area, sampling. He stood now as Maya led Sayffertitz in. "When will you pick up the garbage?"

Sayffertitz sat down on a plystool. "You people amuse me. I haven't agreed to haul your garbage yet. Tell me about it and I'll see if I can take on your account. Do you have any brandy?"

"Maya, get Mr. Sayffertitz a brandy."

Sayffertitz' left eye was not quite the same shade of green as his right. He fixed it on Lon, tossed his hair once. "Just what sort of garbage is it you'd like me to consider?"

"Garbage," said Lon. "Household stuff."

The scavenger stroked one tweedy knee. "What's that in front of you there?"

"My work. I'm a food tester."

"But what is it specifically?"

"Well," said Lon, pointing in turn, "terrapin flambe, shrimp jellyroll, chicken fried halibut and anchovy bisque."

"You intend to include that stuff in my garbage?" asked Sayffertitz. He dropped to the rug, approaching the coffee table on hands and knees. "Which is the halibut again?"

"The orange stuff. It's artificially colored."

Sayffertitz sniffed. "I don't know. You people. Boy, you want me to toss that kind of thing into my truck. That's an awfully persistent odor."

"Seafood. It does have a sort of oceany smell."

"You're used to it. Numbed by your job."

"What days do you pick up? Is there a regular schedule or what?"

Sayffertitz rubbed his lighter eye. "You people." He stretched up, scratched his stomach. "I service my clients in this area on Tuesday mornings at the moment."

"Next week then?"

"Next week. Tuesday morning at 7 A.M." He bent to sniff the halibut again. "I don't know if I can accept you people or not."

"We'll pay well," said Maya, offering him a brandy on a bronzed tray.

"My fee is ten dollars per pickup. In advance."

"Ten dollars?" asked Lon.

"In advance. If I accept the account." He touched the tip of his nose with the brandy glass rim. "Do you have a scale?"

"In the bathroom."

"Remember this then. No more than five pounds of garbage per Tuesday."

"Then you accept us?" said Maya.

"This brandy is not too bad." He drank it down. "Tuesday, seven promptly. No more than five pounds. In boxes. On the left side of the lawn facing the street." He took the money Lon held out, bowed slightly. He went to the door and let himself out into the fog.

Lon picked up the container of halibut and inhaled.

Sayffertitz didn't show up on the following Tuesday. Nor Wednesday. Thursday at 8:17, with nine cartons of garbage stacked in the corner of the cruiser port, Lon called the scavenger. That morning Sayffertitz didn't answer. On Friday he did but he was unhappy that Lon was waking him at 8:14 on his day off. Lon apologized.

Sayffertitz said, "You people and your fish. I refuse to accept any further garbage from you."

"What do you mean any further? I gave you ten bucks and you . . ."

The scavenger went to black.

Using fog as a cover, Lon was able, that night, to toss one carton of garbage into a public disposal at the nearest cul-de-sac. The unit was labelled: FOR LEAVES AND FALLEN GREENERY ONLY. Friday it worked but Saturday the mist was thinner and a mounted android policer, who had been watching from a shadowy gazebo, caught Lon and fined him twenty-two dollars.

Maya found she could flush eggshells and coffee grounds down the toilet. The bowl balked at anything else. Lon dumped four cartons the next Monday night at the beach some eighteen miles from their home. The litter patrol caught him on the third trip and that resulted in a seventy-three dollar fine and the revoking of his sunbathing privilege for a ninety-day period. He was able, by pretending to be strewing the ashes of a loved one, to get rid of three cartons flying low over the Pacific Ocean in his cruiser at sundown. You couldn't do that more than once a month, though.

By the end of August they had twenty-one cartons of garbage in their gingerbread house. When no more would fit in the small cruiser port, Maya started putting refuse in the recreation area cupboards. The house now had a quiet sour-sweet odor most of the time and Terry threatened to have his father pulled asunder by draft horses if the smell didn't stop. Lon called the Bay Area Health Authority but they said they couldn't help him until he had either maggots or plague-carrying rats in his garbage.

He discovered he could get rid of about a half a pound a day by carrying it to work in his briefcase and tossing it in the office disposal when the machine was not being watched. Maya had meanwhile been taking a carton a day over to Carole and Robert, their friends two blocks away. Carole and Robert couldn't dispose of more because the first time Maya had tried to get rid of several cartons at once and the Victorian Village authorities had warned Carole against overloading her appliances again. They knew three other couples in the development and gradually, by using all of their friends' disposal units and with Lon sneaking the more unobtrusive garbage into the office, they got down to only ten cartons stored in the cruiser area.

On the first Tuesday in September Terry decided to drop his left shoe in their disposal hole. The unit roared and thrashed for three and a quarter minutes and then started kicking back. Out came eggshells, orange peels, coconut shreds, soft drink bulbs, teabags, hambones, fishtails, kleenex, back issue magazines, green marbles, cabbage, bandaids, protein loaf, plyogloves, rose petals, tuna fish, melon rinds, a dead canary and Terry's shredded shoe. The kitchen area was a foot awash with old garbage before the machine stopped rejecting.

"Okay," said Lon when it sputtered and stopped. "That's it. I'm going to bury the stuff." He strode into the cruiser area and grabbed up the power shovel.

It was dark and misty. He turned on the lawn spotlights and began to dig. He had a pit about seven inches deep and three feet wide dug when the Victorian Village cop cruised down.

"What are you up to, Mr. Snowden?" asked the cop.

"Burying garbage."

"No, now," said the VV cop. "That's an infraction."

"The whole house is possessed by the stuff," Lon told him. "Besides which I'm starting to feel an enormous guilt over this."

"But you people shouldn't dig up your lawn."

Lon threw the shovel at him.

Victorian Village didn't have its own jail completed yet so Lon was put in the city jail in nearby Sunnyvale. The judge let him off with a $500 fine and twelve days in jail. Maya told him, on his third day in the cell, that since he'd assaulted a Victorian Village staff member the tract people were considering evicting them and had, in the meantime, put their name at the end of the waiting list for repairs. That meant no disposal repairs would be made until October 2nd.

In jail Lon dreamt a great deal about garbage. And he got to know a man in the next cell named Blind John Dove. Blind John said he was one of the few blind private investigators in the San Francisco Bay Area and he solved his cases with his sense of smell.

Lon explained his garbage problem and Blind John, a fat, freckled man with a strip of green plyoglass across his upper face, said, "Know what?"

"What?"

"Playland. Near Playland over in Frisco there's an old bath house that's closed up. By the ocean. From the street level it's three floors down inside. All gutted out. Lots of people with garbage problems throw things there. No guards at night. That part of the city's hardly frequented anymore. Load your cruiser. Fly."

After his release Lon went back to Seawise and found he no longer had his job. That same evening he and Maya, with the house still cluttered with nineteen cartons of garbage Maya hadn't been able to get rid of yet with the neighbors, had a quarrel. Maya took Terry and Pete and walked over to Carole and Robert's to spend the night.

Lon sat in the kitchen area for a while. He was hungry but if he ate it would only mean more garbage. At 10:16 he started loading boxes of garbage into the cruiser. It was a chill, foggy night and he put on a realfleece jacket. He got all the garbage, except for a handful of burnt marshmallows that fell and eluded him in a corner, stowed in the ship.

He took off for the city. By eleven he was parked up hill from the long-deserted public bath house. He quietly carried an armload of garbage up to the marble steps, climbed down and pushed the doors open. They skittered back and he was looking down on a cool hollow. There was a sweet-sour

musty damp smell here. Lon heaved the first batch of cartons.
Heard them hit seconds later and bounce on some kind of
loose metal.

A wind was rising out across the ocean and it blew the lid
off one of the cartons on the next load. In twenty-two minutes
he was at the pit edge with the last three boxes. He threw
them, listened as they hit, bounced, settled.

A truck cut off behind him in the street, leaping feet hit
the misted pavement. "You people," said a voice. "Encroaching on one of my private dump spot. It's difficult enough to
survive in our society without people like you."

Lon turned and watched Sayffertitz approach.

"The fish man," grinned the scavenger. "Well, climb down
there and retrieve whatever it is you've thrown. You
poacher." He pointed at the pit with his Malacca cane.

Lon bobbed, caught the stick away from him. He hit him
several times over the skull with it. Sayffertitz slumped. Lon
flung the stick into the pit. He stooped and grabbed two
holds on the tweed jumpsuit. He braced himself and pitched
Sayffertitz into the dark hollow.

He didn't stay to hear him land.

Fear in the City:
The Problem of Crime

*Fear of crime and criminal assault is almost as serious a
problem in our large cities as crime itself. Many people are
afraid to leave their houses after dark, and the former
American institution of the evening stroll is a thing of the
past for millions.*

*The crime rate in urban areas is growing more rapidly
(although the actual crime rate is controversial, with many
observers maintaining that the rate is rising rapidly only
because more crimes are being reported) than the general
population by a wide margin. In recent years considerable
speculation as to the causes of this increase have been
put forth. Since we live in an era of rapid social change, it*

has been argued that crime is simply a by-product of this phenomenon, one that we will have to learn to live with. With the change in America from a rural to an urban civilization, the pressures of rapid change tend to be exaggerated even further. It is necessary, therefore, to understand crime from a macrocosmic perspective, since it is larger social forces and not local conditions which are producing the dynamics which create criminal activity.

However, crime is not simply a social problem—it is also a political issue. "Law and order" has become a battle cry for two groups—those who are genuinely concerned about crime and criminal justice and those who are using this slogan as a cover for race hatred and who are reacting against what they feel is a loss of traditional national and family values. A number of prominent political figures, especially on the local level, have successfully achieved positions of power in cities like Newark, New Jersey, and Philadelphia through the use of the "safe streets" issue. It remains to be seen if street crime can be used successfully as an issue on the national level.

While the urban dweller fears the (mostly) young mugger with his stereotypic switchblade and leather jacket, criminals also appear in more conventional attire. Members of organized crime in their business suits constitute the greatest danger to urban society both because of the amount of illegal activities they engage in and because so much of the suffering they inflict is borne by the exploited urban poor. In addition, their activities are supported and made possible because of their success in corrupting local political and police figures, a problem whose magnitude is just now becoming appreciated.

The twenty-four "Mafia families" and their more than five thousand members specialize in meeting the needs of people—their need for drugs, their need for sex, and their need for money. Their main "action" involves gambling, narcotics, and prostitution, none of which would be possible without our desires and participation.

In "Undercity" Dean Koontz gives us a glimpse in the day of an urban criminal of the future, projecting a time when most of today's crimes have been legalized. But as the author points out, there will always be human needs that require gratification and there will probably always be *organized groups and individual criminals ready and willing to serve them—for a price.*

The Undercity   Dean R. Koontz

Well, kid, it was a busy day. You might even say it was a harrowing day, and you might be tempted to think that it was somehow out of the ordinary. But you must understand, straight off, that it was perfectly normal as business days go, no better and no worse than ten thousand days before it. And if I live so long, it won't be appreciably different from any of ten thousand days to follow. Remember that. If you want to enter the family business, kid, you have to be able to cope with long strings of days like this one, calendars full of them.

Once, when the cities weren't a tenth as large as they are now, when a man might travel and might have business contacts throughout the world, we were called The Underworld, and we were envied and feared. We are still envied and feared, but now we're called The Undercity, because that is the world to us, and more than we can rightly handle anyway. I, for one, would be happy to roll things back, to break down these hundred-story megalopolises and live in a time where we could call ourselves a part of The Underworld, because things were a hell of a lot easier then for our type. Just consider . . .

Nearly all forms of gambling were illegal back then. An enterprising young man could step in, buck the law, and clean up a tidy sum with a minimal financial outlay and with almost no personal risk at all. Cops and judges were on the take; clandestine casinos, street games and storefront betting shops thrived. No longer. They legalized it, and they gave us bank clerks for casino managers, CPA's instead of bouncers. They made gambling respectable—and boring.

Drugs were illegal then, too. Grass, hash, skag, coke, speed . . . God, an enterprising young kid like yourself could make a fortune in a year. But now grass and hash are traded on the open market, and all the harder drugs are available to all the loonies who will sign a health waiver and buy them from the government. Where's the thrill now? Gone. And where's the profit? Gone, too.

Sex. Oh, kid, the money to be made on sex, back then. It was *all* illegal: prostitution, dirty movies, picture postcards, erotic dancing, adultery, you name it! Now the government licenses the brothels, both male and female, and the wife or husband without a lover on the side is considered a throwback. Is this any way to make a buck?

Hell, kid, even murder was illegal in those days, and a man could buy the big trip for wiping someone off the slate. As you know, some folks never can seem to learn the niceties of civilized life—their manners are atrocious, their business methods downright devious, their insults unnecessarily public and demeaning—and these people need to be eliminated from the social sphere. Now we have the code duello, through which a man can settle his grudges and satisfy his honor, all legally. The once-lucrative career as a hired assassin has gone the way of the five-dollar streetwalker.

Now, kid, you have got to hustle all day, every day, if you want to survive in this business. You've got to be resourceful, clever and forward-thinking if you expect to meet the competition. Let me tell you how the day went, because it was a day like all days . . .

I bolted down a breakfast of protein paste and cafa, then met Lew Boldoni on the fifth subbasement level in Wing-L, where only the repair robots go. Boldoni was waiting on the robotwalk beside the beltway, carrying his tool satchel, watching the cartons of perishables move past him.

"On time," he said.

I said, "As usual." Time is money; cliché but true.

We removed the access plate to the beltway workings, went down under the robotwalk. In less than five minutes, we were directly beneath the big belt, barely able to shout above the roar, buffeted by the wind of its continuous passage. Together, we opened one of the hydraulic lines and let the lubricant spew out over the traffic computer terminal, where it was sure to seep through and do some damage. Before a fire could start, we were out of there, up on the sidewalk again, putting the access plate back where it belonged. That done, just as the alarms were beginning to clang, we went in different directions.

We both had other business.

This bit of sabotage wouldn't pay off until much later in the day.

At 9:30 in the morning, right on time, I met a young couple—Gene and Miriam Potemkin—in a public hydroponics park on the eighty-third level, in that neighborhood they call Chelsea. She was twenty-one and a looker, bright and curious and unhappy. He was a year older than she was, but that was the only real difference between them. They sat on a bench by an artificial waterfall, both of them leaning forward as I approached, both with their hands folded in their laps, more like sister and brother than like wife and husband.

"Did you bring it?" he asked.

I removed a sealed envelope from my pocket, popped the seal and let them see the map inside, though I was careful not to let them handle it just then. I said, "And you?"

She lifted a small plastic satchel from the ground beside her and took another sealed envelope from it, reluctantly handed it over.

I opened it, counted the money, nodded, tucked the envelope into my pocket and gave them the map.

"Wait a minute, here!" Mr. Potemkin said. "According to this damn map, we'll be going out through the sewer! You know that's not possible. Sewage is pumped at pressure, and there's no way to survive in the system."

"True enough," I said. "But if you'll look closely at the map, you'll see that the sewage line is encased into a larger pipe, from which repairs can be made to the system. This larger pipe is everywhere twenty feet in diameter, sometimes as much as thirty, and is always enough larger than the sewage pipe itself to give you adequate crawl space."

"I don't know," he said. "It doesn't look easy . . ."

"No way out of the city is easy, for God's sake!" I told him. "Look, Potemkin, the city fathers say that the open land, beyond the cities, is unlivable. It's full of poisoned air, poisoned water, plague, and hostile plant and animal life. That's why the air freight exits are the only ones that are maintained, and that's why they're so carefully supervised. City law forbids anyone to leave the city for fear they'll return bearing one of the plagues from Outside. Now, con sidering all of this, could you reasonably expect me to provide you with an easy way out?"

"I suppose not."

"And that's damn straight."

Ms. Potemkin said, "It's really not like that Outside, is it? The stories of plagues, poisoned air and water, monsters— all of that's just so much bunk."

"I wouldn't know," I said.

"But you must know!"

"Oh?"

"You've shown us the way out," she said. "You must have seen what's beyond the city."

"I'm afraid not," I said. "I employ engineers, specialists, who work from diagrams and blueprints. None of my people would consider leaving the city; we've got too much going for us here."

"But," she insisted, "by sending us, you're showing your distrust of the old stories about the Outside."

"Not at all," I explained. "Once you've gone, my men will seal off this escape route so you can't come back that way, just in case you might bring a plague with you."

"And you won't sell it again?"

"No. We'll find other ways out. There are millions of them."

They looked at each other, unsure of themselves now.

I said, "Look, you haven't committed the map to memory. If you want, I can take it back and return half your money."

"No," he said.

She said, "We've made up our minds. We need open land, something more than layer on layer of enclosed streets and corridors."

"Suit yourself," I said. "And good luck."

I shook their hands and got the hell out of there; things to do, things to do . . .

Moving like a maintenance robot on an emergency call, I dropped down to the subbasements again, to the garbage monitoring decks, where I met with the day-shift manager, K. O. Wilson. We shook hands at precisely 10:20, five minutes behind schedule, and we went into the retrieval chamber, where he had the first two hours of discoveries laid out in neat, clean order.

Kid, I don't think I've ever talked about this angle of the family business before, because I'm not that proud of it. It's the cheapest form of scavenging, no matter how lucrative it is. And it *is* lucrative. You see, the main pipes of the garbage shuttle system are monitored electronically and filtered to remove any articles of value that might otherwise be funneled into the main sewage lines and pumped out of the city. I've got K. O. Wilson, of the first shift, and Marty Linnert, of the second shift, on my payroll. They see to it that I have time to look over the day's findings before they're catalogued and sent up to the city's lost-and-found bureau. Before you think too badly of your old man, consider that 20 per cent of the family's gross comes from the garbage operation.

"Six valuable rings, a dozen good watches, what appears to be one folder of a top-quality coin collection, a diamond tiara, and a mess of other junk," Wilson told me, pointing to the good items, which he had set aside for me.

I ignored the watches, took two of the rings, the tiara and the damp folder full of old coins. "Nothing else?"

"A corpse," he said. "That'll interest the cops. I put it on ice until you could get in and check over your stuff first."

"A murder?" I asked.

"Yeah."

Kid, the code duello hasn't solved everything. There are still those who are afraid to fight, who prefer to sneak about and repay their enemies illegally. And there are also those who aren't satisfied with taking economic and emotional revenge from those not eligible for the duels; they insist on blood, and they have it. Eventually, the law has them. We're not involved with people of this sort, but you should know the kind of scum that the city still supports.

I told Wilson, "I'll send a man around after noon to see what else you've got by then."

Ten minutes later, at 10:53, I walked into the offices of Boldoni and Gia Cybernetic Repairs, on the ninety-second floor, Wing-B, where I acted very shocked about the break-down in the beltway system.

"City Engineer Willis left an urgent message for you," my secretary said. She handed it to me and said, "It's a beltway carrying perishables in the fifth subbasement."

"Is Mr. Boldoni there?" I asked.

"He accompanied the first repair team," she said.

"Call down and tell Willis I'm on my way."

I used the express drop and almost lost my protein paste and cafa—any inconvenience for a good customer, and the city is the best customer that Boldoni and Gia Cybernetic Repairs has on its list.

Willis was waiting for me by the beltway. He's a small man with very black hair and very dark eyes and a way of moving that makes you think of a maintenance robot with a short between his shoulder blades. He scuttled toward me and said, "What a mess!"

"Tell me," I said.

"The main hydraulic line broke over the traffic computer terminal and a fire started in the works."

"That doesn't sound so bad," I said.

He wiped his small face with one large hand and said, "It wouldn't have been if it had stopped there. We've got the fire out already. The only trouble is that the lubricant has run back the lines into the main traffic computer and the damn thing won't shut down. I've got perishables moving up out of the subterranean coolers, and no way to move them or stop them. They're piling up on me fast, Mr. Gia. I have to have this beltway moving inside the hour or the losses are going to be staggering."

"We'll do the job," I assured him.

"I went out on the limb, calling you before you could deliver a quick computerized estimate. But I knew you people were the fastest, and I needed someone who could be here immediately."

"Don't you worry about it," I told him. "Whatever the B & G computer estimates we'll shave by ten per cent to keep your bosses happy."

Willis was ecstatic, thanking me again and again. He didn't understand that the Boldoni and Gia house computer always estimated an additional and quite illegal 15 per cent surprofit, more than negating the 10 per cent discount I'd given him.

While he was still thanking me, Lew Boldoni came up from the access tunnel, smeared with lubricant, looking harried and nervous and exhausted. Lew is an excellent actor, and that another qualification for success in this business.

"How is it down there?" I asked.

"Bad," Boldoni said.

Willis groaned.

Boldoni said, "But we're winning it."

"How long?" I asked.

"We'll have the beltway moving in an hour, with a jury-rigged system, and then we can take our time with the permanent repairs."

Willis groaned again, differently this time: in happiness.

I said, "Mr. Boldoni has everything in control, Mr. Willis. I'm sure that you'll be in business as usual shortly. Now, if you'll excuse me, I've got some other urgent business to attend to."

I went up in the express elevator, which was worse than coming down, since my stomach seemed to reach the fifty-ninth floor seconds before the rest of me.

I boarded a horizontal beltway and rode twelve miles east the last six down Y-Wing. At 11:40, ten minutes behind schedule, I entered an office in the Chesterfield District where a nonexistent Mr. Lincoln Pliney supposedly did business. There, I locked the outer door, apologized for my tardiness to the two people waiting in the reception area, then led them into Lincoln Pliney's private office. I locked that door too, went to the desk, checked out my bug-detecting equipment, made sure the room hadn't been tapped, then sat down behind my desk, offered the customers a drink, poured, sat back and introduced myself under a false name.

My visitors were Arthur Coleman, a rather successful industrialist with offices on the hundredth level, and Eileen Romaine, a lovely girl, fifteen years Coleman's junior. We had all come together in order to negotiate a marriage between Coleman and Romaine, an illegal marriage.

"Tell me, Mr. Coleman," I said, "just why you wish to risk the fines and prison sentences involved with this violation of the Equal Rights Act?"

He squirmed a bit and said, "Do you have to put it that way?"

I said, "I believe a customer must know the consequences before he can be fairly expected to enter a deal like this."

"Okay," he said. "Well, I've been married four times under the standard city contract, and all four marriages have terminated in divorce at my instigation. I'm a very unhappy man, sir. I've got this . . . well, perversion that dominates the course of my private life. I need a wife who . . . who is not my equal, who is subservient, who plays a dated role as nothing more than my bedmate and my housekeeper. I want to dominate any marital situation that I enter."

I said, "Conscious male chauvinism is a punishable crime."

"As I'm aware."

"Have you seen a robopsych?" I asked. "Perhaps one of those could cure you of your malady."

"I'm sure it could," he said. "But you see, I don't really want to be cured. I *like* myself the way I am. I *like* the idea of a woman waiting on me and making her own life conditioned to mine."

"And you?" I asked Eileen.

She nodded, an odd light in her eyes, and she said, "I don't like the responsibility of the standard marriage. I want a man who will put me in my place, a man I can look up to, admire, depend on."

I tell you, kid, these antiquated lusts of theirs were distasteful to me. However, I believe in rebels, both good and bad, being a rebel myself, and I was ready to help them. Both had come to me by word-of-mouth referral within the past month. I'd researched the lives of both, built up two thick dossiers, matched them, and called them here for their first and final meeting under my auspices.

"You have both paid me a finder's fee," I told them. "Now, you will have sixty days to get to know each other. At the end of that time, you will either fail to contact me about a finalization of the contract, in which case I'll know you've found each other unsuitable, or you'll come back here and set up an appointment with my robosec. If you find you like each other, it will be a simple matter to arrange an illegal marriage, without the standard city contract."

Coleman wasn't satisfied with that. He said, "Just how will you pull this off, Mr. Pliney?"

"The first step, of course, is to have Eileen certified dead and disposed of. My people will falsify a death report and have it run through the city records. This may sound like an incredible feat to you; it is nevertheless possible. Once Eileen Romaine has ceased to exist, we will create a false persona in the name of Eileen Coleman. She will be identified as your sister; an entire series of life records will be planted in the computers to solidify her false identity. She can, naturally, then come to live with you, without the city records people realizing that there is anything sexual in your cohabitation."

"If you can do it," Coleman said, "you're a genius."

"No, just clever," I said. "And I will do it. In fact, on any date you pick, I'll have a man at your apartment to officiate at a clandestine wedding using the ancient, male chauvinist rituals."

"There will be no psycheprobes, as there are in other marriages?" she asked.

"Of course not," I said. "The city will have no reason to psycheprobe you under the Equal Rights Act because you won't, so far as the city is concerned, be married at all."

At that point, she burst into tears and said, "Mr. Pliney, you are the first person, outside of Arthur here, who's ever understood me."

I set her straight on that, kid, believe me. I said, "Lady, I don't understand you at all, but I sympathize with rebels. You're chucking out total equality and everything a normal human being should desire in return for a life-style that has long been shown to be inadequate. You're risking prison and fines for knowingly circumventing the Equal Rights Act. It's all crazy, but you've a right to be nuts."

"But if you don't understand us, not at all, why are you risking—"

"For the profit, Eileen," I said. "If this is pulled off, Mr. Coleman will owe me a tidy sum." I stood up. "Now, I must see you out. I've many, many things to do yet today."

When I was finally rid of the happy couple, I boarded an entertainment beltway into a restaurant district in Wing-P, and there I had my lunch: a fillet of reconstituted sea bass, a baked potato, strawberries from a hydroponic garden immersed in simulated cream. It was a rich lunch, but one that was easily digested.

A warning, kid: Stay away from greasy foods for lunch. In this business, your stomach can be the end of you; it curdles grease and plagues you with murderous heartburn.

By 1:30, I was back on the street. I phoned in to the offices of Boldoni and Gia and learned that the beltway on the fifth subbasement level was rolling again, though Boldoni now estimated permanent repairs as a two- or three-day job. It seemed that one of the B & G workmen had found a second potential break in the hydraulic line just before it was ready to go. He'll get a bonus for that, however he managed it.

At 1:45, I stopped around to see K. O. Wilson again, down at the garbage monitoring decks, picked up the best part of a set of pure silver dinnerware, an antique oil lantern, and a somewhat soiled set of twentieth-century pornographic photographs, which, while no longer titillating to the modern man, are well worth a thousand duo-creds as prime, comic nostalgia. Kid, the strangest damn stuff shows up in the garbage, sometimes so strange you won't believe it. Just remember that there are thirty million people in this damn hive, and that among them they own and accidentally throw out about anything a man could hope to find.

I delivered the dinnerware, lantern and pornography to Petrone, the family fence, and then got my ass on the move. I was twenty minutes behind the day's schedule.

At 2:15, I met a man named Talmadge at a sleazy little drug bar in one of the less pleasant entertainment districts on the forty-sixth level. He was sitting at a table in a dark corner, clasping his water pipe in both hands and staring down at the mouthpiece that appeared to have fallen from his lips to the tabletop.

"Sorry I'm late," I said.

He looked up, dreamy-eyed, smiled at me more than he had to, and said, "That's all right. I'm feeling fine, just fine."

"Good for you," I said. "But are you feeling too fine to go through with this?"

"No, no!" he said. "I've waited much too long already, months and months—even years!"

"Come on, then," I said.

I took him out of the drug bar and helped him board a public beltway that took us quickly away from the entertainment zone and deep into a residential area on the same level.

Leaning close to me, in a stage whisper, as if he enjoyed the role of a conspirator, Talmadge said, "Tell me again how big the apartment is."

I looked around, saw that no one was close to us, and, knowing that he would just grow louder and more boisterous if I refused to speak of it, I said, "Three times as large as regulations permit a single man like you. It has nine rooms and two baths."

"And I don't have to share the baths?"

"Of course not."

He was ecstatic.

Now, kid, this is the racket you'll be starting out in to get some experience in the business, and you should pay especially close attention. Even when your mother was alive, we had a bigger apartment than city regulations permit; now, with your mother gone, it's *much* bigger than allowed. How was this achieved, this lavish suite? Simple. We bought up the small apartments all around this, knocked out walls, refitted and redecorated. Then, through a falsification of land records in the city real estate office, we made it look as if the outsize apartment had always been here, was a fluke in the original designs. Now, although living space is at a premium, and though the city tries to force everyone into relatively similar accommodations, the government repair robots are far too busy to have the time to section up the large apartment, throw up new walls and so forth. Instead, because this sort of thing happens so seldom, the city allows the oversize apartment to exist and merely doubles or triples the tax assessment on whoever lives there. In a city of fifteen million apartments, you can pull a hustle like this at least twice a month, without drawing undue official concern, and you can clean up a very tidy sum from rich folks who need more than the legal living space.

At 2:38, Mr. Talmadge and I arrived at the entrance to his new home, keyed it and went inside. I took him on a grand tour of the place, waited while he checked the Tri-D fakeview in all the rooms, tested the beds, flushed the toilets in both johns, and finally paid me the money yet outstanding on our contract. In return, I gave him his ownership papers, copies of the falsified real estate claims, and his first tax assessment.

At 3:00, half an hour behind schedule, I got out of there. On my way up to the offices of Boldoni and Gia, in the standard elevator, I had time to catch a news flash on the comscreen, and it was such bad news that it shattered the hell out of my schedule. You heard about it. Ms. and Mr. Potemkin, my first clients of the day, were apprehended in their attempt to sneak out of the city through the sewage service pipes. They accidentally ran into a crew of maintenance robots who gave pursuit. They'd only just then been brought to city police headquarters, but they wouldn't need long to fold up under a stiff interrogation.

I canceled my original destination on the elevator board,

punched out the twenty-sixth level and dropped down in agonizingly slow motion, wishing to hell I'd used the express drop.

At 3:11, I rode by the offices of Cargill Marriage Counseling, which was the front I used for selling routes out of the city to people like the Potemkins. The place didn't seem to be under surveillance, so I came back on another beltway, opened up, went inside and set to work. I opened the safe, took out what creds I had bundled there, stuffed half a dozen different maps in my pockets, looked around to be sure I'd not left anything of value behind, then set fire to the place and beat it out of there. I had always used the name Cargill in that racket, and I'd always worn transparent plastic finger tip shields to keep from leaving prints; however, one can never be too careful, kid.

At 3:47, I rode back upstairs to the offices of Boldoni and Gia, checked on the beltway repair job with Lew, who had returned to the office. It was going well; the profit would keep Boldoni and Gia in the black; we're always in the black; we see to that.

I sent a man down to seek K. O. Wilson before shifts changed, then dialed the number for Mr. Lincoln Pliney (who is me, you recall), on the fifty-ninth floor in the Chesterfield District. The robosec answered on a cut-in, and I asked for messages.

In a metallic voice, the robosec said, "Mr. Arthur Coleman just stopped in and asked for an appointment, sir."

"Coleman? I just talked to him this morning."

"Yes, sir. But he left a number for you."

I took the number, hung up, dialed Coleman and said hello and identified myself to him.

He said, "Eileen and I want to go through with the deal."

"You've just met each other," I said.

"I know, but I think we're perfect for each other."

I said, "What does Eileen think?"

"The same as I do, of course."

"In one afternoon, you can't learn enough about each other—"

Coleman said, "It's true love."

I said, "Well, it's obviously true *something*."

"We'd like to finalize things tonight."

"Impossible."

"Then we'll go somewhere else."

"To whom?"

"We'll find someone," he said.

I said, "You'll find some incompetent criminal hack who'll botch the falsification of Eileen's death certificate, and in the end you'll have to tell the police about me."

He didn't respond.

"Oh, hell!" I snapped. "Meet me in my Chesterfield District office in half an hour, with Eileen."

I hung up.

I'd intended to see a man who wanted to purchase a falsified Neutral Status Pass to keep him safe from duel challenges. See, kid, there are a lot of people who are healthy enough to have to go armed but who want to avoid having to accept challenges. The government has no sympathy with them and forces them to comply with the system. I'm always ready, however, to give them a paper disability to keep them whole and sane. I sympathize with rebels, like I said. And there's a profit in it, too. Anyway, I had to call the guy who wanted the Neutral Status Pass and postpone our appointment until tomorrow.

Then I ran off to tie the nuptial knots for Coleman and his lady.

You see, now, why I was late getting home. Scare you? I didn't think it would. Tomorrow, you can come along with me, watch me work, pick up some tips about the business. You're fifteen, plenty old enough to learn. I tell you, kid, you're going to be a natural for this business. I wish your mother could have lived to see what kind of daughter she brought into this world.

Well, kid, you better turn in. It's going to be a busy day.

Rivers of Asphalt,
Oceans of Concrete:
Transportation Problems

*There is presently one car for every two people in the
United States. The number of automobiles has increased
dramatically in the twentieth century, due to the development
of production-line facilities and the incredible demand for
them shown by the public. More than eighty percent of
American families own a car, and a quarter of these own
more than one. These vehicles travel over three million
miles of surfaced roads, highways, and expressways—a
distance equivalent to many dozens of trips around the world.*

*With this enormous automobile infrastructure has come
a number of problems—indeed, the car has been blamed for
a wide variety of social and economic ills. For example,
it is often claimed that the automobile has destroyed the
American city because it made possible the move to the
suburbs. The car is also held responsible for two types of
pollution—visual, because of the tremendous amount of
concrete and asphalt required for roads, and the ugliness of
parking facilities, gas stations, and abandoned cars—and
air pollution, since autos are a prime cause of the choking
conditions in our major cities. Finally, the damage done
to the human mind and nervous system by the noise,
congestion, and tensions brought about by the mass use of
cars is beyond calculation.*

*However, the development and spread of the automobile
has some positive features. More than any other
technological development, the car has created options for
people by providing a degree of freedom from confinement
at home. The psychological benefits which come from
having the ability to pick up and get away from problems
provides a modern parallel to the safety valve of the frontier
in early America. The automobile is almost a mystical
thing to many people, epitomized in song by Phil Ochs'*

refrain, "My kingdom for a car." Whether this is healthy or not is a serious question.

In an urban setting the problem of transportation takes on awesome dimensions. Almost all major American cities were designed before the widespread use of cars. They were not laid out to accommodate the automobile and the network of highways that cars and their users demand. Up until now, instead of developing alternate forms of mass transportation, the response to this problem has been more roads and more parking lots. What is needed for people is efficient, fast, and cheap transportation that is also pollution-free. This does not mean that the car should disappear, but rather that a balanced system of auto, rail, and bus service should be developed. Until now the alternate forms have not been able to compete with the automobile for the patronage of travelers.

It has taken the energy crisis to force a reassessment of the automobile and its role in American life. Long lines at gas stations and car pools have resulted in renewed interest in mass transportation. One of the results of this attention has been an emphasis on the plight of the non-driver in our cities, especially the elderly, the handicapped, and those families with more than one working member but only one car. This situation constitutes a subtle but real form of discrimination, forcing the carless to spend many more hours traveling to and from work than their more "fortunate" coworkers.

The solutions to our transportation problems, like the solutions to all urban problems, will be costly. Science fiction has suggested alternative forms of mass transportation ranging from teleportation to the moving sidewalks of Robert Heinlein's "The Roads Must Roll."

The stories in this section, however, focus not upon solutions; but upon the problems themselves, and do so in a way that only the science fiction short story can. "Traffic Problem" by William Earls presents an urban future in which the automobile is the only major method of transportation in New York. The consequences of this fact may at first appear fanciful, but on closer examination and reflection we can see that the author has taken signs and trends from the present and logically extrapolated them into the future. This powerful story is also impressive for its

skillful weaving of the impact of technology upon the
social and political power structures of an urban center.

"Gas Mask" by James D. Houston is also logical
extrapolation, this time on the environmental impact of a
transportation system still dependent upon the automobile.
It should be required reading for all those who are in a
position to make decisions in the transportation area, and
should be read while sitting in an automobile stuck in
the Holland Tunnel with the windows open.

Gas Mask   James D. Houston

Charlie Bates didn't mind the freeways much. As he often
told his wife when he arrived home from work, he could
take them or leave them alone. He listed freeways among
those curious obstacle-conveniences with which the world
seemed so unavoidably cluttered. Charlie was neither surprised nor dismayed, then, when one summer afternoon
about five-thirty the eight lanes of traffic around him slowed
to a creep and finally to a standstill.

He grew uneasy only when movement resumed half an
hour later. His engine was off; the car was in gear; yet it
moved forward slowly, as if another car were pushing.
Charlie turned around, but the driver behind was turned,
too, and the driver beyond him. All the drivers in all the
lanes were turned to see who was pushing. Charlie heard
his license plate crinkle. He opened his door and stood on
the sill.

He was on a high, curving overpass that looked down on a
lower overpass and farther down onto a 12-lane straightaway
leading to the city's center. As far as Charlie could see in any
direction cars were jammed end to end, lane to lane, and
nothing moved. The pushing had stopped. Evidently there
was nowhere else to push.

He looked into the cars near him. The drivers leaned a
little with the curve's sloping bank. Nobody seemed disturbed.
They waited quietly. All the engines were off now. Below
him the lower levels waited, too—thousands of cars and not

a sound, no horns, no one yelling. At first the silence bothered Charlie, frightened him. He decided, however, that it really was the only civilized way to behave. "No use getting worked up," he thought. He climbed back in and closed the door as softly as he could.

As Charlie got used to the silence, he found it actually restful. Another hour passed. Then a helicopter flew over, and a loudspeaker announced, "May I have your attention, please. You are part of a citywide traffic deadlock. It will take at least 24 hours to clear. You have the choice of remaining overnight or leaving your car on the freeway. The city will provide police protection through the crisis."

The 'copter boomed its message about every 50 yards. A heavy murmur followed it down the freeway. The driver next to Charlie leaned out his window.

"Are they nuts?"

Charlie looked at him.

"They must be nuts. Twenty-four hours to clear a goddamn traffic jam."

Charlie shook his head, sharing the man's bafflement.

"Probably a pile-up further down," the man said. "I've seen 'em before. Never takes over an hour or two. I don't know about you, but I'm stickin' it out. If they think I'm gonna leave my goddamn Valiant out here on the freeway, they're all wet."

His name was Arvin Bainbridge. While two more hours passed, he and Charlie chatted about traffic and the world. It was getting dark when Charlie decided he at least ought to phone his wife. Arvin thought the jam would break any minute, so Charlie waited a while longer. Nothing happened.

Finally Charlie climbed out, intending to find a phone booth. He realized, however, that in order to reach the ground he'd have to hike a couple of miles to an exit. Luckily Arvin had a tow rope in the trunk. Charlie tied it to the railing, waved his thanks, swung over the side and hand-over-handed to the second level. From there he slid out onto a high tree limb and shinnied to the ground.

Gazing up at the freeway's massive concrete underside and at Arvin's rope dangling far above him, Charlie knew he'd never climb back. "What the hell," he said to himself, "I might as well go home. The cops'll be around to watch things. Besides, the car's all paid for." He began searching for a bus or a cab. But everything, it seemed, was tied up in the jam.

In a bar where he stopped for a beer to cool off, he learned that every exit, every approach, every lane in the city's complex freeway system was jammed. "And ya know, it's funny," the bartender told him, "there wasn't a single accident. It all happened so gradual, they say. Things slowed down little by little, and the whole town stopped just about at once. Some guys didn't even use their brakes. Just went from one mile an hour to a dead stop."

It took Charlie two hours to walk home. When he arrived his wife, Fay, was frantic.

"Why didn't you call?"

"I started to, honey. . ."

"And what happened to your pants?"

He glanced sheepishly at his torn sharkskin slacks. "I was shinnying down this tree. I guess somebody left a nail in it."

"For God's sake, Charlie, this is no time to kid. If you knew how worried . . ."

"I'm not kidding. You're lucky I got down at all. Some of the guys are still up there—the older guys—the fat ones—couldn't get over the rails. And a lotta guys wouldn't leave. Probably be out all night."

She looked ready to cry, and she stared as if he were insane. "Charlie, please . . ." He put an arm around her and drew her close. "What happened Charlie? Where have you been?"

He guided her to the sofa and they sat down. His hairy knee stuck up through the torn cloth. "I thought you'd see it on TV or something."

"See *what* on TV?"

While Fay sobbed and sniffled, he told her the whole story. By the time he finished she was sitting up straight and glaring at him.

"Charlie Bates, do you mean you just left our car out on the freeway?"

"What else could I do, honey? I couldn't stay up there all night—not in a Volkswagen. I'd catch cold. I'd be all cramped up."

"You could've got into somebody else's car. This Arvin fellow would have let you. Somebody with a heater or a big back seat or something."

"You can't just barge into somebody else's car and stay overnight, honey. Anyway, I wanted to phone. That's why I came down in the first place."

She rubbed his bare knee. "Oh, Charlie." Leaning against him again she said, "At least nothing happened to *you*. That's the most important thing."

She snuggled next to him, and they were quiet, until she said, "But Charlie, what'll we do?"

"About what?"

"About the car."

"Wait it out, I guess. Wait till tomorrow at least, until they break the jam. Then get back out there. Of course, that won't be as easy as it sounds. Probably have to get over to the nearest approach and hike in—maybe two, three miles of freeway, up the center strip, I suppose—plus getting to the approach itself, which is right in the middle of town. Maybe I can borrow a bike. I don't know quite how we'll . . ."

"Say. Don and Louise have a two-seater. Maybe we can borrow that and both go."

"Maybe," Charlie said wearily. "Let's worry about that tomorrow. I'm bushed."

The next morning Charlie borrowed the big two-seater from Don and Louise, Fay packed a lunch, and they pedaled across the city, figuring to get there fairly early, to be on hand when their car was free, although an early solution was no longer likely. The morning news predicted another 36 hours before traffic would be moving. The jam now included not only the freeways, but all main streets and key intersections, where buses, streetcars and trucks were still entangled. It even extended beyond the city. Police had tried to block incoming traffic, but it was impossible. All highways transversed the city or its net of suburbs. Impatient motorists, discrediting police reports, finally broke the road blocks, and the confusion was extending in all directions by hundreds of cars an hour.

Charlie and Fay smugly bypassed all that, following a devious route of unblocked streets that he mapped out after watching the news on TV. They pedaled most of the morning. At last they mounted a high bluff and decided to ride an elevator to the roof of an apartment building that rose above the freeway where their car was parked. Charlie brought along a pair of Navy binoculars. From that vantage point they ate lunch and surveyed the curving rows of silent cars.

"Can you see ours, Charlie?"

"Yeah. She looks okay. A little squeezed up, but okay."

"Lemme see."

"Here."

"Gee," Fay said. "Some of those poor men are still sitting out there. Don't you know their wives are worried."

"Their wives probably heard the news. Everybody must know by now."

"Still worried though, I'll bet." She hugged Charlie and pecked his cheek. "I'm so glad you came home." Then, peering again, "I'll bet those men are hungry. Maybe we should take them some sandwiches."

"Take a lot of sandwiches to feed everybody stuck on the freeway, honey."

"I mean for the men right around our car. That Arvin, for instance. You know . . . your friends, sort of."

"I don't really know them that well, Fay."

"Well, we ought to do something."

"Red Cross is probably out," Charlie said. "Isn't that a cross on that helicopter way down there by the city hall? Here, gimme the glasses."

"I'll be darned," Fay said. "It is. They're dropping little packages."

"Here. Lemme see. Yeah. Yeah, that's just what they're doing. Guys are standing on the roofs of their cars, waving. I guess it's been a pretty tough night."

"The poor dears."

Charlie munched a tuna sandwich and scanned the city like a skipper. After a few moments Fay pointed. "Hey look, Charlie. Over that way. A couple more helicopters."

"Where? Down there? Oh yeah. Couple of military birds, looks like. I guess the Army's out too."

"What're they doing—lifting out one of the cars?"

"No, not a car. It looks like a long, narrow crate. And they're not lifting it, they're lowering it endways. A couple of guys in overalls are down below waiting for it. There. It's down. They're anchoring it to the center strip. Wait a minute. It's not a crate. One of the guys in overalls just opened a door on the front of it, and he's stepping inside. Hey. People are jumping out of their cars and running down the center strip. They're running from everywhere, climbing over hoods. Somebody just knocked over the guy in overalls. I think there's gonna be a fight. They're really crowding around that door and pushing . . . No . . . I think it's gonna be okay. The guy inside just came out, and he's tacking up a sign over the door. All the men are starting to walk away. The women are lining up along the center strip now."

"The dears."

"A woman just opened the door and stepped inside."

"Oh, Charlie, I'm so glad you came home."

"Me too."

From the rooftop they could hear the police helicopter's periodic messages. By the end of the first day, predictions for clearing the jam were at least two, perhaps three more days. Knowing they should be on hand whenever it broke, yet weary at the very thought of pedaling across the city twice each day to their vantage point and home again, they decided to rent an apartment in the building below them. Fortunately one was available on the top floor, facing the freeway. They moved in that evening, although they had little to move but the binoculars and a thermos. They agreed that Charlie would pedal home the next day to pick up a few necessities, while Fay kept an eye on the car.

The plan worked marvelously. Once situated, they set up a rotation watch—four hours on, four hours off. Charlie figured he could reach the car from the apartment in half an hour if things looked ready to break. He figured he'd have that much warning, by listening to helicopter messages, and watching TV and frequently checking the progress downtown where the cranes worked. Through the binoculars he watched the great jaws lift out cars, van and buses and drop them over the sides of the freeway. Things would loosen up down there first, he figured, giving him time to bicycle six blocks to the pine tree a mile below his car. Scaling the tree he could reach the top of a 15-foot-high concrete retaining wall and drop to the freeway. From there it was an easy jog up the center strip and around the sloping cloverleaf curve to the overpass.

To be safe Charlie made dry runs over the course a few times each day—down the elevator, onto his bike, up the tree, over the wall, along the freeway, to his car. He'd switch on the engine and warm it for a few minutes, then strol

back, waving to waiting motorists who watched his passage
with mixed admiration, envy and disbelief. By the third day
the men were stubble-faced, sullen, dark-eyed from fitful
sleeping. The women were disheveled, pasty-faced, most of
them staring blankly through windshields at nothing. Charlie
felt he ought to do something. Sometimes he squatted on
the center strip to talk to the man who'd lent him the tow
rope.

"How's it going, Arv?"

" 'Bout the same, Charlie."

"Pretty hot out here today, huh?"

" 'Bout like it's been, Charlie. Gettin' used to it, I guess.
You probably feel it more than I do. That's a long pull."

"Not so bad anymore. The old legs are shaping up."

"How's your time?"

"Twenty-eight, ten, today."

"Cuttin' it down, hey boy."

"Poco a poco," Charlie said. *"Poco a poco.* It's the elevator
that really holds me back though. Slowest elevator I've ever
seen."

"You ever thought of waiting down on the sidewalk someplace? The wife could maybe signal out the window when the
time comes."

"Say . . ."

"It came to me yesterday," Arv said, "but I figured you'd
thought of it."

"Never entered my head. That's a great idea, Arv." Charlie
paused. "I've been meaning to ask you," he went on. "Why
don't you come up to the apartment to meet Fay? I've told
her about you. You'd like her, I know. We could have a
couple of drinks and just relax for a while."

"Well . . . that's real nice of you, Charlie. But . . . I'm
not sure. The trouble is, you never know when the thing's
gonna break loose."

"I've got that two-seater, Arv. If anything happens, we can
pedal back over here in no time. Cuttin' it down every trip,
ya know. C'mon. It'd be good for you to get away."

"I'd like to, Charlie, I really would. But . . . to be honest,
I haven't had this car very long. I'm still making payments,
and . . . well, I just feel like I ought to stick pretty close
to it."

"I know how you feel, Arv. In a way I don't blame you.

I get a little jumpy myself—especially at night when I can't see much. But look, if you change your mind, I'll be back this afternoon."

"Thanks, Charlie."

"See ya later, Arv. And thanks for that idea."

"My pleasure, Charlie. Hate to have you miss your car when the action starts."

Taking Arvin's advice, Charlie spent most of each day sitting on a bus-stop bench across the street from the apartment house.

At last, on the afternoon of the sixth day after traffic stopped, Fay's white handkerchief appeared in the 12th-floor window. Charlie's bike stood before him in the gutter. He mounted it over the back wheel, like a pony-express rider. In a moment he was off and pedaling hard for the pine tree.

From blocks away he could hear the now unfamiliar roar of a thousand engines. As he gained the top of the concrete wall and poised ready to drop, a cloud of exhaust smoke swirled up and blinded him. It stung his eyes. He began to cough. He dropped anyway, sure of the route he must follow, even if he couldn't see. Gasping and wiping his eyes he clambered over hoods toward the center strip. The smoke didn't abate. It puffed and spurted, choking Charlie. Every driver was gunning his engine, warming up for take-off. In a panic that he'd miss his car, that it would be carried away in the advancing stream, Charlie stumbled blindly upward, deafened by the sputtering thunder of long-cold cylinders, nauseated by fumes, confused by the semidarkness of gray, encompassing billows.

The cars disappeared. It seemed he staggered through the smoke for hours. He nearly forgot why he was there, until he heard a yell behind him: "Hey Charlie! Where ya goin'?"

"That you, Arv?"

"Yeah. You nearly passed your car."

"This damn smoke."

"Helluva thing, isn't it?"

Arv was elated. Through the veil of fumes that curled up from under Arvin's car, Charlie could see a wild expectancy lighting the haggard eyes. His yellowed teeth grinned behind the beard.

"What's happening?" Charlie said, still gasping, hanging onto Arvin's aerial while his lungs convulsed.

"Looks like we're moving out. Better warm up."

"When did you get the signal?"

"No real signal," Arvin shouted, "but everybody down the line started up, so I started up. Things ought to get going anytime."

"Have you moved at all?"

"Not yet, but you better get the old engine warmed up, Charlie. We're on our way, boy! We're on our way!"

Coughing and crying Charlie staggered to his car, climbed in and started it. He accelerated a few times, then leaned forward to rest his head on the steering wheel, as nausea overcame him. The noise around him would split his ear drums, he thought. He passed out.

When he came to he was staring through the wheel at his gas gauge: nearly empty. He looked around. It seemed less noisy. The smoke had cleared a little. He could see vague outlines of cars in the next lane. None had moved. He switched off his engine. Evidently others were doing the same. The rumble of engines diminished perceptibly from moment to moment. Within minutes after he came to, it was quiet again. There was little wind. The smoke thinned slowly. Only gradually did he discern shapes around him. Behind him he saw a driver sprawled across the hood, chest heaving. In front of him a man and woman were leaning glassy-eyed against their car. And in the next lane he heard the wheezing rattle of a man retching. He turned and saw Arvin leaning out his open car door into the gutter.

The police helicopter droned toward them, hovered, sucking up smoke, and announced, "Please turn off your engines. Please turn off your engines. The deadlock will not be cleared for at least another 36 hours. You will be alerted well in advance of starting time. Please turn off your engines."

No one seemed to listen. The helicopter passed on. Charlie climbed out, still queasy but able to stand. Arvin was sitting on the edge of his seat now, bent forward with his head in his hands.

"Hey, Arv. You okay?" Charlie looked down at him for several moments before the answer came.

"Yeah, I guess so."

"False alarm, huh?"

Arv grunted.

"Looks like tomorrow might be the day, though," Charlie said.

Arv nodded, then raised his head slowly. His eyes were dark, weary, defeated. All hope had left him. Deep creases of fatigue lined his cheeks and forehead. His beard was scraggly and unkempt. He looked terribly old. His voice was hoarse and feeble as he said, "But, Charlie . . . what if it's not tomorrow? What're we gonna do, for God's sake? It's been six days."

Compassion welled up in Charlie. He said, "Look, Arv. You heard the last announcement. It'll be at least another 36 hours. Why don't you come on up to the place and lay down for awhile?"

A little light brightened Arvin's eyes. His mouth turned faintly toward a smile, as if remembering some long-gone pleasure. But he said, "I can't, Charlie." He raised his shoulders helplessly.

Charlie nodded slowly. "I know, Arv. I know." After a pause he said, "I guess I'll see you this afternoon then." He waited for Arvin's reply, but his head had fallen again into the palms of his hands, and he sat there swaying. Charlie walked away.

Most of the smoke had cleared. The heavy silence was broken occasionally by distant groans, staccato coughs. All around him, down the curve he would walk, on the other freeways that snaked so gracefully below him, in among the rows of dusty cars, he saw people sprawled, hunched, prone on the center strip, folded over fenders, hanging out windows, wheezing, staring, stunned.

He picked his way to the concrete wall, scaled it and left the devastation behind. He knew, though, he'd have to return, perhaps several times. No one could tell when it would be over. The police reports were meaningless. He returned to the apartment to console Fay, who felt guilty about sending him on a wild-goose chase. Then he pedaled downtown to a war-surplus store. His lungs still burned from the smoke. He decided to buy Arvin a gas mask and one for himself.

Traffic Problem   William Earls

Davis took the third expressway from 42nd Street to the site of the old Rockefeller Center, dropped down through the quadruple overpass and braked to a halt in the fourth level lot. He paused a moment before alighting from the car, trying to catch his breath—even in the car, with the CO filters on over-duty, the air was terrible. He donned his gas mask before he stepped into the lot, slammed the left-hand door into the unprotected door of the Cadillac parked next to him.

"Serve him right for crossing a parking line," he growled. He jumped aside quickly as a Mustang Mach V whistled past him, slammed around a corner, hurtled down the ramp to the street. He flung a curse after it.

He eased his head out between the parked cars before sprinting across the traffic lane of the parking lot to the elevator on the other side. The attendant rushed to him, tried to demand the $30 daily fee, stepped back when Davis flashed his Traffic Manager's badge at him. The attendant dropped to his knees in salute, stayed down while Davis rushed past.

His office was on the ground level of the Roads and Traffic Building and when he came off the elevator, the hall was full of dust and a jack hammer was going crazily at one end of it. The man behind it was wearing the light blue of Road Construction Unlimited. Davis remembered the spur route of the 2nd level, 57th Street West that was going through the building's corner. He hadn't expected construction to start this soon.

One wall had been ripped out of the office and the derricks were swinging the steel girders for the spur route into place. More men were driving them into the concrete of the floor, slamming them into place with magn-gun rivets. One of the drivers kept walking to the water cooler and Davis stopped him.

"That stuff is three dollars a gallon, buddy," he said.

"Road crew, Mac." The big man tried to push him aside and Davis flashed the badge.

"This is still my office," he said. He crossed to the control board, buzzed the Director.

"Davis in," he said.

I suppose the old bastard will want a report already . . .

"Right," the Director's secretary said, "I'll tell him."

Leingen waved at him from the casualty table and he trotted over, flashed the badge and Leingen nodded. He was off duty now, officially relieved—and he looked relieved.

Lucky bastard will be home in three hours—if he makes it . . .

The casualty report was horrendous, up 4.2% over the day before—with 17 dead on the United Nations area overpass alone. He dialed Road Service.

"Road," the voice on the other end said.

"Traffic Manager. Send a bird. I'm going up for a look." He checked some of the other reports—two breakdowns on the fifth level of the Tappan Zee bridge, both '79 Fords. Goddam people had no right driving two-year-old cars on the roads anyway. He buzzed Arrest Division.

"All 'seventy-nine Fords off the roads," he said.

"Rog." On the board he watched the red dots that were the Fords being shuttled off to the waiting ramps, clogging them. He flipped a visual to one of them, saw the cars jamming in and the bulldozers pushing them closer. The din around him was increasing and pieces of plasta-plaster were starting to fall from the ceiling.

"Slap up a privacy screen," he ordered. He received no answer and looked at one of the workmen driving the rivets for the girders. Jones wasn't there, he thought suddenly. Of course not, that girder is where his desk was. He'd miss Jones.

"That ain't a priority job, buddy," the workman said. "You want materials, get 'em from Construction."

Davis growled, checked his watch. 0807. Things were just moving into the third rush period. Almost on cue the building began to quiver as the lower echelon office workers hurtled by in their Lincolns and Mercuries to obscure little jobs in obscure little offices.

A short buzz came from the main phone. The Director.

"Yes, sir," Davis said.

"Davis?" the palsied voice said. *Die, you old bastard,* Davis thought. "Casualties are up all over."

"The roads are jammed, sir."

"You're Manager. Do something."

"We need more roads. Only you can authorize 'em."

"We don't have any more roads. But that traffic must move. Do what you have to." The voice went into a coughing spasm. "When you're Director, you build roads."

"Yes, sir." He punched off. All right, he'd move the traffic. Say this for the Director—he'd back a Manager all the way.

"The bird's here," the intercom said.

"Smith," Davis said. His assistant looked up from the main board. "You're in charge. I'm going up." He moved to the elevator, bounced up, flipped his telecorder to audio, caught the information as he hurtled toward the tenth floor.

"Major pileup at Statue of Liberty East," the speaker barked. "Seventeen cars and a school bus. Ambulance on the scene. Structural damage on Fifth level East, Yankee Stadium Speedway. More accidents on Staten Island One, Two, Four, Ten, Thirteen, and Twenty-Two; East Side Four, Nine, and Eleven—" Davis punched off. Matters were worse than he had thought.

On the fifth floor he changed elevators to avoid the ramp from the exact-change lane to the fourth level, zipped to the roof and the waiting helicopter.

"Fifty-car pileup on Yankee Stadium Four," the helicopter radio screamed and he punched the button to Central.

"Davis."

"Yes, sir?"

"What's the time on next of kin identification?" he asked.

"Twenty-three minutes, sir."

"Make it nineteen. Inform all units."

"Yes, sir."

"Lift off," he growled at the pilot. He threw his eyes out of focus, watching the cars hurtling by the edge of the roof.

I could reach out and touch them—*and have my arm torn off at 100 miles an hour . . .*

He coughed. He always forgot to don his gas mask for the short trip from the elevator to the bird and it always bothered his lungs.

The smog was fortunately thin this morning and he could

see the gray that was Manhattan below him. Southward he could make out the spire of the Empire State Building rising forty stories above the cloverleaf around it and beyond that the tower of the Trade Center and the great hulk of the parking lot dwarfing it.

"Hook right," he ordered the pilot, "spin down along the river."

There was a pile-up at the Pier 90 crossover and he saw a helicopter swooping down to pick up the mangled cars at the end of a magnet, swing out across the river to drop them into the New Jersey processing depot.

He buzzed the Director as he saw the wrecks piling up in front of the three big crunchers at the depot. They were hammering broken Fords and Buicks into three-foot lumps of mangled steel, spitting them onto the barges. The barges were then being towed out to Long Island Sound for the new jetport. But fast as the crunchers were, they were not fast enough. With a capacity of only 200 cars an hour apiece, they could not keep pace with the rush-hour crackups.

"Yes, Davis," the Director wheezed.

"Would you call U.S. Steel," Davis asked. "We need another cruncher."

"Well, I don't know if we really do—but I'll call."

Davis punched off angrily.

His practiced eye gauged the flow of traffic on the George and Martha Washington Bridges. The cars were eighty feet apart and he ordered a close to seventy-two, effectively increasing the capacity by ten per cent. That was almost as good as another level—but not good enough.

The traffic lane above the piers was packed and smoke from ships was rising between the two twelve-lane sections. Trucks loaded with imports paused for a moment at the top of the ramps were steam catapulted into the traffic. He saw one truck, loaded with what looked like steel safes, hit by a Cadillac, go out of control, hurtle over the edge of the roadway and fall one hundred feet—five levels—to the ground. The safes went bouncing in every direction, slamming into cars on every level. Even two hundred feet above the scene he could hear the scream of brakes and the explosions as the autos crashed and burned. He punched for Control.

"Scramble an ambulance to Pier Forty-six, all levels," he said.

He smiled. It was always good to be the first to report an accident. It showed you hadn't forgotten your training. He had reported four one morning, a record. But now there were bounties for accident reporting and it was rare when a traffic man could actually turn one in. At one time traffic accidents had been reported by the police, but now they were too busy tracking down law violators. An accident was harmful only in that it broke the normal traffic flow.

Traffic was heavy on all levels, he saw—he could actually see only three levels down and there were as many as eight below that—and the main interchange at Times Square was feeding and receiving well. The largest in Manhattan, it spanned from 42nd Street to 49th and from Fourth to Eighth Avenues. There had been protests when construction had started—mostly from movie fans and library fanatics—but now it was the finest interchange in the world, sixteen lanes wide at the 42nd Street off ramp, with twelve exact change lanes. Even the library fans were appeased, he thought: it had been his idea to move the library lions from the old site—they would have been destroyed with the rest of the building had he not spoken—to the mouth of the Grand Central speed lane to Yankee Stadium.

The helicopter banked, headed down the West Side parkway toward the Battery interchange and the Statue of Liberty crossover. It had been clever of the design engineers to use the Bedloe's Island base of the statue for the crossover base—it had saved millions over the standard practice of driving piles into the harbor water. The copper had brought a good salvage price, too.

Of course, the conservationists, the live-in-the-past-people, had objected here, too. But, as always, they were shouted down at the protest meetings. The traffic had to roll, didn't it?

Below the helicopter Manhattan was a seething mass of speeding cars—reds, blacks, blues, and this month's brilliant green against the background of concrete and asphalt. There were quick flashes of brake lights, frightened blurs as a tie rod snapped or a tire blew. Dipping wreckocopters swooped in to pluck cars and pieces of cars from the highways before the lanes jammed. The island was 200 lanes wide at the top, widened to 230 at the base with the north-south lanes over the sites of the old streets running forty feet apart, over, under, and even through the old buildings. It was the finest city in the world, made for and by automobiles. And he controlled, for eight hours a day anyway, the destiny of those automobiles. He felt the sense of power he always had here in the helicopter, swooping above the traffic. It passed quickly —it always did—and he was observing clinically, watching the flow.

"There," he said to the pilot, indicated the fifth lane on the pier route. A dull red Dodge was going sixty-five, backing up the traffic for miles. There was no room to pass, and, with the traffic boiling up out of the tunnels and bridges onto the road, a jam was inevitable. "Drop," he ordered, moved behind the persuader gunsight, lined the Dodge in the cross hairs.

He fired and watched the result. The dye marker smashed on the Dodge's hood, glowed for a moment. Warned, the driver moved to a sane 95. But the dye stayed and the driver would be picked up later in the day—the dye was impossible to remove except with Traffic-owned detergent— and sentenced. For first clogging, the fine was only $200, but for later offenses, drivers were banned from the road for five to 100 days, forced to ride the railways into town. Davis shuddered at the thought.

Battery Point and Bedloe's Island looked good and the copter heeled. He used the binoculars to check the Staten Island Freeway, saw that it was down to sixteen lanes coming into New York from the high of twenty-two. The main rush was almost over and he could start preparing for the early lunch rush.

There was still a pile up at the Trade Center. The one tower, two had been planned, was standing high above the highways around it, with the great bulk of the parking lot building rising above it, the smog line lapping at the seventy-ninth floor. He saw the red lights in the first 92 floors of the lot signifying full, knew that the remaining 40 floors would not take all of the cars still piling in from the twenty-five feeder lanes. He buzzed Control.

"Yes, sir?" the voice said.

"Davis. Get me Parks and Playgrounds."

"Parks and Playgrounds?" The voice was incredulous.

"Right." He waited and when a voice answered, spoke quickly, did his best to overpower the man on the other end.

"Traffic Manager Davis," he snapped. "I want Battery

Park cleared. I'm preparing to dump two thousand cars there in five minutes."

"You can't—"

"The hell I can't! I'm Traffic Manager. Clear the park—"

What there was left of it—the grass fighting for air against the exhaust fumes, dying in the shadow of the interchange above it, stomped to death as the millions of city dwellers flocked to the only green in eleven miles—Central Park had been a bastion for a long time but it was too open, too convenient. It was buried now under a rising parking lot and seven levels of traffic. As a concession to the live-in-the-pasters the animal cages had been placed on the parking lot roof and stayed there for two weeks until they had been hit by a drunk in a Lincoln. There had been a minor flap then with the carbon-monoxide drugged animals prowling the ramps until they had been hunted down by motorcyclists.

"What about the people?" Parks and Playgrounds asked.

"Sorry about that. They have four and a half minutes." He punched off, buzzed Beacons and Buzzers.

"Davis," he said. "Re-route Battery Five, ramps two through ten, into Battery Park."

"Right." He buzzed Lower City, ordered Wall Street closed for seven blocks. Later in the day they'd have to reroute the traffic around it. No matter, the tie-up lasted for four hours anyway.

The big pile-up, as always, was at the Empire State building where the main north-south curved twelve lanes out of the way to avoid the huge building. And, as they curved, tires skidded on the pavement, cars clawed to the side and, day after day, car after car lost control on the corner, went plunging over the side to shatter on the ramps below. It was, in many ways, the best show in town and office workers crowded the windows to watch the cars spin out of control. Today the traffic looked almost good and he clocked the pack at 110 on the corner, 115 coming out of it. Still not good enough, though—they were braking coming into the corner, losing time, and the line was thin as they came out of it. He watched a Buick skid, hit the guardrail, tip, and the driver go flying out of the convertible top, land in the level below, disappear in the traffic stream. The car rolled, plummeted from sight.

"Home," he said. The helicopter dropped him on the roof

and he gagged against the smog, trotted to the elevator, dropped. The building was shaking from the traffic noise and the hammering of rivets. He coughed on the dust.

He checked the casualty lists, initialed them. Above normal, with the Empire State section running 6.2% ahead of last week. He was listed as reporting the pier pile-up, and there was a report stating Battery Park was filled—there was also a note saying that the Director was catching hell for parking cars there. To hell with him, Davis thought. There was another complaint to his attention from Merrill Lynch, Pierce, Fenner and Agnew. Two of their board members were caught in the Wall Street jam and were late for work. He threw it into the wastebasket. Outside (inside?)—hard to say with no wall on one side of the building—the workmen were throwing up the steel plates for the ramp, stinting on the bolts to save time.

"Put the damn bolts in," Davis roared. "That thing will shake enough anyway."

The din was tremendous even now, with seven ramps of traffic passing within thirty feet. It would be worse when the spur route was finished. He hoped that they would put the wall back on the office. He buzzed Smith, asked for a readout on the Empire State complex.

"Fourteen fatalities since nine o'clock."

It was now 10:07 and the pre-lunch rush was due to start in four minutes.

"Damn Empire anyway," he said. The United Nations interchange board went red and he went to visual, saw a twelve-car pileup on the fourth level, the bodies and pieces of bodies, the cars and pieces of cars falling into the General Assembly. Damn! he could expect another angry call from the Secretary General. Damn foreigners anyway, when did they get the idea that their stupid meetings were more important than traffic?

The red phone rang—the Director—and he lifted it. "Davis."

"Everything's running higher," the Director wheezed. "What's the story?"

"Empire's the big tie-up," Davis said. "That and some construction."

"Do something. I gave you the authority."

"Get rid of Empire," Davis said. "Get another forty decks on the Trade parking lot, too."

"Can't be done." The hell it can't, Davis thought. You're just afraid of the conservationists. Coward. "Do something."

"Yes, sir." He waited until the phone clicked dead before he slammed it down. He took a deep breath of the air in the office—it was even better than smoking. Then he began to bark orders over the All Circuits channel.

"Scramble another ten wreckocopters," he snarled. With half again as many copters, wrecks would be cleared that much faster. "Cut next of kin time to fifteen minutes." He was going out on a limb there, but it would speed the processing of accidents through Brooklyn and New Jersey. Now, with the rush hour just over and another beginning, wrecks were piling up outside the receiving centers and the crunchers were idle half the time. "Up minimum speed five miles an hour." That would make it at least 100 miles an hour on every highway, 65 on the ramps. He flipped to visual, saw Beacons and Buzzers post the new speeds, saw the cars increase speed. Wrecks and Checks flashed the going aloft of the ten copters and he breathed easier, flipped to visual at Empire, saw the day's third major pile-up on the third level, cursed. He closed the 34th Street cutoff, ordered three payloaders to dump all wrecks right there, flashed a message to Identification to have a team posted. By midnight, when the traffic eased, they could begin moving the cars and bodies to New Jersey.

The red phone rang, three rings. Double urgent. He grabbed it, barked his name.

"The Director just dropped dead," a hysterical voice said. "You're acting Director."

"I'll be right there." Acting, hell. There were six hours left on his shift and he could get something done now. He turned to Smith. "You're Manager now," he said, "I just got bumped upstairs."

"Right." Smith barely looked up. "Reopen Yonkers Four, lanes one through nine," he said.

He had made the transition from assistant to Manager in an instant. Training, Davis thought.

He took the elevator to the eighth floor, the Director's office. The staff was quiet, looking down at the body on the floor. There were four boards flashing, a dozen phones ringing. Davis snapped orders quickly.

"You, you and you, answer the phones," he said. "You and you, get the boards. You, drag that body out of here. You—" he pointed at the Director's—his—secretary— "call a staff conference. Now."

He looked at the boards, checked Traffic, Beacons and Buzzers, Wrecks and Checks, Gate Receipts and Identification. Fatalities was doing extremely well—Wellborn was the new Manager here. The crunchers were doing well. Wrecks was reporting above normal pickup time.

"The Director's dead," he told the staff. "I'm new Director." They all nodded. "Most departments look pretty good," he said. He looked at Smith. "Traffic flow is lousy," he said. "Why?"

"Empire," Smith said. "We're losing twenty per cent just going around that goddamned building."

"How are your crews fixed for a major job?" Davis asked the Construction Manager.

"Okay." The Manager ticked off eleven small jobs.

"The problem is at Empire," Davis said flatly. "We can't get around the building." He looked at Construction. "Tear it down," he said. "Meeting adjourned."

Later that day he looked south from the roof. The Destruction team had the top ten floors off the Empire State Building and a corner cut of the fortieth floor with a lane of traffic whipping through it. The flow was good and he smiled. He couldn't remember doing anything so necessary before.

―――――――――――――――――――――――――――――――

The Grass Is Never Greener:
The Flight to the Suburbs

The post-World-War-II period has witnessed a great movement of peoples from the centers of American cities to outlying areas which have become known as suburbs.
This has proved to be a shift with profound social, political, and economic ramifications.

People have left the city for a wide variety of reasons. For some, the reasons were negative. The high crime rates prevalent in large American cities and the fear of racial or ethnic minorities forced many to choose flight rather than to attempt to change conditions as city residents. In addition, educational opportunities seemed to deteriorate as tensions gripped urban public schools. But the motives for leaving the city were also positive. Owning one's own home has long been an American dream, and the maple trees and picket fences were hard to find in the canyons of New York or Philadelphia. The cities (at least the largest ones) were old and their once fine mass housing had become decrepit and blighted—and the few "good neighborhoods" were priced out of the range of most people, even those with good incomes. The good life seemed to many to be everywhere but in the cities.

So for a combination of positive and negative reasons millions of families moved to the home in the suburbs and changed the way America lived. Soon, the antiquated highways and roads gave way to modern expressways which were needed to bring the millions to work—for they still worked in the city. The automobile, which was a luxury in the city, became a necessity for suburban dwellers; indeed, without the automobile the whole process could not have taken place.

As new population centers grew in the suburbs they began to attract businesses to serve them, and so the institution of the shopping center was born. It rapidly became apparent that suburbanites resisted returning to the city center for a host of activities; therefore, these services, from restaurants to branch banks, came to them. Eventually, businesses themselves began to locate outside the city, closer to where their employees and customers lived.

These developments were unfortunate for the cities because they had catastrophic economic effects. With the bulk of the affluent population gone, many cities lost the tax base for maintaining and improving municipal services, and further deterioration set in. The suburbs soon could boast higher average income levels, higher educational levels, and a higher level of "safety" than urban centers.

The city still attracted people from other areas, but they tended to be displaced farmers, poor whites, or destitute *blacks. The suburbs soon found that by joining forces in political coalitions with rural interests they could dominate the politics of many states and "rape" the cities, whose political power waned with the departure of its affluent and politically aware population. As housing prices increased in suburban areas the remaining city dwellers found themselves trapped in run-down housing and living conditions. It was not long before the level of protest reached violent levels, peaking during the mid- and late sixties in widespread disorders which were only partially racial.*

In a real sense, then, the development of the suburbs was both a cause and a result of the decay of America's cities. Whether this decay will result in death remains to be seen, but there can be little doubt that the rescue operation to save our cities is one of the greatest challenges facing us all in the years ahead.

"Gantlet" by Richard E. Peck shows us a future when we have failed to meet this challenge and our cities have become fearful places. Each day millions of people ride public mass transportation to their places of work in the downtown areas of our cities and pass through decaying, desolate areas filled with desperate human beings. Some are thankful, saying "there but for fortune go I" while others exhibit a sense of guilt. Whatever their thoughts, at least they do not have to travel this particular "gantlet" of fear and hate.

Gantlet   Richard E. Peck

Jack Brens thumbed the ID sensor and waited for the sealed car doors to open. He had stayed too long in his office, hoping to avoid any conversation with the other commuters, and had been forced to trot through the fetid station. The doors split open; he put his head in and sucked gratefully at the cool air inside, then scrubbed his moist palms along his thighs and stepped quickly into the car. Rivulets of sweat ran down the small of his back. He stretched his lips into the parody of a confident smile.

Most of the passengers sat strapped in, a few feigning sleep, others trying to concentrate on the stiff-dried facsheets which rattled in their hands. Lances of light fell diagonally through the gloom; some of the boiler plate welded over the windows had apparently cracked under the twice-daily barrage.

Brens bit the tip of his tongue to remind himself to call Co-op Maintenance when he got home. Today the train was his responsibility—one day out of one hundred; one day out of twenty work weeks. If he didn't correct the flaws he noticed, he might suffer because of them tomorrow, though the responsibility would by then have shifted to someone else. To whom? Karras. Tomorrow Karras had window seat.

Brens nodded to several of the gray-haired passengers who greeted him.

"Hey, Brens. How's it going?"

"Hello, Mr. Brens."

"Go get 'em, Jack."

He strode down the aisle through the aura of acrid fear rising from the ninety-odd men huddled in their seats. A few of the commuters had already pulled their individual smoking bells down from the overhead rack. Although the rules forbade smoking till the train got underway, Brens understood their feelings too well to make a point of it.

Only Karras sat at the front. The seats beside and behind him were empty.

"Thought you weren't coming and I might have to take her out myself," Karras said. "But my turn tomorrow."

Brens nodded and slipped into the engineer's seat. While he familiarized himself with the instrument console, he felt Karras peering avidly past him at the window. Lights in the station tunnel faded and the darkness outside made the window a temporary mirror. Brens glanced at it once to see the split image of Karras reflected in the inner and outer layers of the bulletproof glass: four bulging eyes, a pair of glistening bald scalps wobbling in and out of focus.

The start buzzer sounded.

He checked the interior mirror. Only two empty seats, at the front of course. He'd heard of no resignations from the Co-op and therefore assumed that the men who should have occupied those seats were ill; it took something serious to make a man miss his scheduled car and incur the fine of a full day's salary.

The train thrummed to life. Lights flared, the fans whined toward full thrust, and the car danced unsteadily forward as it climbed onto its cushion of air. Brens concentrated on keeping his hovering hands near the throttle override.

"You really sweat this thing, don't you?" Karras said. "Relax. You've got nothing to do but enjoy the view, unless you think you're really playing engineer."

Brens tried to ignore him. It was true that the train was almost totally automatic. Yet the man who drew window seat did have certain responsibilities, functions to perform, and no time to waste. No time until the train was safetly beyond the third circle—past Cityend, past Opensky, past Workring. And after that, an easy thirty miles home.

Brens pictured the city above them as the train bored its way through the subterranean darkness, pushing it back with a fan of brilliant light. City stretched for thirty blocks from center in this direction and then met the wall of defenses separating it from Opensky. The whole area of City was unified now, finally—buildings joined and sealed against the filth of the air outside that massive, nearly self-sufficient hive. Escalators up and down, beltways back and forth, interior temperature and pollution kept at an acceptable level—it was all rather pleasant.

It was heaven, compared to Opensky. Surrounding and continually threatening City lay the ring of Opensky and its incredible masses of people. Brens hadn't been there for years, not since driving through on his way to work had become impossibly time-consuming and dangerous. Twenty years ago he had been one of the last lucky ones, picked out by Welfare Control as "salvageable"; these days, no one left Opensky. For that matter, no one with any common sense entered.

He could vaguely recall seeing single-family dwellings there, whether his wife Hazel believed that claim or not, and more vividly the single-family room he had shared with his parents and grandfather. He could even remember the first O-peddlers to appear on Sheridan Street. Huge, brawny men with green O-tanks strapped to their backs, they joked with the clamoring children who tugged at their sleeves and tried to beg a lungful of straight O for the high it was rumored to induce. But the peddlers dealt at first only with asthmatics and early-stage emphysemics who gathered on muggy afternoons to suck their metered dollar's worth from the grimy rubber mask looped over the peddler's arm. All that was before each family had a private bubble hooked directly to the City metering system.

He had no idea what life in Opensky was like now, except what he could gather from the statistics that crossed his desk in Welfare Control. Those figures meant little enough: so many schools to maintain, dole centers to keep stocked and guarded, restraint aides needed for various playgrounds he merely converted City budget figures to percentages corresponding to the requests of fieldmen in Opensky. And he hadn't spoken to a fieldman in nearly a year. But he assumed it couldn't be pleasant there. Welfare Control had recently disbanded and reassigned to wall duty all Riot Suppression teams; the object now was not to suppress, but to contain. What went on in Opensky was the skyers' own business, so long as they didn't try to enter City.

So. Six miles through Opensky to Workring, three miles of Workring itself, where the skyers kept the furnaces bellowing and City industry alive. But that part of the trip wouldn't be too bad. Only responsible skyers were allowed to enter Workring, and most stuck to their jobs for fear of having their thumbprints erased from the sensors at each Opensky exit gate. Such strict control had seemed harsh, at first, but Brens now knew it to be necessary. Rampant sabotage in Workring had made it so. The skyers who chose to work had nearly free access to and from Workring. And those who chose not to work—well, that was their choice. They could occupy themselves somehow. Each year Welfare Control authorized more and more playgrounds in Opensky, and the public schools were open to anyone under fifty with no worse than a moderate arrest record.

Beyond Workring lay the commuter residential area. A few miles of high-rise suburbs, for secretaries and apprentice managerial staff, merging suddenly with the sprawling redevelopment apartment blocks, and then real country. To Brens the commuter line seemed a barometer of social responsibility: the greater one's worth to City, the farther away he could afford to live. Brens and his wife had moved for the last time only a year ago, to the end of the trainpad, thirty miles out. They had a small square of yellowed grass and two dwarf apple trees that would not bear. It was . . .

He shook off his daydreaming and tried to focus on the darkness rushing toward them. As their speed increased, he paradoxically lost the sense of motion conveyed by the lurching start and lumbering underground passage. Greater speed increased the amount of compression below as air entered the train's howling scoops and whooshed through the ducts down the car sides. Cityend lay moments ahead.

Brens concentrated on one of the few tasks not yet automated: at Cityend, and on the train's emergence from the tunnel, his real duty would begin. Three times in the past month skyers had sought to breach City defenses through the tunnel itself.

"Hey! You didn't check defense systems," Karras said.

"Thanks," Brens muttered through clenched teeth. "But they're okay." Then, because he knew Karras was right, he flipped the arming switch for the roof-mounted fifties and checked diverted-power availability for the nose lasers. The dials read in the green, as always.

Only Karras, who now sat hunched forward in anticipation, would have noticed the omission. Because Karras was sick. The man actually seemed to look forward to his turn in the window seat, not only for the sights all the other commuters in the Co-op tried to avoid, but also for the possible opportunity of turning loose the train's newly installed firepower.

"One of these days they're going to make a big try. They'd all give an arm to break into City, just to camp in the corridors. Now, if it was me out there, I'd be figuring a way to get out into Suburbs. But them? All they know is destroy. Besides, you think they'll take it lying down that we raised the O-tax? Forget it! They're out there waiting, and we both know it. That's why you ought to check all the gear we've got. Never know when . . ."

"Later, Karras! There it is." Brens felt his chest tighten as the distant circle of light swept toward them—tunnel exit, Cityend. His forearms tensed and he glared at the instruments, waiting for the possibility that he might have to override the controls and slam the train to a stop. But a green light flashed; ahead, the circle of sky brightened as the approaching train tripped the switch that cut off the spray of mist at the tunnel exit. And with that mist fading, the barrier of twenty thousand volts which ordinarily crackled between the exit uprights faded also. For the next few moments, while the train snaked its way into Opensky, City was potentially vulnerable.

Brens stared even harder at the opening, but saw nothing. The car flashed out into gray twilight, and he relaxed. But instinct, or a random impulse, drew his eyes to the train's exterior mirrors. And then he saw them: a shapeless huddle of bodies pouring into the tunnel back toward City. He hit a series of studs on the console and braced himself for the jolt.

There it was.

A murmur swept the crowded car behind him, but he ignored it and stared straight ahead.

"What the hell was it?" Karras asked. "I didn't see a thing."

"Skyers. They were waiting, I guess till the first car passed. They must have figured no one would see them that way."

"I don't mean who. I mean, what did you use? I didn't hear the fifties."

"For a man who's taking the run tomorrow, you don't keep up very well. Nothing fancy, none of the noise and flash some people get their kicks from. I just popped speed-breaks on the last three cars."

"In the tunnel? My God! Must have wiped them all the way out of the tunnel walls, like a squeegee. Who figured that one?"

"This morning's Co-op bulletin suggested it, remember?"

Karras sulked. "I've got better things to do than pay attention to every word those guys put out. They must spend all day dictating memos. We got a real bunch of clods running things this quarter."

"Why don't you volunteer?"

"I give them my four days' pay a month. Who needs that mishmash?"

Brens silently agreed. No one enjoyed keeping the Co-op alive. No one really knew how. And that was one of the major problems associated with having amateurs in charge: it's a hell of a way to run a railroad. But the only way, since the line itself had declared bankruptcy, and both city and state governments refused to take over. If it hadn't been for the Co-op, City would have died, a festering ulcer in the midst of the cancer of Opensky.

Opensky whirled past them now. Along the embankment on both sides, legs dangled a decorative fringe. People sat atop the pilings and hurled debris at the speeding stainless steel cars. Their accuracy had always amazed Brens. Even as he willed himself rigid, he flinched at the eggs, rocks, bottles, and assorted garbage that clattered and smeared across the window.

"Look at those sonsabitches throw, would you? You ever try and figure what kind of lead time you need to hit something moving as fast as we are?"

Brens shook his head. "I guess they're used to it."

"Why not? What else they got to do but practice?"

Behind them, gunfire crackled and bullets pattered along the boiler plate. Many of the commuters ducked at the opening burst.

"Look at them back there," Karras pointed down the aisle. "Scared blue, every one of them. I know this psychologist who's got a way to calm things down, he says. He had this idea to paint bull's-eyes on the sides of the cars, below the window. Did I tell you about it? He figures it'll work two or three ways. One, if the snipers hit the bull's-eyes, there's less chance of somebody getting tagged through a crack in the boiler plate. Two, maybe they'll quit firing at all, when they see we don't give a suck of sky about it. Or three, he says, even if they keep it up, it gives them something to do, sort of channels their aggression. If they take it out on the trains, maybe they'll ease up on City. What do you think?"

"Wouldn't it make more sense to put up shooting galleries in all the playgrounds? Or figure a way to get new cars for the trains? We can't keep patching and jury-rigging these old crates forever. The last thing we need right now is to make us more of a target than we already are."

"Okay. Have it your way. Only, I was thinking . . ."

Brens tuned him out and squinted at the last molten sliver of setting sun. Its rays smeared rainbows through the streaked eggs washing slowly across the window in the slipstream. The mess coagulated and darkened as airblown particles of ash settled in it and crusted over. When he could stand it no longer, Brens flipped on the wipers and watched the clotted slime smear across the glass, as he had known it would. But some of it scrubbed loose to flip back alongside the speeding train.

The people were still out there. If he looked carefully straight ahead, their presence became a mere shadow at the edges of the channel through which he watched the trainpad reeling toward him. Though he doubted any eye would catch his long enough to matter, he avoided the faces. There was always the slight chance that he might recognize one of them. Twenty years wasn't so long a time. Twenty years ago he had watched the trains from an embankment like these.

Now the train swooped upward to ride its cushion of air along the raised pad, level with second-story windows on each side. Blurred faces stared from those windows, here disembodied, there resting on a cupped hand and arm propped on a window ledge. The exterior mirrors showed him faces ducking away from the gust of wind fanning out behind the train and from the debris lifted whirling in the grimy evening air. He tried to picture the pattern left by the train's passage—dust settling out of the whirlwind like the lines of polarization around a magnet tip. A few of the faces wore respirators or simple, and relatively useless, cotton masks. Many didn't bother to draw back but hung exposed to the breeze that the train was stirring up. And now, as on each of his previous rare turns at the window seat, Brens had the impulse to slow the train, to let the wind die down and diminish behind them, out of what he himself considered misplaced and maudlin sympathy for the skyers, who seemed to enjoy the excitement of the train's glistening passage. It tempered the boredom of their day.

". . . right about here the six-thirty had the explosion. Five months ago. Remember?"

"What?"

"Explosion. Some kids must have got hold of detonator caps and strung them on wires swinging from a tree. When the train hit them, they cracked the window all to hell. Nearly hurt somebody. But the crews came out and burned down all the trees along the right of way. Little bastards won't pull *that* one again."

Brens nodded. There was one of the armored repair vans ahead, on a siding under the protective stone lip of the embankment.

The train rose even higher to cross the river which marked the Opensky-Workring boundary. They were riding securely in the concave shell of the bridge. On the river below, a cat, or dog—it was hard to tell at this distance—picked its cautious way across the crusted algae which nearly covered the stream. The center of the turgid river steamed a molten beige; and upriver a short way, brilliant patches of green marked the mouth of the main Workring spillway.

At the far end of the bridge, a group of children scrambled out of the trough of the trainbed to hang over the side.

"Hey! Hit the lasers. Singe their butts for them." Karras bounced in his seat.

"Shut up for a minute, can't you? They're out of the way."

"Now what's that for? Can't you take a joke? Besides, you know they're sneaking into Workring to steal something. You saying we ought to let them get away with it?"

"I'm just telling you to shut up. I'm tired, that's all. Leave it at that."

"Sure. Big deal. Tired! But tomorrow the window seat's mine. So don't come sucking around for a look then, understand?"

"It's a promise."

Sulfurous clouds hung in the air, and Brens checked the car's interior pollution level. It was a safe 18, as he might have guessed. But the sight of buildings tarnished green, of bricks flaking and molting on every factory wall, always depressed him. The ride home was worse than the trip into City. Permissive hours ran from five to eight, when pollution controls were lifted. He knew the theory: evening air was more susceptible to condensation because of the temperature drop, and dumping pollutants into the night sky might actually bring on a cleansing rain. He also knew the practical considerations involved: twenty-four-hour control would almost certainly drive industry away. Compromise was essential, if City was to survive.

It would be good to get home.

The train swung into its gently curving descent toward Workring exit, and Brens instinctively clasped the seat arms as the seat pivoted on its gimbals. At the foot of the curve he saw the barricade. Something piled on the pad.

Not for an instant did he doubt what he saw. He lunged at the power override, but stopped himself in time. Dropping to the pad now, in mid-curve, might tip the train or let it slide off the pad onto the potholed and eroded right of way where the uneven terrain offered no stable lift base for getting underway again.

"Ahead of you! On the tracks!" Karras reached for the controls, but Brens caught him with a straight-arm and slammed him to the floor. He concentrated on the roadbed flashing toward them. At the last instant, as the curve modified and tilted toward level, he popped all speedbreaks and snatched the main circuit breaker loose.

From the sides of the cars vertical panels hissed out on their hydraulic pushrods to form baffles against the slipstream, and the train slammed to the pad. Tractor gear whined in protest, the shriek nearly drowning out the dying whirr of compressor fans, and the train shuddered to a stop.

Inside, lights dimmed and flickered. Voices rose in the darkness amid the noise of men struggling to their feet.

Brens depressed the circuit breaker and hit the emergency call switch overhead. "Hold it!" he shouted. "Quiet down, please! There's something on the pad, and I had to stop. Just keep calm. I've signaled for the work crews, and they'll be here any minute."

Then he ignored the passengers and focused his attention on the windows. The barricade lay no more than twenty feet ahead, rusted castings and discarded mold shells heaped on the roadbed. The jumbled pile seemed ablaze in the flickering red light from the emergency beacons rotating atop the train cars. Behind the barricade and along the right of way, faceless huddled forms rose erect in the demonic light and stood motionless, simply staring at the train. The stroboscopic light sweeping over them made each face a swarm of moving, melting shadows. Brens fired a preliminary burst from the fifties atop the first car, then quickly switched them to automatic, but the watching forms stood like statues.

"They must know," Karras said. He stood besides Brens and massaged his bruised shoulder. "Look. None of them moving."

Then one of the watchers broke and charged toward the car, waving a club. He managed two strides before the fifties homed on his movement and opened up. A quick chatter from overhead and the man collapsed. He hurled the club as he dropped and the fifties efficiently followed its arc through the air with homed fire that made it dance in a shower of flashing sparks. It splintered to shreds before it hit the ground.

The other watchers stood motionless.

Brens stared at them a long moment before he could define what puzzled him about their appearance: none of them wore respirators. Were they trying to commit suicide? And why this useless attack? His eyes had grown accustomed to the flickering light and he scanned the mob. Young faces and old, mostly men but a few women scattered among them, all shades of color, united in appearance only by their clothing. Workring skyers in leather aprons, thick-soled shoes, probably escapees from a nearby factory. He flinched as one of them nodded slightly—surely they couldn't see him through the window. The nod grew more violent, and then he realized that the man was coughing. Paroxysms seized the man as he threw his hands to his mouth and bent forward helplessly. It was enough. The fifties chattered once more, and he fell.

"But what do they get out of it?" He turned his bewilderment to Karras.

"Who can tell? They're nuts, all of them. Malcontents, or anarchists. Mainly stupid, I'd say. Like the way they try and break into City. Even if they threw us out, they wouldn't know what to do next. Picture one of them sitting in your office. At your desk."

"I don't mean that. If they stop us from getting through, who takes care of them? I mean, we feed them, run their schools, bury them. I don't understand what they think all this will accomplish."

"Listen! The crew's coming. They'll take care of them."

A siren keened its rise and fall from the dimming twilight ahead, but still the watchers stood frozen. When the siren changed to a blatting klaxon, Brens switched the fifties back on manual to safeguard the approaching repair car. The mob melted away at the same signal. They were there, and then they were gone. They dropped from sight along the pad edge and blended into the shadows.

The work crew's crane hoisted the castings off the pad and dropped them on the right of way. In a few minutes they had finished. Green lights flashed at Brens, and the repair van sped away again.

Passing the Workring exit guards, Brens made a mental note to warn the Co-op. If the skyers were growing bold enough to show open rebellion within the security of Workring, the exit guards had better be augmented. Even Suburbs might not be safe any longer. At thirty miles distance, he wasn't really concerned for his own home, but some of the commuters lived dangerously close to Workring.

He watched in the exterior mirror. The rear car detached itself and swung out onto a siding where it dropped to a halt while the body of the train went on. Every two miles, the scene repeated itself. Cars dropped off singly to await morning reassembly. Brens had often felt a strange sort of envy for the commuters who lived closer in; they never had the lead window seat on the way out of City. Responsibility for the whole train devolved on them only for short stretches, only on the way in.

But that was fair, he reminded himself. He lived the farthest out. With privilege go obligations. And he was through, for another twenty weeks, his obligations met.

At the station, he telexed his report to the Co-op office and trotted outside to meet Hazel. The other wives had driven away. Only his carryall sat idling at the platform edge. He knew he ought to look forward to relaxing at home, but the trip itself still preyed on his mind unaccountably. He felt irritation at his inability to put the skyers out of his thoughts. His whole day was spent working for their benefit; his evenings ought to be his own.

He looked back toward City, but saw nothing in the smog-covered bowl at the foot of the hills that stretched away to the east. If it rained tonight, it might clear the air.

Hazel smiled and waved.

He grinned in answer. He could predict her reaction when she heard what he'd been through: a touch of wifely fear and concern for him, and that always made her more affectionate. Almost a hero's welcome. After all, he had acquitted himself rather well. A safe arrival, only a few minutes late, no injuries or major problems. And he wouldn't draw window seat for another several months. It was good to be home.

III. The City 2000 A.D.:
Take Your Pick—or
Alternative Visions of the City

—————————————————————————————

City's End   Mack Reynolds

Bobby was a baboon. He didn't know why they, the main-landers, called them baboons. Perhaps it was because baboons are animals that live in a jungle and Bobby lived in a jungle. His jungle was the ruins of what was once New York City.

He didn't have a last name, or at least if he did, he didn't know what it was. He had become separated from his parents during the gigantic riots which finally led to the all but complete destruction of the city and its abandonment. He had been so young that when the woman who temporarily rescued him asked his name, all he could say was, "Bobby."

He didn't know his age now, but he figured that he was somewhere in his early teens because he was growing so fast that every couple of months he had to steal new clothes from the abandoned shops and department stores.

Well, perhaps steal wasn't quite the word. He had to *find* new clothes. Mr. Thompson, old Fred Thompson, the only real friend he had, had explained it once.

"It's not stealing if it doesn't belong to anyone. The food and clothing and other things that we scrounge out of the ruins no longer belong to anybody and nobody cares. The former owners will never come back—those that are still alive."

Right now, Bobby was disgusted. He glared down at the portable Library Booster screen which sat on his small desk in the living room of his apartment. There was nothing wrong with the set. He had found it in the ruins of the Macy-Gimbels department store and he had an ample supply of the tiny power-pack batteries to keep it in operation for years. The trouble was that as a baboon he had no priority whatsoever. It was as though he were a criminal, a mental defective, a dangerous subversive, or someone on relief, collecting Guaranteed Annual Income.

Without priority, he could only dial books and other information from the Library Banks of the National Data Banks, on the very lowest level. Try to dial any book on the Booster screen that was the least bit advanced and the computer voice immediately demanded his identity and priority rating.

How in the dickens was he ever going to educate himself if he had no priority to dial anything beyond children's books?

He decided to go and consult Fred Thompson. The old man had told him once, "Boy, I'm no font of wisdom. Don't ever believe that hogwash about wisdom coming with age. I sometimes suspect that I'm not nearly as smart as I was fifty years ago. But there's one advantage I have over a young feller such as yourself. I've had the time to accumulate a lot of experience. You haven't been around long enough. So if there's ever anything you need advice about, you might try me."

All right, he'd go over to Mr. Thompson's. He picked up his .22 sporting rifle and slung it over his shoulder by the strap and headed for the trap door he had cut through the apartment floor and through which he could lower himself to the floor below.

He knew that the light rifle wasn't much gun. And he suspected that if he ever had to defend himself against one of the more vicious baboons on the island he'd be lucky if he even dented the man. However, every adult—and you were more or less an adult when you reached your teens—living in the ruins of the city carried at least one weapon, and some, two or three. Even the few women remaining carried guns. As soon as he gained a few more pounds and inches he'd be able to handle a heavier caliber and feel more secure.

Bobby had selected his apartment with care and more with an eye to defense than comfort, although he had furnished it quite well by pirating things from other abandoned flats. It was a house whose front had been demolished by cannon fire from National Guard tanks, trying to put down the rioters. There was no way of gaining entry from the street directly. It was a matter of going down to the basements, then through a hole in the wall to the cellars of the adjoining apartment house. From there you could climb the stairs and emerge in an alleyway and hence make your way to the street.

He had stumbled on the place, quite by accident, while prowling the buildings in the vicinity seeking some kind of stove that would operate on the only kind of fuel available in the city—gasoline taken from the tanks of abandoned cars, buses and trucks. He doubted very much if anyone else had ever been in his building since the riots many years ago. So far, he had been safe here.

However, when he reached the head of the alley, he carefully unslung his rifle and peered up and down East 55th. The once swank residential street was a mass of rubble, overturned cars, cars rammed up onto the sidewalks, odds and ends of personal belongings abandoned by the fleeing population, a baby carriage, small trunks and suitcases, even an antique mirror. It was a mess.

Bobby could see no signs of movement. Had he seen anyone at all, he would have faded back into the alleyway. He didn't want anyone to know where he lived. It was a precaution taken by most baboons, but he had another reason for secrecy. He didn't want to be caught and made a monkey.

The coast clear, he stepped out and started up 55th Street toward what had once been Park Avenue. He customarily left his bicycle in a ruined sports shop there. There was no danger of it being stolen. But if it were, he would simply appropriate another new one from some sports shop. There were thousands of bicycles on Manhattan, more than enough for all. Actually, they were the only practical means of transportation around the island. It would have been easy enough, if you had mechanical ability, to fix up one of the abandoned automobiles. But there were few, if any, places on Manhattan where you could have driven. The city was as if it had been leveled in an all-out air raid.

He had reslung his .22 over his shoulder, the better to make his way over the wreckage. Now a hulking brute of a man stepped out from behind a burned-out car. He said, "Hold up, kid. I want to talk to you."

He was about fifty and must have weighed at least two hundred pounds. He was very well dressed in sports clothes, including a tweed jacket that had probably originally been meant to sell in some swank shop for at least two hundred dollars. There was no reason why he shouldn't be well dressed, Bobby knew, all you had to do was steal . . . scrounge . . . new things from the best shops, once your clothes became soiled or you wearied of them. However, the man's face and hands were dirty. He was obviously too lazy to bother hauling water for himself for bathing from one of the springs in the subway or the park.

Bobby knew him. Or, at least, knew of him. He was called Moose and he was possibly the most notorious keeper of monkeys on Manhattan. There were few children on the island and those that did remain, for whatever reason, were almost all appropriated by some vicious adult as soon as they had become old enough to work. They were forced to fetch and carry, to hunt for the food and other requirements of their baboon. If they tried to escape him, he would beat them. Some were even chained at night, or any other time the baboon couldn't keep his eye on them. If they did escape, invariably they fell into the hands of some other baboon who could be even worse than the one before.

Bobby had been a monkey for almost two years before achieving his independence and running off to live by himself. He had been lucky enough to have had a fairly kindly baboon as his master, but his independence, his frantic desire for freedom, finally led him to the step of escape. He never regretted it.

But this Moose who now confronted him! He had heard of Moose, one of the baboons on the island who remained because the police authorities on the mainland sought him. Since he had no Universal Credit Card—even if he had, and used it, the computers would have been on him like a flash and notified the police of his whereabouts—the only place in the country where Moose could live was in one of the abandoned cities.

His reputation was the worst. His last monkey had evidently been beaten so badly that he had become worthless to Moose (who allowed him to go to the Grand Central Terminal jet-metro station, the only one maintained on the island and ask to be sent to the mainland hospital). The boy had only been about ten.

He repeated, "Hold it, sonny. I want to talk to you."

Bobby shook his head. "No. I don't want to talk to you, Moose. Goodbye."

The other leered at him, displaying broken teeth. It was one of the many shortcomings of being a baboon in the ruins of New York. You might appropriate the most expensive canned foods and clothing on the island, and live in a former mansion, but you had no dental care and only such medical care as you could provide yourself from the medicines in drugstores.

He said, "If you got good sense, kid, you'll become my monkey. I need a new monkey."

Bobby had not survived long years in the jungle of the ruined Manhattan by being a coward. There were no cowards on the island. They had long since fled or perished.

He shook his head again and unslung his small gun. "I'd rather die than be a monkey for you, Moose."

The other laughed scornfully. He carried a semi-automatic carbine, and a heavy automatic pistol on each hip. Then he growled, "Kid, I'd hate to see you have to start off your first day for me with a beating. So far as that peashooter you're carrying is concerned, I bet you don't even know how to shoot well. I'll betcha I can put a slug through your leg or arm before you can hit me with it. Not that it would make much difference if you did hit me. That's a .22, ain't it? Kid, I've been hit with .45s in my time and I'm still around. Tough, see? Now cut out all this crud and come along with me."

Bobby was in his early teens, quick and nimble, and he knew this neighborhood as though he had been born in it. All of a sudden, he blurred into motion—zipped around the back of a car, slewed around a burned bus beyond, and jumped through the broken window of a store.

A voice behind him yelled in rage, "Come back here, you little rat, or I'll shoot!" He could hear the lumbering footsteps of the other chasing him.

He had to laugh inwardly. He knew these houses and ruined stores like a mouse knows the labyrinth beneath a warehouse. He could have run through here almost with his eyes closed. When the house-to-house fighting had taken place between the police, the National Guard and the rioters and criminal gangs, they sometimes blew holes in the walls between the buildings to allow themselves to get through to the rear of their opponent. Bobby knew every hole.

He was three buildings up, scurrying along like a lizard, through the debris, through the wreckage, almost as fast as he could have gone along the street. The sounds of pursuit behind him disappeared.

All right. But did he dare appear on 55th Street again, to get his bicycle?

Yes, he did. By this time, Moose might be anywhere.

He carefully stuck his head out of a doorway, the door itself having long since disappeared.

There was no sign of Moose.

He hurried out and up the street, taking care to use the shelter of abandoned vehicles to the greatest extent he could. He didn't know it but he was using the same tactics as his ancestors in the caves had used fifty thousand years and more before him, when they were eluding a saber-toothed tiger in the wilderness that later became Europe.

He hustled into the sporting goods store, wanting to get out of sight as soon as possible. And, yes, here was his bicycle. He looked at the tires critically. All the glass and rubble were awfully hard on tires. And it was sometimes hard to find new ones in good shape. They were so old that the rubber was beginning to rot.

He wheeled the bike out onto the sidewalk, mounted, and headed down Park Avenue. It was usually easier going on the sidewalk than the street, since there was less refuse.

He came to a sudden halt, dismounted and pushed the bike behind a car. He peered around the side of it. Two blocks ahead, he could see a man. A man dressed in khakis and high leather boots, with a safari hat on his head and rifle in hand.

A hunter! The first one Bobby had seen in months.

There was no law on Manhattan. No police, no courts, no judges, no jails. In short, no law at all.

If anybody was foolish enough to remain on the island he could expect no protection whatsoever from the authorities. If you were robbed, hurt, or even killed, it was your own bad luck. Hence it was that the ruined cities, such as New York, Chicago and Los Angeles, were possibly the only places in the world where a thrill-seeker could actually kill someone for the sport of it and never be apprehended.

The hunters took advantage of this. They would get permission to visit the island on the excuse of attempting to find some object in one of the museums, the library, a private home, or perhaps some record lost in a law office. They would fully arm themselves with the latest weapons, and wear bullet-proof clothing. Then they would come seeking victims. Victims to kill for the fun of it, the thrill of it.

Bobby couldn't imagine more disgusting human beings.

But the problem now was getting past this particular one. He was certainly having bad luck today. First Moose and now a hunter. He must take it carefully. Hunters almost always came in a group, at least two or three, for mutual protection against the baboons. Most baboons went around singly, as did Bobby, and were seldom a match for hunters in a group.

Waiting until the other's back was to him, Bobby quickly remounted his bike and returned to where East 53rd cut over to Fifth Avenue. He peddled over to Fifth and carefully looked around the corner before entering it.

No one in sight. He peddled on.

This was a route he didn't usually take, due to the fact that quite a bit of the fighting had taken place at Rockefeller Center and the rubble of that once fabulous complex of buildings made the street just short of impassable. He would have to push his wheel through it.

When he reached the public library, something came to him. He dismounted and pushed the bicycle up the steps, past the shattered stone lions, and into the building. He left it just inside the crumbled doors, where no one would see it, and headed for the rooms with the shelves of books. There weren't too many of these rooms left undestroyed, but he thought he knew what he was looking for. So far as Bobby knew, he was the only baboon on the island who ever came in here. Few of them were the type who did much reading, and those who did had Library Boosters and could dial their low-level reading material from the National Data Banks, just like respectable citizens throughout the rest of the country.

Sure enough, he found the two books he had in mind without too much difficulty, and headed back for his bicycle.

Fred Thompson's apartment wasn't too much further now. On East 37th, to be exact. The old man lived on the eighth floor, which made it a hard climb for a man his age, but it afforded him quite a bit of protection from his fellow baboons and from hunters. There was only one stairway intact and most of the way up it was quite dark. Thus Fred Thompson could rig the way with various little warning devices, so if anyone started up, without shouting his identity first, Fred could take his shotgun and fire a few warning shots down the stairwell. That invariably warned them off.

Bobby stopped a few moments at the nearby grocery store and selected a dozen or so cans of pork and beans and corn, and another dozen of sardines. It would save his friend a load the next time he wanted to replenish his supply of canned goods. The old man was fond of beans and had a plentiful supply available, since most baboons were inclined to steal more luxurious foods from the ruins of the grocery stores. Bobby also picked up a few cans of fruit juices. He put the things in a plastic shopping bag.

He pushed his bike into the ruined foyer of the apartment house his friend lived in, went over to the stairway and started up, yelling as he went, "Mr. Thompson! Mr. Thompson. It's me. Bobby!"

By the time he got to the fourth floor a weak voice called down to him, "Come on up, Bobby."

Fred Thompson's apartment was the only one on the eighth floor that had survived sufficiently to be habitable. Bobby had been there so often that he knew the place almost as well as his own. Sometimes when he got caught by the night he stayed, rather than risk returning home in the dark.

He put his parcel of food on the kitchen table and returned to the living room where the old man was seated in a comfortable chair. Like Bobby, Fred Thompson had pirated excellent furniture from other apartments and was thus well equipped.

He said, "Well, how've you been, son? Haven't seen you so far this week."

"I've been trying to study," Bobby said.

Fred Thompson had gotten to that period in life where he looked as though he might be anywhere between seventy and ninety. His hair was still full but completely white, his hands trembled a bit, and his voice was wavering. Otherwise he seemed to be in reasonably good shape for his years.

Bobby walked over to the one window that still had glass in it—the others were boarded up with cardboard. He stared down at the street, not expecting, really, to see the hunters this far away from where he had spotted them, but one never knew. They sometimes had hover cars or even helicopters and could travel much faster than someone on a bike.

He said, "On the way over, that big one called Moose tried to grab me. Wanted me to be his monkey. Then I spotted a hunter on Park Avenue."

"This town gets more dangerous, not less, as time goes by," the old man grumbled.

From this height, Bobby could see over a considerable section of this part of the city.

He said softly, "Was it pretty in the old days, Mr. Thompson? New York, I mean."

"Eh? Pretty?" The old man scratched his chin. "Why, I suppose so. This part of town, at least. A lot of the nice buildings, nice homes were around here. Up where you live, too. But there were a lot of parts of town that were terrible. Harlem and so forth."

Bobby left the window and went over and sat at the table near his friend. He knew the story, more or less, but he said, "Mr. Thompson, what happened?"

The other knew what he meant. He pursed his aged lips before answering. "Why, I suppose a lot of things, son. The big cities were doomed for years before they finally collapsed. For one thing, poor people from the South, from Puerto Rico, and other places where it was hard to make a living, moved to the cities to get on relief. So the better-to-do people moved out into the suburbs where they could have better schools, better police protection and so forth. The cities had to raise the taxes so they could support those on relief. So more of the better-paid people moved out, to escape the taxes. So did a good many businessmen, with their businesses. And that meant even less work, and more people on relief. Crime went up and the city couldn't raise enough money to pay more policemen. The population of the slums increased but the city couldn't raise enough money for more teachers to educate the kids, more and more of whom dropped out and got in trouble in the streets."

Bobby said, "But I mean, how did the final riots start?"

"Actually, over a period of time. There were smaller riots, between blacks and whites, students demonstrating against their schools, riots between pro- and anti-war folk, demonstrations of people on relief who wanted more money. Everybody was up-tight, everybody was frustrated.

"Then came the water shortages and the breakdown in the supply of electricity. The city went broke. Police, firemen, garbage collectors and the rest went unpaid. Many of them quit their jobs and left town to get work somewhere else. Then all of a sudden it popped. Everybody who could afford to, for all practical purposes, had left to live in the suburbs or smaller towns. The big fires started and there weren't enough firemen, and the water supply broke down. Half the city had no electricity. Mobs of unemployed kids and criminals began prowling the streets. Some of them broke into gun stores and stole guns. Some of them mobbed police stations and took the guns. Before you knew it, thousands and then tens of thousands of people were trying to get out of town. Hundreds of gun fights were going on. The subways stopped—too many of the employees had joined the people escaping the city. The traffic lights went out. Traffic piled up until the whole place was clogged. People left their cars and, hysterically, started walking, heading for the bridges. The fires got worse and worse, and then the looting. Practically everybody seemed to be looting. The National Guard was brought in, including aircraft to drop first tear gas, then high explosives on areas where the gangsters, the rioting kids, the looters had taken over completely. And still the fires got worse.

"It lasted for a couple of weeks, I suppose, and finally, even the police deserted the city. There was no city left. No water, no transportation, no electricity—no people. Only we baboons remained."

"Why?"

The old man shrugged. He didn't mind talking about it. He liked company and Bobby was his only visitor, these days.

"Why, some were criminals. Some were mental cases. Some liked the looting." He pursed aged lips again. "I suppose possibly I come under that heading. I'd never had much money, son. I lived in the poorest neighborhoods, ate the cheapest food. All of a sudden, I was able to move into a swank apartment, scrounge the best food available from the gourmet stores. I'd never tasted caviar before, for instance. I got myself the fanciest of clothes. For the first time, I was living it up. Of course, there were disadvantages. No lights, so I had to find camping lanterns in the sport stores that burned gasoline. No water in the plumbing, so it had to be hauled up from the springs that busted out in the subways. And no fresh food at all, so I had to supplement my canned food with vitamins and minerals from the drugstores. But it was kinda fascinating. In a way, I suppose I'm sorry to see it all end. I'm afraid I'm going to have to go back to the mainland like so many of the older baboons have to sooner or later. I don't think I can spend another winter with this kind of heating."

The old man looked at the boy. "How about you, son?"

Bobby put his chin in his hand and his elbow on the table. "Well, I was just a child when it happened. I suppose I got separated from my parents, or they were killed. I can't remember. An old woman picked me up and took me to her place. She lived in a cellar at that time. I can barely remember it. Later, we moved to an abandoned apartment. Now I realize that she was crazy. Her mind must have slipped in the rioting. She died, just a few years ago, and then one of the adult baboons made me his monkey and I worked for him for about two years before I escaped. Then I found the place I'm living in now. I guess that's about it."

"No, I meant, why didn't you go back to the mainland? Most of the folks who remained dribbled back over the years. Living is too tough here. And the only new recruits we get are either criminals hiding from the police, or aliens who aren't eligible for Guaranteed Annual Income and this is the only place they can make a living—scrounging in the ruins."

"Oh," Bobby said. He thought about it. "Well, when I was living with the old lady, I didn't know about anything else. Then when I was a monkey, I couldn't escape. Now, I'm in kind of a pickle."

"How do you mean?"

"Well, suppose I went back to the mainland. I have no parents. They'd put me in some sort of an institution. They wouldn't let me have the kind of freedom I have now. But besides all that, I haven't the education that others my age have. I wasn't even able to read until three years ago, when I met you and you helped me."

"You've sure done a lot since."

"Yes. But if I went back, I wouldn't know the things that kids are taught in the schools over there. I'd have to start in where five-year-olds are. They'd make me. I'd never catch up to the point where I'd learn enough to hold down a job."

"Yeah," the old man said unhappily. "However, there's a lot of advantages to getting the kind of education you are getting. You're getting your own, studying what you want; you're not on a treadmill."

Bobby said, scowling, "That's what I wanted to talk to you about. Listen, why am I not able to get any book I want from the National Library of the National Data Banks? The computers won't let me because I have no priority rating."

The old man frowned, too. "I know," he said. "It's kind of a long story, son."

Bobby waited.

"Well," the old man said, "the way I figure it, it's because The Establishment, the powers that be, or whatever you want to call it, don't want anybody to rock the boat."

"The Establishment?"

"That's a word they used to use maybe thirty years ago. It meant the men at the top, the men who run things. You see, son, all down through the ages the men on top have fought change. They don't want their applecart upset."

"I don't understand."

"Well, along about the end of the Second World War, about fifty years ago, the second industrial revolution came along. Automation and computerization and the knowledge explosion. At first, it led to a lot of new jobs, building new factories and new machines. But then it hit. Half a dozen technicians can run a factory now, where it used to take thousands of men. As far back as the 1950s, when I was still fairly young, we began to have unemployment and one of the think-tank men predicted that by the year 2,000, two percent of the labor force would be all that was needed to produce everything the country needed. Well, he was right. They had to bring in Guaranteed Annual Income—sometimes they called it Negative Income Tax—to keep the unemployed going. They merged all local relief with Social Security, old age pensions, Medicare, and all the rest, and practically everybody wound up on it."

"But what's that got to do with me not being able to get advanced books?"

"Son, the present-day Establishment, the two percent who do work and get fabulously high pay, want to remain in that spot. And they want their children to, as well. So the children of the present well-to-do get the best education available but the children of those on Guaranteed Annual Income are given a ridiculously inadequate education, most of it devoted to keeping them from thinking about changes—about changing or reforming the government. Not only schools they attend, but the books they read, the TV shows they see, even sometimes the sermons they hear—all are devoted to making them conformists, happy with things the way they are."

"What changes are you talking about?"

The old man looked at him questioningly. "I don't know, son. And perhaps I'm too old to have an opinion. But I'd say that when a nation has ninety-eight percent of its population on what amounts to relief, and only two percent of the population works at all, then something very basic is wrong with that country and it'll never really progress. Idleness isn't good for individuals and it isn't good for a nation."

"What should I do to help change it?"

Fred Thompson shook his head. "That's not for me to say, son. It's for you to find out on your own. I was born in 1920. It was my generation who gave our country the Great Depression and later the Second World War. The next generation gave the Asian wars to us, pollution of our country, the race riots and the chaos in the schools of that time, among other things. Obviously, we didn't do so well."

He thought back to the time when he was younger. "In my day, the kids used to have a slogan. You can't trust anybody over thirty. At the time we either laughed at the kids, or got mad at the way they refused to do things the way we always had. But you know, Bobby, I've about come to the conclusion that they were right. We weren't to be trusted."

He looked at the books the boy had laid on the table. *Collected Works of Thomas Jefferson and The Speeches of Abraham Lincoln.* Fred Thompson nodded. "Were these some of the books you couldn't get on your Library Booster screen?"

"Yes."

The old man shook his head. "So they've got to the point where they consider even the two greatest presidents the country ever had to be subversive, eh? Afraid that if the common people read what they had to say, they might start thinking about real freedom and real liberty, instead of the gobblydygook the politicians hand out these days."

"Then you think these books would be worth my reading?"

"They're certainly as good a place as any to start. Bobby, one of these days, when you're a few years older, you're going to have to return to the mainland. And when you do, you're going to be confronted with the same problem the rest of your generation has: How to get the country back on the path of progress. Not just material progress. Real progress. Like I say, I can't tell you how to do it. My generation didn't. We failed."

Bobby picked up the two books. He said, "I'd better get along, Mr. Thompson. I want to start wading into these, if they're not too hard."

The old man saw him to the door. "I suspect that they won't be too hard, Bobby. And that before the year is out, nothing will be. The person who has the thirst for knowledge can somehow manage to find drink. The public library isn't the only source of your material, you know. Half of the old mansions in town that have remained comparatively whole, have big private libraries. You might try scouting around in them when there's something you want."

"Goodbye, Mr. Thompson. Thanks a lot." Bobby started down the stairs.

The old man looked after him. "Thanks for what?" he said softly. "Your generation is the hope of the country. If we don't get out of this rat-race soon, mankind will disappear."

Bobby found his bike where he had left it, put his books in the luggage rack and wheeled it out onto the street. He looked up and down carefully for hunters or other baboons. Ordinarily, the baboons on the island didn't bother each other. There was no reason to and so there was an armed truce. But since he was in the ideal age group to be made a monkey, he couldn't take any chances. He was growing rapidly but he was still too slight to resist one of the burly toughs such as Moose. And, actually, most of the men remaining on the island were large, strong specimens. The weaklings had been weeded out long ago.

The return to his own place was uneventful. To make doubly sure he would avoid the hunters, he went over to the Avenue of the Americas before heading north. As he peddled, it came to him that in this whole day, the only living things he had seen were Moose, the hunter and Fred Thompson. He hadn't spotted, even at a distance, another baboon. There must truly be few left. How many? Nobody knew, but he suspected that there were less than a couple of hundred on Manhattan. Each year some returned to the mainland, due to age or whatever, and each year some died, particularly in view of the lack of medical care. And few indeed were the newcomers.

He thought over what the old man had said and he realized that in one respect his way of life was an advantage. Except for the members of—what had his friend called it? The Establishment, he was one of the few in the whole country who had access to what The Establishment considered dangerous books. Real books were no longer printed. The rest of the country depended on the National Library of the National Data Banks. And you were only allowed to dial for your home screen those books that they thought suitable for you to read. Bobby didn't know it, but the system was one of the most effective systems of censorship the world had ever seen. But he, Bobby, was able to beat it. He wasn't dependent on the National Library. In the ruins of New York, he had real books at his disposal.

He reached 55th Street and turned right, being doubly cautious now. He was entering the vicinity where the hunters had been and where Moose had accosted him that morning. He prayed inwardly that Moose hadn't seen the alleyway from which he had emerged.

So far, so good. He reached the corner of Park Avenue and wheeled his bike into the sports shop. He began to leave, but then hesitated and looked at the gun rack. Some of the rifles and shotguns that had originally been there had been taken, particularly the heavier caliber ones. But there were still some of the lighter models. He took down an automatic chambered for the .22 Magnum bullet. It wasn't much heavier than his own .22 Long Rifle gun. He searched about and found a couple of boxes of cartridges and loaded the gun. To make sure it was still in working order, he emptied it into the wall, then reloaded it. It was still in order all right, and he liked the feel of it, and realized that its high velocity made it almost as powerful as a higher caliber. He left his own gun in the rack and turned to go.

The way was clear, but he approached his apartment house very slowly, so as not to be surprised. Moose might be waiting for his return. He might be behind any burnt out vehicle or in any doorway.

But he wasn't

Bobby reached his alleyway, looked up and down again to check if there was anyone who might see him enter. Then he hurried up it, gun now slung over his shoulder, his books in hand.

The reason Moose had not been seen on the street was because he was in the basement of the apartment house adjoining that of Bobby. He was sitting on a wooden crate, next to a furnace, and his carbine was held on his lap, ready for action.

There was no retreat; Bobby was past Moose and had his one exit cut off before he saw the man.

Moose grinned nastily and said, "Hello, kid. I told you not to run this morning, but you did. That means you're going to start out being my monkey by taking a beating. First of all, drop that gun. From now on you don't carry no guns. If you need any protection, Moose'll protect you."

Instead of dropping the gun, Bobby dropped the two books. He took a deep breath and said, "Moose, a friend of mine, Fred Thompson, once told me that no man has to become a slave if he doesn't want to. He can die first—and a dead man isn't a slave."

"Don't be crazy, kid. I don't want to kill you. But if you give me any trouble I'll put a slug in your leg. It'll lay you up for a while, might even cripple you permanently. But that'd just make you easier to keep herd on. So drop that little peashooter and come along."

Bobby unslung the gun and the other must have thought he was about to drop it, as ordered. But that was where Moose made his final mistake.

Bobby shot him three times. *Bang. Bang. Bang.* Once in

the upper chest, once in the throat and once square in the middle of the forehead.

The big man doubled forward, his reddish eyes popping surprise, even as he died.

Coldly and efficiently, Bobby dragged him out into the alley. The man was heavy, and it was difficult, but he managed. He could take him no further, he didn't have the strength, but he knew it wasn't necessary. When night came, the other inhabitants of Manhattan, other than the baboons, would take care of the problem of disposal; the wild cats, the wild dogs, and, above all, the rats.

Bobby turned and made his way back into the interior of the building. He took up his gun and the books, and through the devious holes and passageways, returned to his apartment.

He was feeling very empty. He had never hurt another person before in his life, even in self-defense. He did not believe in harming other human beings. But he believed even more strongly that everyone has a right to his freedom and must be willing to fight and die for it.

He leaned his gun up against the wall and took his books over to his desk. He sneered at the Library Booster sitting there and, instead of activating it, opened one of the books— *Jefferson's Collected Works*—at random.

He came upon the first inaugural address and the first lines that hit his eyes were:

. . . let us hasten to retrace our steps and to regain the road which alone leads to peace, liberty and safety.

He knew that old Mr. Thompson was right and that there was hope.

Surprised, he reached up to wipe away some tears.

The Slime Dwellers   Scott Edelstein

SHARTAR

He stood on the crest of a small hill, alone, looking across the long grassy area at the city. Sun gleamed off the metal dome enclosing one of the city's residential areas. Huge construction derricks hovered above the dome and above other parts of the city, waiting to begin the dismantling and the demolition.

Most of the city would be carefully taken apart, and the sections would be transplanted elsewhere, in urban and suburban areas that had grown up with little or no planning. Other sections of the city which had not been built from pre-fabricated units would simply be demolished, and the materials recycled and used elsewhere. To accomplish this demolition, many of the derricks were fitted with giant booms.

Shartar took his camera from its case and hurriedly took several shots of the city. He put the camera away and looked back across the grassy expanse at the huge metal structure. He saw some of the booms and hooks and electromagnets begin to sway. The tearing down had begun.

HENSHAW

"It's kind of small, isn't it?" the wrinkled, well-dressed woman said. "Don't you have anything bigger?"

"I'm sorry," Henshaw said, imperceptibly straightening his tie. "It's the largest model available. Six rooms is the maximum. One of the most important concepts of Basin City has been to make the best use of space."

"This room, I mean," the woman said. "It's not very big for a living room. The one we have back home is a lot bigger, isn't it, Rod?"

Her husband was a decaying, flabby man, with thick spectacles that made his eyes look huge. "Yeah," he said slowly, uncertainly. "Yeah, I think so."

She nodded her head slightly. Frosted hair bobbed up and down. "Show us the kitchen."

"Over this way, please." Henshaw led them through the low doorway into the kitchen.

The couple stood just inside the doorway, surveying the room. "It looks pretty nice, doesn't it?" the husband said.

"I don't really like the way it's laid out," his wife said. "I'm used to the refrigerator being right next to the sink, not the stove." She turned to Henshaw. "I notice the stove's an electric. Are there any gas ones in the city? I like cooking with flame a lot better."

Henshaw shook his head. "All the appliances in Basin City are electric, as well was the climate control system and the recycling system. It's much less expensive than gas; all the electricity the city needs is generated in a big power plant underground."

"What does the recycling system do?" the husband asked.

Henshaw strode across the kitchen, stopped next to five small metal drawers set into the wall. "Whenever you finish with what you're using, you just dump it down one of these chutes." He pulled open a drawer and a faint rumbling filled the room. "This drawer is for organic wastes—you know, rotten food, banana peels, apple cores, things like that. The others are for aluminum cans and containers, for glass, for plastic, and for paper."

The woman said, "What happens to those banana peels and things? They don't grind them up and make them into food, do they?"

"Of course not," Henshaw said. "They use them for compost."

"What's that?"

"Compost? It's used as fertilizer for the farms outside of Basin City."

"What about trash?" the husband asked. "Is there an incinerator in the apartment?"

"There's a central incinerator for each community," Henshaw said. "There's no need for an incinerator chute in each apartment. The only things that don't get reused are cigarette butts, used paper towels, things like that. You'll only have to take out trash once a week, at the most."

"Do all the apartments look like this one?" the woman asked.

"No, this is one of nine basic models. This is one of the most expensive units available, because of its size and location. As you can see, we're located on the next-to-top level of the dome, with what's probably the best view of the countryside in the whole city."

The woman walked tiredly to the picture window in the living room and looked out. "There's not much to the countryside," she said. "Just farms, and past that, desert."

"How much is this going to run us?" her husband said.

SHARTAR

The city had been his life's work. Appalled at the conditions existing in the growing megapoli, terrified by the prospect of the entire Eastern Seaboard becoming one giant, dirty, urban prison, Shartar had set about to create a livable city. He began with a degree in architecture and another in human ecology. He drew up the plans for the city over a period of seven years; designs for living units, recreation areas, cultural centers, laboratories, industrial areas, gardens, all fitted together into a huge mechanical gestalt.

He had supervised every step of the city's construction, had watched the megastructure slowly rise from the desert, had seen the land become irrigated, then plowed, then planted. The entire construction process had taken over nine years.

Meanwhile, the existing cities, the sprawling, wasteful urban centers, had swelled to unbearable size.

HENSHAW

"All of the homes in Basin City are very reasonably priced," Henshaw said. "For something like this, including all utilities for a period of three years, the price is $19,500. I can draw up the papers right now. If you'll sign them today, I can cut the price by a thousand."

"I don't know," the man said. "I don't like to jump into things. I'm not sure it's what we want at all."

"Where are you from?" Henshaw asked.

"Los Angeles. Why?"

"Basin City's services were modeled after those of Los Angeles, New York, the biggest cities in the country. It was designed to fulfill every need of its community members. And everything is much closer to you than it would be in Los Angeles. Transportation is easier and more efficient, too."

"I don't know," the woman said. "It just seems . . . uncomfortable, somehow, you know? I mean, we've lived in L.A. all our lives. Basin City just isn't what we're used to. It's not what we're used to at all."

"Cars aren't allowed to Basin City, are they?" the man said.

"They aren't necessary. You can get anywhere you want within the city in fifteen minutes on the electric shuttles."

"I know. It's just that I like driving. It helps me relax."

"You can keep your car in the underground garage—with no fee charged for it—and you can drive around the countryside whenever you like. If you'll look at the map I gave you when you first arrived you'll see there are quite a few picnic areas right by the road, and a park and an artificial lake are being planned."

There was a moment of silence.

"Do you have any children?" Henshaw asked.

"Three," the wrinkled woman said.

"Think of how much nicer it will be for your children to grow up in Basin City. There's no smog, no filth, no congestion, a lot less noise."

"That's true," the woman said slowly.

"No outdoors, either," her husband said. "You're stuck inside all day."

"Not at all," Henshaw said. "The outside is never more than ten minutes away by shuttle."

"But we're out in the middle of the desert." Energy seemed to flow into the man's flabby face. "When you go outside, it's only a few minutes before you get so hot that you have to go back in, so why bother?"

"It's not only that," his wife said, almost pleading with Henshaw. "All our friends live back in L.A. You said we should think of our children. How do you think they would feel, knowing that they'd have to make new friends all over again? Remember how lonely you were as a child when your family moved to a new town?" She stared past Henshaw, out the picture window.

"There'll be lots of children in Basin City," Henshaw said, following her gaze, himself looking at the newly-planted crops. "That's one of the major purposes of Basin City—to provide a healthy environment for children. Do you realize that sociologists predict that in Basin City there will be only a tenth a much crime as in most urban centers? And so far this has held pretty much to be true. Think of the protection it will afford your children."

"I don't know," the man said. "It's so far away from everything. It's over a hundred miles just to the nearest town of any size. We'd feel so isolated."

"A hundred thousand people will live in Basin City eventually," Henshaw said. "This town will *become* your home. You'll have a lot more community ties than in Los Angeles—and probably a lot more personal ties, as well. You may just find the people here to be a lot friendlier. One of the main reasons people come here is to get away from the isolation, the coldness of the big city. Basin City is designed

to provide big city facilities with a small town atmosphere."
Henshaw stopped himself there; carried away by his own
sales pitch, he had repeated Basin City's principal advertising
slogan.

"There aren't a hundred thousand people living here," the
woman said, suddenly turned cold by Henshaw's remarks.
"There probably aren't even ten thousand."

"There are over nine thousand living here right now,"
Henshaw said, carefully keeping his voice genial. "And we
expect the population to rise greatly in the next few years."

"What if it doesn't?"

SHARTAR

A boom pounded against the structure's metal side. The
earth shook. Shartar nearly fell.

He was forty years old. Within the next thirty years he
would see the cities grow still larger, grow more wasteful and
crime-ridden, more infested with dirt and disease. At the age
of forty he had already spent a lifetime's energy at work on
a solution to a tremendous problem, and had had his expectations crushed. He would live another thirty years, observing
with disbelief the style in which Western man had chosen to
live.

He felt as if death had already overtaken him.

HENSHAW

The man shook his head. Fat jiggled on his neck. "We'll
have to think about it," he said hurriedly. He guided his wife
toward the apartment's front door.

"Well, look," Henshaw said. "Are you interested in hiking,
horseback riding, any of those? Are your children interested
in them?"

"No, I'm sorry." The man had opened the door and his
wife was already through it, into the courtyard outside. She
was speaking to him, urging him to leave. "We'll be back
next week," he said. He shut the door, hurriedly.

Henshaw turned and glared out the picture window at the
grain fields. He listened and heard the very faint hum of the
city's environmental systems working a dozen levels beneath
him. Idly, he scratched the back of his hand, then turned
and strode across the room. He opened the door and looked
out at the courtyard, its screens and fountains and subdued

lighting. A shuttle was just pulling away from the courtyard. He stared at it, dazed, until it rounded a corner, then shut the door behind him and walked to the courtyard's center to catch the next shuttle.

SHARTAR

He remembered a talk he had given, many years before, when his plans for the city had been perhaps half completed. He was speaking to a group of students at a small liberal arts college somewhere in the midwest. He had just finished relating how the city was to be structured, and had emphasized its independence, its superiority to the urban structures then —and still—in existence.

A student had raised his hand. He was small and thin and had beady eyes that gazed out at Shartar through thick glasses. Shartar called on him.

"Granted," the student said, "that all you've been talking about is a far better alternative than rotting away in smog and slag and your own urine. Granted that your city will be cleaner and less wasteful and more compact and better planned than anything we've got now. I understand what you're trying to do, and if it works it'll be the best thing that's ever happened to man since the industrial revolution.

"But Mr. Shartar, *what in God's name makes you think that people are going to be willing to live there?*"

HENSHAW

When he entered his office seven levels down, Henshaw was confronted by an excited babbling. The other three brokers were huddled together around a desk. One was on the phone talking quickly. The other two were smoking cigarettes, talking to each other.

"What happened?" Henshaw asked, striding inside.

Dave Snyder walked over to him. "They're closing Basin City down."

"What?"

"They're dismantling all the residential sections but one. Everyone will have to move into that section or move out completely. We're going to lose a lot of commissions because of that. The whole city's going to be turned into an industrial complex. Even the farms won't be used; food is going to be shipped in."

"But . . . all of a sudden, like this?"

"Basin City's been operating at a loss for two years. Money ran out and the government won't give them another grant."

Henshaw was quiet for a moment. Then he said, "I thought we'd at least have until the end of the year."

Snyder shrugged. "What difference does it make? If people aren't going to move into Basin City in two years, they probably never will. The whole complex can't be operated very economically with a population of nine thousand. And that's forgetting about all plans for future development."

Henshaw stared at Snyder. "When we were granted a real estate license to Basin City, we thought we'd gotten the biggest break of our careers." He strode to his desk and sat down wearily. "For two years we've barely been able to keep this office open." He lit a cigar and exhaled the smoke noisily. "Maybe it's better this way. Now at least I'll be able to spend the whole week with my family again. Driving from San Diego to here on Mondays and back again on Fridays takes all the energy out of me."

"I'm shot," Snyder said. "It's Thursday. Let's call it a week and go home, okay?"

SHARTAR

He watched a boom crash against the straining metal one final time and thought about the hundreds of millions of city-dwellers choking to death on their own wastes. Then he turned, feeling the trembling beneath his feet, walked down the gentle slope to the road, got in his car, and drove away.

——————————————————————————

A Happy Day in 2381   Robert Silverberg

Here is a happy day in 2381. The morning sun is high enough to reach the uppermost fifty stories of Urban Monad 116. Soon the building's entire eastern face will glitter like the sea at dawn. Charles Mattern's window, activated by the dawn's early photons, deopaques. He stirs. God bless, he thinks. His wife stirs. His four children, who have been up for hours, now can officially begin the day. They rise and parade around the bedroom, singing:

"God bless, God bless, God bless!
God bless us every one!
God bless Daddo, God bless Mommo, God bless you and me!
God bless us all, the short and tall,
Give us fer-til-i-tee!"

They rush toward their parents' sleeping platform. Mattern rises and embraces them. Indra is eight, Sandor is seven, Marx is five, Cleo is three. It is Charles Mattern's secret shame that his family is so small. Can a man with only four children truly be said to have reverence for life? But Principessa's womb no longer flowers. The medics have said she will not bear again. At twenty-seven she is sterile. Mattern is thinking of taking in a second woman. He longs to hear the yowls of an infant again; in any case, a man must do his duty to God.

Sandor says, "Daddo, Siegmund is still here. He came in the middle of the night to be with Mommo."

The child points. Mattern sees. On Principessa's side of the sleeping platform, curled against the inflation pedal, lies fourteen-year-old Siegmund Kluver, who had entered the Mattern home several hours after midnight to exercise his rights of propinquity. Siegmund is fond of older women. Now he snores; he has had a good workout. Mattern nudges him. "Siegmund? Siegmund, it's morning!" The young man's eyes open. He smiles at Mattern, sits up, reaches for his wrap. He is quite handsome. He lives on the 787th floor and already has one child and another on the way.

"Sorry," says Siegmund. "I overslept. Principessa really drains me. A savage, she is!"

"Yes, she's quite passionate," Mattern agrees. So is Siegmund's wife, Mattern has heard. When she is a little older, Mattern plans to try her. Next spring, perhaps.

Siegmund sticks his head under the molecular cleanser. Principessa now has risen from bed. She kicks the pedal and the platform deflates swiftly. She begins to program breakfast. Indra switches on the screen. The wall blossoms with light and color. "Good morning," says the screen. "The external temperature, if anybody's interested, is 28°. Today's population figures at Urbmon 116 are 881,115, which is + 102 since yesterday and + 14,187 since the first of the year. God bless, but we're slowing down! Across the way at Urb-

mon 117 they added 131 since yesterday, including quads
for Mrs. Hula Jabotinsky. She's eighteen and has had seven
previous. A servant of God, isn't she? The time is now
0620. In exactly forty minutes Urbmon 116 will be honored
by the presence of Nicanor Gortman, the visiting sociocomputator from Hell, who can be recognized by his outbuilding
costume in crimson and ultraviolet. Dr. Gortman will be the
guest of the Charles Matterns of the 799th floor. Of course
we'll treat him with the same friendly blessmanship we show
one another. God bless Nicanor Gortman! Turning now to
news from the lower levels of Urbmon 116—"

Principessa says, "Hear that, children? We'll have a guest,
and we must be blessworthy toward him. Come and eat."

When he has cleansed himself, dressed, and eaten, Charles
Mattern goes to the thousandth-floor landing stage to meet
Nicanor Gortman. Mattern passes the floors on which his
brothers and sisters and their families live. Three brothers,
three sisters. Four of them younger than he, two older. One
brother died, unpleasantly, young. Jeffrey. Mattern rarely
thinks of Jeffrey. He rises through the building to the summit.
Gortman has been touring the tropics and now is going to
visit a typical urban monad in the temperate zone. Mattern
is honored to have been named the official host. He steps
out on the landing stage, which is at the very tip of Urbmon
116. A forcefield shields him from the fierce winds that sweep
the lofty spire. He looks to his left and sees the western face
of Urban Monad 115 still in darkness. To his right, Urbmon
117's eastern windows sparkle. Bless Mrs. Hula Jabotinsky
and her eleven littles, Mattern thinks. Mattern can see other
urbmons in the row, stretching on and on toward the horizon,
towers of superstressed concrete three kilometers high, taper-
ing ever so gracefully. It is as always a thrilling sight. God
bless, he thinks. God bless, God bless, God bless!

He hears a cheerful hum of rotors. A quickboat is landing.
Out steps a tall, sturdy man dressed in high-spectrum garb.
He must be the visiting sociocomputator from Hell.

"Nicanor Gortman?" Mattern asks.

"Bless God. Charles Mattern?"

"God bless, yes. Come."

Hell is one of the eleven cities of Venus, which man has
reshaped to suit himself. Gortman has never been on Earth
before. He speaks in a slow, stolid way, no lilt in his voice

at all; the inflection reminds Mattern of the way they talk in
Urbmon 84, which Mattern once visited on a field trip. He
had read Gortman's papers: solid stuff, closely reasoned. "I
particularly liked 'Dynamics of the Hunting Ethic,' " Mattern
tells him while they are in the dropshaft. "Remarkable. A
revelation."

"You really mean that?" Gortman asks, flattered.

"Of course. I try to keep up with a lot of the Venusian
journals. It's so fascinatingly alien to read about hunting
wild animals."

"There are none on Earth?"

"God bless, no," Mattern says. "We couldn't allow that!
But I love reading about such a different way of life as you
have."

"It is escape literature for you?" asks Gortman.

Mattern looks at him strangely. "I don't understand the
reference."

"What you read to make life on Earth more bearable for
yourself."

"Oh, no. No. Life on Earth is quite bearable, let me assure
you. It's what I read for *amusement*. And to obtain a necessary parallax, you know, for my own work," says Mattern.
They have reached the 799th level. "Let me show you my
home first." He steps from the dropshaft and beckons to Gortman. "This is Shanghai. I mean, that's what we call this block
of forty floors, from 761 to 800. I'm in the next-to-top level
of Shanghai, which is a mark of my professional status.
We've got twenty-five cities altogether in Urbmon 116. Reykjavik's on the bottom and Louisville's on the top."

"What determines the names?"

"Citizen vote. Shanghai used to be Calcutta, which I personally prefer, but a little bunch of malcontents on the 775th
floor rammed a referendum through in '75."

"I thought you had no malcontents in the urban monads,"
Gortman says.

Mattern smiles. "Not in the usual sense. But we allow
certain conflicts to exist. Man wouldn't be man without conflicts, even here!"

They are walking down the eastbound corridor toward
Mattern's home. It is now 0710, and children are streaming
from their homes in groups of three and four, rushing to get
to school. Mattern waves to them. They sing as they run

along. Mattern says, "We average 6.2 children per family on this floor. It's one of the lowest figures in the building, I have to admit. High-status people don't seem to breed well. They've got a floor in Prague—I think it's 117—that averages 9.9 per family! Isn't that glorious?"

"You are speaking with irony?" Gortman asks.

"Not at all." Mattern feels an uptake of tension. "We *like* children. We *approve* of breeding. Surely you realized that before you set out on this tour of—"

"Yes, yes," says Gortman, hastily. "I was aware of the general cultural dynamic. But I thought perhaps your own attitude—"

"Ran counter to norm? Just because I have a scholar's detachment, you shouldn't assume that I disapprove in any way of my cultural matrix."

"I regret the implication. And please don't think I show disapproval of your matrix either, although your world is quite strange to me. Bless God, let us not have strife, Charles."

"God bless, Nicanor. I didn't mean to seem touchy."

They smile. Mattern is dismayed by his show of irritation. Gortman says, "What is the population of the 799th floor?"

"805, last I heard."

"And of Shanghai?"

"About 33,000."

"And of Urbmon 116?"

"881,000."

"And there are fifty urban monads in this constellation of houses."

"Yes."

"Making some 40,000,000 people," Gortman says. "Or somewhat more than the entire human population of Venus. Remarkable!"

"And this isn't the biggest constellation, not by any means!" Mattern's voice rings with pride. "Sansan is bigger, and so is Boswash! And there are several bigger ones in Europe— Berpar, Wienbud, I think two others. With more being planned!"

"A global population of—"

"—75,000,000,000," Mattern cries. "God bless! There's never been anything like it! No one goes hungry! Everybody happy! Plenty of open space! God's been good to us, Nicanor!" He pauses before a door labeled 79915. "Here's my home. What I have is yours, dear guest." They go in.

Mattern's home is quite adequate. He has nearly ninety square meters of floor space. The sleeping platform deflates; the children's cots retract; the furniture can easily be moved to provide play area. Most of the room, in fact, is empty. The screen and the data terminal occupy two-dimensional areas of wall that once had to be taken up by television sets, bookcases, desks, file drawers, and other encumbrances. It is an airy, spacious environment, particularly for a family of just six.

The children have not yet left for school; Principessa has held them back, to meet the guest, and so they are restless. As Mattern enters, Sandor and Indra are struggling over a cherished toy, the dream-stirrer. Mattern is astounded. Conflict in the home? Silently, so their mother will not notice, they fight. Sandor hammers his shoes into his sister's shins. Indra, wincing, claws her brother's cheek. "God *bless*," Mattern says sharply. "Somebody wants to go down the chute, eh?" The children gasp. The toy drops. Everyone stands at attention. Principessa looks up, brushing a lock of dark hair from her eyes; she has been busy with the youngest child and has not even heard them come in.

Mattern says, "Conflict sterilizes. Apologize to each other."

Indra and Sandor kiss and smile. Meekly Indra picks up the toy and hands it to Mattern, who gives it to his younger son Marx. They are all staring now at the guest. Mattern says to him, "What I have is yours, friend." He makes introductions. Wife, children. The scene of conflict has unnerved him a little, but he is relieved when Gortman produces four small boxes and distributes them to the children. Toys. A blessful gesture. Mattern points to the deflated sleeping platform. "This is where we sleep. There's ample room for three. We wash at the cleanser, here. Do you like privacy when voiding waste matter?"

"Please, yes."

"You press this button for the privacy shield. We excrete in this. Urine here, feces here. Everything is reprocessed, you understand. We're a thrifty folk in the urbmons."

"Of course," Gortman says.

Principessa says, "Do you prefer that we use the shield when we excrete? I understand some outbuilding people do."

"I would not want to impose my customs on you," says Gortman.

Smiling, Mattern says, "We're a post-privacy culture, of course. But it wouldn't be any trouble for us to press the button if—" He falters. "There's no general nudity taboo on Venus, is there? I mean, we have only this one room, and—"

"I am adaptable," Gortman insists. "A trained sociocomputator must be a cultural relativist, of course!"

"Of course," Mattern agrees, and he laughs nervously.

Principessa excuses herself from the conversation and sends the children, still clutching their new toys, off to school.

Mattern says, "Forgive me for being overobvious, but I must bring up the matter of your sexual prerogatives. We three will share a single platform. My wife is available to you, as am I. Avoidance of frustration, you see, is the primary rule of a society such as ours. And do you know our custom of nightwalking?"

"I'm afraid I—"

"Doors are not locked in Urbmon 116. We have no personal property worth mentioning, and we all are socially adjusted. At night it is quite proper to enter other homes. We exchange partners in this way all the time; usually wives stay home and husbands migrate, though not necessarily. Each of us has access at any time to any other adult member of our community."

"Strange," says Gortman. "I'd think that in a society where there are so many people, an exaggerated respect for privacy would develop, not a communal freedom."

"In the beginning we had many notions of privacy. They were allowed to erode, God bless! Avoidance of frustration must be our goal, otherwise impossible tensions develop. And privacy is frustration."

"So you can go into any room in this whole gigantic building and sleep with—"

"Not the whole building," Mattern interrupts. "Only Shanghai. We frown on nightwalking beyond one's own city." He chuckles. "We do impose a few little restrictions on ourselves, so that our freedoms don't pall."

Gortman looks at Principessa. She wears a loinband and a metallic cup over her left breast. She is slender but voluptuously constructed, and even though her childbearing days are over she has not lost the sensual glow of young womanhood. Mattern is proud of her, despite everything.

Mattern says, "Shall we begin our tour of the building?"

They go out. Gortman bows gracefully to Principessa as they leave. In the corridor, the visitor says, "Your family is smaller than the norm, I see."

It is an excruciatingly impolite statement, but Mattern is tolerant of his guest's faux pas. Mildly he replies, "We would have had more children, but my wife's fertility had to be terminated surgically. It was a great tragedy for us."

"You have always valued large families here?"

"We value life. To create new life is the highest virtue. To prevent life from coming into being is the darkest sin. We all love our big bustling world. Does it seem unendurable to you? Do we seem unhappy?"

"You seem surprisingly well adjusted," Gortman says. "Considering that—" He stops.

"Go on."

"Considering that there are so many of you. And that you spend your whole lives inside a single colossal building. You never do go out, do you?"

"Most of us never do," Mattern admits. "I have traveled, of course—a sociocomputator needs perspective, obviously. But Principessa has never been below the 350th floor. Why should she go anywhere? The secret of our happiness is to create self-contained villages of five or six floors within the cities of forty floors within the urbmons of a thousand floors. We have no sensation of being overcrowded or cramped. We know our neighbors; we have hundreds of dear friends; we are kind and loyal and blessworthy to one another."

"And everybody remains happy forever?"

"Nearly everybody."

"Who are the exceptions?" Gortman asks.

"The flippos," says Mattern. "We endeavor to minimize the frictions of living in such an environment; as you see, we never refuse a reasonable request, we never deny one another anything. But sometimes there are those who abruptly can no longer abide by our principles. They flip; they thwart others; they rebel. It is quite sad."

"What do you do with flippos?"

"We remove them, of course," Mattern says. He smiles, and they enter the dropshaft once again.

Mattern has been authorized to show Gortman the entire urbmon, a tour that will take several days. He is a little apprehensive; he is not as familiar with some parts of the structure as a guide should be. But he will do his best.

"The building," he says, "is made of superstressed concrete. It is constructed about a central service core two hundred meters square. Originally, the plan was to have fifty families per floor, but we average about 120 today, and the old apartments have all been subdivided into single-room occupancies. We are wholly self-sufficient, with our own schools, hospitals, sports arenas, houses of worship, and theaters."

"Food?"

"We produce none, of course. But we have contractual access to the agricultural communes. I'm sure you've seen that nearly nine tenths of the land area of this continent is used for food-production; and then there are the marine farms. There's plenty of food, now that we no longer waste space by spreading out horizontally over good land."

"But aren't you at the mercy of the food-producing communes?"

"When were city-dwellers not at the mercy of farmers?" Mattern asks. "But you seem to regard life on Earth as a thing of fang and claw. We are vital to them—their only market. They are vital to us—our only source of food. Also we provide necessary services to them, such as repair of their machines. The ecology of this planet is neatly in mesh. We can support many billions of additional people. Someday, God blessing, we will."

The dropshaft, coasting downward through the building, glides into its anvil at the bottom. Mattern feels the oppressive bulk of the whole urbmon over him, and tries not to show his uneasiness. He says, "The foundation of the building is four hundred meters deep. We are now at the lowest level. Here we generate our power." They cross a catwalk and peer into an immense generating room, forty meters from floor to ceiling, in which sleek turbines whirl. "Most of our power is obtained," he explains, "through combustion of compacted solid refuse. We burn everything we don't need, and sell the residue as fertilizer. We have auxiliary generators that work on accumulated body heat, also."

"I was wondering about that," Gortman murmurs.

Cheerily Mattern says, "Obviously 800,000 people within

one sealed enclosure will produce an immense quantity of heat. Some of this is directly radiated from the building through cooling fins along the outer surface. Some is piped down here and used to run the generators. In winter, of course, we pump it evenly through the building to maintain temperature. The rest of the excess heat is used in water purification and similar things."

They peer at the electrical system for a while. Then Mattern leads the way to the reprocessing plant. Several hundred schoolchildren are touring it; silently they join the tour.

The teacher says, "Here's where the urine comes down, see?" She points to gigantic plastic pipes. "It passes through the flash chamber to be distilled, and the pure water is drawn off here—follow me, now—you remember from the flow chart, about how we recover the chemicals and sell them to the farming communes—"

Mattern and his guest inspect the fertilizer plant, too, where fecal reconversion is taking place. Gortman asks a number of questions. He seems deeply interested. Mattern is pleased; there is nothing more significant to him than the details of the urbmon way of life, and he had feared that this stranger from Venus, where men live in private houses and walk around in the open, would regard the urbmon way as repugnant or hideous.

They go onward. Mattern speaks of air-conditioning, the system of dropshafts and liftshafts, and other such topics.

"It's all wonderful," Gortman says. "I couldn't imagine how one little planet with 75,000,000,000 people could even survive, but you've turned it into—into—"

"Utopia?" Mattern suggests.

"I meant to say that, yes," says Gortman.

Power production and waste disposal are not really Mattern's specialties. He knows how such things are handled here, but only because the workings of the urbmon are so enthralling to him. His real field of study is sociocomputation, naturally, and he has been asked to show the visitor how the social structure of the giant building is organized. Now they go up, into the residential levels.

"This is Reykjavik," Mattern announces. "Populated chiefly by maintenance workers. We try not to have too much status stratification, but each city does have its predominant populations—engineers, academics, entertainers, you know. My Shanghai is mostly academic. Each profession is clannish." They walk down the hall. Mattern feels edgy here, and he keeps talking to cover his nervousness. He tells how each city within the urbmon develops its characteristic slang, its way of dressing, its folklore and heroes.

"Is there much contact between cities?" Gortman asks.

"We try to encourage it. Sports, exchange students, regular mixer evenings."

"Wouldn't it be even better if you encouraged intercity nightwalking?"

Mattern frowns. "We prefer to stick to our propinquity groups for that. Casual sex with people from other cities is a mark of a sloppy soul."

"I see."

They enter a large room. Mattern says, "This is a newly-wed dorm. We have them every five or six levels. When adolescents mate, they leave their family homes and move in here. After they have their first child they are assigned to homes of their own."

Puzzled, Gortman asks, "But where do you find room for them all? I assume that every room in the building is full, and you can't possibly have as many deaths as births, so—how—?"

"Deaths do create vacancies, of course. If your mate dies and your children are grown, you go to a senior citizen dorm, creating room for establishment of a new family unit. But you're correct that most of our young people don't get accommodations in the building, since we form new families at about two percent a year and deaths are far below that. As new urbmons are built, the overflow from the newlywed dorms is sent to them. By lot. It's hard to adjust to being expelled, they say, but there are compensations in being among the first group into a new building. You acquire automatic status. And so we're constantly overflowing, casting out our young, creating new combinations of social units—utterly fascinating, eh? Have you read my paper, 'Structural Metamorphosis in the Urbmon Population?' "

"I know it well," Gortman replies. He looks about the dorm. A dozen couples are having intercourse on a nearby platform. "They seem so young," he says.

"Puberty comes early among us. Girls generally marry at

twelve, boys at thirteen. First child about a year later, God blessing."

"And nobody tries to control fertility at all."

"*Control fertility?*" Mattern clutches his genitals in shock at the unexpected obscenity. Several copulating couples look up, amazed. Someone giggles. Mattern says, "Please don't use that phrase again. Particularly if you're near children. We don't—ah—think in terms of control."

"But—"

"We hold that life is sacred. Making new life is blessed. One does one's duty to God by reproducing." Mattern smiles. "To be human is to meet challenges through the exercise of intelligence, right? And one challenge is the multiplication of inhabitants in a world that has seen the conquest of disease and the elimination of war. We could limit births, I suppose, but that would be sick, a cheap way out. Instead we've met the challenge of overpopulation triumphantly, wouldn't you say? And so we go on and on, multiplying joyously, our numbers increasing by three billion a year, and we find room for everyone, and food for everyone. Few die, and many are born, and the world fills up, and God is blessed, and life is rich and pleasant, and as you see we are all quite happy. We have matured beyond the infantile need to place insulation between man and man. Why go outdoors? Why yearn for forests and deserts? Urbmon 116 holds universes enough for us. The warnings of the prophets of doom have proved hollow. Can you deny that we are happy here? Come with me. We will see a school now."

The school Mattern has chosen is in a working-class district of Prague, on the 108th floor. He thinks Gortman will find it particularly interesting since the Prague people have the highest reproductive rate in Urban Monad 116, and families of twelve or fifteen are not at all unusual. Approaching the school door, they hear the clear treble voices singing of the blessedness of God. Mattern joins the singing; it is a hymn he sang too, when he was their age, dreaming of the big family he would have:

> *"And now he plants the holy seed,*
> *That grows in Mommo's womb,*
> *And now a little sibling comes—"*

There is an unpleasant and unscheduled interruption. A woman rushes toward Mattern and Gortman in the corridor. She is young, untidy, wearing only a flimsy gray wrap; her hair is loose; she is well along in pregnancy. "Help!" she shrieks. "My husband's gone flippo!" She hurls herself, trembling, into Gortman's arms. The visitor looks bewildered.

Behind her there runs a man in his early twenties, haggard, bloodshot eyes. He carries a fabricator torch whose tip glows with heat. "Goddam bitch," he mumbles. "Allatime babies! Seven babies already and now number eight and I gonna go off my *head!*" Mattern is appalled. He pulls the woman away from Gortman and shoves the visitor through the door of the school.

"Tell them there's a flippo out here," Mattern says. "Get help, fast!" He is furious that Gortman should witness so atypical a scene, and wishes to get him away from it.

The trembling girl cowers behind Mattern. Quietly, Mattern says, "Let's be reasonable, young man. You've spent your whole life in urbmons, haven't you? You understand that it's blessed to create. Why do you suddenly repudiate the principles on which—"

"Get the hell away from her or I gonna burn you too!"

The young man feints with the torch, straight at Mattern's face. Mattern feels the heat and flinches. The young man swipes past him at the woman. She leaps away, but she is clumsy with girth, and the torch slices her garment. Pale white flesh is exposed with a brilliant burn-streak down it. She cups her jutting belly and falls, screaming. The young man jostles Mattern aside and prepares to thrust the torch into her side. Mattern tries to seize his arm. He deflects the torch; it chars the floor. The young man, cursing, drops it and throws himself on Mattern, pounding in frenzy with his fists. "Help me!" Mattern calls. "Help!"

Into the corridor erupt dozens of schoolchildren. They are between eight and eleven years old, and they continue to sing their hymn as they pour forth. They pull Mattern's assailant away. Swiftly, smoothly, they cover him with their bodies. He can dimly be seen beneath the flailing, thrashing mass. Dozens more pour from the schoolroom and join the heap. A siren wails. A whistle blows. The teacher's amplified voice booms, "The police are here! Everyone off!"

Four men in uniform have arrived. They survey the situation. The injured woman lies groaning, rubbing her burn. The insane man is unconscious; his face is bloody and one eye appears to be destroyed. "What happened?" a policeman asks. "Who are you?"

"Charles Mattern, sociocomputator, 799th level, Shanghai. The man's a flippo. Attacked his pregnant wife with the torch. Attempted to attack me."

The policemen haul the flippo to his feet. He sags in their midst. The police leader says, rattling the words into one another, "Guilty of atrocious assault on woman of child-bearing years currently carrying unborn life, dangerous anti-social tendencies, by virtue of authority vested in me I pronounce sentence of erasure, carry out immediately. Down the chute with the bastard, boys!" They haul the flippo away. Medics arrive to care for the woman. The children, once again singing, return to the classroom. Nicanor Gortman looks dazed and shaken. Mattern seizes his arm and whispers fiercely, "All right, those things happen sometimes. But it was a billion to one against having it happen where you'd see it! It isn't typical! It isn't typical!"

They enter the classroom.

The sun is setting. The western face of the neighboring urban monad is streaked with red. Nicanor Gortman sits quietly at dinner with the members of the Mattern family. The children, voices tumbling one over another, talk of their day at school. The evening news comes on the screen; the announcer mentions the unfortunate event on the 108th floor. "The mother was not seriously injured," he says, "and no harm came to her unborn child." Principessa murmurs, "Bless God." After dinner Mattern requests copies of his most recent technical papers from the data terminal and gives them to Gortman to read at his leisure. Gortman thanks him.

"You look tired," Mattern says.

"It was a busy day. And a rewarding one."

"Yes. We really traveled, didn't we?"

Mattern is tired too. They have visited nearly three dozen levels already; he has shown Gortman town meetings, fertility clinics, religious services, business offices. Tomorrow there will be much more to see. Urban Monad 116 is a varied, complex community. And a happy one, Mattern tells himself firmly. We have a few little incidents from time to time, but we're *happy*.

The children, one by one, go to sleep, charmingly kissing Daddo and Mommo and the visitor good night and running across the room, sweet nude little pixies, to their cots. The lights automatically dim. Mattern feels faintly depressed; the unpleasantness on 108 has spoiled what was otherwise an excellent day. Yet he still thinks that he has succeeded in helping Gortman see past the superficialities to the innate harmony and serenity of the urbmon way. And now he will allow the guest to experience for himself one of their techniques for minimizing the interpersonal conflicts that could be so destructive to their kind of society. Mattern rises.

"It's nightwalking time," he says. "I'll go. You stay here . . . with Principessa." He suspects that the visitor would appreciate some privacy.

Gortman looks uneasy.

"Go on," Mattern says. "Enjoy yourself. People don't deny happiness to people, here. We weed the selfish ones out early. Please. What I have is yours. Isn't that so, Principessa?"

"Certainly," she says.

Mattern steps out of the room, walks quickly down the corridor, enters the dropshaft and descends to the 770th floor. As he steps out he hears sudden angry shouts, and he stiffens, fearing that he will become involved in another nasty episode, but no one appears. He walks on. He passes the black door of a chute access door and shivers a little, and suddenly he thinks of the young man with the fabricator torch, and where that young man probably is now. And then, without warning, there swims up from memory the face of the brother he had once had who had gone down the same chute, the brother one year his senior, Jeffrey, the whiner, the stealer, Jeffrey the selfish, Jeffrey the unadaptable, Jeffrey who had had to be given to the chute. For an instant Mattern is stunned and sickened, and he seizes a doorknob in his dizziness.

The door opens. He goes in. He has never been a night-walker on this floor before. Five children lie asleep in their cots, and on the sleeping platform are a man and a woman, both younger than he is, both asleep. Mattern removes his clothing and lies down on the woman's left side. He touches her thigh, then her breast. She opens her eyes and he says, "Hello. Charles Mattern, 799."

"Gina Burke," she says. "My husband Lenny."

Lenny awakens. He sees Mattern, nods, turns over and returns to sleep. Mattern kisses Gina Burke lightly on the lips. She opens her arms to him. He shivers a little in his need, and sighs as she receives him. God bless, he thinks. It has been a happy day in 2381, and now it is over.